W9-AGB-358

STELLA LANDRY

Also by Robin McCorquodale

Dansville

STELLA LANDRY

A Novel

Robin McCorquodale

William Morrow and Company, Inc.
New York

It is the policy of William Morrow and Company, Inc., and its imprints and affiliates, recognizing the importance of preserving what has been written, to print the books we publish on acid-free paper, and we exert our best efforts to that end.

Library of Congress Cataloging-in-Publication Data
McCorquodale, Robin.
Stella Landry / Robin McCorquodale.
p. cm.
ISBN 0-688-11528-4
I. Title.
PS3563.C3446H4 1992
813′.54—dc20 91-42918
CIP

Printed in the United States of America

2 3 4 5 6 7 8 9 10

BOOK DESIGN BY M 'N O PRODUCTION SERVICES, INC.

For Malcolm and our children,
Angus, Wilmer, and Malcolm III

For once I did not feel the pang of the empty house. It welcomed me, and after an hour (I had been watching for her) the wild cat came and I fed her. It set a seal on all I had been feeling, for there is no doubt that this shy, intense, starved creature had become an alter ego. I have identified with the perpetual hungerer after comfort, the outsider watching lighted windows.

May Sarton, *Journal of a Solitude*

STELLA LANDRY

I

If anyone had told me that one day I'd marry, I wouldn't have believed it, and that's because people like me don't. They may talk awhile with a man they like, dream up a family history to pass the time, but they never go further than that, and they don't make plans. Because marriage is a place where someone like me can't go, a place I'd closed the door on five years before on that fall afternoon.

But that came after I got to Fort Worth, and I'd gone there because it was where I could lose myself, go out whenever I wished and never see the same person twice. And I liked the room I rented in a cottage in a settled neighborhood near the center of the city, a part of town with brick streets and shops with plate-glass windows right in peoples' houses, where the ones who lived there used their living room for a beauty parlor or a store to sell used goods. Mr. Perez, my landlord, was an old man who listened to the radio all day from a wheelchair, played it loud, except when his daughter came over from next door to give him a bath and make dinner, so it was as if he were yelling for her all the time, a baby crying for company. And that made me offer to cook for him regular or just every once in a while, but he said it was her job, and he kept to that firm.

The house was old, no telephone or modern gadgets, but my room was bigger than any I'd had before, a corner room at the back, the long side of it facing east into the morning sunshine. At Christmastime, one of the kids on the block was selling pine wreaths off a wagon, and so I bought one, found a red ribbon for it, and hung it on the inside of my door, making the whole room smell like a forest.

During the week, I took the bus downtown. I'd eat somewhere, a cafeteria or a hamburger stand, though my favorite place was a café with a pool table, a little hole-in-the-wall named Curly's, where you could get a bowl of chili or a chicken-fried steak, all the coffee you wanted to drink with it, and when business was slow, the company of a waitress named Phyliss, who talked to you about her vacation in Florida, her husband and son and their pet collie who won medals and prize money in dog shows. And then one evening, when Phyliss told me she was quitting because she was pregnant, it popped into my head to ask her if I could have her job, and she told me to talk to Mabel, Curly's wife.

I liked working at the café. For one thing, Mabel and Curly asked no questions, and that's probably because they paid me in cash, no benefits or anything. And the place was comfortable, not fancy, with plain people, like the ones I'd seen around Anderson, particularly those who were passing through, men doing three- or four-day jobs, so they were coming to a café like this to drink beer, eat, and play pool, betting small stakes they could stand to lose, talking to people they'd never met before, putting their arms around one another's shoulders, bragging about the money they'd made, the women they'd had, and the war they'd won. And after, they would pay for their drinks and food, tell their new friends good-bye, and leave with no responsibility toward any of it.

Curly's wife, Mabel, was the one who did the cooking and ran the café. Curly only opened the doors and the beers and talked to customers, mostly about violent crimes or people in public office. He knew a lot of dirt on all of them, and he liked to tell it whenever anyone would listen.

So, for me, working at Curly's was good. It kept me out of my room, away from staring out the window all day at the Perezes' pink plaster flamingo and toy windmill, remembering too much, thinking about how I'd had to leave Prentice, packing so quick in one suitcase that I had to leave half my things, then walking up to the gas station and getting a ride with a man who was going home to a town called Palo Pinto. I asked him what the nicest city near there was. He said Fort Worth. When we got to Palo Pinto, I took a bus here.

And then, since I hadn't hoped for anything out of Curly's other than money and a means of seeing people, when I'd otherwise be by myself for so long that I'd start thinking too much and crying, I was surprised at what happened next and really on an evening when I expected nothing other than my routine: clearing off dirty glasses and plates, taking orders, remembering them long enough to get them back to Mabel, talking to the customers, but not so much that I'd make Curly mad. Since we were busy, I hadn't noticed who was coming in, just catching the shape of people as they came through the door, seeing out of the corner of my eye where they'd sit, so I could get to them quick.

But I had noticed one man, and I guess that was because he had red hair and was good-looking, too; and that's rare. Most red-headed men look so washed out that you'd think they'd been shut up since birth in a room with the shades drawn. But not this one. He had real looks and a manner that I liked from the minute I was standing beside his table, and his gaze had risen into mine and mixed with it right, him smiling by then and me not being able to keep from it, either. He was with another man, older than him by a good bit, someone he'd met at the fat stock show, he said, and who was so close to drunk that I didn't want to serve him, but Curly gave me a nod, and so I took each of them a beer.

Anyway, I liked the redhead's blue eyes and freckles and ready smile, how young he was, and how old he tried to act. He said he was here for the show and that his name was Jim Lester. He reminded me of a boy I'd once known from the Tabors' ranch, healthy and strong and treating everyone like a friend. And so when the place wasn't busy, I stood near him and talked. Then, when someone new came in, or someone called to me, I felt him watching me and listening with only half an ear to what his friend was saying.

After a while, he stopped drinking beer and asked me to bring him a coffee, and while he was pouring sugar in it, letting the sugar heap over his spoon, watching it careful, he asked, "You married?"

"No."

He pointed to the sapphire ring I wore. "Then why do you wear that?"

"It doesn't mean I'm married. It's just jewelry."

"Good. So when you get off, I'll take you home. I got my truck parked outside."

"No."

He looked surprised. "You got someone else?"

"No."

He reached out for my hand, but I held it back. "I'll wait on you then," he said. "What's that going to hurt?"

I liked him and I hated to do it, but I wasn't disturbing my peace of mind for a day or so's attentions from a cowboy who'd come here to Fort Worth for the fat stock show, who lived in a town that was probably like Anderson, dusty and lost, all the people harsh with you if you were the least bit different. So, at quitting time, I went out the back door, down the alley, and walked along the dark sidewalks like I always did, then crossed the park where it was lighted, and climbed the back-porch steps to my room, drinking in with my eyes how comfortable it looked: the bed and easy chair and standing lamp, all worn but clean and neat. Mr. Perez's radio was playing through the walls, Spanish songs that made you want to dance.

The next evening, a few minutes before five, when I turned the corner, I saw a pickup truck parked across the street from the entrance of the café. A man got out, dodged a cab with the driver sitting on the horn, came to me, and took my arm. A loose lock of red hair was dangling near his eyes. He spoke close to my face, bending down some to do it, since he was tall. "How come you didn't tell me nothing last night?" he asked. "I waited for you. Why didn't you meet me like you said?"

I saw immediately that he was hurt more than mad, and I knew I could handle that.

But I didn't answer. I guess I'd just gotten tired of people trying to take me over, and I wasn't going to put up with it from anyone

I served in the café. And that was because the café was special to me. "I didn't promise anything," I said.

I turned the corner into the back alley and entered through the screen door. Mabel was already up front taking some beer orders from a couple. Curly was standing at the counter, tall and fat, so you could hardly see the two men sitting before him, chatting with him about something the pope in Italy had said in the news. The conversation was sure to be against Catholics, and I wasn't up to hearing that. I could see that Mabel was busy setting up beers for a table in the back, and that I'd better get out there quick. I put on a red apron with the letters in big swirling script saying CURLY'S, then went to the jukebox and put in a handful of quarters I'd taken from the register.

In the top center of the front door, there was a diamond-shaped window. People could stand there and see if their friends were inside without coming full into the room. And that's where Jim was. I caught his eyes, knowing them before I knew him, and that made me look down. Then he was holding the door half-open, watching me. "You coming in?" I heard Mabel ask.

Jim nodded.

She had one hand on her hip. "Well, do it, then. You're letting out the air-conditioning."

She motioned toward a place next to the pool table.

Mabel was never friendly with the customers. She believed that if your café had a good location, a beer license, and you could make a French fry crisp on the outside and cooked all the way through, people would come to you no matter what.

Jim sat down, his eyes following me to the pass counter, or into the kitchen, back into the room, to each table I served. Two men came in, went to the pool table, and picked up cues. One of them broke the balls apart, cracking them loud, a sound I'd gotten used to and liked. It meant something was going on, meanness in a way, one man beating up on another, but all of that controlled by rules and happening in the open.

I brought each of the men a beer, the brand I remembered they liked. I was good at that kind of remembering. I knew one of them, Harry Swenson, a truck driver always trying to make a date and me always turning him down.

When I got through there, I went over to Jim. "What do you

want?" I asked, saying it nice. I wasn't mad at him, then or ever.

"I want you to sit down here with me and talk," he said.

"What do you want to drink, I mean." My eyes flowed quick into his. "I'm not allowed to sit down."

He smiled. "Never?"

I bit my lip to keep from laughing, but I know I had it there in my eyes. "No, I mean here at work," I said.

"Well, what's it going to hurt?"

"Me. I'll lose my job."

"Maybe you can get another."

"You going to find one for me?"

I gazed at him for a moment, waiting for him to answer. He dipped his head and ran his freckled hand through his hair, curls like Joylyn's. "A Schlitz," he said. "No glass."

"Please?"

He laughed. "Sure. Please."

I swiped at the table with a damp rag, though there was nothing to clean up. "You're easy to take care of," I said.

"That's what I've been telling you."

But he didn't smile with that last, so I knew that the patient way he said that was different from the way he felt.

I got him the beer, then went back to stand beside Curly in case I had an order. Curly made a motion toward a back table where a hand was raised for me. I went to serve the people there, stopping by the pass counter to pick up three thick white plates that each held a hamburger and dozens of hot, smoking fries.

Jim sat quiet, nursing his beer, and reading something out of a paperback book with a cowboy on the cover, the horse rearing up like it planned to trample the whole group of cruel-looking men who were running before it. Jim couldn't have been able to see the words very well in the light he had, but if that bothered him, he didn't let it show. It was his pale-colored eyes that made him able to see without much light, he was to tell me later. He said that this kind of vision was good for deer hunting in the early morning, just when the light starts, though bad for working in any kind of summer glare. His eyes were a beautiful color, though, the finest kind of blue, like sometimes the sky is on a cold day, just calling out for something to get it warm.

He ordered a coffee, then read his book folding the cover back on itself so he could hold it in one hand and manage his cup with the other, me filling it from a glass Silex pot whenever it got down. Occasionally he looked away from the book's narrow white pages and stared at me. Then, at quitting time, when I brought him his check, he laid the book down and took my wrist in his hand. Gentle, though. And I know he would have let me go if I'd looked a certain way or asked him. But I didn't. Then I was letting myself down in the chair beside him, talking a little but mostly listening, then starting to dream, just the seed of it coming into focus in a way I'd never let it come before. The smoke in the room started to burn my eyes so that tears formed, and Jim pulled me out a napkin to use for that and made me promise, if not to let him take me home, then to meet him sometime, because (his glance took in the room quickly, and he smiled), after all, we couldn't spend all our time here in the café. And anyway, Mabel was calling me. "You have to work," he said, "so if you—"

I got up to go. "All right," I was saying, not able to smile back because Mabel was watching.

He read his book until at last I came out, dressed to leave. He wanted to walk me home, he said. I told him no, but when he asked me to meet him the next day, I said I would.

"You promise?" he asked.

"Yes, I do."

"I guess I shouldn't believe you."

I smiled. "I guess you should."

That night I caught the bus back to Mr. Perez's, a warm night but fresh with breezes. Every second of the ride, I was thinking about Jim, imagining his going home to some girlfriend in that town where he lived, his driving his truck up before her house, a porch light going on, her shouting his name, then running out to him as fast as she could get down the front steps, her parents looking on happy and smiling from behind. Then his marriage with her, the wedding, long dresses, and a tall cake; later, their family, three or four kids, all freckled and clear-eyed like him.

2

The next evening, Jim took me to a movie. I didn't let him pick me up at the house. I told him that Mr. Perez's daughter was funny about men coming around and that I'd meet him at the show if he'd tell me the theater. He was there when I came. I had waited a minute on the far corner watching him gaze up the street the opposite way from where I was coming, his body strained and his face worried. Then, when he saw me coming up from a couple of storefronts away, he broke out in a smile and started walking fast to where I was. He tried to kiss me light on the lips, but I turned my head so his mouth touched only my cheek. He felt cool and he smelled good, not like perfume or anything, but fresh like a boy who's not yet full come into being a man.

He took my hand then, and we walked together over to the poster that showed a couple running scared down an alley where the street was black and wet. "You want to see this?" he asked. "I think it's about some longshoremen who get in trouble with the union bosses. I believe I heard that most of it was filmed in Boston, but maybe it was New York." He motioned toward the poster. "You like him?" He was talking about Marlon Brando.

I smiled. You almost had to when you were with Jim. And then he was talking about the woman in the picture playing opposite

Brando, and that was Eva Marie Saint. "Her hair's the same color as yours," he said. The wind was bothering my hair, and I pushed it back away from my face so that it would look more like hers.

"You want to see it?" he repeated.

"Sure."

I opened my purse to take out my money. He touched the hand that was reaching down. "Put that up," he said.

"I like to pay my own way."

"It'd make me happy to pay for you."

I stood quiet, thinking, standing near him. I decided to pay, because then things between us wouldn't get confused. "No, I'm paying for myself," I said. And I did. I bought my ticket, then stood back away from the ticket booth while he bought his.

Inside the lobby, there was the smell of popcorn and melted butter. We each ordered a bag of it, and then got a Coke in a paper cup with a lid on it and a straw sticking through. And it seemed strange, me walking down the aisle of a movie, then sitting beside a man who had invited me there. Sometimes I went to the show alone and sat in the back. And that was all right. What I liked about it was that it would seem to others that I had time to waste, nothing to do on a weekday afternoon but go to the show, buy popcorn with money I'd begged off my daddy; and then, when I was walking home, I could criticize the story of the movie, telling myself where it was good and where it wasn't.

Marlon Brando played the part of a prizefighter who had to work on the docks after he'd failed in the ring. By nature, he was honest, but since his older brother was a member of the ones that ran the local, he had to do what he was told. . . . The nicest thing about him was how much he loved some pigeons that he kept in a coop on the roof of a building. When someone killed them, after Brando had informed on the mob, I thought about a cat I'd once had, and how much you could love a pet.

"The show's real sad, isn't it?" Jimmy whispered.

"Yes, it is."

"You want to leave?" I guess he'd seen that I was wiping tears from my eyes.

"No," I answered, since I could never bear for any story to be unfinished in my mind. "I want to see what happens."

I cried again after Marlon Brando was beaten up; and then, with the help of the priest and Eva Marie Saint, rose and walked into the warehouse to work, though his body was broken and his face was bleeding and cut. But he had to do that so the other workers could follow him in and get their rights, too. At the close of the show, I felt as if all of them had entered the Kingdom, a place where they'd be safe behind that enormous corrugated door.

About halfway through the movie, Jim put his arm around me, and I let it stay there. From the first, he made me feel like I was good and deserved to rest against someone, and that he had come to me just for that. Jim was like having a recess in my life, and right then it didn't matter if I deserved it or not, or if I could make it last.

When we came out of the movie, it was nearly eight o'clock but still light, so we walked along the streets talking about the show, then stopped to look in shop windows and talk about what they had. I glanced up at Jim. "My legs are tired," I said, smiling. I guess I was always smiling at him, from the first and forever. He was the kind of man who made you want to do that. If he liked you, he had all day for you, listening to you or just looking into your eyes, knowing what you were thinking before you said it but not letting on because he wanted you to enjoy your own time of talking or of just being quiet and savoring things.

He pointed to a diner across the street. "You want to go in there?"

I nodded and let him take my hand.

The diner had booths with red plastic benches and plastic table covers crinkled to look like leather. For a minute, I thought they were. Pots of ivy hung in each of three plate-glass windows, their heart-shaped leaves dripping down nearly to the sills. Someone took such good care dusting them that the leaves shone as though they'd been oiled. The handwritten menus were in plastic frames. A man at another booth held an opened newspaper, and you could see only his fingers. It was nicer here than at Curly's and more comfortable, the waitress in a newer dress than Mabel gave me, though that's not to say that I wasn't satisfied with what I had.

Country music was playing on the jukebox. "You like that?" Jimmy asked me.

"I don't know about much else."

"Not Beethoven?"

"No."

"Who's your favorite singer?"

"I don't know. I like country, though."

I looked down at Jim's hands. They were big, with thick fingers and flat white nails. He was wearing slacks, a shirt with pearl snaps. A flower was embroidered on the yoke in back and one flower on each side of the divided yoke in front. His boots were new, a shiny brown leather, tooled with green insets at the top. He'd probably ordered them special months ago and picked them up here. I guess he thought he was dressed up. In any case, I liked the way Jim looked better than anybody I'd ever seen. And it wasn't just those looks, it was what he said, how he reacted to whatever news you gave him; and I believed, without knowing many steps in his history, that he was good, and that, if I could only know him long enough, he'd be very good to me. "How many days are you spending in town?" I asked him.

"Three more. I'm helping my brother show his calves."

"He going to win anything?"

"Sure—he's got good stock. The judging's tomorrow; then, on the last day, they award the prizes. The results will be in the *Star* if you want to look. Buck Lester's his name."

Buck Lester, I was thinking, planning by then to remember everything Jim said. "You help raise them? The calves, I mean?"

He nodded. "I help him with everything, as much as I can."

"You live with him?"

"Not anymore. I used to, but now I rent a room of my own in town. I go out there whenever he needs me."

"What kind of work do you do?" I imagined Jim just as he was. I could have almost spoken his answer myself.

"Car mechanic," he said. "I work in a garage. But I'd like to get out of that for a while, drive a truck, see some parts of the country I've never seen, go up East and visit cities. I'd come home, of course. It's just that I'd like to see things, get me some memories, go somewhere. In the meantime, I'm doing okay, and I've got a salary."

"This is somewhere. Fort Worth, I mean."

He smiled. "Yes, it is."

"You good at fixing cars?"

"I've been doing it all my life. Buck and me built us a car once from what we found left in a ditch, and what we could beg off our dad's friends."

While we talked, I played with the sugar jar, turning it slowly in my hands, running my fingers up and down the surface, but thinking, not about my slim hands and softly painted nails, but about Jim's hands, how they seemed right for a mechanic; or for a man holding the wheel of a truck; or even for one holding the reins of a horse and riding herd, and then hunting when he could, killing deer out of season, and not because he wanted to break the law, only that he lived in a country wild enough, so that when you need something special to eat, you can kill it on your own land.

"Where do you live?" I asked.

"Winston Valley."

"Where's that?"

"Not all that far from San Antonio. When I want to make trouble, that's where I go."

"San Antonio," I repeated.

He sighed and looked away dreamily as though going there gave him particular pleasure, and it didn't happen often enough.

"And what do you do when you get there?" I asked.

He blushed easily. "Have fun. I go with friends."

I tightened my lips at the corners to do the way I like when I want to tease. "Your girlfriends?"

"No, guys I knew in high school."

I supposed that was like the boys I'd known about in Anderson, who drove to El Paso or Del Rio to spend their money for beer and clothes and radios for their cars, doing that every three or four months, then stopping off in Juárez or Villa Acuña, buying mixed drinks and a woman, and coming home broke.

The waitress came, and I ordered a hamburger.

"Take a steak, Stella Jean," Jimmy said. "That's what I'm having. And let me buy you something this time. Please."

"I don't need that much," I whispered.

"Sure you do. Everyone needs to eat good." Jim glanced up at the waitress, a fat girl with shaggy black hair and thick hips. If she'd been dressed differently, she would have looked like a girl I'd once known named Roseanna, though Roseanna was always smiling as sweet as a little child, and this girl looked like she never did. "Bring us both the T-bone," Jim said.

"And how do you want it?" She kept looking at Jim. I was going to see that a lot more, but I didn't mind, because after we met, Jim never looked at anyone but me, at least not in my presence, and I never heard any rumors about him doing it elsewhere.

"Medium," he answered. Then he changed his mind. "No, medium well."

"You, too?" asked the waitress, whom I kept wanting to call Roseanna.

"Yes."

When she left, I looked out the window, trying to think of something to say, something about ranches and stock, but I hadn't been around any of that for the last little while, so I asked him about something I'd heard Mabel say. "You ever go to an encampment? A Baptist one, I mean?"

"Are you Baptist?"

"No. I'd like to be baptized though, so I'd be sure about something. I mean, belong to something."

"Didn't your folks ever take you to church?"

"When I was real little, but not after."

"I'll take you to church sometime."

"All right." I looked down at the table, feeling bad about making plans with him I couldn't keep.

Then we talked about Jim's brother, Buck, and his sister-in-law, June, and the place they had, how after their parents got killed in an auto wreck, Buck had kept him until he was eighteen on the ranch Buck's in-laws gave him and June; and then, when June had had the third baby, and their first child was nearly fourteen and able to do every chore that Jim could, he'd known it was time to give Buck's family some privacy, and for him to take a job in town and a room as well. When Jim asked me about myself, I told him about being born in Ozona, making up that my father had passed away there, and then my mother; and that I'd come here, rented a room, and found a job.

The waitress came with the steaks, charred on the outside and half-covered with thick fries, glittery with salt. While we were eating, Jim was talking about seeing me again. "No, not tomorrow," I said. "I'm going with a friend to see her people in the country."

"Then Monday. I'll come by the café, and we'll go somewhere after you get off. You decide what you want to do."

"All right."

I knew I wouldn't be there, Monday being my day off and I knew he had to leave on Tuesday. I'd known that all along, and I was just enjoying what time we had left, in the same way that I enjoyed talking to some of the people at Curly's who didn't know more about me than what I told them, and never would. I knew I was going to think about Jim for a long time, that I'd get a lot of memory out of having sat in such a good movie with his arm around me, then window-shopping with him, looking at cameras and photographs of people on vacation; people laughing and running toward the water on a white beach scattered with umbrellas; then Jim and me ordering a dinner as nice as this, and my having the company of a man so gentle.

Then I thought of something else. "You got a picture of yourself?" I asked.

"Why?"

"So I could have it."

He smiled. "Sure."

He reached into the back pocket of his slacks and pulled out a wallet. The pictures were in plastic covers. "Here's one of me playing baseball in high school. It isn't recent, so I look a little different. But it's sure me."

"It that your only picture? I don't want to take the only one you have."

"No, I've got a whole album at home. June made it up for me on my eighteenth birthday."

"You just eighteen?"

"Twenty-one," he said.

"Then you're a year more than me."

"I don't mind that."

"I don't, either."

As he was handing me the picture, I was wiping my fingers on a napkin; then I took it carefully by one of its white corners. It was a color photo, an even younger Jim dressed in a baseball suit: knickers, special shoes, red hair sticking out from under his cap, one of his cheeks swollen. "You chewing tobacco?" I knew that baseball players did that.

He looked down, shy. "Yeah."

"You chew it now?"

"Sometimes. You mind that? I'd quit."

"Why should I mind? I like people to do what they want. You make people unhappy, and they'll take it out on you."

"That's smart to know."

I put the picture in the zipper pocket of my purse. "I won't hurt it," I said. "I'll take real good care of it." I planned to buy a frame for it and keep in on my dresser.

I finished my steak, all of it, then picked up the bone and gnawed around it like Jim was doing. "Best part's the bone," he said, finally getting all the juice out of it that he thought was there and wiping his greasy fingers on the bunch of paper napkins he'd pulled out of the metal container. I did the same, as if I were looking in a mirror. He made me wish I had red hair and freckles and big hands, wish that we were twins or just as close. As soon as I could, I was going to buy myself a western shirt like he had and a belt with pretty leather work and a silver buckle.

"You coming back to Fort Worth regular?" I asked.

"Maybe. I want to."

"I may be going to school when you come back," I said.

"Where?"

"Secretarial, I think. Or beauty college."

"You want to work in a beauty shop, making women pretty?"

"That would be all right."

Then I got from him that smile, where the skin around his eyes crinkled and made dimples on both cheeks. "Well, you sure don't need it for yourself."

The waitress came to us, clattering the plates as she stacked Jim's on mine, one of the forks falling on the floor, and Jim having to reach down under the table to pick it up.

"You want pie?" the waitress asked when he handed her the fork. She didn't even say thank you. At Curly's I would have been nice about a thing like that.

"What kind of pie you got?" Jim asked.

She looked back toward the counter on the far wall where there were slices of pie under a slanted glass case. "Chocolate meringue's left," she said. "Or there's a couple of slices of Dutch apple."

"Can you heat the apple and cut us each a wedge of cheese?"

"We don't have no Cheddar," she answered. "But I can give you what we use on the cheeseburgers."

He shook his head. "I'll take the chocolate." He looked at me. "What do you want, Stella?"

"I'll take the chocolate, too."

The pie looked old, the filling cracked and the meringue drawing back, but it tasted delicious, a full cup of sugar I'd bet; and I let it melt in my mouth so all I had to do was swallow it. I ate slow, making it last as long as I could.

We parted on the corner, although he'd asked to walk me home. "I'll see you Monday," he said, squeezing my hand.

When I went to work on Tuesday evening, it was raining, and I got my shoes wet. I shook out my umbrella and left it open near the back door. "You're late," Mabel said. "You know I need you at five." But she wasn't mad, just fussing at me because she was irritated with Curly's laziness. At that hour, there wasn't much to do. Mabel and Curly could take care of it easy, and why should they care? They only paid me for the exact time I worked.

"It was the rain," I said, pulling off my damp cotton sweater and slipping my uniform over my head. Then I arranged my hair at the mirror and went out to the tables.

One of the men at a corner table made a pass at me, inviting me out after work to the motel where he was staying. He was with another man, and that man laughed. "Go to hell," I said quickly, meaning both of them. On my way back to get a customer a beer, Curly stopped me, stretched out his arm before me so I couldn't pass. "Don't start bitching the customers," he said.

"He was asking me out, talking dirty."

I was looking up at Curly. I hoped Mabel didn't see the way that he was staring at me.

"Mabel says I don't have to do no more than wait table," I said softly.

By that time, Mabel had come out of the back room, and Curly had managed to change his expression, but I knew it wasn't over, and I thought with a sharp pang that I might have to look for other work, and that maybe I wasn't as near to being secure as I'd thought. I had money in the bank. Sure. That was from what I'd saved. But I had a thing about keeping my nest egg in case I got hurt again or sick. I thought about Curly and how free he was getting with me. I guessed that Mabel might have fired girls before me for that same reason. I noticed that Curly's hand was trembling on the bottle of beer he was opening.

In a minute, Mabel was calling me to take out an order of a chicken sandwich and a burger in a basket. "A man was asking for you yesterday," she said. "He seemed to think you were working."

At moments like this, my blood heats up quick and flows into my cheeks. "He say who he was?"

"No, but he left you a note."

"Why didn't you tell me before?"

She shrugged. "I just thought of it."

Mabel was never fast about anything. I suppose that's why they needed to hire a waitress. She went to the back room and came out with a paper napkin. "I didn't have nothing else for him to write on," she said.

I put the note in the pocket of my uniform, made the rounds of the tables to make sure no one needed anything, then stepped to the back to read what I had.

I came for you like you said. How come you lied to me? Jimmy.

If you want to make the person receiving it feel rotten, it's always the fewest words that say it best. If you write a lot, you soften things and ruin the effect. I kept staring at the crumpled napkin until one of the men at the pool table called me. I felt like walking out the back door, going home. But staying seemed usual for me, and that's what I did, even when the tears started coming in my eyes, and I had to wipe them away on my fingers. I don't cry often, actually. I learned long ago that crying doesn't get you anywhere.

The man called again. I wanted to tell him to go to hell, too; but, instead I started toward him, moving among the tables to where he was, knowing that my shoulders went back and my hips swayed, whether I meant for them to or not. Sometimes I try to hunch over a little and keep everything about me quiet, but that never seems to work for long. I'm just shut inside a package that makes people want to act in a certain way with me, and all I can do is tell them that they're wrong.

3

It was Joylyn who told me how I was found, told me in bits and pieces, her sewing and me stroking our cat, Grisha; or her cutting up vegetables for soup and me dressing a paper doll; me holding the scattered facts in my head in the way that about that same time I was learning to play jacks, to hold them in my fist until I had them all, playing that game with my best friend, Susan Noble. Sometimes Joylyn was squinting when she talked about it; sometimes her voice broke. Then again, she'd be calm, so I'd hardly realize that she was going into that again. And she never would have told me, if Susan hadn't said that I was adopted, that her mother knew.

They got me from a minister, Joylyn said, and not from Doc's father, the minister who lost his church and died of grief for it; but from one in Victoria who not only had a church, but a brick house as well. Because I was found in the hotel there, a room clerk using his pass key when people heard me howl too long for what was normal. And I was sitting up in the middle of the floor in nothing but a diaper, one of the pins unfastened and sticking in my side. There was a swelling on my face and bruises on my legs, but that could have been from falling off the bed rather than from anyone hurting a baby.

I asked Joylyn what the clerk did.

She said that when he got close, I cried more, so he sent for the minister, Dr. Whitley; and Dr. Whitley sat on his heels and said, *Oh, baby, now there, honey, don't cry.* And he jerked the pin out of me, then wrapped me in a hotel towel and took me home, me yelling steady until I got rested and fed. His wife would have kept me, added me to the four other kids she had, but I fretted too much, and she didn't like children who did.

When Joylyn heard about me in church, she kept on her best dress and went to their house to see. She tried to play with me, she said, to know if I could laugh, but I just laid my head on her breast like she was already my mother. Then Doc came, and he said I was about eight months, because I could sit up good, though I might have been younger since some girl babies learn fast. Doc had a job then, so they got me over another couple who weren't working.

"Do girls learn faster than boys?" I asked.

"Yes, they do."

Joylyn and I were in the hammock then, and she was smiling, her white teeth catching the light from the pure part of the sunshine that was pushing through the limbs. "It was me taught you to walk," she said, "holding on to both your little hands. And you were fast at that. Well, you're smart at everything you do. Can't you braid your own hair quick?"

I said I could.

"And did the ones who left me ever come back?" I asked.

"No."

I was touching Joylyn's mouth, tracing her full upper lip with my finger, bringing back the red of her lipstick and rubbing it on my own mouth. "Then how did you know my name?" I asked.

She talked against my finger. "We didn't know it, so we had to make one up; and that came to us on the night when we were taking you home, Doc carrying you, and you gazing up, like your eyes were drinking up the sky. 'Let's name her Stella like the stars,' I said, and Doc said fine."

Joylyn was working now at a chain she was weaving from a bunch of daisies I'd picked so she could. The chain would be for me, she said. "A necklace for my pretty." And I was pretty; I had straw-blond hair that Joylyn washed in rainwater, rinsed in lemon juice, and curled on bobby pins for church, then gave me the hand mirror to see.

Later, Doc came home from work and brought a can of beer outside, so I went to the tube chair where he was sitting, and he took me on his lap, while Joylyn braided the daisy chain, her hands trembling now as if she'd gotten cold from telling me about my name; so I had to climb away from Doc and go to her, stretching out beside her to get her warm like she did for me on winter nights. She didn't say anything. She could be like that, dreamy, getting away.

I got stomach cramps that night, and I lost my supper of chicken and rice. Doc said it was a bug. He said probably I'd be sick three days, but the next morning I got up fine.

"You see?" Joylyn said to him. "Stella never gets sick."

She hugged me and took me on her lap. "Aren't you my healthy girl?"

Our house was in the old part of Ozona, a cottage built back so far from the street that you had to walk on a path through bushes and trees to get to the porch. Joylyn wanted the bushes cut low, but Doc never got to it. Our front door had two glass panes at the top, so on tiptoe Joylyn could see anyone who knocked. In the living room, there was a fireplace with an iron basket, three gas logs, and a black tile hearth. Beside it lay a kapok bed for Grisha. We had two bedrooms, the front one for Doc and Joylyn, the back one for me, each room papered different, mine with roses, Joylyn and Doc's with bluebirds in cameos of braided flowers. Venetian blinds hung on the windows. We had to dust each slat, each of us with her own pink feather duster, mine a little smaller then Joylyn's. When the wind blew, the blinds clanked against the window frame, so Joylyn fastened them with clips on either side of the sill. "Now they won't keep us awake," she said.

Between the bedrooms, there was a bathroom that had a toilet with a tank up high and a flush chain I couldn't reach. "Call me when you're through," Joylyn said, and I always did. Beside the toilet was a tub with lion-claw feet. When Doc said that every night after we were asleep, the tub walked out the front door and took a stroll downtown past the bank and courthouse, Joylyn laughed, but I didn't.

I though about the lion. "I'd better not go in the bathroom

when it's dark," I said to Joylyn, while we were saying my prayers.

"Oh, I think you'd better," she said.

But that night I didn't go, and near morning I was crying, and Joylyn heard.

"Poor baby," she said over and over, while she was getting me dry and settled on the couch, speaking to me soft so Doc wouldn't know. "You call me when you're scared"; and after that I did.

We lived in the part of town where there were shady streets, so you could go out walking any time of year. Sometimes Joylyn walked with me, holding my hand. "Mind the cracks and the oak roots," she said, when I broke away on my own. Other times she pulled me in the red wagon. Once I told Joylyn that I wanted my name drawn on the wagon. She said she'd do that, and one Saturday afternoon she drew it on, me kneeling beside her to help. "Stella Jean Landry," I said, but she wrote too big and only had room for STELLA JEAN.

When Joylyn was sick with asthma, and work or walking made her choke and lose her breath, Doc and I ate from cans; and it was he who took me on my walks, his eyes searching the limbs for birds. And when he'd see one, he'd crouch beside me, his eyes wrinkled tightly in the glare, him showing me, then telling me its name. "That's a yellow warbler," he said once. "That's rare."

I tried to catch it; and, afterward, another day, a sparrow, by sprinkling salt on its tail, but Doc didn't know I was hunting, and he scared it.

"The blue ones are scrub jays," Doc said. "They're friendly, but they don't sing well." He pointed his finger toward the top of a tree. "And the gray one with the white is a mockingbird. The state bird, honey. He can sing any song he wants. He just has to hear it once. I wish I could do that."

"You can," I said.

"Don't I wish," he said soft. "Joylyn can."

"*Mama* can," I said to correct him.

He smiled on one side of his face. "She's not my mama."

"No, but she's mine."

He came close to me then and straightened the bunch of cloth violets that Joylyn had sewn on my straw bonnet. "The mockingbird steals songs from other birds," he said. "And from people, too. A woman I knew was singing a hymn, and the bird got it."

"How?"

"He stole it from her."

The corners of his mouth trembled. I believed he'd laugh, and he did, then he kissed me and threw me up above his head. When I came down, I hung on his neck. "Give Doc a kiss," he said. Each time I kissed his mouth, the bristles of his mustache bit into my face. My eyes teared.

"You going to cry?" he asked. "You going to be a crybaby?"

On the way home, he taught me a poem: "Birdie with a yellow bill . . ." I taught it to Susan Noble, then took her to see Grisha's kittens, where they were next to the hot-water heater, sucking at Grisha's stomach. I bent over Grisha and tried to pat her head. She bared her teeth. "Better be careful," said Susan.

The next week, when Joylyn and I were sitting together at a card table on the front porch, our chairs so close together our skin touched, she drew the Texas flag. There were forty-eight states, she told me, each with a flag, and this one was ours. It had two fields painted in, and one star.

"The star's in the blue sky," I said. I couldn't draw very well then, but I could color, so Joylyn let me color in the flag with red and blue pencils that she sharpened with a metal sharpener she held in her hand. The shavings fell on the porch floor, then the wind came and eased them along until they dropped among the hydrangea leaves.

"Watch the flag's borders," she warned me. "Don't color over them, honey." After that, I didn't. She thought I colored like some older child, and she said so to Mrs. Noble, Susan's mother, when she was keeping me for Joylyn on the Wednesdays that she went to the beauty shop. Then later she told Doc.

"That's nice," Doc said, passing us on his way in from work. He had his blue seersucker jacket thrown over his shoulder. His tie was loose; his shirt stuck to him in places from sweat. In a minute, Joylyn got up because Doc had called out to her about dinner.

Doc was as tall as Joylyn in her high heels. He was thin, and he had veins in his arms that you could trace with your fingers. Sometimes after work, when he was reading in the easy chair that was his, Joylyn stood behind him and rubbed his shoulders, getting her fingers down deep, so he shut his eyes, and the corners of his mouth tensed. I liked to rub his shoulders, too; but it didn't do the same, since my fingers were still weak and small.

He was a doctor, and a good one I thought for Susan when she had mumps, for Joylyn when she had pneumonia, and for the people who sometimes dropped by, frowning and limping and talking about pain. But he didn't work at a clinic; he worked up at Mr. Able's hardware store. It wasn't nice there, he said, and sometimes, when he came home, his face looked limp and hanging down like mine did when I got punished for riding my trike off the yard. "It's a job," Joylyn said, whenever he said he was going to quit.

He was one of the clerks, and I liked to go with Joylyn to Mr. Able's and see him sell things. Sometimes when Mr. Able wasn't looking, he would give me some of the rock candy that was a present for the customers who bought things. He'd reach into the glass jar with the pig's face on it and hand me three or four, and I'd slip them quick into the purse that Joylyn spent a week crocheting for me, me smiling at Doc like we knew something no one else did, Doc looking regular so Mr. Able wouldn't guess.

But he hated the job there, and not just because he had to stand up all day, but because he couldn't be a doctor, since he'd never passed the tests. "I just can't take exams," he explained once to a couple from church whom Joylyn had invited to dinner. "I shake. At least my hands do, and then I get cold and can't think. Some people just can't take tests." He talked about another person like him. "It's not unusual," he said. Doc spoke with a lisp, but he always said the right words and was careful to correct Joylyn and me when we didn't.

"You didn't study," Joylyn said.

"I did," he said. "For weeks at a time, I sat at my desk."

Her lips pulled down at the corners. "Okay, you did."

I went to Doc and stood beside him, so he'd have something to look at besides the couple staring at him, but he picked at the doily on the arm of the chair and didn't take me on his lap.

Then once, when Susan Noble and I were in the living room working a picture puzzle, I heard him and Joylyn talking on the porch. Doc wanted to buy into a store that a friend of his wanted to start. "We'd own half," he said. "I'd manage it."

But Joylyn said she thought that the idea was a bad one. Why didn't he stay with what he had? Didn't we rent a nice house? She liked being able to pay the bills.

"I want to own something," Doc said, whining like I sometimes did to get something. When she didn't answer, he came inside, filled a jelly glass with whiskey, and went to bed.

Once I asked Joylyn where she'd met Doc, and she answered that it was at a church party in Lufkin where he'd come with his cousin.

"Did you love him?"

"I dropped out of school to go with him."

"Was that okay with Dad?"

"No."

Each summer, Joylyn's father, Dad, came to visit us for six weeks. The day he came, Joylyn kissed him and gave him a hug every chance she got. "It's just as hot here as Lufkin," he told her, "but it's a hell of a lot dryer. Great for you, Joylyn." He knew we'd moved here for her health.

During the day, I helped Dad fix the holes in the screens, and make the faucets tight, and the cabinet doors shut without squeaking. Then at night he always asked me to go with him to the drugstore, where we bought a quart of peach ice cream, took it home, and dished it up fast in bowls so it wouldn't melt before we got to the porch to eat. After that, he went to sleep on the sleep sofa that pulled out to the opposite wall of the living room and blocked the front door. Sometimes he talked wrong like Joylyn did, *bad English,* Doc said, but I didn't mind. Dad ran a motor court in Lufkin and sent Joylyn money in letters. On the day the money came, we always went to eat at a restaurant downtown.

One summer when Dad had seen that our oven was burned out, he bought Joylyn a copper Chambers range. On Joylyn's twenty-seventh birthday, he sent her her mother's upright piano, and then a new guitar for Christmas when she asked him to give her that, too. She could play them both and sing. "Did you just now learn to play it?" I asked her when the piano came, and she played some songs I'd heard in church.

"No, I learned when I was little. My mother knew."

"Will you teach me?"

I learned "Chopsticks" first, and, after I did, she and I played it together faster and faster, as loud as we could, until Doc told us no. "There's lots of music for four hands," Joylyn said. In her desk, she had a yellow copy of "Easter Parade," with the name *Jean Fisher* written on it in longhand, a way to write that I didn't know yet. "That was my mother's name," Joylyn answered to my question.

"My second name," I said.

"Yes. That's why."

Joylyn's mother was in a brown photograph, where she wore a big hat and stood beside a skinny man that Joylyn said was Dad at twenty-three. "They were on their honeymoon in New Orleans."

"Did she die, your mother?"

"Yes."

When I'd learned "Easter Parade," we played it for Grisha and Susan and Mrs. Noble, them sitting side by side in chairs like the audience would be for the talent show at church. On cool evenings, after we'd eaten and cleaned up, Joylyn was always with the guitar as if it were a part of her body. "Sing 'Gloryland,' " I'd say, since that was my favorite hymn. I learned it, too, and one Sunday morning, when we sang it for Dad, his eyes got hazy, and Joylyn said it was because he was thinking of his wife, Jean, who was with God.

Dad could hardly walk. His joints were big like fists, and he moaned in his sleep, so Joylyn had to wake up and give him aspirin. I'd hear her cloth slippers on the floor, then water from the sink filling a cup. When Dad worked in the garden, he couldn't kneel, so he'd ask me to bring him out a kitchen chair. Then he'd bend down, breathing heavy, and his hands would work as fast and regular as a machine. "That's good," I'd say.

"I know damned well."

After dinner, he liked to sit and talk to Doc about the motor court and how he made such a success of it, then tell Doc how maybe he could get ahead; but usually Doc would say he had to work early the next day, and then he'd go to bed. After that Dad would tell Joylyn and me the story about how, when he was fifteen, he'd seen a man killed in a duel fought on the Main Street of Crockett, and how, when he was a year older, he had tamed a wild horse that an Indian gave him.

When I was seven, the war came in Europe, then two months after Joylyn's brother, Eugene, got killed, Dad died, too, and left Joylyn the motor court. She thought that we should move to Lufkin and run it, like Eugene would have done if he'd lived, but Doc wanted it sold. In part, he said, to pay what we owed for furniture and at the grocery; in part to buy savings bonds, so in five years he could quit working for Mr. Able. From the bed in my room, I heard Joylyn crying softly. Doc was speaking slow and easy.

"You wanted to run your own store, why not the motor court?" Joylyn asked.

"I have my own ideas," Doc answered.

Then one Sunday, after Joylyn and I got home from church, Doc talked of a ranch he wanted to buy near a town out west called Valentine. Raising cattle now, with the United States in another war, couldn't be anything but profitable, he said. People were telling him that with even a small property, you'd be able to make a fortune selling beef to the army because they'd take care of most of the overhead. With what he and Joylyn had in the bonds, they could easily buy it. Joylyn didn't like the idea, but it sounded good to me, ranching, supplying soldiers with food, and living near a town with a name like that. Doc glanced over at me. "Hey, Stella, wouldn't you like to own a ranch? You want your own pony?"

I could hardly breathe. "Sure," I said soft. "Can we take Grisha?" Grisha was curled in my lap, purring and sleeping heavy as a stone. It had been a long time since we'd given her kittens away, but Joylyn thought that after all the howling outside for several nights running she might be expecting more.

"You can take any damned thing you want, honey." His eyes were shining.

"You've got work here," Joylyn said. "You don't know ranching."

"I don't know running a motor court, either, and you wanted that."

"I couldn't live in the country. I need people." Then she pulled me up near her. Her face powder smelled like the gardenia bush that Mrs. Nobel kept in her yard. "I'm a people person," she crooned, like she sang. "Isn't that what you and I are, Stella? People persons?"

4

I'd known boys in school who were something like Jim; quiet, contented ones from the country who did their chores, rode the school bus into town, then in their free time fixed up cars and trucks, their fathers and older brothers teaching them until they were so good with their hands that there wasn't anything that they couldn't put together with nearly nothing at all. They'd be outside in the yard or in the barn, squatting on their heels, studying bolts and wires, then reaching for some tool, trying, failing, cursing quietly when things got too bad, going away discouraged and ashamed; then coming back, seeing the problem fresh, and solving it soon.

At school, they did their work, using the study-hall time, their heads low over their papers, the pencil moving fast, them knowing that they had to finish before they went home because their chores left no time for study, and anyway there was no place to do it but on a table in the one big room that was the hub of the house and never got quiet. If they were strong, they played football when the coach asked them, doing that as well as they could, too; not minding getting hurt, at least never showing it if they did. And if they managed either the schoolwork or the sports better than average, the praise never went to their heads; and that was because they didn't see the future as any leap from what they had now, but only as a continuation of the life they knew. What it came down to was that they wanted to be like their fathers and grandfathers, no better and no worse. Born into a life that they saw no reason to change (their fathers had jobs good enough to provide food and a roof), their pride was in how well they were able to copy the men who had come before them.

I couldn't imagine Jim ever being rough or mean, or just walking over my feelings, either, like I supposed he thought I'd walked over his when he couldn't find me at Curly's and wondered why, if I liked him even as a friend, I'd lie. But women you want to love can be like that, I'd heard men say, though I'd never thought I might be one of them.

"Stella Jean!" he called out that morning before he caught up with me, just as I was going into the entrance of the house where I lived. He was coming toward me, his arms bent and swinging as though he were going a long way, when he wasn't going far at all.

"Oh, Jim," I was saying under my breath. "Oh, my God, Jimmy."

He stood before me, me not knowing how he'd found out where I was but knowing what it meant, and knowing for thereafter how carefully I would have to handle this miracle that was happening to me.

He stared at me, trying to smile steady, succeeding, then failing, the fair lashes that sheltered his eyes catching the glints of what sunshine there was under the latticed, vine-tight roof of the porch. Then he'd taken the grocery bag I was holding and carried it around to the back, following me inside and to my door, where I'd stopped, unlocking it the best I could, having to try three times since my hands were tied up too closely with my mind to do it. The day was sunny and cool, not yet late enough in the year to be hot, so I'd left the windows open. The curtains billowed into the room, then lay back against the sashes after Jim shut the door behind us.

The bed was rumpled a little, so I went quick to smooth the covers. "I didn't know anyone was coming," I said.

Jim put the grocery sack on the table and spoke soft. "This is a nice room," he said.

"It's just fine."

He paused a moment, and then he said, "You didn't work last weekend, Stella Jean."

I looked around at him and said weakly, "No, I didn't."

"Were you here?"

"Yes," I said. "Did you come over?"

"No, I went home."

"All the way to Winston Valley?"

"I had to get back to work, but I've taken off now, till I get this thing fixed up with you."

"What thing?" I whispered.

He had sat down on the arm of the easy chair, frowning, in one of those moods related to big things in your life that have to come out right. "Whatever it is that keeps me from sleeping and working good. I just keep seeing you, Stella, picture you sitting with me at the show, and then eating dinner."

He got up and tried to hold me, but I backed away, asking him if he wanted me to make some coffee.

"Yes," he answered.

"I bought sweet rolls at the bakery. You want one?"

"Sure."

"I could heat them."

He shook his head with his eyes shut, so I could see he wanted to get on to discussing what he'd come for, and not take too much time talking about breakfast. Not that he was annoyed. Not at all. I saw that clear. I asked him to sit down again, and then I served him on a decorated Mexican tray that I'd bought the week before.

"That's pretty," he said about the tray.

"I bought it in case I ever had a guest here," I said. I smiled. "I guess you're the first."

"I'm glad I am."

He acted pleased, and I imagined that he was thinking about how nice I'd been brought up.

While Jim was drinking his coffee and helping himself to the sweet rolls, dabbing the glazed sugar off his mouth with the napkin I'd given him, neither of us talked very much, Jim's eyes taking in what he saw: the zinnias I'd picked from the Perezes' garden and put in a jar, the flower prints I'd bought and hung over the bed.

When he saw his photograph on the desk beside the door, he gestured toward it. "You put it in that frame?" he asked.

"Yes."

"I guess you like it."

"I sure do."

"And what does that mean?"

I was quiet. I couldn't answer him anymore for thinking what was happening and thinking about what had happened, how I'd been here nearly eighteen months and how I liked the room well enough; yet whatever I did to fix it up and make it nice like my home, it always still came around to being the place where I was going to have to live the rest of my life alone.

"Nice place," Jim said. "You have trouble finding it?"

"No, I got off the bus, walked around, and saw the For Rent sign."

"And you've lived here since you came to Fort Worth?"

"Yes."

"This your furniture?"

"No, it belongs to my landlord."

Jim glanced at me over his coffee cup, and then he set it down. His face looked serious and still. "Why'd you lie to me about last Monday, Stella Jean? I thought you liked being with me. I don't think I'd have done that to you."

I was sitting then in a chair across from him. I glanced down at the flower print upholstery that covered its arm, right into the center of a big, wide-open rose. I'd studied those flowers many times before. When I was troubled, I tried to look at things like that, focus on something so long that I could nearly climb into it, pretend I was sitting in a field somewhere, nothing around me but flowers. "I'm sorry," I said, looking up.

"Why did you do it?"

"I thought you were getting serious."

"And what's so bad about that? People do."

"I don't want to."

"You don't like me?"

"No, I like you."

He laughed. "You think you're too young or something? I don't worry about it, so why should you? I told you I have a job. Is that what's worrying you? How we'd eat?"

I liked what he said, teasing me gentle like that. As far as I was concerned, he could go on forever telling me about his plans for us, how we could live where he did at Mrs. Slover's house, until we found our own place, and then paid down. I felt as if I could sit there listening the rest of my life, never troubling about anything more, just letting Jim handle things, as a knight does in the movies, and then the girl goes off with him into some shiny kingdom. I knew better, but I knew about moments, too; and this was one.

"How did you find this?" I asked. "My place, I mean?"

"Mabel knew."

"So you went on home?" I was beginning to smile. "How come you came back?"

"I love you," he said.

Well, I guess what I was feeling for him was love, wanting to be with him, missing him till it hurt my heart; but it had been better not to let on until I knew what he was thinking entirely. I thought he might kiss me then, but he didn't.

After he finished his coffee, we went out into the sunny air, walking for blocks without worrying about how far or where, not talking much, then stopping under some trees, where there was a bench covered with red and gold tallow leaves that looked like they'd been torn out of the shiny pages of a magazine. Jimmy brushed the leaves away with a swipe of the brim of his hat, and we sat down, each of us staring out at the lake, watching the big white geese swimming paths through the silver water, then walking up to us in a group and begging for food that we didn't have. I held my hands outstretched empty to show them, then I pulled on Jimmy's sleeve. "Let's go get some peanuts for them to eat," I said.

We walked over to where there was a vendor and bought some, then went to the edge of the water and called to the geese, me holding up the bag and them getting out and coming toward us, shaking water off their tails and waddling fast.

Jim and I divided what was in the bag. I hollered when one of the geese caught my finger with his bill; then again, when the peanuts were done, and another of them snatched the paper from me and shredded it into pieces that were hard to collect. Jimmy shooed them away, and we went back to our bench, Jim taking my hand and kissing it, then easing me into his arms, his eyes on me like there was nothing else in the world to see. "I love you, Stella Jean. I don't want to leave you." He ducked his head down quick and kissed my mouth, and afterward I laid my head on his shoulder, and he was kissing my hair and face. I heard people talking, heard the rattling wheels of a baby carriage, saw the feet of people as they passed, one set of them in brown shoes stopping and pausing before it went on.

"We going to get married? That's what I want. That's why I came back, and I don't want to leave here until you tell me we can." He was whispering against my cheek.

"Jimmy, I don't want to marry. It's not you. It's that I don't think I want—"

I was talking when I glanced up at him, so much hope in his face, him looking out at a future with a house and friends. I saw tears in his eyes from what he felt, and I know I was crying then, too—crying and nodding my head.

He put his hand under my chin so I'd look at him. "That mean yes?"

I said it did.

That afternoon, just after we'd stopped in a jewelry store and bought two gold rings, Jim telephoned Curly's Café from a pay telephone in the courthouse rotunda and talked to Mabel, telling her our plans. I don't know what she said, but I guess she was glad to see me gone—not that she hadn't liked me at first. "Yes, I know," Jim told her. "We decided quick, and I'm taking her home. . . . Yes, that's right, it's pretty fast." He nodded twice more and said yes, then told her good-bye, hung up the receiver, and took me in his arms, laughing, and not at Mabel or at me, but at our good luck at having everything go along so smooth, and that every time he asked me a question, I answered that I wanted to or that I would. We bought the marriage license, then went to a clinic and took the test that one of the clerks who waited on us had said we had to have.

Jimmy was staying with a friend of his brother Buck's across town, someone who'd gone to school with him in Winston Valley, then moved here to work. Every day for the next three, he picked me up in the morning; we went walking, out to lunch, to the movies. All I knew was that I loved him, that I'd never been loved by a man before, and that it was bringing out in me something so calm and happy that it made me smile even in my sleep.

"I love you," he kept telling me, and I told him I loved him, too.

During that time, I got to know him a little, not so much in what he said in his stories about hunting, bagging birds and deer, bringing them home to his sister-in-law, June, as offerings for her care of him; and not at all in what he told me about his dead parents, or how kind his landlady, Mrs. Slover, was; but more in the watching of him talking about what was important to him, the sweetness of his face, the gentle tone of his voice, the feel of his arm around my shoulders.

Then we cleared the room of the things I wanted to take: my clothes, the Mexican tray, and the pictures. When Jim was out buying gas in the truck and some soft drinks and ice for the cooler, I paid Mr. Perez's daughter the balance on my rent and explained that I was getting married.

So it was October 3, 1954, when I was riding in a truck with a man I'd promised to marry, doing what I said I'd never do but wanting so badly what I knew others had inside the houses we kept passing, where now during the day, there were flowers in the windows, and tonight there'd be wispy curtains glowing soft from lamps. And I knew about those houses, about what the people would be doing in there and saying, and that was some because of Ozona, but mostly because of Anderson and my eighth-grade teacher, Mrs. Bell. Because it was Mrs. Bell who once invited me to dinner at her house during the Christmas holidays. And I was remembering now as I was sitting beside Jim, thinking of our future, how nice her husband and kids had acted, how before the meal Mr. Bell had sat in an easy chair, talking to me about my studies and current events and the president, as though I were an adult, the way Doc tried to but couldn't anymore because his mind—his train of thought, he said—wouldn't stay long enough with him. Then Mr. Bell had leaned forward to tap his pipe on an ashtray, filled it, and lighted it, the smoke curling up toward the ceiling. The Bells had two little girls, one, Berta, in the second grade, who always took me first thing when I was in the house to see her room and her toys; the other one, Vale, in a high chair eating with us, hitting her spoon hard against the tray edge, practically right in my ear. But I didn't mind that—I just smiled at Mrs. Bell when she said, "You have to excuse Vale; she's just a baby."

"It's okay," I said. "I like babies."

Mainly I tried to answer the Bells' questions and talk about what Christmas meant, instead of staring too much at the table with its china dishes and silverware, the paper tablecloth with poinsettias printed on it. For food, we'd eaten the backstrap off a deer that Mr. Bell had shot in the fall and that they'd saved in the freezer for the holidays, marking on white freezer paper in red ink, CHRISTMAS. For dessert, there were individual ice creams in the shape of decorated spruce trees. "Would you like a second one?" Mrs. Bell asked me.

"Yes, thank you," I said, using the politeness I knew from Joylyn, though it might have been politer to refuse. And I'd kept staring at the Christmas tree, too. I could see it from where I was at the table (Mrs. Bell had given me that place beside Berta so I could), set up in a corner with a white bedsheet draped around its base to look like snow. It was decorated in red balls and red velvet bows, and strung with colored lights so that later that evening, when we were sitting in the living room with the lamp turned off so we could see better, I was imagining that the lights were stars, only more perfect, since they were placed at regular intervals instead of just scattered.

And in the weeks and months that passed, and finally nearly a whole year, I had the fantasy that one day the whole family of Bells, Mr. Bell, Berta, Mrs. Bell carrying the baby, would come together to the trailer, Mr. Bell in a business suit and Mrs. Bell in one of the blue wool dresses she wore to school, and they'd sit down outside the trailer in the aluminum chairs. "We'd like to have Stella," they'd say, then ask Doc if they might not adopt me. And though I couldn't have left off caring for Doc then since he was sick, maybe at least I could have gone over to the Bells' every afternoon to help Mrs. Bell with dinner, and help her in her garden on weekends, so people would have believed I lived there and shared that bedroom with Berta, as Berta had once asked me to do, when I was playing with her, sitting on the hook rug, helping her set up the furniture in her two-story dollhouse, me arranging each room just as she told me she wanted it done. And after, when we were looking at it, Berta climbed on me and kissed my cheeks. "I want you to stay on here as my sister, until Vale gets old enough to play."

All that winter, I went over to the Bells' several times a week, just dropping by; and Mrs. Bell let me play checkers or dominoes with Berta, and watch the baby while she was grading papers or cooking. "I need you here, Stella," she said; and that made me feel warm no matter what I was wearing.

But then that spring, Mr. Bell was transferred to Midland in his job, and the Bells left early in the summer, Mrs. Bell having found a new teaching job in the high school there. "It's wonderful for me," she said; and I guess she thought I'd be thrilled for her, instead of believing that the bottom had dropped out of my life. "The new job means a promotion for my husband," she said, "and I'll be happier in a bigger school with more advantages for myself and my students. We just don't have the equipment we need here, or the library. You can't teach without good reference books. She was telling me that while I was pouring some apple juice for Berta, and of course I spilled some and had to say I was sorry."

She laughed. "It doesn't matter at all, honey."

Then, when they'd gone, after that day when I'd watched the baby while the Bells and their friend were loading the van, then watched Mrs. Bell and the kids leave in the car that would follow, I wished there had been a little more of a holding back on Mrs. Bell's and Berta's part, not wanting to leave Anderson so fast and all their friends. And after, I used to walk by the vacant house, painted as white and pure as they were, soft wildflowers growing up in their garden after a rain, remembering the Bells talking soft and moving around and putting down dishes on their table with hardly any sound at all.

In a few days there was a For Rent sign hammered onto the picket fence, and while I was looking at it, I had another fantasy: that Doc got a letter with a check in it from something he'd won, and he'd had me call the number on the sign and ask to rent the house; and after I could move into Berta's room and fix it up with furniture for someone my age, then invite over Roseanna Klepper or some other girl to do homework, or just to drink a cold Coke with me and talk.

And now I was shutting my eyes and taking my chances with Jim, now for the second time and in sharp reverse of what I'd done before. But if I was ever tempted, it was by this: having the honor and glory that goes with being the one who runs a home and puts children in it. For almost everyone, it's the treasure at the end of the rainbow, and I had it; and though I've sometimes been sorry for what I did, I'll never believe I could have done different. I thought then of my meeting Jim at Curly's as having holy direction, more than anything since Joylyn took me from the minister's house and promised to keep and raise me.

We planned to go back to Winston Valley and marry there among Jim's people, but then changed our minds and decided to do it as soon as we could so that things would be all right with Mrs. Slover. That is, married, we could go straight to Jim's room in town. He didn't want me staying away from him for the week or so we'd have to live apart, maybe me having to move in at the ranch with Buck and June and him not even being able to see me if he had to work late at the garage. We were riding on the highway when we decided, the truck running along past some painted barrels, orange, white, and black to mark some construction. All at once, Jim pulled off the road and took the turn into Waco.

As soon as he could, he stopped in a booth to look in a phone book for a justice of the peace; then, with the help of a map tacked to the wall of a service station, we drove down some wide streets crowded with Saturday cars going on errands, then into a neighborhood with cottages set on slopes, the morning light hard on the drives and sidewalks so you had to shield your eyes. Jim had memorized the turns we had to take, and we missed only one, the truck going into a city park beside a river, then Jim turning back, retracing our path into the neighborhood, and seeing the street sign, WILLOW'S END.

When we got to the address, a blue shingled cottage with a sign in front with metal letters, I sat in the truck while Jim went to the door, knocked, waited with his hands in the pockets of his slacks, until someone answered, Jim standing straight. The door opened, and Jim took off his hat, his hands tight on its curved brim, his red hair ruffled by a breeze off the vacant lot next to the cottage. A short, stocky woman was gazing up at him and listening; then, in a moment, he turned toward me, jogged down the steps, coming back, opening the door, and offering me his hand, being silly by making a bow that made me laugh, swing into him, and kiss his cheek.

The woman invited us in. She looked about Joylyn's age. She had a small nose like Joylyn's, too, and her hair was shot through with streaks of gray like Joylyn's had to be if she didn't dye it now; and I didn't believe anyone as religious as Joylyn would. The woman (her name was Mrs. George) wore a white dress with small sailboats on it and a blue sailor tie in the front over her breasts. On her shoulders, she had put a flowered sweater; she was the kind of woman who, from the minute she has breakfast until she goes to take her bath before bed, wears chunky-heeled shoes and stockings. Different from Joylyn there, since Joylyn liked big, full, cotton dresses and sandals.

Mr. George came out of a back room, probably a bedroom he'd fixed up for an office. He was nearly as tall as Jim, with hair a purer gray than his wife's, cut short around his ears, a crest like a rooster along the top of his head, but the same slow, soothing way of speaking as Mrs. George.

"Do you have the license?" he asked. He was pulling on the knot of his tie to get it tight under his collar.

Jim reached in his pocket for the paper we'd bought. He unfolded it. It had a wafflelike seal pressed in the corner, and both our names on lines one above the other, Jim's first. Mr. George looked at it and nodded, then signed another paper, something he'd taken from his desk. "Now you and the lady sign this," he said. He laid the paper on the piano and handed me the pen. "Stella Jean Landry's going to become Mrs. James C. Lester," he said. When I glanced up, my hand still shaking with the pen, and me trying to hand it to Jim, Mr. George was smiling, and his wife had picked up the smile, so I knew they were one of those couples where the woman feels safer copying the man. *Mrs. Stella Jean Lester,* I was thinking, that name as fresh and new as the light on the other side of the window panes that was lighting the garden, a few flowers still left red on the geraniums, and then a plant I didn't know but whose yellow flowers looked as happy as I felt, standing before the Georges and leaning a little on Jim.

"Join hands," Mr. George was saying. He coached Jim to answer the first question, and he answered it; and then me, me whispering mainly, though loud enough so that Mr. George could hear and nod and go on to ask Jim whatever came next.

The Georges had some wine, and when the ceremony was finished, after we'd said all the words he had for us and Jim had slipped the ring on my finger and I'd done that on him and we'd kissed (Jim drawing me up too close and holding me too long, I thought, for being with the Georges), Mr. George divided the wine among us in bell-shaped glasses, then offered a toast to our happiness and to that of our children.

Mrs. George went to the kitchen. I heard her moving around, opening a cabinet and closing it, then she brought out a plateful of white cookies glazed with sugar. I took one bite into a cookie and drank a sip of wine. I saw the others do that, too.

A bit of the sugar got on my dress. I brushed it off with the side of my hand.

"I forgot the napkins," Mrs. George said; and she was back in her kitchen getting them, bringing more cookies. I was sitting on the sofa, listening to Mr. George talk about the garden, when Jim nudged me and said we'd better be getting on.

We thanked them and said good-bye; and then the Georges stood on their porch, waving at us even after the truck started up, and we were pulling away. I looked back to see them as long as I could. That was my wedding, and I'll never forget it, or the Georges' house, which I would ride by again much later in my life, the fine light of that day, picking out everything so clear, especially the gold wedding band I wore and that was now keeping my full attention.

We drove on, passing open fields, high black rows filled with bushy cotton plants, then pastures as green as the lakes and ponds that lay among them. Sometimes Jim put his arm around me. We rode for miles like that, my head on his shoulder. Then he would kiss my forehead, take his arm away, stretch, and breathe deep. I played the radio, changing the station to wherever he suggested when I'd start to lose it. We drove on into late afternoon, me watching the heather color of that autumn, the shadows from trees and buildings flung long as towers across grasses glowing bright orange in the slant of the sun; then, later, watching the lights on the dash strike Jim's face and catch on his teeth when he smiled.

We were near San Marcos when Jim said we should stop for the night. I saw the pretty town coming up quick. Jim pointed out the college, its buildings perched high on a hill, one of them like a palace. In a minute, we were passing motels on the right of the freeway. "Where you want to stay?" Jim asked, bending over me and pointing across the car at a motel with a big red sign. "You pick the one you think looks the nicest. You like that one?"

"Aren't we going on to Winston Valley?"

"You want that, Stella Jean? I thought you'd like a motel room on the first night. Something pretty. My room at Mrs. Slover's isn't all that much."

"I want to go on to Winston Valley," I said softly. I wanted to start living where he did just as soon as I could, have everything starting over for me, as though I'd been born when he'd come for me that morning. "Let's go on," I said.

We stopped in a café on the west edge of San Marcos, a place with paper lanterns strung above the tables. "I hope your landlady's going to like this," I said. "Me coming and moving in, I mean."

"She will. She's been telling me I ought to get married; June and Buck's been telling me that, too."

I teased him. "Is that because you're so wild?"

"No, I'm not wild. They just didn't like seeing me lonely."

"Why?"

"They love me."

"That's nice having everyone love you so much."

"I know it."

"It wasn't nice having your parents killed."

"No, but it didn't take me under, either. I had June and Buck and a lot of others distracting me."

"You go to church, Jimmy?"

He laughed. "Sure. When I think about it, and when I don't sleep too late Sunday mornings. . . . You like going, Stella Jean?"

"Yes, I do."

"You care where? Everyone's Baptist or Methodist in Winston Valley."

"No, I don't care where." I thought about the church in Anderson, the altar with its huge wooden cross, the incense I liked to see so much, coming out of the swinging brass lantern in its soft silver puffs, but I'd let Jimmy choose the church, since then he'd be more likely to go.

"You like dancing?" he asked me.

"Yes."

"All right, we'll do that, too; but we won't tell it at church."

"They don't dance?"

"No. And we won't tell Mrs. Slover, either."

"She Baptist?"

"Yes."

The way he answered, I knew she was strong that way. Well, I would be, too, if that's what they liked in Winston Valley, and that made you fit in.

It was dark when we arrived in town, everything empty except for a few pickups parked before a café that already had red and green Christmas lights strung across the porch, twinkling their reflections in the two plate-glass windows. I remarked on it, and Jimmy said they weren't really Christmas lights, but decorations left there all year to attract attention to the place. Only the main street was lighted, and the park with stone benches and tables down by the river. I liked the square with its inn and stone walls. "People used to have to fight off Indian attacks," he said. "Under the ground, there were supposed to be tunnels for escape, but no one's ever found them. Buck and me and some friends looked for them when we were kids, but the search never came to nothing. My father didn't believe they were there, just something to keep people worrying so they'd forget the real things."

And then Jim had had the loss of his father to worry about and his mother, too. That was a real thing.

I was staring at the town we were passing through, liking the way the windows of the shops looked with their quilts and pottery and cedar furniture that Jim said city people bought to furnish their vacation houses on the bluff along the river and on the banks of Cyprus Creek. He was nervous then. I could tell by his voice, how it was catching in the shortness of his breath.

He took a turn, the truck tires slashing at the gravel cover of the road, the truck lights beating like wings on the black-green coves that the oak trees made. "We're nearly home," he said, patting the pair of hands I had folded tight in my lap. "I love you."

5

The Nobles had dinner for us to leave by: barbecued lamb and blueberry pie with whipped cream, the smell of the meat and baking fruit filling up the whole neighborhood. That night I kissed Susan good-bye. We both sat on the Nobles' back steps and cried, and I promised to send her a greeting card from Valentine and ask her to come stay with me that summer. "As soon as school's over," I said. "You want to ride my pony?"

Early the next morning before the sun, we left Ozona, three of us riding out in the pitch-dark, Joylyn holding Grisha, who was meowing and clawing at her dress, me holding my storybook doll, trying to keep her net skirts away from the wind and Grisha's claws. We drove away from the dawn, through the purple hills and mountains, then south toward Mexico. We stopped at a roadside park to eat our box of chicken sandwiches on a stone table that Doc said was Indian, probably Comanche; then we turned off the main road to the only town we'd see after that, and it was small, a few houses spread out, a wood church without paint, part of its steeple broken off and just left lying in the yard, and a store with ripped screens and concrete blocks for steps. The land that Doc had bought started at a wire fence just past a creek full of stones and grizzly huisache. Even Doc hadn't imagined it would be so dry.

"Is this Mexico?" I asked.

"No, it's still the U.S. of A., but we're only thirty miles from the border and cheap labor." He looked at Joylyn. "That's one reason I chose it."

"It's not worth near what you paid," she said. Her voice quivered as if she might cry. "Hill Country land's less money than this, and it's got green grass. What are the cattle going to feed on?"

"They ranched this land before we did."

"But look at it."

There were no willows or sycamores on the land Doc said was ours, only dwarf oaks and cedars. Doc liked the cactus flowers, but when he pointed out some yellow ones, Joylyn wouldn't look. She was worried about Doc's agreement to buy more cattle, she said; worried about all Dad's money going into a place like this.

I had no bedroom there because the house was only two rooms: the big one where the front door opened, and a bedroom for Doc and Joylyn. The bathroom had a concrete floor and cinder-block walls. There was no window in it or glass cover for the light above the sink. "It's like an air-raid shelter," Joylyn whispered.

My bed was in the corner of the big room. My toy box still had to be the table for my lamp, but there was no room for the bookshelf that Dad built me, so Doc and Luis, the hired Mexican, dragged it to the shed out back, and I put my books in the bedroom with Doc's. "You'll have to keep your part of the room neat," Joylyn said to me when we moved in. She had her hands on her hips while she looked around the house and yard, shaking her head. She had spoken harsh to me, but it wasn't me she was angry at. "This place has no shade trees for the hammock, no porch for the swing, and Stella Jean has no bedroom," she told Doc.

"She'll be all right," he said.

Joylyn turned to me. "We'll add a bedroom. We'll hang wallpaper, if you want. I promise you that."

She and I drew a sketch of the room, filling in the spaces with my furniture, including the bookcase, and coloring the walls with rosebuds like my room in Ozona, where Susan Noble and I had counted the roses once, gone over 650 before we realized we might be counting some we'd done before. I showed the sketch of the room to Doc, and he liked it, but when I asked him when it would be ready, he answered impatient, "We'll do it when we can. Other things have priority."

"Like what?" I said, impatient, too.

He was silent and I was, then he bent down eye level. "I promise you I'm putting your room high on the list," he said. "I'll have someone up from town and do it as soon as I get our bills cleared."

"Why don't you build my room yourself?" I remembered that Susan's father, a truck driver and gone most of the time, had added a playroom onto their house.

He laughed. "I'm not so good with these," he said, holding out his slim, sunburned hands for me to see.

I nodded. Then he had to go outside because Luis was calling him, asking about which animals were supposed to get the feed we'd had to buy when it didn't rain as much as Doc thought it would.

Our house had thick adobe walls and a red tile floor. Since there was no sill, you walked in from dirt. "Don't wear your shoes inside," Joylyn warned me. But I'd already left a trail of dust along the tile.

I got the mop still damp from morning and cleaned the streak. "Doc does."

"Does what?"

"Makes a trail."

I hadn't meant to forget to change into my terry slippers as soon as I came in the door.

"Mama loves you," she said.

I looked up into her face. "I love you," I said.

"I'm sorry you have to live out here."

"I don't mind."

I picked up Grisha and rubbed my face into her long gray fur. She was fat now with new kittens inside. She meowed as if I was hurting her, so I put her down gently on her kapok bed beside the stove.

"Well, I mind for you," Joylyn said.

Then she held out her arms, the two of us rocking back and

forth sideways, my cheek on her breast where it came when we stood close, because by then I was over six, and as she said, not tall. I was average in first grade, and that meant right in the middle. The children measured by a ruled-off place that we'd marked in pencil on the door of the classroom. "Is that tall?" I asked the teacher. She was Mexican, but she spoke English. "Average," she answered, and Joylyn said that, too.

By then I had the school bus coming for me, Joylyn standing outside with me until it did. "I can wait alone," I told her when once she had the flu and Doc didn't want her leaving the house. It was fresh outside that morning, a dry wind coming off the hills.

She shook her head, and her short blond curls danced. Her face was red with fever. "No, I don't like you being out on the road alone."

"Why? I'm a big girl." I had smiled at Doc because he'd said so.

"All right, but don't speak to anyone out there. If anyone stops, you run back home. You hear?"

I nodded.

The next Friday, when I came home from school, I couldn't find Grisha. She should have been sleeping in her bed or on mine, but she wasn't. Her bowl stayed filled with cat food bought in Valentine. I threw away the old food and put in new, but still she didn't come. Joylyn prayed for her and told me to. Doc went out on horseback looking for her, then one evening Luis's grandson brought her home. I could see from a distance her stiff legs and matted hair. At first I thought she was a rabbit he'd killed, then I saw her collar and that her chest was open and her stomach gone. "A mountain lion," Luis said.

"A mountain lion wouldn't have left this much," Doc said.

Luis shrugged. "Maybe it don't like the taste."

I pulled on Joylyn's sleeve. She bent down. "Where are her kittens?" I whispered. I said they might be where Grisha was found. Joylyn shook her head.

Doc buried Grisha, then Joylyn put her kapok bed and toys in the can where we burned things.

Doc brought them back to the house. "We'll get another cat," he said.

"Not out here," Joylyn said.

That night, instead of sitting outside with Joylyn and staring into the dry stars, I took the Parcheesi game out of the sideboard, spread it on my bed, and played both parts until I fell asleep with the dice in my hand.

After that, I was nine and nearly ten and all we heard on the radio was about the war, the Japanese all over the Pacific like a swarm of bees. Doc said it was a good thing he was forty.

"Why?" I asked.

"Because that's too old to go."

"It's a good thing you don't have to fly a plane." I was thinking of Uncle Eugene.

A couple of years later, the war was over, the drought came again, and Doc had to sell half the cattle before they got their weight. But that met the back payments on our debt, and Doc had cash money. "I need a sewing machine," Joylyn told him. "I have to make clothes for Stella. She's growing. She needs things. I thought we had a thousand dollars saved in the account that Dad—"

Doc broke in on her, saying there was less in the bank than she thought and, after she'd stayed quiet awhile in her room, she came out and asked him and Luis to wrap the piano in a blanket, tie it on the truck bed; and she and I drove to Fort Stockton, where we traded it for a sewing machine, a Singer built inside a table, so you could swing it down and make it hide. That night we went to a dance hall where Joylyn danced with a brown-skinned man. When the band played a waltz, he danced with me.

I liked the sewing machine, and after a time, I learned to make it hide without jarring it, and also to make it run. "Let me," I said to Joylyn. "I can thread the needle for you."

"You have hawk eyes," Joylyn said, grinning. "You could soar and dive and catch a field mouse." She made a high swoop with her hand to show how that would be done. I did that, too, and then I made a shrieking noise for the dive. Joylyn ducked her head low to her lap and held her ears.

I learned to sew on buttons, too. "You do that good," Joylyn said. "Better than your mama." She was running her hands through my straight hair that we kept shiny with washing.

"I wish my hair was like yours," I said. Her curls jiggled when she walked fast or shook her head.

Joylyn was tall, and her arms and legs were long. "You won't be like me when you grow up," she said. "I mean, you may talk like me, since I'm your mother, and think like you think I think, but you won't be as big."

"Well, I want to be big," I said. I was hemming the skirt of a corduroy jumper then, blue for me since blue matched my eyes. We'd gotten the material and pattern in the mail. I was trying to use Joylyn's silver thimble, but it kept dropping off my finger.

"You can't be big," she said. Then she put her foot on the pedal of the machine.

"I'll change the way I grow," I said loud above the roar.

Sometimes Joylyn played with me, hide-and-seek. I covered my mouth with my hands, ashamed that I couldn't quit laughing at how I loved her, and me playing this game, and me winning so much. "I can always find you," I told her, "because I see your hair or your arm."

"It's not fair," she moaned, covering her lip with her teeth. "You're a little girl and you can hide easy." There was no place to hide in the desert.

"But you know where I am. You always know."

Afterward, Joylyn made purple or red Kool-Aid for us in a pottery pitcher that we'd bought in Ojinaga from women who sold things off blankets. We had no ice block like we'd had delivered in Ozona, but there was cool water from the well. Joylyn laughed and said the Kool-Aid tasted like Mexican clay, but I liked it, and I believe she did, since she always finished her cup.

That year at roundup, when extra men came up from the Estes ranch to help Doc, we still didn't have a bunkhouse, so they slept outdoors under a roof that Doc and Luis made from tarps, and Joylyn cooked special treats of cakes to have after the *faquita* and *frijoles,* and I helped her. We even made angel cakes from mixes we bought in Valentine; and they were tall and light, though they didn't have as much taste as the apple cake, Joylyn said. "You have to make cakes from scratch," she said. *Scratch* meant sifting the dry ingredients together four times and stirring the egg whites as fast as you could until they turned white. And Joylyn didn't have the angel-cake pan, either, since in the move from Ozona, we'd lost it, so we baked them in bread pans.

"It doesn't matter," I told her. She and I sampled all of the cakes from licking the bowl. She laughed when she saw my face, and I laughed, too, when I looked in the mirror. I had a mustache nearly as wide as the mustache of Bernie, the cowboy who was my boyfriend and was teaching me to barrel-race on my pony, Jay.

Then I saw Doc watching Joylyn too close, and I ran to him and climbed on his lap. "Doc!" I said. "That's no name for a rancher! You should work in a hospital!" I was fooling with the buttons on his shirt, pearl buttons, a good shirt that had once been Eugene's—too good for roping steers, so I teased him about dressing up for Joylyn. I looked at her then, but she didn't smile.

Doc set me down on the floor, and soon Bernie called me outside to the chairs and set me on his knees and said the rhyme: "This is the way the lady goes; trot, trot, trot," his legs moving faster and faster until the gallop, when my teeth hit together, and I was leaning back holding his hands. And he didn't drop me or let me fall, so I went down gradual between his knees, inching to the floor, my skirt coming up and covering my face, him laughing and bending over me. He was gathering me up in his arms, when Joylyn came for me and led me away.

"We were playing!" I said shrilly.

But she held my arm tight and took me to the Singer and got me busy running long seams on a piece of scrap material. I tried to sew them straight, so she wouldn't make me rip them out and do the work over, but this time she liked my seam, even though there was a crimp in the stitching. "That's beautiful," she said, then she pressed her cheek against the top of my head, and she smelled of soap and the baby powder she used, not like Doc, who smelled of horses and cigarettes and of the beer he drank starting in late afternoon. "Don't drink before five," he said to Joylyn, laughing. "Five till four."

A few days later, Joylyn and Doc argued strong, and I heard her say she was going to leave and get a job if this money thing didn't straighten out.

"We have food," Doc said.

"We gotta have cash," Joylyn answered, rubbing her fingers together before his eyes, her mouth like she'd tasted something bad.

I went crazy with fear then, and I felt sweat come out on me. Then, when Bernie and the other cowboys left after roundup, and Doc said the white-faces had to be sold short, and that meant adding our neighbor Mr. Estes to our list of people we owed money, Joylyn went down with such a sickness that we had to keep her propped on pillows so she could breathe, so I took her food and cooked for all of us—which I knew how to do from her teaching. When she got a little better, she said, "You can do anything, Stella. You're the best little girl I know. Give your mama her kisses." And that meant the "Eskimo" with the tip of my nose rubbing against hers, then the "butterfly" with my eyelashes fluttering against her cheek.

"Not a movie-star kiss," I said, laughing, since I *could* laugh, now that she was breathing good.

"No," she said. "That's for when you meet your man." She looked sly then, and when I made no reply, she tickled me to get me laughing again. I liked it whenever she touched me, and sometimes I lay next to her in bed, playing with the curls on her head and listening to her breaths, imagining that they made my heart go.

Doc was working hard then, not sitting around anymore reading and letting Luis do the work. When I wasn't in school, I helped him. "I'll bet you wish you had a boy," I said, because I wasn't all that strong.

"No, you're a good worker and you do just fine. You're good with animals, Stella, and that's a gift."

And I was good with them, whether it was rabbits shut up in the hutch or something wild. But it wasn't any gift. It was just giving them water and food, and being halfway polite.

About then, Doc taught me to rope and catch calves on horseback, though most often the rope went down limp. Then, one day, when Doc was chasing a Brahma dogie to bring him home, his horse, Pete, shied and fell. Pete raised himself and waited, pawing by the fence with his reins hanging down, but Doc had hit on his shoulder and face and cracked his collarbone. He was lying facedown when he told me to pick up Pete's reins, so he wouldn't tromp them and make them snap. "But go easy," Doc said. "Don't scare him more than he is."

I calmed Pete by clucking to him like the Mexican mothers do to their crying babies, then I looped the reins over the saddle horn. For nearly a month, Doc had to sit still.

Joylyn could get up now, but she would wheeze if she did too much and would have to sit down, so I still did most of the cooking, which was tuna casserole or *huevos rancheros,* since Luis's family still had hens. For lunch I made canned pimiento or lunchmeat sandwiches, depending on when our neighbor had gone into the store in Valentine. Doc complained of his pain and cried out in the night in dreams, but Joylyn was quiet, and I knew she was thinking.

Then, one morning, just before Doc limped out to tell Luis what to do, she told him again that she was leaving. "You're losing everything. I'm not staying here to watch it. I'm going to do something. I've already waited too long."

He said she wasn't leaving. She said she was, and then she began folding clothes into an old suitcase of Dad's, dresses of mine and hers from the wardrobe. But Doc pulled my clothes out and put them back.

"If you go, you leave Stella Jean," he said, cold and swift as hail.

She stood still, watching him like a rabbit does when it doesn't know which way to run. "She goes with me," she said soft, her hand trembling.

"Not while I'm alive," he said, the way he'd spoken before. "You can't even take care of yourself. How are you going to take care of her? And you're sick now, or you wouldn't be talking this way. . . . You want everything good, Joylyn. You want to get off the train whenever there's a little trouble. You won't stick by the ones who are trying. They teach you that in church?"

"I'm not sick," she said, but she started to cry.

I thought he might try to hug her then, as he hugged me when I cried; but he didn't. "You stay here where you belong," he said firm.

So she didn't go. On and off during the days that followed, I heard her saying again that she was and him threatening her with me; so I kept close to her, following her in the house and yard, not sleeping much for watching the door and listening for sounds of her changing her mind.

6

Second to June and Buck and the kids, I loved Mrs. Slover. Maybe I really loved her better but felt a duty to Jim's family to care for them in a way that's different from those who aren't kin. I never knew exactly how old Mrs. Slover was. She wasn't the kind of person you could ask direct, and she didn't volunteer, but she had an older woman's face with loose skin around her neck and chin, and an older woman's hairdo. That is, she braided her white hair tight, then coiled it up on her head and fastened it with a handful of ripply silver pins.

She didn't welcome me right off that night when we drove in from Fort Worth. After she came out of her house, she stood on the porch, then came down the steps into the side yard and stood before the truck, staring at me a minute or two, at this girl who Jim helped out of the truck cab as if she were a child who couldn't quite make it down to the ground on her own. Then, while Jimmy was taking Mrs. Slover's hand and telling her what we'd done, and that I was his wife now, she was biting on her lip, frowning, the tears coming. Jim hugged her, smiling so she would; but she broke his embrace and acted like she was straightening her clothes, saying to Jim, "I guess you didn't need any old friends standing up for you at your wedding."

"Now don't feel bad," Jim said.

She glanced away into the dark garden. "I don't."

Jim had turned off the truck lights, but there was a yellow light on Mrs. Slover's porch. She stood still a moment, and we said nothing or even moved. Then she turned her eyes and looked me over so close that my hands moved quick over the skirt of my dress to get out the wrinkles.

At last she reached up and gave Jim a pat on the shoulder. "Well, she's pretty," she said. "You can't say she isn't."

"I guess you can't," he said.

She put her hand on my hair and smoothed it. "It must have been a fast decision."

"It was," I whispered, wondering how much I should tell, glancing at Jimmy, and when he didn't make a sign otherwise, saying, "It wasn't even two weeks. Jimmy came back for me." I wanted to tell her how my heart had jumped up hard when I'd seen him outside the house, about how I never thought he'd return, that the most I could ever do to remember him was to stop at the service station I passed on the way to work and get them to tell me where Winston Valley was, and how, if you ever needed to, you might get there.

Mrs. Slover was talking about how the kids would surely be towheads. I smiled. I wanted to talk about kids, mine and Jim's; and I liked her hand on my hair. I wanted it to stay there, and I'd just go to sleep standing beside the truck in the cool backyard, lighted by the yellow glow from the porch. The big silk-hair dog that had barked at the truck ambled up to us, licked Jim's hand, stood quietly to be petted then took a step toward me and put its head in the cup of my hand.

"Her name's Alley," Mrs. Slover said. "I named her that because she looks like an alley cat." And she did. She had broad marks on her that you could have called stripes, though they were golden instead of black. "She can fetch good. There's a tennis ball for her on the back porch. You play with her whenever you want. She never gets tired."

I was letting Alley's ears slip through my hands. She closed her eyes and pushed her lean body against my leg. Jimmy was talking to Mrs. Slover about paying her more now, but Mrs. Slover was saying no. "It's still only one room. I guess I'd have to heat it anyway." She looked at me in a way that made me know that she thought I was skinny. "And she doesn't seem like she eats all that much," she said.

"Oh, she does," Jim warned her to tease me. "She's not shy." He hugged me. "Are you, honey?"

"I guess I'm not."

Jim carried our grips inside; I brought the two plastic bags filled with throw pillows and the storybook doll I still had. There was too much for Jim's room, so as the days passed, Mrs. Slover put some of the things I'd stacked against the wall in a closet she said we could use until we had our own home. "Though I don't want to lose you," she told me and Jim, while we were thanking her.

Well, I wasn't thinking of leaving. That was the furthest thing in my mind. The room was small at the back of the house, but it was plenty for us, happy as we were simply being anywhere then. It had a strong wood bed that Mrs. Slover said her grandfather made for her grandmother, while they were waiting out the long engagement that was customary then. Beside it, there was a matching dresser whose drawers stuck so bad when it rained that Jim and I laughed tugging at them, nearly pulling the dresser down, muffling our laughter so Mrs. Slover wouldn't hear us and have her feelings hurt. Because it wasn't that the dresser was ugly or anything. Not at all. I wished Jim could make me something so good. I told Mrs. Slover that the dresser was a real treasure, and I meant it. There was a chair in the room and a small cotton rug. The windows faced in such a way that in the morning the sun came in bright and early. I kept the shades pulled, but still it came in the cracks, touching Jim and me like it was saying, *That's enough. Come on now. That's plenty.*

"I added this room on for my son," Mrs. Slover told me. "He wanted to be in a far part of the house where he'd have his privacy. So I guess he had it. My husband said it was so he could bring in girls without our noticing it, but to my knowledge he never did." She walked over to the window and raised it to freshen the room. I could smell the breeze going through the pear trees and picking up their scent. "Men like to believe things like that about their sons," she went on, "but I never did. I wanted Henry pure till he married in church. Like a girl has to be." She sighed and looked away. "Why not? It ought to be the same."

I was standing by the bed, leaning over to open my grip and take out the dresses, so they wouldn't look so mashed. I didn't want to ask her anything. I guess I didn't want any sadness on that night, and I saw it coming, whirling around near me like it always did.

"Henry's a friend of mine and Buck's," said Jim. "He got wounded in Korea. They keep him in a hospital near San Antonio."

"The army does?"

He nodded, his expression like he didn't want to stay on this too long.

"I see him every weekend that I can get a ride up there," Mrs. Slover said. "Jimmy takes me sometimes, but I guess he'll be too busy now."

"No," Jimmy said, leaving the room to make one final trip to the truck to get the cooler. "We'll take you. I don't think Stella Jean'll mind riding up there with us some Sunday when I'm off. Will you, honey?"

"No," I said after him. "I'd be glad." I was smiling. I didn't care what we did, just as long as we did it together.

When Jim got back that time, Mrs. Slover left us, shutting the door, me stopping my work of unpacking because I felt Jimmy's eyes on me serious, and so I knew to put aside what I had until tomorrow and go to him. I noticed his hand tremble when he reached down to switch off the lamp. But it didn't tremble when he held me. It was me that started to shake, him telling me up against my neck that it was going to be all right, saying he wouldn't hurt me for nothing.

The first thing I heard the next morning was Mrs. Slover, busy in the kitchen where I was going to have to go in a few minutes. Jim had gone to work, so that had me and her moving close together right from the start, her treating me like a relation, keeping me nearly as close to her as she did Jim. When Jim was working, I helped her in the kitchen, peeling vegetables, stirring what she asked me to, setting the table and helping her wash dishes. Then, when a few days after I got to Winston Valley with Jim, she went down with the flu, I fixed her trays of food and took them to her, her saying no all the time and trying to get up, but me not letting her do anything after I found her fainted on the bathroom floor one morning, and Jim and I had to rub her hands and feet to bring her to herself, then pick her up and carry her back to bed. "You just stay here real quiet," I said. She kept wanting to do things for herself, and I kept reminding her that Dr. Moor said she couldn't.

Six days a week, Jim had to be at the garage by six-thirty.

"Six-thirty!" I hollered when I knew.

"Ranchers get up early," Jim said. "Their animals don't keep no debutante hours, honey."

So as soon as I felt him stirring and stretching, I was up on my feet and in the bathroom, splashing water in my face, then barefoot or in my terry-cloth slippers, padding across Mrs. Slover's rugs and fixing his breakfast and mine, then setting the tray for her and waiting until I heard her get up to use the toilet; and when I did, I'd start breaking the eggs for her in the bowl, while the bacon fried to crisp like she fried it for us, since when she'd been well, she'd gotten up before us and had the food fixed by the time we came in, us still looking sleepy and wearing our robes, and her stirring her coffee and waiting for us as if we were her children and she might need to give us instructions before sending us to school.

Then, while Jim dressed, I'd sit with Mrs. Slover, reading the paper and drinking coffee, making another pot if she asked me for it. After that, we'd usually talk awhile, our elbows and arms on the checkered oilcloth, the fall sun streaming past the shriveled leaves of the pear trees, in across the dry grass, hitting the rusty poles of the swing set that had belonged to Henry and his sister, Jessica. Jessica had married a sailor, and they lived up North. "I went to visit her once," Mrs. Slover said. "Spent two weeks one spring. I guess she wants me to come live with them, but I don't like the damp cold; and, of course, I can't leave Henry."

"Maybe they would move Henry up there," I said. "The army, I mean. Don't they move people if they need it? I mean, if their folks want them moved?"

"No and he's better staying where he is. They get him sitting up in his chair. He can't talk or anything, but I believe he knows me when he sees me. Every time I go there, I notice some light in his eyes that says he does, and that he's glad I've come to look after him awhile. I think he'd be scared if I didn't, so I couldn't move away."

Hearing Alley bark and leave her dugout under the house, Mrs. Slover glanced out the window into the yard, and my eyes went with hers, so I could watch Alley chase a squirrel up a dead tree in back beside the garage.

"How do you know what Henry's thinking, if he doesn't talk?" I asked.

"Oh, I know, that's all."

After she said that, tears came to her eyes, and she had to wipe with her napkin up under the oval lenses of her glasses, and in a while she was looking on the wall at a photograph of Henry and his father. They were out on the front walk, dressed up for church. Henry looked about fifteen or sixteen, and Mrs. Slover told me that that was the best picture she had of him from before he was hurt. "He was too young to go to war or anywhere," she said when she could, "but he wanted to, because two of his friends were going. He was big, heavy, no fat on him, like my husband's people that way; so he played football in his sophomore year, junior, too. He was getting real good. The coach said he might get him a college scholarship if he kept it up. He was seventeen then, but at the recruiting office he told them he was older, the same as the others, boys who'd graduated the year before. I told him he couldn't go, but then he was gone, telephoning me from where he'd enlisted, saying it was done. Then right away I started getting letters from California." She paused. "Jimmy was lucky, having his knee torn up playing football."

Jimmy had told me about that injury, his disappointment about not being able to finish out the season his senior year; then the guilt and pain he had felt when Henry and some others enlisted and left Winston Valley, and he had had to stay behind.

"Thank God," I whispered. I had thought about that, what if Jimmy had been hurt, put in a hospital, and I had never met him. And that was not only because he was all I had, but that he was so much more than I ever expected.

Mrs. Slover glanced back at me. Her shoulders hunched, and by her eyes I saw again how old and troubled she was. "Henry wasn't ready," she whispered. "None of them were. No training. He was strong, but he didn't have judgment, and they don't teach it."

I patted her hand. She slipped it out and covered mine with hers. "You have any brothers, Stella Jean?"

"No, ma'am."

"Sisters?"

"No, not that, either."

I told her the story that I told everyone, except a little more, but saying Doc died in Valentine instead of Anderson. I told her how I'd screamed when I'd first seen he wasn't going to wake up that morning before I went to school, and me throwing down the books I had in my arms and going for the hired man, and his coming in the house with me and saying Doc must have died in his sleep. "It took my savings to bury him," I said. "But I wanted the grave marked, and I got that."

"You ever go back there and visit the cemetery?"

"No ma'am."

"Maybe Jimmy can take you one day."

"Maybe he can," I whispered.

"And so what were you doing in Fort Worth?" she asked.

I lied then. I don't know why. "Working," I said. "A girlfriend wrote me and told me to come there."

When she heard I had somebody, I saw something come up bright in her eyes that I hadn't seen before. I guess it had her worried that nobody ever wrote me or phoned. "Oh? Well, is your girlfriend ever going to come down here and visit?"

"I don't know."

"Do you write to her?"

"I will. Well, I haven't yet."

"If she comes to visit, she can stay here. There's that bed in the sewing room, and if we air the mattress a little, it'll be just fine. You tell her she's welcome." Then she asked me my friend's name as though I'd told her before and she'd forgotten.

"Shirley," I said. "Shirley Berg."

That was the name of a woman who worked in the bank in Fort Worth. She'd never told me her name, but I'd seen it written on the plaque below the glass panel that separated her from me. I liked the way she wore her black hair, pulled back tight in a French twist, and how she wore white shirts and tailored suits just like a man.

"She Jewish?"

I paused, and for a moment I felt uncomfortable without knowing exactly why. "I don't know," I said soft.

Mrs. Slover shook her head. "Well, it doesn't matter." Her glasses were flashing in the light from the outside, and I couldn't see her eyes to know if they were hard or not from what she was thinking. "It's just that you can't always trust them."

"Why not?"

"Because they stick together and only take care of their own."

"I don't think so," I said firm.

I was starting to argue, when I heard Jimmy's truck coming in, the tires bumping over the ruts in the drive. I looked outside and saw the sun hitting the shiny fenders and making starbursts over the hood. The door slammed, and Jim was running toward the porch; then he was inside, lifting me to twirl me around and say good morning again. "How are you, Stella Jean?" he was leaning over me then, waiting for my answer, but I was embarrassed in front of Mrs. Slover. I wanted her to think I was brought up right, that I'd been taught to cook and keep house and care for children and act shy around men, especially the one who was my husband. "I'm fine," I said. "You feeling okay?"

"Sure, why wouldn't I?"

I looked at him like I thought he was crazy for saying that, then he drew me up in his arms and kissed me again. "You ever going to get up?" he asked.

"I *am* up, Jimmy."

"I mean get dressed and start your day." He was fooling with my hair, running his fingers through my bangs, each time causing me to shut my eyes.

I glanced toward our room. "I was just going to, when you came."

"I'll bet." He kissed me again and grinned. "I don't care how long you laze around, honey. You do what you want."

What I wanted was to put my arms around him and keep him there with me, but I had to step back because I knew he hadn't come to stay.

"Well, walk on down to the garage when you can," he said.

"And what would I do there?" I asked.

He laughed. "That's a smart question. You can talk to me while I work, tell me stories, jokes."

"And why would I do that?"

"Because you love me."

"And why else?" I asked, forgetting myself, since he had. Then I was kissing his hand over and over, my lips pressing into his skin.

"To keep me company."

Mrs. Slover had looked away to give us privacy, but I knew she was smiling. She loved Jim, too; and I think she had sparks of love for me that kindled real big sometimes, though it's hard to know exactly what people are feeling, since they don't always know fully themselves.

"He's just a kid about a lot of things," she said when Jimmy was gone, after he'd let the screen bang and then waved through the kitchen window, putting his thumbs in the corners of his mouth and making a face like the pumpkin jack-o'-lantern, the one we were going to make in a few nights and set on a plate on the front porch, "but that just reminds me of how Henry was. He used to come in here hollering, dragging his dirty boots all over the floor, then kissing and teasing me, when I told him he was going to have to clean up."

"And did he clean up?"

"Not so you could tell it. He never learned to hold a broom, none of the good ones do."

I stood at the opened door and watched Jimmy stride to the shed to get some tool he needed. I saw him feint and pull his arm back like he was getting ready to throw a football pass; then he threw it, opening his hand, standing still as if he were waiting for it to land, then jumping for joy when the imaginary runner caught it and ran over the line. "You see that, Stella Jean?" he yelled from the yard. "You see that, honey?"

"I saw it, Jimmy!" I was trembling with delight over his love for me, not minding a bit now that Mrs. Slover could see. I wanted her to tell people that Jimmy loved Stella Jean, and because of that, they had to love her, too.

In a minute, Jim had disappeared inside the shed, come out with what looked from a distance like a wrench, then climbed back in the truck, slammed the door, and driven off. "He's never quiet, is he?" I whispered.

"No, he isn't," answered Mrs. Slover. "And you be glad of it."

"I am."

Then she was talking about Henry, how much he and Jim were alike—not in looks but in personality—how she'd never been enough to Henry, since he was a late child for her and her husband, born when she was past forty. I was turned from her, sitting down again but still gazing outside, watching the dust at the bend in the road, seeing that the cloud that had been solid earlier had broken up and was hanging there over the hedge in a nearly straight line, as if it were still trying to watch what was going on here but its power to do that was dimming with every moment that passed. I was hoping I'd never have regrets like Mrs. Slover had, but I guessed that most likely I would.

We were going to a football game that night. The high school was playing the one in Boerne, thirty miles away, and the game was supposed to be the best of the season. Winston Valley had straight wins so there was excitement in town, people at Bearden's Café even placing bets, I'd heard. I asked Mrs. Slover if she wanted to go with Jimmy and me. We liked to take her places. Sometimes we took her to the movies or down to the river for a picnic on Sunday, where after we'd eaten, we'd sit in the twilight and feed the birds from the bag of bread that she always saved for them whenever she got a chance to go down. "No, I don't like the cold," she answered. "There's going to be a wind tonight that I wouldn't want to be sitting still for."

I don't know anything about weather. I just notice when it's beautiful, and then I let myself drift into it and try to become a part of what it is. "How do you know there's going to be a wind?" I asked. "It isn't all that windy now."

"How do I know?" She paused, staring past me at the outdoors framed in the window. "From thirty years of living through the seasons in Winston Valley."

I thought about my living through thirty years here, how easy it seemed now. She got up and started running the hot water for the dishes. I got up, too.

* * *

The first thing that Buck and June did, after that Sunday morning when Jimmy had taken me out to the ranch, after we'd gone into their big, rambling house and they'd heard the news and taken turns hugging me as close as they could, was to give a party for us, a supper and dance starting in the early evening, with friends bringing music—a drum, a harmonica, two accordions, and two violins—so that we could dance on the floor of the barn. June and her girlfriends fixed just about everything you can think of to eat, starting with grilled bass the men caught in the Blanco River, then going on to barbecued ribs and beef and chicken and rich sauerbraten, dumplings, bowls of steaming sweet-and-sour cabbage, hot potato salad, slaw with dill weed. Then pies and cobblers with the fruit bursting the crusts. The dishes were on a half-dozen long tables set under the trees, covered with white cloths and decorated in the center with crepe paper, crimped and pulled and stretched and tied to look like bouquets of flowers. Ribbon streamers were caught up with bows and hung from the rafters in the barn.

Jim and I stood in the front yard, just inside the gate, a table behind us for presents. And the people came, each one of them stopping to congratulate Jim and meet me, then to give us what they'd brought in the way of cookware and china. One couple brought a lamp, another a corner table, each gift wrapped up in white paper and ribbon, some of them with a paper orchid or lily of the valley. The men, ranchers and cowboys mainly, with coarse hands, their faces and necks still showing the sunburns left over from summer, were hitting Jim on the back and shoulders, grasping his hand tight, whispering to him sometimes, then laughing and kissing me. And I smiled back at them and at their wives and children until my cheeks ached and my mouth trembled and the bones in my feet were breaking. But I wanted to keep on. I'd hardly ever even been to a party, much less had one given for me, not since I'd lived in Valentine.

"Jim known you long?" one of the women asked me. Her name was Joyce Cooper, a woman not much older than myself and who had been Jim's girlfriend in high school. He'd already told me that when he'd graduated, they'd talked of getting married, but he hadn't thought he was ready, nor had he really loved her enough that way. Then late that summer, she'd eloped with Shelley Cooper. Joyce was a small, pretty woman, and now she was smiling up at us, holding a baby in her arms, and when I asked her to let me see it, she lifted the corner of the blanket to show its face. Jim looked at it, too, without flinching, so I took that to be a good sign that he'd forgotten whatever had gone on between them before me.

"Where did Jimmy find such a pretty thing as you?" one of the men asked. He'd been Jim's football coach at the high school.

I looked up at Jim.

"Not here," Jimmy said, and then he blushed for the mistake he made and tried to correct it. "I mean, I had to leave town. Nobody here would have me. Isn't that right, Lucy?" Lucy Bearden ran the café in town.

"No, it isn't right, Jimmy. I guess you had plenty of choices, but you weren't happy with a country girl."

I looked down at my dress, white like Mrs. Slover had told me to wear, and then made it for me, too, telling me I could use her machine but doing most of the work herself. I'd been afraid about wearing makeup, and so I hadn't used much until I'd seen what the other women did. The young ones wore it, most of them more than I had on. It worried me that Mrs. Bearden didn't think I looked like a country girl. I guess my eyes flashed too quick on the new faces, studying too closely each guest who stepped out of a car and started coming my way, afraid one of them might know me and say from where.

They came early while it was still day and drank beer as the sun went down, the light fanning out orange over the hills, the trees blackening into it, then sinking into the sky, one planet sitting so close to the moon that Mrs. Slover told me it was a good sign for Jim and me.

It was a cool evening. "Go in and get your sweater, honey," Jim told me when I complained, and when his arms being around me and the fast dancing hadn't been enough. "Or you want me to do that for you?"

He started out, but I called him back. "I'll go," I said. He'd been talking to some men who'd just arrived, driven a long way, and I believed he wanted to go on talking.

I went in the house and found my sweater. As I was coming back, I noticed the guests looking at me, since I was the bride, dressed like I was in white, with pearl earrings that Jim had given me and a wreath of chrysanthemums in my hair that June had made for me and put there as soon as I was dressed.

That night was the best one of my life. Geraldine Moss, the lady who ran the library and had gone to school with June, had even made us a wedding cake, three round layers, each one of them smaller than the one below, and then a bride and groom doll on top, black and white plastic, staring at Jim and me and the guests out of the black dots that were their eyes, the little dolls placed under a spun-sugar trellis that Jim and I broke and divided before we began cutting the slices, putting the pieces of it in some of the little children's outstretched hands.

Then Buck and his friends began opening the champagne, bottles and bottles of it popping and fizzing over the sides of the circular mouths of plastic glasses. We danced until my dress was wet with perspiration, and Jimmy had taken off his jacket, and we knew we'd have trouble finding it the next morning since it had fallen between two bales of hay and gotten caught. We were twirling around, I was dizzy with dancing waltzes and *Ten Pretty Girls,* laughing at Jimmy's jokes before he'd even finished telling them, feeling his hands on me, hoping they'd keep me up forever, support me, never let me fall. Then he was holding me around the waist, giving my mouth quick kisses whenever neither of us was speaking. People were probably looking at that, but I didn't care, if Jim didn't.

The music started up again. It was four o'clock in the morning. Most of the guests had left long before, but we had a solid line of about twelve of us, and then five or six couples for the waltz; a new couple joining us for the polka. I thought I'd die catching my breath, my lungs hurting, me holding my hand to my chest like my heart was pushing out of it with each beat, and I wished I would die. I wished that everything would stop that night, that I could slump to the floor of the barn and feel my life go out while I was happy.

"I never was so happy," I kept telling Jim, when I could get my voice out again and he was holding me and talking about what fun we were having and were going to have for the next fifty years. "Fifty," he said, touching the end of my nose with the tip of his finger. "I promise you a whole half-century, honey."

I started teasing. "A whole half? Well, how can that be?"

And I was so glad that I kept telling him, repeating it even as we were climbing the stairs to June and Buck's spare bedroom, all decorated with wildflower wallpaper and real garden flowers that June and her girlfriends had picked especially. "I never was happy before I met you," I said. "I never knew anything about it before now."

7

It was the summer after I had come to Winston Valley when we found out that living at Mrs. Slover's wasn't going to be enough; and that was on a morning I had set aside to work in the garden until it got too hot, then in the afternoon to help Mrs. Slover can the figs we had put in plastic containers in the pie safe that she kept on the back screened porch.

First thing I did after breakfast was to go outside with an empty basket to collect any new figs that hadn't been quite ready the day before. There were a few, and I gathered them carefully, knowing now from Mrs. Slover's teaching to avoid the ones not yet soft enough under gentle fingers, and lacking enough of the rose color that was supposed to be shooting through the green. The big dog, Alley, was with me, prancing at my side, her bright yellow tennis ball in her mouth, staring at me and whining so much that I had to stop and throw it to her three or four times, then finally tell her firmly that we had to quit till I got through.

When I had put the figs inside with the others, I went to the vegetable garden, planning to clean the twenty-odd rows of weeds and then attach the sprinkler and water the plants, watching the timer clock inside for when to change it. The hoe was in the shed behind the garage. I moved small as I could among the stacks of musty clay pots, reaching for it in its place on a hook on the rafters. Then I put on Mrs. Slover's canvas gloves, pulling them on my hands slowly so as not to split the seams. I started out behind the garage, where in March, after Mrs. Slover had said she wanted us to stay on with her that year, Jimmy had made the garden nearly twice as large, breaking up what we needed for us to plant, so we wouldn't be taking so much from her.

I glanced at the watch that Jimmy had given me for Christmas, a small gold one with a narrow ribbon band. It was nine o'clock, later than I planned, since I knew that it being August, it would get hot early. I put on a straw hat and suntan lotion. I didn't want to get a sunburn. Once when Jimmy and I had been canoeing in the Guadalupe with Buck and June Lester, and Jimmy'd told me to put on a shirt and I wouldn't, I'd burned my body so badly that I could hardly move and I sure hadn't wanted Jimmy anywhere near me—though he didn't get mad about that. He just turned over away from me a little quick, not saying anything, and in a while I heard the deep, regular breathing of his sleep.

I never quarreled with Jim. Quarrels started to happen a couple of times; and after that, I did all I could to avoid them. I knew that it hurt me too badly; and, really, Jim didn't quarrel with people anyhow. When he was angry, he got quiet. He would lie on his back on the sofa, reading some book that used to belong to Mr. Slover; or maybe he would turn on the TV, then ignore me when I tried to make up, me snuggling up to him and him just keeping his hands to himself and his eyes on what he was reading or watching. I knew it was losing his parents in an accident that made Jim like that, knowing that he couldn't trust anybody because he might wake up one morning and find them gone.

And I really couldn't get to him then, unless with loving him, but I was good at that, and it didn't much matter what time of day. The troublesome thing was that the bed Mrs. Slover's grandfather had made creaked whenever we moved on it steady, and that embarrassed me when I had to see Mrs. Slover the next time, since, though our room was to the back of the house, she must have heard us; and I knew it didn't matter what she thought about Jim since he was a man, and people think that men have that kind of pleasure and mischief coming to them, but it mattered what she thought of me—though, in general, the days had passed fine, me pretending to be a different person, a preacher's daughter or a girl born into a quiet family like Dr. Moor's. Maybe I'd gone to high school here, and Jimmy had come by in his truck on Friday nights to drive me to a movie in Kerrville, take me to dances, then park on one of the roads back of town, us listening to the river while we were learning about one another, taking weeks, months, even a year if we wanted to, going a lot slower than we'd had to on that first night for us together in the private back room that the Slovers once added on to their house for Henry.

And then, when the spring had filled out with days gorgeous with light, Jim ordered me a pink bicycle from Sears, and we took rides, fifteen or twenty miles, and had picnics by the river's edge, or under the trees of an orchard, where Jim always knew the name of the rancher and every member of his family. Then, in summer, we'd settled down some, Jimmy working hard at the garage, and me taking on the garden. The weeds had been bad, and he hadn't had time to get to them all. Hardly a moment since he'd been working alone at the garage since Sweeney Hendrick, who owned the garage and the pumps and the food store that his wife ran, had broken his leg jumping down from a truck bed (a sixty-year-old man, acting like a kid, Jimmy said), and so Jimmy had no one there to help him, though sometimes I walked up to the store and ran the pumps and checked the oil. Jimmy had taught me to do that, and it hadn't taken an hour for me to learn, though for the first couple of hood checks, I'd had to call him to come help me, since in the different models the oil stick isn't placed the same.

That summer, I asked June to cut my hair short, and I let my face and shoulders get freckles. I even put a rinse on my hair to make it look brown; but Jimmy didn't like it, so I let it wear off and didn't put on more. I thought of gaining weight, but I'm not good at that; my breasts have always been full, but my arms and legs stay skinny no matter what I eat. Mrs. Slover said most of that was a question of age: As the years go by, keeping off weight gets hard. At nineteen and then at twenty, she didn't have to worry much about weight either, she said.

"But you're not fat," I reminded her. Except outdoors in winter, when she wore a coat, you could see Mrs. Slover's sharp bones showing through her clothes.

"I don't let myself get that way," she said. "I never let things go." She talked about the good health her family had always had.

I'd gotten through chopping the first rows, aiming the sharp, pointed side of the hoe at the small green tendrils and young, leafy stalks, tearing them from the even slopes, watching grains of earth crumble into the bottom of the trenches. Alley had been pushing near me, trying to get me to play ball, so finally I had to scold her—and I was sorry to be mean, sorry to see her slink away ashamed and lie down in the hole she'd made under the hedge, then put her face on her paws, watching me with sad eyes. On the other hand, I wanted to get my work done, and I knew I'd be sorry about that, too, if I didn't. It was going to be a surprise for Jimmy, and I didn't want anything going wrong with that. I chopped fast, pretending the weeds were the foe and I was a warrior sent out here by Jim and Mrs. Slover to get them. I went down one row, cleaning it of my enemies, then started down another and then another. The sun shone definite on the slanted, rippling tin roof of the shed, then slipped down onto the grass, making the shadows wave and change like an eager face that's listening to what you're saying. The air was quiet and hot, and it seemed as though the more I waited for the cool breezes to blow up across the back of the yard and refresh me, the less they did. I stopped and wiped my face, then drank some water out of the pint Mason jar that I'd brought from the house, watching the sun bobbing brightly on the curve of the thick glass while I drank. Since I'd made the mistake of setting the jar in a place that too soon got the sun, the water was warm; but I drank half of it anyway because my throat was dry and I was sweating.

When I felt the dizziness, the first signal of it no more than a shiver, I went on working, thinking that I'd had my head bowed too long. I'm strong, and I don't worry a lot about my body getting discontent with heat or cold or even sickness. But then quickly, without much warning except the churning of my stomach, I felt my legs go weak, and in a moment, I was down on my hands and knees, vomiting in one of the trenches, seeing the crumbled earth sucking up the liquid part. I reached over with my hand and covered the other with a clod, then I called to Mrs. Slover, though I knew that my voice was too weak for her to hear and that there was no way in the world I could get it stronger. Then I remembered that she was away at her flower club. She wouldn't be home till lunch. So I curled up in the dirt, waiting for the spell to pass. Alley came to me and licked my cheek. I reached around to pet her for her sweetness, then felt the sour waves going through me once more and had to rise again to my knees to keep from soiling myself. I started to cry, quick, jerking sobs like babies do. The next few times I retched, nothing came up. My head ached at the back of my neck. I kept arching into the spasm, then being pulled down to the earth that was warming and drying quickly, everywhere that my hoe had exposed it to the sun; and seeing on the level of my eyes the weeds I had hacked and feeling that they had brought me down with them in revenge, wanting me there with my cheek against the slope of the trench, my skin pinched by the clods. I lay there, I don't know how long, but long enough that when I lifted myself, my legs ached.

"Jimmy," I whispered, and then I was getting up and knowing where I had to go, and what I had to tell.

I ducked my head and went through the hedge, taking the shortcut at the open place where Jimmy and I always walked when we needed to get out on the road to town, Alley pacing beside me, her thinking, I guess, that we were just going up to the corner on the road. I watched my feet, one of them pushing out before the other, knowing what to do, though my aching head couldn't insist on a direction for them. I moved aside for a car; someone called to me from its window. The voice wasn't one I knew. Then I was stumbling on the gravel shoulder to the horse path, trying to miss a wild daisy; but my foot didn't obey me that time, so the toe of my shoe hit the base of its stem and snapped it off.

The service station and garage were at a bend in the road just before the town square comes into full view with Mrs. Bearden's café and the shops.

I heard someone shouting "Stella, Stella!" And then I heard another voice: "Isn't that Stella Lester?" A stout woman was running toward me, her breasts bouncing, her arms outstretched, the soles of her shoes hitting the road like clapping hands.

"Hey, Jimmy!" And that was a man's voice coming up from the side. "Where the hell's Jimmy?"

And then I went down hard on my knees, someone catching me under my arms before my face hit; and then two people working with my tangled limbs and laying me down flat. I saw all the eyes above me straining, the hair and shirts blurring, then those heads were pushed aside and replaced by red hair, and unruly pale eyebrows that nearly came together in the center. "What is it, honey? Stella Jean? Somebody hurt you?" There were tears in Jimmy's eyes, and I wanted to say something to help him, but I couldn't because of my throat.

"That's it," the woman was saying, "just slip your hands up under her. Easy there. You see?"

And he had done that, lifted me, then said where we were going, but already I couldn't remember. Someone pushed my arms up around his neck and told me to hold tight, and I think I did.

The sun was hitting my eyes from on top, then not hitting them except in quick, surprise glances like blanks in a slide show. We turned, then went inside a building, and I heard a woman telling him where to go, while he told her all that he knew. In a moment, we'd gone through a couple of inside doors, and I was lying on a table under a light, a man speaking softly; and I recognized the voice of Dr. Moor and heard him tell everyone except Mrs. Moor to leave us now, because if this was what he thought, then we'd need a little privacy. And I guess Jimmy and the ones who had followed him in agreed, because pretty soon no one was in there with me but the Moors, Mrs. Moor helping me get ready, then Dr. Moor doing what he had to do and, after only a little more discomfort for me, telling me the news.

Mrs. Moor opened the door; and Dr. Moor, stepping out on the threshold of the room, said, "Come on in, Jimmy. I'm going to let Mrs. Lester tell you herself what I guess you've been hoping to hear."

I was home in bed when we decided about the house, me eating chicken soup made by a friend at church and sent over in a blue-and-white tureen. Behind my head were our pillows and one off Mrs. Slover's bed, too; Jimmy's hand dipping a spoon into the soup, dabbing at my mouth with a napkin, so I wouldn't drip anything on the bedcovers. I saw light on Jim's face, light from the lateness outside lying on his red hair like his head was part of the setting sun. You would always remember Jimmy's hair, the way it looked in that kind of light, and also in the early morning hours when it was against a white pillowcase. "I can get up," I said, though I had no idea where I meant to go. Maybe to pick up the tools I'd left in the garden.

"I know. But maybe you don't want to. Is the soup going to stay down, you think?"

"Sure."

He handed me a soda cracker, and I bit down on it. The salt in it tasted good. While I ate, I stared at him, trying not to smile until I was sure everything was all right with him about what we knew, since before now, he and I were like two kids playing house, living with our mother, Mrs. Slover, and not bothering about getting anything of our own, just letting her take care of us, not sponging off her, I always like to think, but getting what we needed; though we paid the rent on our room and for the food we ate, and we did our part of the work, whatever we thought of to help her and whatever she might ask us to do, including taking her on hospital trips every two weeks to visit Henry.

I guess we thought I'd get pregnant that first month we were married, and then the second and third; and when I didn't, we quit expecting it. We hadn't talked about it, either, though I'd done nothing to prevent its happening and I knew Jim hadn't.

So, all of a sudden now, with me sick today and all the town knowing why, I was making plans and including in them what I knew about, but couldn't see or even feel yet, except in the sickness I had which Dr. Moor said would probably continue for at least a few more weeks. I could just hear it being said in all the houses and in the drugstore and the grocery store: *Stella Lester's pregnant; Jimmy and Stella Lester are expecting.* It was always like that, people telling it and knowing the final truth of a couple, that at last they were getting out of what they did what God intended, instead of perpetually answering to some call their bodies made, and which had nothing to do with anything except this.

My eyes took a quick study of our room, the chest of drawers filled to breaking, more clothes folded on a table in the corner, Jim's and my books and magazines stacked against the wall, our coats not even in here but on the coatrack by the front door, where they'd been since the last chilly spell in April. "You know of anything we could rent?" I asked Jim. "I guess we're going to need more than just this room."

"The Caters are going to put up their house for sale," Jim said. "Mrs. Moor says they're moving, and they have to be gone some time before school starts."

That was all right with me. Kitty and Orman Cater had a cottage not much farther from town than we were now, just enough farther to be quieter and a little more isolated. The cottage was in the center of a block, with two houses across the street and one behind it, but none on either side. It probably needed work on the roof and the garage, and the outside was too shady, but Jimmy and Buck could make the repairs, and then cut down the smaller trees and trim the larger ones so the sun could come through. Once I got well, once my mornings cleared up to normal, as Doctor Moor said they would, I could make curtains and spreads. It was then that I told Jimmy about a savings account that I had in a bank in Fort Worth, some my father had left me, I said. "I'd meant to tell you about it before, but I guess we didn't need it until now."

Two days later, we were in the Caters' yard. "Mrs. Lester," I heard Kitty say. I guess she was being extra polite with me, not using my first name because she wanted me to buy the house.

"My name's Stella," I said to her; and I was smiling because I wanted the house, and she was smiling because she knew that she was going to sell it that afternoon and have that worry behind her. And I was smiling, also, because I was having a baby, and if it were a son I was going to call it Darrell after a man in Jimmy's family who'd come to Texas from Tennessee and had to fight Indians; and I figured that any child of mine would need a spirit strong like that behind him.

All of us went to see how the garage was. Jimmy thought it needed some better support in the center, the two-by-fours replaced there; and I was sure he planned to paint it and the toolshed as well. Then, when we weren't looking at that anymore, we stood in the center of the backyard, each with his arms folded across his waist, each staring at the back fence, the bottom of it hidden by Johnson grass, the top tangled with trumpet vine and ivy. The yard had been mowed short, for our visit, I guess, since it still smelled fresh-cut; but no one had raked it, so that some of the damp green clippings stuck to our shoes. A cloud was blowing across the pasture out back, turning the grass blue.

Orman was speaking about the mayor and the new paved street that the council planned to have run along the west end of town to connect the farm road that ran along Cyprus Creek. I knew not to interrupt him, so I didn't say anything to Jimmy. I just snuggled near him, so he draped an arm around my shoulders and pulled me up close, me resting my head on his shoulder. And when finally Orman had quit talking, Jimmy moved just slightly so he could look directly into my eyes. By then I had been holding some cone flowers in my hand that the Caters' little boy had brought to me; one that had just the yellow center now, since, while Orman was talking, I'd pulled off the petals one by one to see if Jimmy loved me and had that come out right.

"How do you like it, honey?" Jim asked me. "You want to live here?" He wasn't smiling, and I knew that was because having me and now this baby and buying a house meant working harder and steadier, and not buying a hauling truck, and not being able to wander over America—hard on a man who's planned it, even one as reliable as Jim.

"Sure, I do."

He put his hands on my shoulders, his eyes taking me with him wherever he was thinking of going. I know that Jim loved me that afternoon, and not just by the cone flower's saying it. "You want the house, I'm asking you," he said softly, so that the question would seem only between the two of us.

"Yes, I do."

Then, while Jim and Orman sat on a bench beside the fence, drank a beer, and talked about the money, Kitty invited me into the house again; and in a moment I was standing in the narrow hallway with the cozy living room on the right side and the Caters' sunny bedroom on the left, wide sash windows in each of those rooms; and as I moved farther on, Kitty was talking and holding her baby on her hip, the baby's eyes round as buttons with interest in me, while it closed its gums on a graham cracker, the dark brown crumbs leaking thickly down its chin, Kitty telling me the good of the house. And I was feeling the hardwood of the floor beneath my feet, how solid it was and well built, then looking in at the smaller bedroom on the right, then the bigger one on the left, then behind me to the kitchen, not a large room, but plenty for anything I'd ever need to do; and, beyond, an alcove large enough for an eating table that would hold two people, maybe even four, and space enough for a high chair.

I stood at the back door, gazing through the torn screen. I wanted to repair it right then, to make this solid house perfect, give it what it deserved for the hard work and good materials someone had put into it apparently with so much care.

"Oh, I should fix that," I heard Kitty say from behind me. "I've been meaning to, but the kids don't give me time." She started to laugh, then seemed to decide that making excuses to me wasn't worth the trouble. I guess Jim and I didn't appear all that good, living with Mrs. Slover in one room and owning nothing more than two gold wedding bands and a six-year-old truck.

Kitty mentioned the attic. We walked back down the hall. One of the kids' bedrooms was full of toys and rumpled flannel bedclothes. The other, smelling of urine and sour milk, had a baby bed beside the window and a stack of packing boxes against one wall. "My husband's taken a job in Schulenburg, where my family lives. I'll be glad to get there where I have people to help me with the kids. My baby just turned one year, and here I am already having another."

Kitty Cater was pregnant, but much farther along than I was, her belly so big it strained her dress; and she breathed so fast when she walked any distance at all that I told her please not to climb the stairs to see the attic and storage room with me. "I can go up there alone," I said.

"Well, be sure you look at everything, Stella Jean. You just take your time."

The stairs were steep and slick, and so I held on tight to the banister, knowing what could happen if I fell. The dark storage room was filled with boxes. I pulled on a string dangling from the ceiling, but the light only blinked a few times and never came on full. The attic was heaped with things, too: an old wooden radio; blankets stuffed in a wicker basket; a huge cardboard box filled with scraps of material probably meant for quilting, but whose corners had been gnawed by a squirrel or rat so that some of the scraps trailed across the floor like water flowing from holes in a barrel.

I stood at the dormer window and gazed into the black branches of a live oak tree. A woodpecker was hammering at a dead limb, its red head like a hood someone made it for Christmas. I must have made a sudden motion that scared it, because it stretched its wings, flapped them a couple of times to steady its flight, then disappeared. I was sorry. I would have liked to stand there in the warm space and watch it, working out in my mind how I was going to fit what I had now with what I'd had in the years before, maybe people thinking that I wasn't quite the quality of the Lesters and Slovers, that there was something missing about me that they couldn't fully learn, but could only imagine and regret.

But right then, standing there looking out, hearing the faint buzz of Jim's and Orman Cater's voices in the yard, then Kitty calling out so friendly to them from the kitchen window, asking if they'd like something to eat, it seemed like an invisible hand had passed over and made me a promise. And I vowed that as soon as Jim and I were settled, we'd never miss church, never get up too late for the service, as we sometimes had in the past months. We'd go to Sunday school, too, because I'd need to know the Bible. With a child, I'd have to know some quotes from *Psalms* and *Proverbs*—not by heart, of course, because I'm not good at memorizing, but at least know the sense of them, be able to find a passage and read it aloud whenever I needed to, so I could guide my child in the paths Mrs. Slover tried to live by, and that Joylyn had tried so hard to understand.

8

It's odd the things I remember from the best days of my life: the way the clouds appeared, Jimmy saying one looked like a camel, another like a clipper ship; the striped silk umbrella of a black woman in town; what flowers were blooming in the window boxes on the square; what trees were out full and which were holding back; the baby book I got at the shower June Lester gave for me, me leafing through it while I was waiting for Jimmy to come, thinking about what I'd be writing in it tomorrow.

It was on a Monday after a weekend of Jim and me putting in some bedding plants I'd grown under glass; and I was feeling good, strong like I always do. I had started cramping, but the pains came and went. And anyway, I'd welcomed the first one and said a prayer of thanksgiving because hurting like that meant I'd soon see the baby.

On the phone, I told Jim that I could walk to the clinic and meet him there, save him time since I knew he had a full day and didn't need to be bothered. He was an experienced mechanic now. I believed he knew all that Mr. Hendrick did, and that the news of his good work was bringing in more business than they could nearly do. With part of the money I'd had for the house, he'd thought to ask me if he could buy into the garage and store so he'd be half-owner with Mr. Hendrick. And that was fine with me. "You have to own what you do," Jimmy'd said, when we were talking about it one night, having coffee in the kitchen while we were still living at Mrs. Slover's. "You can't always be working for somebody else. Though it's your money, Stella. So it's going to have to be you who decides. I wouldn't touch it if you didn't think it was a good idea."

Well, I didn't know enough about business to give an opinion, but I knew this: Everything I had, I meant to share equal with Jimmy, and so I moved the money into an account where he could draw on it the same as I did. And now that he owned half the garage and service station, he and Mr. Hendrick were planning improvements, and talking serious about hiring someone else on at the garage.

"You stay put, honey," Jimmy said on the phone, when I mentioned walking. "Just wait on the porch; I'm coming. You won't leave, Stella Jean? I don't want you going up there alone."

"I can meet you at Dr. Moor's."

"You want to take a chance of hurting the baby?" He was speaking firm and steady, and I knew he wasn't hanging up till I agreed.

So I stayed home, and when he arrived, screeching the truck, jumping out of the door and leaving it open, then coming up the walk fast, frowning, I was sitting in the white wood armchair on the porch. I'd just come out from lying on the sofa. "Well, you were right," I said, waiting in the chair, shutting my eyes until a new trouble passed. "I guess I couldn't have walked."

He got me to my feet. "You crazy or something," he whispered, hugging me, "thinking you could get over there by yourself?"

When we walked down the steps, he held me close; when he helped me up into the truck, he boosted me from behind, pretending that I was too heavy for him, groaning, teasing me like he had for the last few weeks. Buck had teased me, too, saying when I walked, I looked like a battleship in high seas. "You're going to get swamped, Stella, if you can't keep any straighter than that. I hope we don't have no rain."

From the truck window, I could see azaleas in fancy yards, blooming pink and white, purple iris standing stiff in shallow bordered beds, the air still light and cool, so that when we stopped for the traffic light in town, I pulled my sweater tight around my shoulders. We passed one block vacant of houses, then another, vacant except for Dr. Moor's one-story clinic. There was a trellis of roses over the entrance to the walk, but no blooms yet or even buds, just leaves starting on the stumps of the pruned branches, and getting thicker every day. Jim came around for me and lifted me down, catching me under my arms; then he opened the gate for me and took my hand while we walked together up the walk to the porch, a cement slab, one side of it higher than the other, a lightning-bolt crack shooting across, so that Mrs. Moor had to warn the patients to be careful stepping in and out the door. "Thank you for doing this for me," Jim said.

"For doing what?"

"For carrying the baby, for what you're going through now."

I laughed. "What else could I do?"

We were inside the waiting room. Julius Bearden was sitting on the sofa, reading the morning paper. I heard him wheezing like he always did and guessed he had an appointment to see Dr. Moor. "Hi," he said and waved at us with a hand that held a lighted cigarette. "Looks like we got a baby soon," he said, especially to me.

I smiled as well as I could, since I was hurting then.

Jim answered for me. "I guess we do."

I liked Julius Bearden. Whenever you went into the church, you could count on his being in one of the pews, his wife in a lace-collar print dress sitting beside him, Julius with his asthma, his pigeon chest, his neck thick from the high breathing he had to do. I don't think he or his wife ever missed church or Bible study or picnics or revivals, or anything else Dr. Tillerson organized or told us about; but with all that, it seemed to me that his faithfulness hadn't blessed his life like Dr. Tillerson said it should. More than once, I'd seen him lift his eyes to the roof of the church when Dr. Tillerson called to the Savior, pleading with Him to bless and save us. And then I'd hear Julius sing, his voice on-key but wispy and shrill because of his thin breath.

Jim walked up to the desk in the corner of the waiting room and pressed the heel of his hand flat on the silver, dome-shaped bell. Mrs. Moor came out and had me sit down while Jim filled out a form, Jimmy writing slow and careful like he always did, the way he'd signed our marriage certificate and then the loan papers to finish off the portion on the house we still owed at the bank.

While I waited, breathing deep, some of the time hurting, some of the time free of it, I was watching Jim in his work shirt and Mrs. Moor in her white uniform, but I was thinking about church, of all those people praying and singing, going down to where Dr. Tillerson was standing and saying they were saved; his putting his hands on them to tell them that if they truly repented of their sins, they were forgiven them, and that God would never think about those sins again.

After I heard about the baby, I knew I was going to have to go down there to Dr. Tillerson. Now that my body was blessed that way, I'd have to try to get pure. And so three Sundays before, I'd done it, amazing myself that I had the nerve. I imagined that while I walked down the steps, the Mosses and Pickenses and Beardens, too, were staring at my body, at how big I was and at how the skin on my cheeks was blotched and how I was breathing nearly as heavy as Julius Bearden. And when Jim had seen the thing I was going to do, he'd risen, too, and taken my arm and held it the whole time we were going down the steps to where Dr. Tillerson would bring Jesus' grace and mercy into us both.

The Moors weren't Baptist like Mrs. Slover and us. They were something else, or maybe like Doc, they never went to church at all. Doc believed that there was nothing after this life, just sleep and rest for wounded people like himself. The universe wanders blind, he said, and he and Joylyn argued.

I glanced around the clinic waiting room, thinking about the Moor family and how this was their home as well as Dr. Moor's clinic, so that only about half of the rooms beyond this one were for the patients. June had told me that when Dr. Moor built the clinic, he planned to live elsewhere, but when his partner had gotten an offer to work for a college in Denton and Dr. Moor couldn't attract another doctor to the town, he'd had to sell his house to pay for the clinic and move his family in there, too.

"He's a grand doctor," June had told me. "You won't find better anyplace you go." That was on a Sunday, when we'd been having dinner at the Lesters' ranch and Jimmy had just told her and Buck about the baby we were expecting. "Well, you'll be plenty safe with Dr. Moor," June had told me, and then she'd glanced around the table at her children. "He delivered Trix and Nancy and just look at them."

I shut my eyes and bowed my head. A pain was coming, and I didn't want anyone to see my face.

"It was bad?" Julius said, when my head raised up.

"Not too. I'll be all right."

And I knew I would. I'd gone through too much in my life to worry seriously about something like childbirth, which nearly any woman on earth could do.

When the form was filled out and Jim had pushed it back across the desk, Mrs. Moor took me to a white room, one with two beds, a chair beside each, and a table for a glass jar with cotton and a nest of metal containers. On a bar with hooks, there was a white canvas curtain, but since no one else was in the room, the curtain remained pulled back to the wall. "Take the bed nearest the door, Stella," said Mrs. Moor. "Jimmy, you go back and wait where Julius is. There's some magazines, and you can turn on the TV if you want. But keep the sound low. Mr. Harmon's got pneumonia in the room next to this one, and he needs his rest."

Jimmy nodded, then came over to where I was and kissed me. "You going to be okay, Stella Jean?"

I nodded.

"I'm going to phone June and Buck," he said.

"Call Mrs. Slover, too."

"You can use the phone on my desk," Mrs. Moor said, "but tell them not to hurry. She's going to be here awhile, and we'll want her to have quiet. No visitors at all."

"Tell them I'm doing fine," I said.

I undressed and put on a white gown that Mrs. Moor tied for me in three bows behind. The bed she put me on was flat and hard, a white sheet tucked in tight around it. There was a folded sheet at the end of the bed and a blue blanket folded on a shelf above. The room had only one window, at the far end. When I turned, I could see the trees, pecans not yet making full shade, so that when the sun came in, the shadow of the panes was etched clear on the white cover of the other bed. In the fall, we'd picked pecans, not only in our yard and in Mrs. Slover's but everywhere we could find them on sidewalks or roads, loose and unclaimed. Then we'd put them in mesh sacks in the root cellar, bringing them inside whenever I needed them for what I was cooking, Jim and I cracking and picking them on Sunday afternoons while we watched football on TV.

We had moved into the Caters' house in October, when it was already cool, but with the coralvine still blooming like a pink cartoon fire all over one side of the front porch. Buck had thought we ought to pull the vine down because it might rot the wood trim, but I'd screamed *no* when he'd started to yank on it. One streamer fell and curled in the dirt, and when Jimmy picked it up and wound it so careful again among the others, I put my arms around him and hugged him tighter than I ever had. That was a windy day, the wind blowing hard on Jimmy and Buck and Junior as they carried in the heavy things: the bed we'd bought, the chest of drawers and the sofa that June's mother, Mrs. Ambler, was lending us, until we could afford to go to San Antonio and buy one of our own.

Then that evening, after I'd cooked hamburgers outside on the grill the Caters left behind, and Jimmy had gone to the drive-in grocery for fudge-ripple ice cream; and when, at last, June and Buck had left and Jimmy and I were alone, it began to rain, a sprinkle at first, raindrops splashing off the porch steps, then so hard that some of the tallow leaves fell to a drenched carpet on the lawn, and the hanging basket on the oak began to spin, one way and then the other, some rain spattering on the floor before an open window; then Jimmy and me going down on our knees with a new towel because I didn't have any rags yet, us rolling out part of the new rug and laughing and playing on it, because this was our house in here and our garden out there, wet as it was.

Mrs. Moor put a thermometer in my mouth. It tasted bitter of alcohol. She waited, read it, and wrote something down, then put a band tight around my arm and stuck a needle in a vein she'd searched for with her thumb. Dark red blood inched into one glass tube and then a second. When she'd set that aside and was doing the other preparation, she had to stop because I'd pulled my legs together and turned my body to the side. By then I was biting my lip and groaning louder than I meant to. I didn't want to make any kind of trouble for the Moors, and I tried to think of Mr. Harmon resting.

When my body was quiet again, and Mrs. Moor had finished her job, I thought of Mr. Harmon, how he lived on our block, his house on the opposite corner, shaded in, so that his front yard was nearly bare of grass but thick with a kind of hard-leafed ivy that he let wander where it would, so that even the stone walk to the front was overrun. He wasn't old, but he had that kind of wrinkled skin from always being out in the sun, and something was wrong with his face, so whenever he came outdoors, he wore a scarf over his mouth and chin. Jim believed he might have cancer, but he wasn't sure. Mr. Harmon was retired, and even Mrs. Slover didn't know about him, except that he'd come to Winston Valley with a daughter named Oona, who had slanted eyes, a round face, and thin brown hair, and hadn't been to school past the first grade, where they found that she couldn't learn or talk right, either, mostly groan and point to things. Mr. Harmon kept her up as best he could, but sometimes she'd get out by herself and wander down the street, so he'd have to come find her, or one of the neighbors would take her home and leave her on the porch.

Then, once, when I was painting the frame of the window in the baby's room, I heard a noise in my kitchen like someone stealing from me, so even without closing the paint can or wiping my hands, I ran in there and found Oona taking the pots and pans off the hooks that Jim had fixed for me over the sink. She was looking at them, saying words about them that meant nothing to me. It was like hearing a mockingbird changing its song, and you don't know why it does. I made her a glass of lemonade, let her ruin a few lemons trying to help me squeeze them. Then I sat with her at the kitchen table, holding the glass for her to drink. After a while she looked toward the door to the hallway, and I figured that meant she wanted to see the rest of my house. The room she liked best was the nursery. She kept rocking the cradle that Jimmy and Buck had made from a picture I'd seen in a magazine. She seemed to want to stay there forever, with her hand on the rocker, rocking it so hard I had to tell her to stop. Her face drew up then, and I thought she was going to cry, but she seemed quickly to forget, and after, to stare calmly at the cotton spread with the tiny bears printed on it and the stuffed goose that June made for me and left one Sunday as a surprise, leaning it up against one corner of the cradle. At one point, she picked up the goose and kissed it, her mouth wet from drooling, since she never really closed it.

I had let her see everything I had for the baby. I even opened the drawers of the dresser so she could look at the flannel gowns and batiste diaper shirts that Mrs. Slover and I had made on the new machine that Jimmy bought me for Christmas. And when she'd seemed to have studied them to her satisfaction, touched them all she wanted, I had taken her hand and started leading her out of my house, making her careful of the stairs. "I don't want you to fall," I said. "That's all you need, huh? To hit your head."

She laughed, her small eyes glittery with pleasure at my attention; and I laughed, too, thinking about the Bells and my visits there.

From our porch, I saw Mr. Harmon walking the street about a half-block down, his face turning from one side to the other, searching the yards; and I heard him call Oona's name. She didn't reply, so I answered for her, and he came toward us along the side of the ditch as quick as he could, the handkerchief lifting in the rough winter wind, exposing some of his hollowed-out face, the flesh like rotten fruit. He took her hand from me, and I said, "I want her coming to see me whenever she likes." And looking deeper into his eyes, I added, "I like her, Mr. Harmon. She doesn't bother me at all."

He stared at me nearly hard enough to make me look away. "Why should she bother you?"

I blushed. "I want her coming back, that's all."

That was only a few weeks ago, and I was full-out pregnant then, walking heavy and flat-footed, sometimes having to hold my back with one hand to ease the weight; and I thought, *Well, here we are, a girl who hasn't brain enough to pass first grade; a man with a sour nature and a face so eaten away that he has to hide it; and a pregnant woman praying to God every night till she falls asleep that she'll never lose this precious society.*

"No," Mr. Harmon said, "I keep her home."

"Maybe she'd be better seeing friends."

"No one can be her friend."

I meant to argue, but Mr. Harmon was leading Oona away. For a moment, I stood against the breeze, the hem of my skirt tight against my legs. I caught Oona looking back at me like a puppy that you're leaving at the pound and it doesn't want you to go; and I knew I was going to look for Oona whenever I could, that I was even going to teach her to help me with the baby. Women always like babies, I knew. No matter how strange or crippled or ugly the woman is, she wants to nurse a child and watch it grow.

And now I began to wonder about Mr. Harmon's being sick with pneumonia, because who would take care of Oona? And I started to ask Mrs. Moor, but I couldn't because the pains were coming on me harder now, Mrs. Moor letting me hold her hand when I asked her if I could.

All that morning, I watched the sunlight cross the bed beside me, then in the afternoon it spread wide on the wall, fading slowly toward four o'clock; after suppertime, it left the room altogether. I noticed the haziness, and after a while, when Mrs. Moor had gone away and come again, I asked her to turn on the light. When I started crying, she gave me a shot that stung but made me better and then sleepy.

When I moaned, Mrs. Moor wiped the perspiration off my face with a piece of gauze, then gazed at me worried and left the room. I was scared while she was gone. The time I was alone seemed too long. Then she came back with Dr. Moor, who'd put on a white coat and a cap that completely covered his hair. "How do you feel?" he asked, smiling and pulling the sheet away and easing me onto my back.

"Fine," I answered, polite as if I were at a party.

"Well, let me take a look to see how far along we are."

Mrs. Moor stood beside him, a wisp of hair fallen on her forehead, so I was going to reach up and pin it securely with one of the big hairpins that held the heavy brown braids laid side by side on the top of her head; but just then I felt the beginning of a pressure I knew I couldn't bear. I waited for it to let up, but it didn't. "It can get real bad toward the end," June had said, "but then you're nearly through. Scream if you want to. That's what helped me."

One thing about this pain: Under it, for the first time since I'd come here with Jim, memories weren't edging into my mind and ruining everything positive I was trying to build up. Through my pregnancy, I hadn't dwelled much in the past. It seemed that the fact of the baby freed me from the nightmares that I couldn't drive out before. I sat for hours at my sewing or reading and never thought once of any of it, and I was glad because I believed that such pain going through my heart and then down into my blood to the center of my body might make me have a baby like Oona, and then I'd have to raise it closed up like Mr. Harmon had done with her, and not because he wanted to at first, I believed, but because he had learned that people like her remind others too much of their own failure and sin.

"I don't like being on my back," I whispered, and tried to turn, but the straps they'd fastened held me firm. Then I screamed because I couldn't stand being bound helpless; and Jim was standing inside the door, the color out of his face, his shoulders slumped as if the frame of his body had collapsed on his way to me. I saw Mrs. Moor put her hand on him gentle, and say something to him as if she was explaining. But he pushed past her, coming full up to the bed, tugging on a strap, and loosening the first one. Dr. Moor stepped in front of him, explaining more of what his wife had tried to say.

"Well, nothing could be worse than this," Jimmy said; and when he'd done loosening me, I quit thrashing and screaming, and lay still. Jim stood beside me, trying not to cry, I believe; then Dr. Moor touched him and said something that soothed him, so that in a moment I was hearing his footsteps retreat, the soles of his shoes screeching on the linoleum of the floor. I watched the top of the door open and close slowly.

"Not too much longer," I heard the doctor say. "Not long now."

The faces of Dr. Moor and his wife fell away from mine, them talking together, trying to decide something. I felt pain rise over me so bad that I thought my baby must have been born. "Is it all right?" I asked. I was thinking of Oona Harmon.

"It's not here yet, honey."

Then I was praying aloud, prayers by rote, mixing Catholic ones with Baptist. I wanted to yell, curse the Moors for hovering around me and curse myself and all of it; and then I was feeling the taste of blood in my mouth as I had one time when I'd been running fast and fallen in the dirt.

A bright light switched on; the glare of it came close to the foot of the bed. I thought it was Mrs. Slover bringing me something cool to drink, but it was Mrs. Moor coming near me to place a cup over my mouth and nose. The cup was damp and smelled of silver. "Take a deep breath," she said, and I did.

I needed to yell out, but I couldn't anymore; it was as though my teeth were locked together for a pain that would shatter my body into so many pieces they'd never be found. I wanted to warn Mrs. Moor, but when I tried, no sound came.

"Fine, honey." I heard an echo. "And now another."

And that was all.

I slept. When I was awake good, someone pulled up the window shade. I squinted. The sun was coming in on the bed a bright yellow. Jimmy was sitting in a chair, bending forward, yawning, his hands on his knees. He got up, came to me, and kissed my hand. Then one of them brought the baby to me, wrapped in a flannel blanket. His eyes were open, alert, his mouth pursed almost for a kiss.

"You want to hold him?" Mrs. Moor was asking.

"Sure." I reached out.

9

In the springtime, when Doc had gone to El Paso to sell Dad's collection of rifles, Joylyn called me in to her from where I was jumping rope outside. I'd stood in the bedroom door, the skip rope Doc cut for me dangling from my hand. Joylyn's clothes lay folded in the open leather suitcase, done careful this time. She was dressed as if for Sunday in Ozona, a small felt hat holding down her curls, a thin blue dress, high-heeled shoes.

"I'm leaving to fix up something for us," she said. "When I have all we need, I'll send you the bus money to come where I am."

I went cold all over and dropped the rope, then I took her hands and pressed them to my cheeks to make her remember how much she loved me. "Doc won't let me go with you," I said. "He'll—"

"I know, not now. But he will when I send you the money."

"I don't think so," I said, stuttering like a baby when I needed to be old.

"Then I'll come for you."

I held to her, but she shook me off gentle, then closed the suitcase lid and snapped shut the metal clasps. When she was pulling on her white gloves, I saw her hands were still weak. "I have to go, Stella. When the ranch is gone, there'll be nothing left for us. I'll get a job and then come get you. We'll make a nice place."

"Without Doc?"

She was looking around the room as though for anything she might have left. "Yes, without him," she said.

She walked through the house quick, not glancing back once, the heels of her shoes clattering on the red tile. She stopped on the dirt outside, the suitcase at the end of her arm.

"I know I can find something, Stella Jean; and when I have us a place, you'll come live with me, and we'll fix it up like what we had before." I thought she was talking about Ozona. "I'll get us friends, too. Remember Susan Noble?"

I told her I did.

"Won't we need the sewing machine?" I asked.

"Yes, but I can't take it now. You take care of it, honey."

She had shown me how to dust the inside with a special brush and to oil the motor with a clear yellow liquid.

"What about your guitar?"

"I'll get it later, too." Then she smiled for the first time. "You play it for me while I'm gone. Be sure and keep it tuned."

I knew hymns from Joylyn, though I still didn't have all the chords. She was walking along the path to the road, and I was trying to help her carry the suitcase, our fingers tangling. "You better take me now," I said, my heart throwing itself against my chest like a wild dog Luis and I caught once and tried to cage. "I don't believe that Doc can keep me good. I might get sick. . . ." Then my voice trailed off, since I'd been well all my life, and no one knew that better than Joylyn.

She stopped at the road, set down the things she carried, and bent over to look in my eyes direct. "You'll be okay here, Stella," she said, speaking slow and taking more time, since she was wheezing now from the walk and breathing fast. "You have a roof over your head, and you won't be hungry. I may have trouble awhile before I find work. Not even a place to sleep. And that's all right for a grown-up, but not for a child who's getting her growth." She patted her purse. "I only have a little money here. But when I have a job and a place, I'll come to get you, and then we'll take the machine and the guitar with us. You hear me, darling? Did Mama ever lie to you?"

"No," I said, since I couldn't remember that she had. Just the same, I searched her eyes for the truth and hoped I was right in believing her promise and all the good about her that I did.

A truck beaded out on the horizon. She watched it. When it was close enough, she held up her thumb like I'd seen the cowboys do when they needed a ride to town, though I'd never seen a woman do that and I wouldn't have believed Joylyn could. The truck braked, then pulled up to the shoulder, a greenish pickup, scratched and dusty like everything else out here. There were two men in the cab, one of them young, the driver older than Joylyn, but not old. Both of them wore hats with sweat-stained bands. Doc wore dark glasses when he was outside, but these men dealt with the sun by squinting. The older man had wrinkles shooting back into his hair. Joylyn smiled at him so he'd take her. "The little girl ain't going?" he shouted over the sound of the truck's engine. He'd been smoking a cigarette, but he threw it out on the road. Its smoke curled downward into the ditch.

I saw Joylyn's mouth form the word no; but I didn't hear it because of the engine.

The young man got out and swung Dad's suitcase over the side of the truck. Joylyn climbed in quick and slid to the middle. The truck jerked to start. Joylyn's hand waved through the back window, her face turned to me. Then, suddenly, her expression changed like she'd made a mistake, and that's when I started running after them, bawling like a calf.

The truck slowed. I was laughing when I reached for the fender. I would grab on and climb up beside Dad's suitcase. I was nearly there, then I saw her shake her head and duck her face in her hands. The truck dug out, skidding, spraying dust. I tripped. Blood oozed from my knees like my skin was a strainer. Dirt got on my dress, and my eyes stung. I ran after them till I couldn't.

When Doc came home, I said, "Mama went somewhere."

He threw down his hat on one of the tube chairs and ran inside.

"She's gone for good," I called after him, wondering if he'd understood. I must have looked funny, because in a moment he came out of the house smiling crooked and gazing at me like something was wrong with *me,* not with what he knew. His skin looked pale and wrinkled in the moon's whiteness, but that was because we were in the desert. Under the trees at school, he looked darker and younger. I didn't think of him as old.

"Most of her clothes are gone," he told me, speaking hollow, "but she won't stay long."

On hearing that, I drew in my breath fast, and for the first time since Joylyn left, the corners of my mouth tipped up in a smile. "Why?" I asked soft.

"She left her guitar."

"She couldn't take it," I said. "But she means to later. And the machine. She'll take them when she comes back for me." I was sorry to have to tell him that both of us were leaving him. I wished I'd waited, then I said there was a letter for him in the center of the table, and his face went paler still. Without speaking, he went inside again. I followed closely.

He read all the pages of the letter, crumbling each of them in his fist as he finished.

"She go with a man?" he asked.

"There were two of them in the truck."

The gun rack was empty now, except for a carbine that a few days before Doc had said was worthless but now lifted and brought down, fumbling with his fingers through a cardboard box half-filled with shells. While he did that, I explained as careful as I could about the men.

The rest of the day, I stayed inside waiting for him to get back, praying for Joylyn to come first. When he came home that night drunk and crying, the carbine left somewhere, I stayed stiff in bed until I heard him snoring from his place in Dad's old chair.

Dear Stella Jean:

Like I said in my letter, I haven't a definite job yet, but this time there's a good chance of one in a nursery. And that's not a place for taking care of babies, but where they sell plants. It's a job a man used to have, but they can't get one now for the wages. So the salary's low, and I have to share the room that goes with it with another woman, but I'll be able to save half of what I make, and when I have enough, I'll rent us an apartment. The people are nice who run it. The Bronsons. You'll like them and their place, fresh and open. You should see the pretty plants, some of them tall as the greenhouse, hibiscus, bougainvillea. (Can you spell those? Mrs. Bronson did for me.) You know I love flowers and you do, too. And won't you be a help to me here? Well, I have to go for now. More later. I'm still in El Paso. You noticed the postmark?

I kept my clothes ready. I had two plans: one to take just a few things if I had to get the bus in Valentine; the other to take all my things if she came for me. I thought she might not phone first, so I watched the road for any car I didn't know. I had an idea that she might come in the green truck she'd left in, so I looked especially for it.

Dear Stella Jean:

I was at a clinic for two days, but I'm out now. The Bronsons are holding my job. When I get back to work, I'll write again. This sets back my plans for having you here. I wish you could come for Christmas, but you can't. I sit in bed listening to story programs on the radio. I don't like them, but I'm too weak to read. Are you being a good girl? Lily (that's a friend) sends you a kiss. I do too. I meet nice people. It won't be long. They want to see you. All for now so I can get Lily to put this in the mail. She found me a kitten for company. I don't know what to call it. Think of a name.

There was no return address. Every day I went to the mailbox on the road. All Christmas holiday from school, I would watch for the mail truck.

Once, Doc went to find Joylyn in El Paso, but he couldn't with what little my letters were to go on. No one there named Bronson had a nursery. She must have made the whole thing up, he said. And, anyway, he didn't believe she could ever work. "She doesn't have the constitution," I heard him tell a cousin of hers who phoned from Tennessee. "She might get a job, but she won't keep it. She'll be back." While he talked, he was staring at a snapshot of Joylyn near the phone. "She said she'd be gone only a few months," he continued. "She wanted to experiment with being away on her own." He had taken the cousin's telephone number on a scrap piece of paper, so once when he and Luis were outside mending a pen, I phoned the cousin myself, telling her I was sick and asking if I could come live with her. She said she'd come for me, and when she didn't, I called again, her husband taking the call and telling me to wait till Joylyn came home. I was trying to explain why I needed to leave now, when we got cut off. I dialed right back, but no one answered.

Twice I took some money of Doc's and tried to leave. He stopped me both times: once when I was waiting on the road, the next in Valentine when I was at the café asking strangers to take me with them. After he brought me home, we didn't talk about it. Unless he was drunk, we never talked at all.

I quit going to school. In the mornings, from the bedroom window, I watched the bus stop for me, heard it honk, watched it wait a moment or two, then go on. After a few days of that, it drove on by. Doc got a call from school and said I'd come.

The next word I got from Joylyn came in May and was postmarked *Galveston*. She said she had gone there because the doctor had told her she'd benefit from the sun and salt air. She'd hitched a ride with some people passing through on their way to Florida. I looked on a highway map for Galveston. It was an island on the Gulf of Mexico, six hundred miles from Valentine.

I wrote to Joylyn, keeping the letters in the bottom drawer of my dresser ready for when I got any address. In the letters, I told her to send for me. I reminded her of what housekeeping I could do and told her that if I was with her, I'd do the cooking. We didn't have the sewing machine anymore because Doc sold it to pay on the bills, but I knew how to hand-sew and I knew she did, too. I was sure she'd be sorry she hadn't taken the machine while we had it. I didn't think she'd be able to buy us another one any time soon, because it looked like, since she was moving around, she'd lost her job. She was already probably living in a cottage with Venetian blinds and a garden. I told her that I hoped so and asked her if she'd named the kitten. I was thinking of names. It would help if she'd tell me how it looked. If it had stripes, we could call it *Tiger* like a cat we'd known in Ozona.

I live where there's a vegetable garden, she said on a postcard that I got that summer. *I'm a part-time farmer, but I still can't work, and I can't get the doctor here to say when. It won't be any heavy work like I had in the nursery though. Something where I can sit. Well, I don't know what I can do that way, do you?*

The letter was postmarked *Cameron.*

"That's in Louisiana," my teacher said, when I showed her the card at school.

I was in sixth grade when two men in business suits came to the ranch and, without even getting out of the car to visit or drink the tea I'd fixed on a tray with napkins, gave Doc some papers to sign and told him that the ranch wasn't his anymore because he'd failed to pay the taxes, once, then twice. On the fender of the car, they made him sign a typed paper and three blue copies, then told him to return all but one to the driver.

"What does that mean?" I whispered when they were driving away.

"That we move," he answered. His hands were in his pockets, and he was watching after the car, it throwing up pink dust because it was sunset.

My heart went darkest then because I didn't see how, if we left here, Joylyn's letters would reach me. I hadn't had a letter in nearly two months, not since the second hospital visit where she told me she was getting tests and that the nurses kept bothering her whenever she tried to sleep. *You can't get any rest in a hospital,* she said. *I've learned that.*

It wasn't her handwriting.

That winter, a dealer from Midland came to the ranch house, loaded up the furniture, most of Doc's books, and the Chambers range, and gave Doc two hundred dollars in cash.

The next day, I met the postman out by the road and told him that we were moving to a town called Anderson where Doc had a job clerking in a railroad station. The postman said that Anderson was nice, and not only because the train stopped there every day, but because there was a college. I'd never seen a college, and I couldn't remember if there'd been a railway depot in Ozona, but I think there was.

I told him that I was worried about my mother finding us if we moved, and he took a little book from his pocket and wrote down *General Delivery* and *Anderson.* "Now you be sure and go to the post office and ask at the window for your letters," he said. "And if I see your mother or hear anything about her, I'll write you myself."

Three days before Christmas, the new owner's son drove us to Anderson with the few things Doc judged we could take and let us off at the depot. "My job with the railroad's not anything much," Doc had told him on the way over, "but I'm tired of going without the basics. It's a new start for me and my daughter, and I'm looking forward to it."

But that move to Anderson made me believe that it's harder to give up a place you're used to than give up food, and I knew Doc was wrong to change: When the new people took over the ranch house, we should have asked if we could live in the shack above the arroyo, me and Doc working for them, doing what they said, servants really; but at least being in a place we knew. True, I went to bed hungry at night out there, and sometimes I couldn't sleep for it, but I knew our place; I'd seen it dry and in thunder and lightning. For weeks at a time, I'd seen the land like a stack of dead cattle bones, then I'd seen the riverbed flooding and Doc afraid that one day it was going to wash us on down with it, and it slapping its waters past the windows, us up on the roof for nearly a full day, the sun blistering my skin, then the waters not taking the house after all, and us going down and drying our things in a sun that was already hot, so that steam came off the ground, and Doc said that was like everything under it was boiling. And then I'd watched from my place on the cedar fence for the last of the cattle to be sold off to a rancher come up from across the border; Doc's sorrel, Pete, sold to a vaquero who came with him; and finally my pony, Jay.

We stayed a night at the depot on cots behind the ticket booth, red and green Christmas lights twinkling above the counter, keeping me awake. In three trips, we carried our clothes, the box of kitchen things, and Joylyn's guitar to the trailer that Doc had rented from a woman named Mrs. Whitcomb. The trailer stood on a bare lot behind a section of clapboard houses, machines broken and rusting in other yards, a toilet on its side with what Doc called barley weeds growing out of its bowl. We had a full lot to ourselves but no trees or lawn. "It's too expensive to water," Mrs. Whitcomb said. "Unless you want to pay the bill."

"I can't," Doc said.

A few yards from the trailer was an outhouse. "Will you put in some shrubs to hide it?" Doc asked. Mrs. Whitcomb raised up her hands like he'd asked for the moon. That was the first time I'd ever lived in a place without a bathroom, and I knew Joylyn wouldn't like it when she came, but after Mrs. Whitcomb left, Doc said that when he was a kid, his grandparents had an outhouse, and it served just as well as anything else for what you have to do there.

For a few days, he quit drinking; the whites of his eyes stopped being so red and watery, and I thought that was what a new start meant. And he was cheerful about fixing up the trailer. "We'll be snug and comfortable in here," he said when I was standing in the dirt yard, hugging Joylyn's guitar to me as close as it'd go, thinking of what we'd come to and where we'd been. And after his days working, Doc was too tired to start the garden, so he worked with it on Sunday afternoons, digging at the hard ground that had no shade; then gradually he gave it up, and I tried to keep it going until the antelope got the young plants because the money that might have paid for the goods for a fence Doc spent on a game he planned to win to make something fast for us, telling me about it beforehand, but breathing funny so I knew he'd lose.

I didn't sign up for school, but I had to go anyway because after New Year's a lady from the government came to the trailer to visit. I started at midterm, the worst time, since the kids had already picked friends. By then, I was wearing clothes split out in the seams, sometimes with the skirt hem hanging. I wore them dirty. Not all at once; it came on gradual.

At first I was loud and hollering, wild, breaking in on the teacher to make the kids laugh, then having to sit in a corner, face to the wall; and when that did no good and the principal couldn't whip me because he was a man, he sent me to the rest room with the gym teacher, a big woman with short gray hair, who, each time I got in trouble, gave me more strokes of a round, flat paddle than the time before. But I still burst out talking when someone was reading aloud, and I still wasted the new chalk out of the box just to watch the pieces fall and break. Then once, when I came home with my buttocks bruised, and crying there because I'd held back crying at school, Doc visited the principal and the teacher both; but neither of them listened because his speech blurred and because he walked down the hall having to brace himself against the lockers to keep from falling down, the boys snickering to see it.

"Anything wrong going on at home?" one of the teachers asked me.

I kept my eyes down. "No."

"Your father good to you? I mean—"

"Yes, he is."

After that, I said nearly nothing but waited out the school days for the sound of the bell, letting the information the teachers tried to give me churn through my mind until I could get sixteen and quit school and find a job waiting tables in Cameron, or wherever I heard Joylyn was.

It was the next fall when I got back to school, age thirteen, just a few months before the Christmas when Mrs. Bell asked me over, that I started finding trash in my locker. Once a horned toad, smashed flat by a car and parched stiff, so that when I was trying to take it to the wire garbage can at the end of the hall, it fell apart all over the floor. I got in trouble for that, too (not for the mess but for screaming the words I did) and when I was sitting in the principal's office, I heard a boy laugh in the hall behind me, and though my head jerked around fast, I couldn't see who. Another time, two paper dolls without clothes, one with *Stella* written on it, the other with *Gabe,* the name of a big boy who couldn't get out of kindergarten and sat taking up all the space in the sand pile from the little ones, ruining their forts and tunnels, and then their hitting him for it till he cried, the two dolls facing one another, stuck together with a straight pin at the top of their legs. And then once a rubber sheath filled with something, though I don't think it was that, but milk.

I figured some of the boys had done it, ones who were stupid in school, because none of the smart ones would, and no girl. But I knew I wouldn't get whipped now. I was too old. I had things starting now like a woman, and you can't whip anyone grown. I got a lecture, then after, when the principal said I was excused, I walked home with my back as straight as I could make it go, my strides even and not fast; and those pranks against me happened, I knew, because I'd lost my mother and lived in the Whitcombs' leavings, and because Doc stayed at home when he was laid off by the railroad. Theft was the reason given, though I knew he never stole anything past rock candy favors from Mr. Able. It was just an excuse to get rid of a man who drank on the job and was never on time.

I believe that was about when he started begging money downtown, though I never saw him do it. I think he did it while I was at school, then brought home food, though it was never chicken. We ate macaroni mostly, seasoned with salt and mixed with whatever cheese we had, and sometimes diced Spam and canned peas.

"I want to move," I told Doc.

"We will. And soon. I think I have a chance at a job in Davis."

"Back to Ozona." I thought Joylyn might be in Ozona now, since she loved it there. "Will you write to Mr. Able and ask him for your old job back in the feed store?"

"I did that. I told you. He said no."

"Try again. Other people change their minds." I was thinking we'd get our house back, with the footed bathtub, and of how nice it would be in winter to sit in warm water with bubble-bath foam lilting and whispering around my shoulders.

"Well, maybe we can," Doc said, but then he'd grabbed his jacket from among his tangled bedcovers and left the trailer, and I believed I'd seen tears in his eyes.

So I thought when I was eleven or twelve, the kids avoided me for my temper; when I was thirteen and fourteen, for how quiet I was and for staying to myself without seeming lonely; and though I couldn't keep my hair too clean without much hot water and only the soap I could take from the rest room at school, I did the best I could, so that when I looked in a mirror, either the piece of one I had in the trailer, stuck on the wall of the upper bunk, or the one at school, I was pretty. My features were soft and regular. My eyes melted into things harder than they were and sometimes made them soft, too. And my body was not there yet, but it was going in the direction of a woman's photo on a calendar they had in a place in town where Mr. Phil Ashton and his son repaired guns and did taxidermy. I was skinnier than she was, but I had the other things getting as full and pale. And my skin stayed fair, and what the wind did there was only to brush it at the cheekbones and make me look healthy.

And I guess the boys feared my quietness, too, though now and then one of them came after me: "Hey, Stella Jean, walk with me." But I wouldn't, so he'd follow me on the dusty paths and sidewalks as I'd once seen a pair of cats, the female turning to the male and making her own decision about what to do. And I supposed then that it's the same as the mystery of why a girl takes on one boy and not another, stretching her arms toward him, her hair tumbling like rolling water, lolling back over itself in orderly waves no matter how long she combs it with the little piece of comb found in the school play yard at the end of a seesaw where it likely dropped out, and where she put it quickly in her skirt pocket, hoping that neither of the girls having lunch on the stone bench saw.

I was never with girls now. Only a few of them ever talked to me, mostly new girls, and then just long enough for one of the others to tell them not to. I believe now that they feared me for the wildness they thought I had, and for the courage I showed in asking the teacher for any leftover half-pint cartons of cold milk or packages of saltines that the school gave free at midmorning. Sometimes I heard them whisper about me when we were walking home for lunch on clear winter days, where you need a good thick cap because the wind crosses the prairies from the mountains and burns your face, especially your ears, so that you nearly can't stand the pain. Though, except for that, there was no reward then in the change of the seasons, except for summer at those times when I could be by myself in the trailer, lying in my top bunk staring at the ceiling, or taking out Joylyn's guitar and just tuning it because I didn't feel like singing. And Doc had gone wandering up to the road to drink beer and talk to the truck drivers who stopped at the café on the highway, and I sat gazing out the window at a stalled tumbleweed, watching up the path for Joylyn.

That spring, Doc took a job on a crew digging ditches down by the creek, working until his hands and leather jacket cracked the same, and his skin bled at those cracks so bad that he had to soak in a metal tub outside the trailer, asking me to carry out a kettle of hot water to warm what other water he had. And then I walked the twelve town blocks from the trailer to the store and bought the skin cream he told me to get, then walked twelve blocks back; and Doc was sitting on the trailer steps in his jeans, no shirt, him shivering.

Late that evening, I took the money they gave him for the ditch and walked the twelve blocks again and bought some eggs and potatoes for supper and was taking them back, when one of the boys at school, Farley Baugh, started nagging me to go out with him Saturday. He was angry, too, because I still wouldn't, though he had asked me on hot summer evenings when he'd followed me on my walks. But I didn't like Farley. His hands were clammy, and he cheated in school.

When he grabbed me and his lips grazed mine, I turned on him and stared him down, my eyes starting to hurt from lasting so long without blinking. He backed off, jabbing at me, not striking, only punching through the air with his fingers and spitting words through his teeth, some of them true of me, some not. But I didn't like any of them said and I didn't like it that he'd caused me to drop my grocery bag.

I shook my head and picked up the bag. "You owe me for this," I said, showing him how the bottom of the bag was wet and yellow from the eggs.

"The hell I do! You're a whore, Stella Landry."

I drew up like he'd hit me. "You don't know nothing," I said.

"I do know," he answered. "And I know who."

"Well, that's better than what you are." I couldn't think of the name for a man who was asking for it. I don't know it now.

I watched him leave, the back of him in a thin wool jacket and baggy slacks. I paused a moment more to see his form disappear, even his shadow go skinny as a stick, then get eaten away by some shade.

10

I loved holidays for Darrell more than for me, because it was his chance to celebrate within a family, all of them loving him and treating him special because he shared their blood. That first year of Darrell's life, I was looking forward to Christmas, the decorations and presents, anxious to watch his reaction to the glitter and sparkle, the wrapped toys and the house smelling of spiced and sugared foods, the party at church where his photo would be taken on the lap of Dave Cooney, the foreman from one of the big ranches, who'd promised Dr. Tillerson that he'd dress up like Santa Claus. I'd already bought some ornaments and a string of lights and I planned to buy more, some special ones in spun glass that were coming into the variety store after the first of December. And I wanted a big tree for us. I'd already told Jim, and I knew he'd talked to Buck about where they could drive northeast of San Antonio to a friend's place to cut it—a pine or even a young cedar, if they could find one with good enough balance and a thin trunk.

But first we had Thanksgiving, the beginning of the cold weather —turkey, trimmings, and prayers.

It was one o'clock on Wednesday when Buck came by to take Darrell and me out to his place, so I could start helping June with the food. We'd been talking back and forth for weeks about the meal, either at my house or in the church garden after Sunday services, which was where we usually met to discuss what we needed to do for a holiday or celebration. And we were always looking for those because it gave the family a chance to be together and something for me and June to plan. When Jim finished work, some time after dark, he'd drive to the ranch. Till then, June and I would fix the food, mind the kids, talk about who was coming and what might have changed for them since the last time we'd been together. Jim and Darrell and I had been invited to spend the night. At noon Thursday, June's parents and her cousin would come out for the feast. By then, I felt safe being in Winston Valley, that nothing could harm me as long as I was part of a big family like this one, all of them, even June's parents, accepting Jim's choice so well. Mrs. Ambler once told June that I seemed to have been just made for him, and June told me.

We can have some warm Thanksgivings in Central Texas, nearly hot, but this year the days were bright and sparkling—not cold, but cool enough for a jacket, red and orange leaves nearly covering the road, the tires on Buck's truck turning them up and sending them toward the ditches in spiraling swirls. While Buck and Darrell and I rode past the farms and pastures, Buck talked about how fine Darrell looked, mentioned how nice I was to come out and help June, then he turned on the radio, letting me think my own thoughts while he enjoyed his. Buck and Jim were alike that way, and so I felt comfortable with Buck—Buck a darker, heavier, older version of my husband, but just as hardworking and nice in his ways.

"You and Jimmy going hunting in the morning?" I asked, when Buck had climbed back in the truck after stopping a minute to see if there was mail in the box out on the road.

"Sure. You want to go, Stella? June will."

"I never shot a gun."

"Nobody ever teach you?"

"Sure . . . but I didn't like the noise cutting into my hearing like it did; and anyway, my mother was against hunting."

"She liked to eat meat, didn't she?"

"She didn't like to kill it."

"Well, that's just letting somebody else do the dirty work, isn't it? People enjoy eating meat. It's good for them. Someone's got to kill it."

He looked at me with his eyebrows raised, then he smiled. But I couldn't smile back because I wasn't sure; and, also, I didn't much like what Joylyn thought being talked against.

Buck turned the truck into the lane that led to the ranch. I held Darrell up to the window, so he could look out at the cows. "See them honey? See them watching us, wanting to know what we're doing in this truck?" I kissed his cheek, and he laughed. "Maybe they think we're bringing them some hay."

Buck leaned toward Darrell. "You'll be helping me one of these days, won't you, Darrell? I can just see you out here riding herd for me, throwing a steer."

Darrell turned his head and looked at his uncle, his mouth open, his eyes wide, me hoping that he didn't understand a single word. Because I didn't want him wrangling. I knew too many people hurt that way, especially kids who thought they knew how but hadn't learned the first thing. I set him on my lap, but he stiffened his knees and drew back up standing, pulling at my hair, trying to see more of what there was outside.

At the turn in the lane, the house came up ahead, the Buck Lesters' rambling frame house, newly painted blue with navy shutters, Buck and the boys doing all of it last spring, Jimmy helping them on Sunday afternoons, me coming out and sitting under the trees, nursing Darrell and talking to June. Smoke was coming out of the chimney, a gray ribbon cut off nearly as short as the trees by gusts of wind. My mind went inside, where I could imagine June sitting before the fire, knitting a sweater for Buck, then when she heard the truck, hiding it quick under a throw pillow on the sofa, since she meant the sweater for Christmas. She'd shown it to me last Sunday after church, pulled it out of her knitting bag, a kelly-green wool with a white snowflake design. I thought it was just beautiful, and I'd made her promise to teach me to knit as soon as she could find time.

I swung Darrell around on my lap so he could see the house. "See where Uncle Buck and Aunt June live, honey? See where your cousins are? In a minute, you're going to be with Junior and Trix and Nancy. You remember your cousins, don't you? They're going to be your best friends all your life."

And Darrell was looking where I showed him; then he glanced back at me and smiled with his mouth open because mine was.

That afternoon, starting about four, June and I stayed in the kitchen, making what we needed to get ahead on for the next day, first the dough for the pies, fixing the pastry, sprinkling flour out on the wood table and rolling the dough in it until our arms were covered up to the elbow, a light film of flour sticking to the apron June had lent me, the flour looking like the only kind of snow I knew anything about, and June said that was true. While we worked, we could look out the window to the pasture, Trix and some friends of his playing football, tackling one another, falling down in the mud that still hadn't dried after nearly two days of sunshine.

I kept glancing back at Darrell, who was sitting in Nancy's high chair, chewing on the edge of a graham cracker, and, when it broke, rubbing the brown pieces into the crevices of the tray, pushing them in as hard as he could, filling everything as though he were packing grease in some machine, just as his daddy worked at the garage. And I wanted Darrell to be like Jim. I was thinking of Trix and the game outside, the boys pulling one another down, coming in bruised, sometimes bleeding, their faces twisted in rage at someone who, five minutes before, they'd hugged and called their friend.

"I don't want Darrell rough," I said, keeping my eyes on the circle of dough, watching it get rounder and fuller with each stroke I made. "I want him sweet like he is now."

June stopped rolling out the dough she had, the rolling pin staying in the center of the board. "You don't want him a sissy, Stella, the other kids teasing him."

I glanced up. June was frowning and waiting for my reply. "They won't tease him," I said. "He's going to have plenty to do, but safe things, fixing cars, being Jimmy's partner when Mr. Hendrick gets too old."

June went back to the rolling, her back bent, her shoulders hunched, her hands pressing down until the flesh on them was as white as the flour she worked. "You want him to be just like his daddy then."

"Yes."

"Well, that's sure all right. But Jimmy's no angel, Stella. He used to play real rough, honey. They have to grow up. They need to learn to take care of themselves. Darrell's world is going to be a lot different from yours and mine, you know."

Not really, I was thinking. I didn't believe you could make a boy weak just by keeping him away from rough company. So I kept looking at June; but she didn't glance away from her work, so I figured she thought she'd convinced me. And that was all right. I didn't mind it if she believed her philosophy was getting through to me. For most things, it was.

"You going hunting in the morning?" she asked me. "If you want to, I'll stay here at the house with Nancy and Darrell."

"No, thanks. I'm too lazy to get up that early." I didn't feel like going over again what I'd said to Buck.

She smiled, and we both looked outside at the sunset coming in strong and red, covering the pasture low like a spread hovering over a bed, waiting for you to let it down.

I had just started to lift my circle of dough into the metal pie pan, when I saw Nancy standing at the kitchen door. She was two years older than Darrell, and she talked real well. Her coveralls were dark blue, the color of her eyes, and on her feet were tiny white tennis shoes, laced and tied tight in two lumpy knots. She was a plump, pretty child, with brown hair like her mother. I saw her screw up her eyes to study Darrell. "Darrell's making a mess," she said. "Mama, look what he's doing to my chair." I could see how glad she was to be pointing that out to June.

"I'll clean it up," I said, before June could answer.

"He throws his food down on the floor," Nancy said.

"You do that," I said.

For a moment, Nancy tightened the corners of her mouth and frowned. Then her face went quiet, she tipped her chin to the side and stared at me, her blue eyes calm. "Not anymore," she said softly.

It was getting close to seven o'clock when Jim arrived, but he hadn't forgotten the food. We had all we could do that night with cooking lunch for the next day, so I'd asked him to stop by the café for hamburgers. "Use the drive-in window," I'd told him. "That way, if it's cold, you don't have to get out." I knew the kids would love the idea, and that June wouldn't fuss about wasting money, because she'd feel as tired as I felt.

I went out in the lane to meet Jim, not taking time for my sweater; and when he scolded me for that, I said, "Then you keep me warm, honey." And he kissed me, too, me biting down gentle on his lip to tease him. Then I broke away and ran toward the house, as if I were going to hide like we sometimes played at home; and he came after me, grabbing me from behind, me yelling and him catching me by my waist, picking me up, and turning me over his shoulder. My head was down, I was laughing and beating my fists on his back, saying it wasn't dignified for a mother to be carried into a house like a sack of grain.

"I'm taking you upstairs," he said. He wanted to do that even before he said hello to Darrell, but I said no. We were in the hallway, and I was laughing and shrieking for June; but she didn't come. He let me down, and we were whispering. "Let's go up for just a little while," he said, but I said no, and I had to quit laughing and look serious so he'd stop what his hands were doing in my clothes. Then he picked me up under my shoulders and knees, held me in both his arms, my arms around his neck, him kissing me in the way he knew would make me want to go upstairs, but I still said no, so he carried me into the living room and dumped me on the sofa, and then went to Darrell and picked him up, singing to him, playing with him, Darrell squealing with delight.

In a while, all of us were sitting at the kitchen table, eating and talking and smelling the yeast growing in the dough for the cloverleaf rolls, watching as an hour passed, while it stretched its dome against the tea towels that covered the glass bowls, us seeing it rise as though it had a life and breath of its own.

After we put the babies to bed, singing to them awhile and getting them quiet, June and I shaped the rolls, put the pans of them in the refrigerator, then shelled the peas on a newspaper. While we listened to our voices talking about the food and our children, we peeled the sweet potatoes and boiled them, mashing them with butter and cinnamon until they were fluffy and could be spooned into the buttered Pyrex pans. The men were sitting on the glassed-in porch, watching a comedy show on TV, talking during the ads about the price of beef and lamb, then of anything of interest that Jim had experienced at the garage. I could hear the pride in Jim's voice and knew it wasn't just his success at work, but that he had me and Darrell, too.

When the food was done, we all went outside to the bonfire that Junior and Trix had made, sat on blankets near it, talking about hunting and the weather and the college teams, joking and singing songs until the moon had risen full and made the pasture white, the cattle moving slowly across it, grazing because the brightness reminded them of a hazy sun. Then, as the wind came up, strong and cold, Jim and Buck and Junior went out to round them up and bring them into the barn.

We had a norther that night and a freeze down into the teens, the wind chilling the house, especially the upper part where Jim and Darrell and I were, the walls being frame there instead of stone. I kept getting up to make sure Darrell was covered, then I lay in bed, listening to Jimmy beside me, his long, quiet breaths telling me how happy he was and free of trouble.

Later, I heard sock feet climbing the stairs as softly as they could; the beam of a flashlight bobbed around the hall ceiling and walls, Buck coming into our room to waken Jim. I turned my face into my pillow, while he touched Jimmy's shoulder and whispered to him that it was time to go if they were going to get into the deer blinds before sunrise.

Jimmy drew up on one elbow. "What time is it?"

"Four-thirty."

He groaned. "God a'mighty, Buck." But it wasn't a complaint. Jim was always glad to get up before dawn if hunting was the reason.

Through a slit in my eye, I watched the light waggle back to the door, then I felt the mattress change weight, and after covering the part of my shoulder that he'd bared of blanket by his movement, Jimmy groaned again; and I felt him shiver with cold. Then his bare feet were padding along the wood floor to the table, where he was pouring water from the pitcher into the basin so he could splash his face and rinse his mouth. Later, I heard them downstairs murmuring their plans, quieting Trix and Junior so as not to wake

"Nancy and Darrell and Aunt Stella Jean." I heard the guns come down, clanking against the gun rack, someone pulling back a bolt to check the chamber. June said something about which gun she wanted, she and Buck arguing. Then I heard the furnace cut on, and the dogs whine, anxious to go. The front door opened quick and shut firm, hushing the voices. There was the sound of the engine turning on the Jeep, failing to catch; the second time, catching good.

I slept on till late, lying on my stomach, burrowing in tight, cold because Jimmy was gone and I was missing his full-length warmth. Then, after a time, Darrell began to croon, and I heard the beads shake inside the rattle that I'd tied to the leg of a chair and set on the pallet near his head. It was nearly eight-o'clock when he left the pallet and crawled over to me.

"Good baby," I said, "letting your mama sleep. Come on here, honey."

I eased my arm over the side of the bed, beckoning to him with my finger. Right away, I heard his knees sliding along the wood planks, the palms of his hands slapping flat against the floor. He caught my hand, pulling up on my arm, causing the cover to slide back from my shoulder where Jim had covered me. I turned on my side. He took my face in his hands and squeezed my cheeks so my mouth puckered. "Quit it, honey," I complained awhile before I inched up in bed and drew him to me, letting him climb all over me while I dropped my head back on the pillow and tried again to close my eyes, hoping he might fall asleep beside me, clutching his daddy's pillow and shutting his eyes; yet me smelling and feeling the wetness of his gown, and the knowledge coming to me that I had to get up and change him. And after I'd done that, I carried him over to the window to watch the red ribbon of the sun streaming across the back lot, the grass glittering from the frost not yet ready to melt, glaring with its silver eye at the sun, saying no, not yet knowing it didn't have the same power it had during the night, no power at all over the warmth that was rising fast over the shoulder of the farthest hill, then taking in the next hill and the next until it reached June and Buck's valley.

"Look at it, Darrell. Did you ever see anything so pretty?"

Darrell pulled at my lip and made me laugh. I stroked his hair, the way it grew, and then the wrong way. He made a face, and I tickled his tummy. I put on my robe, having trouble getting it over my arm, since he didn't want me to set him down. Then he and I went downstairs to wake Nancy, to fix us something to eat, and start the coffee.

I had the food ready when the hunters drove in, all but the eggs. The biscuits were in the oven keeping warm on Low, the grits over a pan of water, butter melting in pools on top. I went out in the cold to see the deer, hugging my arms around my chest. "Twelve points," Jim called to me from the Jeep.

"Who killed it, Jimmy?"

"I did. Over at the lake."

Buck's eyes looked red and watery, and the sleeves of Jim's jacket were splashed with blood. June and the boys were in the backseat, looking sleepy, windblown, and cold. Jimmy was speaking across at me through the wind. "Get your coat, honey. Haven't you got any sense? I can't get off from work to nurse you sick."

I went inside to get it, then came out again. By then the animal was hanging on the limb of a tree, its belly slit, its tongue hanging loose and thick. After breakfast, and after they warmed up, Jim and Buck would hook the skin up to a chain on the pickup and pull it off, all in one piece. Then while June and I were arranging the lunch and setting the table, they'd butcher it on a table in the barn and bring the wrapped pieces to the freezer, Jim giving half of everything to Buck, the same way Buck shared when the kill was his. I knew how proud of it Jim was. I turned and hugged him, knowing that the blood was still damp on his jacket, staining my robe, but I held on to him just the same, kissing him full on the mouth, him kissing me back and holding me so tight I quit feeling the cold that I'd felt ever since he'd left me that morning.

"Hey, cut that out!" I heard Buck say, clipping Jim's shoulder as he passed on his way to the house. "Maybe you'd better do that upstairs."

"We'll do it there, too," Jim answered. He glanced down at me and whispered, "We do what we damned please."

"We're not home," I said.

Buck laughed; his voice caught in the air behind us and hung there in spite of the wind trying to sweep it away.

We crossed the lawn with our arms around one another, my forehead pressing into the sleeve of Jim's jacket. He left his boots outside on the steps as Buck had, then left me and went to clean up. Buck was already running the water. I heard it pound loud on the shower's metal floor. Jim went into the bathroom with him. I heard them roughhousing, which meant that Jim must have pulled Buck out from under the shower head before he was clean.

Darrell, hearing his father and Buck, laughed and screeched and hit the side of the high chair with a spoon. His bottle was on the floor where he'd thrown it. I lifted him out of the chair, put him in the warm living room on a plastic pad, and dumped Nancy's box of toys before him. He reached into the pile, took up a truck, and ran the rubber wheels along his leg. I went into the kitchen and broke the dozen and a half eggs in a bowl, whipping them quick since it was nearly ten o'clock and June's parents would be arriving soon. I told June to sit at the kitchen table and be served; she protested a little but yawned her big, wide yawn and let me work so she could smile at Buck, who, still flushed from his scuffle with Jim, was standing in the doorway in a green tartan robe.

They came at noon, June's parents, Angie and Claude Ambler, with Angie's cousin Maureen McAuley. I liked Angie and Claude. They were cheerful people, easy company for me. Angie must have been pretty once, but she was pudgy now, her features too small for her face, her flesh too tight for her wool crepe dress. She probably wasn't much more than fifty, but the weight made her look a decade older. When they'd first met me, the Amblers had lots of questions, then gradually their interest eased into just letting me be Jim's wife, and now they left me alone, hardly doing more than saying hello. It was Buck and June and their kids who got the attention, Angie always bringing them gifts from the drugstore and some special food or drink.

I didn't know Maureen. She was their guest for the holidays. She lived in a town west of here, whose name I'd never heard. Her face was small and delicate like I thought Angie's would be if she were thin. Her dyed hair was teased full, then pulled back to her neck and fastened with a pink bow that matched her dress. Her body smelled of baby powder and lilac cologne—the kind of woman you can't imagine crying, or laughing much, either, just letting other people's lives attract her, while she watches television or talks on the phone.

After they came, the house party got formal. We quit joking so much and being loud. Jim stopped coming up behind me, holding me around the waist, and nuzzling my neck. I knew the Amblers didn't make him feel self-conscious, so it must have been Maureen.

"You're sure happy," June had said to him after breakfast. "That your pretty wife that does that, or is it because you just killed something so fine?"

"Both."

Jim had laughed then, his eyes coming through my hair to look at June. I'd known he'd wanted to say then what he could say only to Buck, but wouldn't because of June and me, and that was why he was staying still.

I'd dressed Darrell in red corduroy overalls that I'd made for him for Christmas Day but wanted to see on him now. Under them, he had a starched white shirt with a round collar on which Mrs. Slover had appliquéd a red clown. We sat in the living room, the women drinking the homemade wine that Angie had made for June. The men drank a dark German beer that a farmer in Luling had given Buck. Then, when Jimmy and Buck started talking about getting hungry, June and I set the hot dishes on the table in the dining room and called the family.

The dining room was the only formal room in the house, and June used it for special occasions. It had a flowered carpet and curtains in a material that picked up the color in the rug. The wallpaper was blue and had silver birds drawn on it—pheasants, June said. Over the table was a brass chandelier with small, clear light bulbs shaped like candle flames. While June was telling us where we were to sit, my eyes eased over the room, picking up the footlong candles lighted even though it was only two o'clock in the afternoon; the crocheted tablecloth that Angie had brought out with her that morning; the silverware gleaming from June's and my polishing it yesterday until it did. For the iced tea, we were using goblets that June and Buck had received for a wedding present from Jim and Buck's parents, and none had ever been broken, thin etched crystal with long emerald-green stems, all of them matching, even Trix and Junior getting to drink out of them because it was Thanksgiving. "If they break, then they break," June had said, when I'd spoken against letting the kids use them. "Better for them to know good things early and feel at home with them."

While the rest of us unfolded our napkins and talked about how pretty everything was, Buck stood at the head of the table, his broad back curved over the roast turkey. He was dressed as he was on Sundays for church in jacket and tie, his big hands holding the fork up to the hilt in the breast of the bird to steady it while he separated the joints with the sharp point of the knife, then turned the blade at an angle and sliced into the white breast, the crisp curls of golden skin and the slices of meat falling to the side on pickled peaches and curly sprigs of parsley.

"I admire your being able to do that so well," Claude said.

Buck kept his attention on the turkey, lifting some of the meat on the edge of the knife and putting it on a plate. "This is nothing," he said. "My dad was the one could carve. I wish you could have seen him cut up a bird cooked as pretty as this one." He glanced down the table at June; she smiled back.

"I remember that, Buck," Claude said. "I remember seeing your father carve a turkey one Christmas at the Smiths'. He was doing it for Chester Smith, after Ches was taken ill."

Buck nodded. He often talked about his parents, complimenting them, saying that his father was a better man than he was, though I didn't believe it, since Mr. Lester never owned any land or even a shop, but was always doing jobs for other people. You have to own things, is what I thought then, own what you put your life's work in, as Buck and June owned the ranch now and Jim owned half the garage, enough so our name was on it, *Hendrick-Lester*. Then, when the time came, you needed to bring your kids into that, as Mr. Ambler had done for Buck and June. I glanced over at Jim. Jim was tucking a white napkin in the neck of Darrell's shirt. Darrell kept pulling it out and laughing. I laughed, too.

So the lunch should have gone fine and particularly for me, since it was showing me, as nothing else could, how far I'd come and how lucky I was. And it wasn't just the food we were going to eat for which I was thankful. It was everything I had: Jimmy and

Darrell and this family, days like this, nights like I'd had yesterday with all the love around me that anyone could ask for. And me, Stella Jean Landry, a key part of it ever since I'd given a baby to the Lester family. But something always happens in my life, something coming along to hurt it, like Doc making us leave Ozona, or the Bells moving away from Anderson. This time it was Maureen McAuley.

When I first noticed her staring at me, Buck was serving the plates. I thought she was going to say something right then, but she didn't. And then I remembered that ever since this morning when she'd arrived, or at least since I'd come downstairs after dressing Darrell and been introduced to her, she'd been giving me more interest than was normal for someone you hardly know. On and off, all morning, I'd caught her eyes fixed on me and holding, mine catching hers, then pulling away as quickly as they always did whenever people studied me too long.

When the filled plates were being passed around and Maureen kept the one that Buck said was hers, I noticed her staring at her food but not seeing it, her eyebrows drawing together, as though she were trying to pry a piece of hard stone out of her mind, her worried face framed by her teased hair and the wing tips of that huge pink bow. I tried to relax. I couldn't imagine how she might know me. Where would I have ever met a woman like her? I knew she'd never lived in Anderson.

I got up and moved behind the chairs to where Darrell was sitting next to Jim. Nancy was in her high chair, so he was in a regular chair, perched on a stack of books and tied in with a towel. Jim had made a game of getting him there, so he'd stay still long enough for him to make the knot. But Darrell didn't like to be kept still. He was curious about everything he saw and wanted to touch it. Keeping him in one place was about as easy as holding down a wild bird. "What is it, honey?" Jim asked me. "I'm watching him. He's doing fine."

I reached for Darrell's cup of juice and held it to his lips, tilting it and letting him drink, holding the corner of his napkin under his chin to catch any of it he might miss. "Be sure and mash the dressing," I said to Jim. "And don't let him have any of the tomato aspic; he might choke on the chopped celery we put in there."

"You want him sitting up there by you, Stella?" asked Jim. "I thought you wanted him by me."

Jim's question confused me. For once I wasn't really thinking about Darrell, I was thinking about Maureen and the Amblers. "Yes, I do," I said. "No, that's right. I want him to learn to sit by his daddy. Well, he shouldn't always be with me." I bent my face close to Darrell's. "Isn't that so, my precious? You don't want to be a mama's baby? No, a big boy." I was shaking my head and replacing the trouser strap that had fallen off his shoulder.

Darrell frowned and threw his empty cup on the rug. I picked it up and held it.

Jim touched my arm. I bent down, and he kissed my cheek, then I glanced up the table at Buck. "No meat for the baby, thank you," I said.

"He's eight months, honey," said Claude. "You don't have to be so timid with him."

"Well, I don't want him choking." I'd read in magazines about what to feed babies Darrell's age, and I knew.

Claude looked away, grimacing like he always did when he thought he was right and you weren't. "He won't choke," he said. I knew he and Angie thought I was spoiling Darrell, but I didn't care. He was my baby. Likely they had spoiled June. Wasn't that spoiling her to give her and Buck their ranch, half their furniture, and move into town into a brick cottage with a yard no bigger than a postage stamp?

Buck was serving Claude's plate, heaping it high with chunks of dark thigh meat and paper-thin slices of light, then pouring over it a ladleful of brown gravy, floating thick with giblets. When the plates passed by Angie, she piled them with sweet potatoes, the browned crust of marshmallows crackling each time she cut through them with the edge of the spoon. "Don't give me so much," June said, when hers was going by.

"It's Thanksgiving," Angie said.

"Well, I don't want to be sick."

At last Buck sat down, bowed his head, and led the blessing, then after the prayer mentioned the good things that had happened over the year, about some important cattle sales he'd made, about the birth of Darrell and Jim's progress in his work, and Claude getting over a heart attack, exercising, losing weight, and looking better and younger than he ever had.

While Buck was giving thanks, we were silent. While he said the prayers, our lips moved, even Junior's and Trix's. There was a murmuring of sound around me. I had my eyes closed at first, as I believed the others did, then I opened them narrow and glanced at the food on my plate, thinking how thankful I was to be sitting in a decorated dining room with glasses and silverware passed down from grandparents, and listening to the man of the house saying God's words, thanking Him for all of us and begging Him to keep helping us. I was always thanking God for what I had now, for His lifting me up and keeping me there; thanking Him every day for what my child had, knowing that Darrell was part of this family, as much theirs as Nancy was. "You're Jim Lester's son," I'd say to him sometimes, when we were alone and I'd be fixing his food, or we'd started to play. "And Buck and June Lester's nephew. That's the main thing you are. I got that for you, my pretty; and you won't ever be without it."

I pressed the palms of my hands together, glancing above the tips of my fingers at Darrell. He was reaching into his plate for the dressing, making a fist when he had it, so that it oozed out the side of his fingers, him catching what he could with his lips sucking, the rest falling back onto his plate. He opened his hand and looked at it fascinated, his blue eyes fixed. Then he brought his hand to his mouth, licking what he could, spreading the rest on his lips.

I wanted to say something, but I couldn't, not while Buck was finishing the grace, his bass voice getting lower and softer as he reached the final thought. I glanced around the table. All the others had their eyes shut, the food steaming up. Only Maureen was doing different, and she was staring at me. I shut my eyes and bowed my head as low as Buck's.

When the prayer finished, Claude stood up, reached over, and shook Buck's hand. "Fine grace," he was saying. There were tears brimming over the puffy lids of his eyes, then trailing down his wrinkled cheeks, so he had to reach for his handkerchief. "If I'd had a son, I couldn't be more grateful to God than I am for you."

Buck blushed and cleared his throat, glancing at June and his kids. "Now you all start eating this fine food our girls have prepared for us. Don't let any of it get cold."

We began at once, all of us staying as quiet to eat as we'd been for the prayers, the silence broken only when someone complimented June and me on the lunch. Jim kept having to clean Darrell's face, Darrell whining and trying to free himself from the towel that held him. I wasn't half-finished when I saw that I was going to have to untie it myself, then take him in my lap or else put him down on the rug to crawl.

"Darrell's wet," I heard Nancy say.

I got up and went to him, sticking my first finger under the rubber pants and seeing that this was so. I picked him up and started for the upstairs bedroom.

"Darrell's always wet," said Nancy. I turned back. She was in her high chair, gnawing like a puppy on the drumstick bone that June had given her. It almost hid her face.

I shouldn't have said anything, but Maureen's staring had spoiled most of what I'd looked forward to. "He's not *always* wet," I said sharp. "And anyway, he can't help it."

Everyone looked at me then, Jimmy's eyes wide, his mouth open a little. But I didn't care. I disliked Nancy. She was whiny and cruel like all little girls of her kind, and I believed that she was jealous of Darrell because he got more time from me in one week than she'd ever get in her whole life from June. June liked her kids; I don't mean that. It was just that she preferred being out on the land with Buck, driving cows, riding fence, hunting with him like she'd done this morning. There are some women who love their husbands more than their kids, and you can always see the kids trying to break into that, restless and grouchy, pulling at parents who care more for one another than they do for them.

As I was walking through the living room, I heard June speak: "Nancy, I don't want you saying things like that about Darrell in front of Aunt Stella Jean. She doesn't want to hear them."

I stopped still and listened, Darrell staying quiet and playing with the gold buttons on my dress. "But he *was* wet," Nancy said. "He's nothing but a baby."

"You were a baby," said Buck.

"He messes in his diaper; it stinks and ruins your food," Nancy insisted.

"Shh!" I believe that was Jim. And he must have startled Nancy, because in an instant she started crying, and then I heard June.

* * *

That afternoon, when Darrell was napping, and after the dishes were washed and dried, the leftover food wrapped and put away, some of it in plastic dishes for Jim and me to take home, we sat on the porch, an electric floor heater humming, its coils glowing orange and warming our feet and legs. We were watching a football game on television, Buck wanting A&M to win, Jim favoring U.T. They made a bet on it, small so neither of them could lose more than a few dollars, but a bet just the same. "Dr. Tellerson wouldn't like that," I heard June say.

"What?"

"Betting."

"Who's going to tell him?" It was Buck who spoke. He was smiling, his eyes moving rapidly from Jim to June.

Jim glanced at me. "Stella Jean might," he said. "Isn't Dr. Tellerson your best friend, honey?"

I felt the heat rise in my face. "Yes, he's my friend."

"He should be, for all you do for him."

I was looking down at a magazine. "I don't do so much for him, Jimmy. Mrs. Slover's the one. She made Thanksgiving dinner for the Tellersons. They're at her house now."

"Phoning sick people, taking them food, going over to recreation in the afternoons and helping with kids . . . Isn't that doing something?" He laughed. "He ought to pay you a salary."

I looked down closer at the pages, flipping one hard. "I've got all I want. You make enough. You want me working instead of taking care of Darrell?"

Jim sat down on the arm of the sofa and put his arm around me. "I didn't say that." He was still smiling. "You aren't mad, honey?"

"No," I answered. "Why should I be mad about helping Dr. Tellerson?" I was acting like the magazine was more interesting to me than Jim trying to make up, but I didn't like him teasing me about church.

"Come on, Stella Jean," he whispered, so sweet that I had to smile. Then we exchanged one of those kisses where your lips hardly touch but the softness of it lasts with you a long, long time.

When the halftime came, I left my place and went to check on Darrell. I passed through the kitchen to the hallway, feeling the emptiness of the house now, how still it was after the laughter and yells while we were all in the kitchen doing the dishes, June washing and me and June's kids drying and putting away, Jim and Buck sitting in kitchen chairs telling jokes, the Amblers and Maureen in the back bedrooms taking naps. I went upstairs as quietly as I could, listening for my baby, then standing in the doorway, gazing at him sprawled on the bed in his rumpled red overalls, his chest rising slow and steady, his mouth open, a trickle of saliva on his cheek. I stooped and wiped it away with the hem of my slip. When I did, he wriggled his mouth, then turned his whole body to the side, smiling, knowing I was there, yet not knowing. He might have been dreaming about me, of us in the backyard picking flowers; or us lying on the grass at Mrs. Slover's, gazing up at the sky, me holding back Alley from licking our faces; or maybe dreaming of the sparrow we saw the other afternoon, its feet skimming over a birdbath like a skater, ducking its head in the water and shaking all over, the water lower after it left, though not as low as a moment later when a blue jay did the same thing.

I felt Darrell's legs and found them cold, so I pulled the afghan up to his waist, then tiptoed downstairs as silent as I could, though in that old house the stairs creaked no matter what you did.

At first I hadn't seen Maureen. Maybe it was because I was still thinking about Darrell, keeping my mind on how perfect he was, how happy he made me and Jim, our plans for his Christmas, all of that running through my head like a second happy song tuning up against this first one here at June and Buck's before the Amblers brought Maureen. When I did see her, she was standing before me, blocking my path back to Jim, or else threatening to catch me, I believed, if I tried to return to Darrell. I started to turn back anyway, but she touched my arm, and I knew then that I had to stand still and wait for what she had to say, sensing that she was going to hit me with something, seeing it coming in the same way that, once when I was in school and playing sports I'd seen a ball coming, and there was no way in the world I would have time either to lift my hands to catch it or step aside to avoid the damage it was going to do.

"Stella Jean," she said. Even in the dimness of the hall, I could see how bright her eyes were and that her expression was eager to press on me what she knew. "I remember now where it was I saw you. At my sister's dress shop, several years ago before Christmas when I was helping her out. Prentice. That's where she lives. Since my husband's death, I always spend Christmas in Prentice."

She paused, and when I didn't reply, she said, "You bought some lingerie. Just beautiful. We thought you were getting married. I remember how my sister and I talked about it afterward, how pretty you were, but how young to be settling down."

I felt cold, much colder than the unheated hallway should ever have made me feel. I thought of the deer outside, hanging there, all the blood run out of it, not able to save itself once it had heard the click of Jim's rifle, only moments before thinking it had reached that lake with the water it was so thirsty for. "I've never been to Prentice," I said. "You're mistaking me for someone else."

"No, I'm sure it was you. I wouldn't forget. Did you know Jimmy then? It must have been for him that you bought those things."

"I've never been to Prentice," I said, my voice sounding hoarse and thick. "I don't even know where it is."

"Well, I don't think—"

I put my hand up to my face as though I was showing her more clearly the features she'd mistaken. "I look like a lot of other girls," I said, interrupting her. "There's nothing very different about me."

I pushed past her then, moving toward the voice of the sports commentator on television and the howling of the crowd. Passing through the living room, I walked as though I were on a swaying raft, holding on to the back of the sofa, then each chair, the gun rack and pictures rising and falling like the banks of a river.

"I need to go, Jimmy," I said, when I was standing beside my husband on the porch. The hand that I placed on his shoulder fluttered like an injured bird.

While I spoke, June rose from her chair, came toward me, and touched my arm. "I'm so disappointed," she said. "I thought you and Jimmy would stay with us all evening . . . have a light supper, I mean, before driving back." She glanced over at the TV screen. "Well, at least stay till the game's over. I know Jimmy would like to."

"No," I said, in a tone of voice hard enough so she'd know I meant it firm. "I can't."

In the corner of my eye, I'd seen Maureen enter the room. She seemed again to be blocking my way, ready to grab me, and while she held me, tell Jim's family that she believed that I'd once come into her sister's store.

"No," I repeated. "I've got to get back. I don't want Darrell—"

I forget how I finished that sentence. In any case, I was already off the porch, crossing the living room, then taking the stairs to wake my baby, making him cry when I hadn't intended to, saying with every step I took: *Stella Jean, you get calm. Stella Jean Lester, you just relax, honey.* Because I meant to protect what I had as long as I could, and right then, that meant whispering prayers to God and Joylyn and Dr. Tellerson, even to the Spanish priest on the church steps in Anderson, his black robe fluttering in some new, fresh breeze coming off the hill.

11

Maury Abrams and Link Kittley were the names of the ones who I went with. Both of them played football, basketball, shifting as the seasons changed to whatever sports there were. Maury was dark, big in the shoulders and back, strong, not too tall; Link had brown hair, tall, most of his height in his legs. When they walked down the halls, they talked loud and acted rough, hitting other boys on the arms, telling jokes, getting quiet if a girl came by. Once Link took out a boy named Jarod Sweeney, got him drunk on tequila, and left him sleeping in a garbage dump at the trailer park in Telingua. Some woman preacher lent him a blanket and brought him home, coughing and sunburned. I didn't like it, and once, when we were riding together in the truck and Link was bragging, I said so. He replied that a similar thing happened to him when he was a freshman, so why not Jarod? "We just take turns, Stella; and that was his." I didn't understand that kind of meanness. I never have, but I guess I understood Maury and Link. What I did proved it.

It was at the high school initiation that I met them. And you had to hate the initiation. I dreaded it all spring of the eighth grade and through summer. The first days of school were hell waiting for it, my mind switching between wanting it finished and wanting it canceled. I thought of staying home, saying I was sick, but I didn't dare. If anyone mentioned the initiation, the teachers said it wasn't bad, but I knew it was. The object was to herd the freshmen through town, making them carry buckets of whitewash so they could paint the *A* for Anderson up on the hillside. And that wasn't the worst of it. Before you left, you had to stand in line to have your face painted with water paint that dried quick and made your skin itch, so you scratched it with your fingers and spread the color. Then one of them broke a raw egg in a paper cup and made you drink it, hoping you'd gag. Though I didn't gag, and that made them want to give me a second, but the coach said no. "She don't have to eat but one," he said.

It was a girl who painted my face, wanting it as ugly as hers, I thought, since she had a swollen purple birthmark on one side of her neck. Then, afterward, she dipped a horseshoe in paint and marked two prints on the back pockets of my jeans. I stood around awhile, waiting for the others to get their faces done, then the seniors in charge of organizing the parade lined us up outside school and made us march through town, carrying buckets of whitewash, brushes, and rags. Some of the seniors held brooms, and if you lagged or complained, they hit you. "We're just sweeping up trash," one of them said.

The hardest was climbing the hill, because since you were carrying things, you couldn't break your fall if your feet slipped on the rocks. We'd been told to wear hiking boots, at least tennis shoes, but I didn't have anything but the moccasins I wore every day, and that meant that I was not only slipping every few steps but had rocks pushing up into my feet.

Then once, when I tripped, a boy grabbed me and held me up, catching me quick so my knee wouldn't hit the ground. That was Maury Abrams. I knew him as all the freshmen knew the senior leaders, but I didn't think he knew me. I glanced up at him. He was good-looking enough: his face shaved close, his clothes tailored, his black hair cut plain.

"I'll help you carry some of that," he said, reaching for the bucket I had.

"No, thanks," I said, pulling it away from him, thinking that the others might punish me more if they saw a kindness done to me.

He reached again. "Here, let me have it."

"No."

He started to say something more, but I looked at him cold, and he didn't. Then I think he was waiting for me to talk, and when I was quiet, my attention on the path, he fell back with some other kids, one of them teasing him about me, but him saying nothing I could hear. I went on with my work, bending over and replacing rocks in the section of the *A* assigned to me. It didn't even look like a letter up here close, just a low wall. At first I was cold from the wind, but after I'd replaced the scattered rocks, I started sweating, and my breaths came quick through my opened mouth. Maury was there again, offering me water from a cup.

Next time I saw him, he was standing with some boys, one of them Link Kittley, both of them staring at me, Maury smiling when I looked up, Link studying me, and too close for just being interested in the boring thing I was doing. Then Link moved away toward some boys who were piling up rocks. I heard him curse and kick the rocks, scattering them. I figured he might take it in his head to come over to me, and he did. "Can't you work any faster?" he asked.

"I might," I answered, "if you'll stay out of my way and let me."

After the work and we'd gone back down the hill, the kids talked about getting cleaned up and going to the supper and dance at the recreation center. I didn't go. It wasn't just Doc telling me I was crazy to let them paint my face, or my skin looking raw from scrubbing the paint off; but more me not having a floor-length dress, and no way of getting one.

That was Friday. On Monday, when Maury Abrams passed me in the hall at school, he called me by name, just *Hi, Stella,* but speaking; and I got his smile, which was wide and white and strong and told me more about him than he ever would. That first time, I didn't think he meant me, and I glanced around for someone else. But it was me, and after that I answered him, first giving him a nod and then a half-smile, then later a full one because he did. The only time he didn't speak to me was when he was with Betty Elias, a dark-haired senior girl that I'd heard someone say he meant to marry.

It was five days later when I met Link on my way to school, and he invited me to go with him to the Sweet Shop in the afternoon, telling me that Maury was going to meet us and that the two of them would buy me something at the fountain. I told him I would, and then we walked there, using the alleys mostly, him saying that was quicker, though I knew it was the same. On the way, I glanced at him a time or two. He had a heavy face and pale eyes, but he dressed nice, his clothes pressed and clean. Some people were afraid of him, I knew; and I believed he was conceited: Before initiation he never said anything to me at school; now, if he saw me coming, he glanced at me quick, then frowned because he had.

I asked him if he was going to get anything to eat. He said no. So while he was looking at the gifts and boxes of candy, I sat at the counter and ordered what he told me I could: a chicken-salad sandwich on toast and a chocolate soda with double scoops of vanilla ice cream, soda squirted slow and perfect over the chocolate syrup, so it would rise like hills past the top of the glass; whipped cream hissing out of the nozzle of a cylinder, causing the soda to run over the side of the glass, and then a wet red cherry with its stem stuck up stiff and straight.

I saw Maury come in and stand by Link. They talked together, glancing at me but not too much. I got my sandwich and soda, and as I ate them, watched myself in the mirror, turning the half-sandwich sideways, licking at the mayonnaise that was oozing out, then taking every spoonful of ice cream to my mouth and letting it melt slowly while the boys talked, not to me but to one another. Then, on the way out, after Link had paid my check, I asked him if he'd buy me a lipstick in the drugstore at the corner.

"A lipstick?" he asked. "What the hell do you want with that?"

"To make me look nice."

"You look fine."

"Okay." I pretended that I was going home, leaving the Sweet Shop without either of them.

Link was beside me, holding my arm. "What kind? What one of them you want?" He was breathing quick. I looked at his hand without smiling. He let my arm go, and I turned into the drugstore, went over to the counter, and picked up a marbled green plastic tube marked *Cherries in the Snow*; then the owner's wife came over quick to where I was, probably thinking I was going to steal it; and though I'd never stolen anything out of her place or anywhere, I guess I was dressed like I would. "I'll take this one." I said it quiet in the same way in which, while I was drinking my soda, I'd heard the lady who owned the beauty shop say she wanted a box of pralines to take to her mother.

Link pulled out his wallet and paid. "You want something else?"

I could see other money in his wallet, green bills like a closed hand of cards. I wanted one of the bottles of hand cream beside the display of lipsticks, and I said so. He paid for it and gave it to me.

I opened the lipstick tube, bent down to a mirror that was there for trying the cosmetics, and put some on, following the curve of my lips. It was a bright pink and made me look older, I thought. I dropped it and the hand cream into my purse, pushing them below the other things so they couldn't slip out.

"Thanks," I said, and I was going on.

"We'll walk a ways with you," Link said. And when they had me nearly home, and we were crossing along some high shrubs that hid the battered oil drums, Link stopped and kissed me. Then I was shaking my head and pulling back, my heart beating fast like it does after I run. Maury came close, so I was between the two of them, not wedged, but nearly. "I've got to go," I said. "Doc's going to be worried."

When I turned, they were looking at one another, then Link shouted something after me. I thought they might be chasing me to where I lived, so I ran the two blocks home; and when I looked back before shutting the door of the trailer, I saw that they had followed me and were watching from the far corner of the lot across the road.

Doc was in his bunk, his eyes shut, his mouth pulled to the side so he looked hurt. I tried to be quiet, but I wakened him when I shut the door. He must have seen my face when I turned to see how I looked in the mirror. The lipstick was smeared. "Where'd you get that?" he asked me.

"What?" The top button on my blouse was undone. I fastened it quick.

"What you're wearing."

"Lipstick?" I was looking in the mirror, my eyes moving toward him, though I tried to keep them steady on me, while I was rubbing at the smear that Link caused. "A boy bought it for me," I said.

"Who?"

"Link Kittley. You wouldn't know him."

"He like you?" Doc laughed as if he didn't think it possible, but there was something in his voice that made me know he didn't like me accepting gifts.

"No," I said. "Why would anyone like me?"

I started to try to lead him off it, to get him talking about himself, but I saw I didn't need to since he'd already shut his eyes and begun to breathe deep, his chin sinking down on his chest.

The rest of the week, I hardly saw them. I knew Maury's schedule, so I could avoid him easy; and whenever I saw Link between classes in the hallway, I glanced the other way, pretending I'd seen someone else, a boy I thought more of. Then on Monday, I found a note in my locker from Link, saying he needed to talk to me, and that that afternoon he'd take me for a drive. The note was carefully printed on nice paper, and I appreciated that; but I wasn't up to going with him, so at midmorning, when I was in one of the toilet stalls, I tore the note up fine, flushed it, and tried to forget. I left school as early as I could, having my books stacked and ready so that when the bell rang, all I had to do was grab my jacket out of my locker and go. I walked home fast, keeping my eyes on the sidewalk before me. I was more than halfway, nearly where the sidewalk ran out and became a dirt path just wide enough for one person, when a red truck came up beside me. Maury was driving. Link opened the door, reached for my books, then pulled me across his lap into the center.

On the rear window, there was a gun rack with rifles. "We going hunting?" I asked.

"That what you want to do?" Link asked.

The cab smelled of beer and cigarette smoke, the black seat cover was mended in crisscrosses of sticky green tape. "How do you like the truck, Stella? It belongs to a friend of Maury's dad. A real chariot. That's what I think."

There was a six-pack of beer on the floor under Link's legs. He reached down and twisted a can from the plastic holder. "You want one?"

"No, thanks."

"We bought it for you."

"No."

"Teetotaler, huh? Your dad drink too much, turn you off? Well, we'll teach you. Start you out slow."

I knew then that they'd asked around and learned about Doc. I sure hadn't told them. Link opened a beer for Maury and then one for himself, while he talked about binges he'd been on, how much he'd drunk and hardly felt. He told a long story about him and a friend on a pack trip, mixing beer and tequila, then walking along a narrow ledge above a canyon, later stopping in a cantina and telling everyone they could get to listen. "The next morning, we drove home fine, but I had an awful head. It's not worth it," he said.

"It can be," said Maury.

Then Link put the beer can to my lips, pressing to make me open my mouth. I tried to move my head away, but he kept on, holding the back of my head, so finally I had to take a swallow to make him stop, some of it spilling down my chin. He wiped the spill with his hand. "See, it's not so bad."

"I don't like it," I said, and I reached across him to open the door and get out. I didn't care that the truck was moving.

"Okay, okay," he said, pushing me back and patting my hand. "I know now." He winked at Maury. "She can sure get mad," he said. "We'll have to watch out for that."

While he finished his beer, I sat quiet. He squashed the can in one hand, glanced my way to see if I was watching, then threw it out the window.

"You like to go riding?" Maury asked.

I nodded. I never went anywhere in cars now. Doc couldn't afford one, and he had no friends anymore who would loan him anything.

"We'll take you whenever you like. Something in particular you want to see?"

I shook my head. I wanted to see it all, yards and houses passing by fast; clouds hanging over the mountains and mesas; maybe a herd of antelope or deer racing away at the sight of us, or crossing the road and leaping a fence, graceful, perfect.

Maury headed the truck for the low-water bridge, taking the downhill so fast that if someone else had been trying to cross, he'd have hit us head-on. I cried out, laughing, holding my fists to my cheeks. "Go faster!" I shouted. I wanted to drive on like this forever, never stop, the noise of the wind, the yelling, the ocotillo streaking past. Link put his arm around me, then turned me to him and kissed me—gentle at first, then opening my teeth with his tongue. When I tried to get away, he let me up for air, but then he came after me again, going under my clothes, his hand broad and slow. I told him to quit.

A sandstorm was blowing up, dust all over the road, making it hard to see what we were passing or what we were going toward. The dust boiled before us, miniature cyclones hitting one against the other, a gritty, burnished color that made you feel sick. Link rolled up the window beside him and asked Maury to roll up his. That made it warm and close inside the cab. Link was trying to take me up on his lap, his hands under my skirt. I told him no.

"Leave her alone," Maury said.

"You change your mind?" Link asked.

Maury shook his head. "It's up to her."

I thought we weren't going anywhere definite, that they just wanted to drive around, taking the loop up by the college, bearing down again on the bridge, the truck rattling like it was falling apart; then going around again by the grammar school and out on some of the unpaved roads behind town. Every time we came to a quiet place with some bushes and no houses, I was thinking that Maury might pull the truck over and park, and let Link try to do what in a minute he was almost going to have to do, but he didn't stop or even slow down all that much.

Then, at once, Link let me go, opened a second beer, and began to talk to me loud over the engine of the truck. "Maybe you need us to help you out some," he was saying. "Give you money. What with your father being sick and all, you may need it."

I nodded and listened. "There's a stone house down by the creek bed, where nobody's lived for years," he said, "and where nobody ever goes anymore. It's all grown up with juniper and cottonwood, and you can't see it from the highway." He told me what they'd pay me and what they'd expect for their money. He made it clear.

Nothing vague. I could appreciate that. And then, also, my life had taught me that when surprises come in the form of bad news, it's best to get all the facts straight off. At first I just listened to the wind squealing through the cracks in the windows, letting what Link was offering set in good; and when I was silent too long, Link eased my face around with his hand and asked if I'd ever done this before. "Been with someone, I mean, because if you haven't, we don't want—well, I won't be responsible for anything like that." He stopped talking and flashed a glance at Maury. I did, too. Maury was watching the road, his hands tighter on the wheel than I believed they needed to be, his eyes squinting more than ever to see through the dust.

"Yes," I answered.

The house was dark inside. For a moment, I had to stand in the door to let my sight adjust. Just one room. I could see that there had once been a partition, but it was mostly down now, except for a portion in the back. I kept thinking of the money, the trip to the drugstore, the ride in the truck. I wouldn't let myself think of the rest. I knew that if I did, I might pass out or something, and I couldn't let that happen, since if I did, I'd have no say about what they did to me, and even whether they paid me or not. And I sure wasn't doing this for nothing, not with the kind of people they were to think it up. Yet I did have some plan, one I'd made quick when Link first put his hands under my skirt. "Not with my clothes off," I said. "And no light on me, you hear?"

The boys glanced at one another. Link turned his face away.

I looked around the room, my eyes not resting too long on anything.

"You make the rules," one of them said quietly. I believe it was Maury. "We're not here to do anything you don't like."

"I mean it," I said.

"Sure."

A hand came from somewhere and tousled my hair. I straightened my back and shoulders as if I were one of their kid sisters, and we were going to play. But my heart was beating like a drum up high in my throat. I tried to breathe quiet. Maury kept my arm, so I knew he'd be with me first. Link shut the front door, pushing it hard with both hands; then with his boot heel kicking it at the bottom to make it shut good. I shivered when I heard the bolt shoot into place. I swallowed hard, like I would if I was preparing to speak. I meant to say that I'd decided I didn't want to do what I'd nodded to in the truck, but nothing came out of my mouth. And anyway, Maury was coaxing me with his hands—not mean, just guiding me toward one of the back corners of the room where two mattresses were stacked, no springs or frame or anything, the top mattress partly covered by a stained quilt.

In the center of the room stood a black chiffonier, and that and a damaged partition hid the mattresses from the rest of the space. The chiffonier looked as though it might once have been nice, but not now. An animal might have climbed it, scratching it with its claws; one of the small top drawers was broken, wood splinters scattered on the floor. High above the bed was a window. The room might once have been a cellar, dug out from the banks of the dry creek. When we'd been walking down here, I'd noticed a bridge outside. I pulled the curtain closed.

Link stood away, near where there was an old sofa; one corner, where there should have been a leg, was sitting on a broken piece of stone. While Maury was with me, Link sat on the arm of the sofa, watching out the front window to warn us if someone was coming.

Maury tried to hold me then, but I pushed him back because I wasn't ready. I mean, the place wasn't. I reached out and pulled the quilt tight over the mattress, and brushed away bits of dirt and straw fallen from the roof. Some time after, as Maury watched me, somber-faced, his arms to his sides in a way that made him look helpless (and I didn't mind that), I lay down. My panties were off like I knew to do, but my skirt was pulled down so someone above me still couldn't see what I had. I closed my eyes. There was movement above me, clothes being undone and slipped off. When Maury came down to me, the mattress rocked to the side. He tried to put my hand on him, but I pulled it away in a fist. "You going to do anything?" he asked.

"No," I answered. "That's not part of it."

He sat up a little. I felt him pull up my skirt, tuck it under my waist. He hesitated, then cleared his throat softly. I felt his fingers touch me where my hair grew, but that didn't help my legs. When he opened them, they stayed stiff. I'd meant to bend them for him, but I couldn't because I believed they'd tremble. He waited, I think for me to try to do something more to help him, and when I didn't, he gave up thinking I should. Because in an instant he was hunched over me, making his way.

Then at once he quit, eased down on the mattress, turned from me, and lay still. "You want to stop?" he asked.

His face turned back to mine. For a moment, he looked in my eyes steady, then he took me in his arms, petting me slow, giving me time, before he raised up and started in again, going at me serious then and not stopping until he was where he needed to be. I might have cried out, but I knew better. I did stiffen up, though, and then he stopped an instant, sighed deep against my neck; and when I nodded to his question, he took up again until his breathing jerked and got fast. I could feel the sweat breaking out on him, him out of control, whimpering, trying to say my name. And then he was lying on me full weight, sweat thick between us, him thanking me in whispers for what I'd let him do. In a moment, he lifted himself from me, glancing down at my face; he patted my thigh and kissed me light on the cheek. The mattress changed position as he rose off it and turned from me. Moving slowly, unbalanced, tripping over a shoe, he stooped to pick up his pants, getting five $1 bills out of his wallet and leaving them on the dusty top of the chiffonier. He paused, staring at me, his eyes soft. "You okay?" he asked.

"Yes."

"You want Link in here or not?"

"It's all right."

"What?"

"Yes."

I closed my eyes again, pulled down my skirt, and listened for the sound of clothes being put back on; and then, in a moment, for a few whispered words between the boys across the room.

"That's not my problem," I heard Link say. "She said different." Maury said something back. I couldn't hear it. Link said no. Then he was coming around the back of the chiffonier in nothing but his briefs, dropping a crumpled five-dollar bill beside the money

Maury left; then sitting down on the mattress and starting to unfasten the front of my shirt.

"I said no!"

"You say a lot of things," he whispered.

It was an old shirt of Doc's and not all that fresh—no stains really, but dirty on the collar where my neck had been. He raised me, slipping off the sleeves, dropping the shirt on the floor, having trouble with each of the bent hooks on my bra, then taking the straps down over my arms. For a moment, he didn't touch my breasts; he just stared, then covered them with his hands, squeezing them like a man thinks he should to make you want him. He lowered his head, his mouth everywhere he could think of, doing that until my head went back, and I was holding his face and asking him to stop. He kept on, though, as long as he was having to unfasten my skirt and slip it over my feet. I didn't say anything more. I listened to him grunting, then crying out wild, me hating it that the other boy could hear.

When he was through, he lay there; when he started to breathe quick and touch me again where he did, I said no. He asked a couple more times. When I didn't give in, he got up as Maury had, turned toward the chiffonier, his back to me, hunching down enough to see the reflection of his face in the narrow mirror and to pat the top of his hair. I saw the form of him, his long legs slipping into the briefs he'd gathered up, the swell still there like he'd never even come back here and done with me what he had; and then him in the semidarkness moving over by Maury, who was sitting in a corner of the broken sofa on the other side of the room. Maury said something. Link laughed, and I heard a quick exchange of whispered words; after that, silence. I lay quiet a minute, my head pounding, tears running down my cheeks.

"Anything wrong?" Link called into me from the sofa.

From where I was, I couldn't see him, or Maury, either. "No."

I sat up and looked between my legs, put my hand there, my palm coming back with what they'd left.

"You ready to leave?" I heard Link ask, his voice like it was at the initiation.

I said I was; then I rose and dressed and took the bills from the top of the chiffonier, reached for my purse, and stuffed them into it. On the way out of the house, Maury tried to slip his hand under my arm as if to help me along; but I pulled away, drawing my jacket around me close, then opening the door, tugging on it and having it yield. Maury and Link followed me into the milling particles of yellow dust, into the daylight that was only a few minutes from being over, nighttime coming up fast in the sky over the mountains behind the hill with the whitewashed letter *A*.

12

A week later, I had a new sweater, one that Maury brought me from his family's store, a long-sleeved blue wool that fit close. I think it was the first new thing I'd had since Doc had bought me an embroidered peasant blouse in Juárez. When Maury gave it to me at the stone house, I'd started to put on my bra so I could see. "No, without that," he said. He took the bra from me and held it behind him, feinting and teasing.

"Give it to me, Maury." I caught it once, but he pulled it away.

"No, I want to see you without it."

"For what?"

"For fun."

"I don't know what's fun in that."

I was talking impatient to keep on playing. He kept the bra from me, changing hands when I'd just about gotten it again—him laughing, and I was laughing—and, finally, when I had the sweater on, he put his hands under my breasts and lifted them, studied how that was, then covered them as completely as he could, trying to get them all under; and when he couldn't, he smiled, pleased, me breathing fast for his touching me there, and prying all the time at his fingers. "Don't let anyone else do this," he said, as if there'd never been anyone but him.

The next day I wore my new sweater to school, and when my math teacher, Mrs. Phillips, called on me, I guess I was daydreaming about Maury and me standing there together in the stone house, both of us smiling, while I'd opened the box and stood staring down at the sweater in the tissues. That was usually the way it was: When I was in school, I'd have something strong on my mind that had nothing to do with the lesson, but rather was some part of my life that I had to watch out for. I wanted to learn, though, especially figures, since after I knew enough, I'd get a job somewhere, standing behind a counter, operating a cash register or waiting on people in a store, something real.

"Stella," I heard Mrs. Phillips say.

I looked up. "Yes ma'am?"

She was asking me a question about the homework.

I glanced down at my notebook. "I don't have that one, ma'am," I said quietly.

She left the front of the room and walked up the aisle to the back of the class where I was. I always sat in the back, since you don't get called on as much from there. Her shoes had stack heels, and the sound of each step nearer me was like a warning, worse than anything she ever said from her desk, when she had to lean to the side even to see me. "You're going to have to do your homework, Stella. Did you understand what to do?"

"Yes, ma'am." I tried to let my eyes meet hers, but they just kept going past her face and focusing on the bare tree in the yard and on a crow that was sitting on a limb of it, steady and sleek in spite of the wind.

I heard one of the boys start to snigger, then stop suddenly, as though someone might have punched him. As Mrs. Phillips walked down the rows back to her desk, glancing down at papers on all the other desks she passed, commenting now and then, I moved my pencil on the page and pretended to write something. This afternoon I'd go home and do my work. If Maury or Link left a note in my locker, I wouldn't answer. Every time I was with them, after I had my money and was walking home, I'd be promising myself that I wouldn't go back, even if they told and Doc got strong enough to whip me, even if we had to move. Then, by the next morning, I'd started thinking about what I'd do when my money was gone, and by the time the note came, I'd do what it said. The trouble is, you get used to having money, and when someone starts buying you nice things like the sweater I was wearing, and you're feeling its softness on your skin, the newness of its smell coming up to you with every breath you take, like flowers in a garden you had once but lost, it's even harder to think back on when new things were out of your reach.

The bell rang. I picked up my books and left the room, looking down at my sweater, at the smooth weave of it, the nice way the sleeves fit over my wrists and turned back, making cuffs.

"That's pretty," Sarah McCloud told me when we were on the way to Spanish class, and she was walking beside me.

"Thank you." I looked around, hoping someone was seeing me with Sarah.

"Was it a birthday present or something?"

"No, I just bought it."

"Where?"

I hesitated. I shouldn't lie. If I did, she could find out. "Abrams's," I said. Well, that was better than telling her who had given it to me.

"It's nice."

I noticed that none of their sweaters fit as tightly as mine. Maybe Maury hadn't meant for me to wear this to school, but only for him at the stone house.

Sometimes I heard girls talking about buying clothes, a new wardrobe, they said, putting the things they'd selected on lay-away and paying on them when they could. One of them, the daughter of a professor at the college, bought her clothes in El Paso. She didn't shop here at the store that Maury's family owned; the quality wasn't good enough, she said. But I thought it was. Once I'd stood in front of the display window watching Mrs. Abrams change the clothes, strip the dresses off the six wooden mannequins, all of their skins painted cream, their eyes shining with attention, though they were just staring across the street at the dust-streaked windows of the lumberyard.

Then, one afternoon, the day after Anderson had won a basketball game, Maury told me that he'd give me a dress for Easter. If I'd walk by the store, I could look in the window and see what

I liked, and then if he could find the dress in my size, he'd go inside and buy it for me.

"What will you say to your father?" I asked him.

"Nothing. He won't know."

"How are you going to fix that?"

"You want the dress?"

I nodded.

So Maury got me the dress, one that I'd picked out, not in the window but off the racks, after I hadn't seen what I wanted and dared to go inside, then met Maury in the alleyway behind the store and told him how the dress looked, blue with a small flower print and lace on the collar, size ten—something right for Catholic church, I thought. And that's where I intended to go.

From where Doc and I lived, it was a long walk to the church, first to town, then across its width to the railroad track and uphill on the other side, people moving before me on the path in a loose broken line, some of them holding the hands of children, the men in clean khakis and jackets, the women wearing mantillas, me watching the rocks so I wouldn't scuff the shoes I'd gotten at a shop that had secondhand goods, new-looking; and I'd found Doc some shoes there, too; though Doc said he wouldn't go to church even on Easter. "I never have," he said. "There's no point in starting now, when I haven't got anything to offer. And that's all they want. You better have something when they start shaking around the change in that basket." He had passed his arm under my chin to show me where the basket would come.

I don't know if I looked good, walking up to the church on a path that was sometimes steep, seeing from as far as the station the priest in his black robe that hung down to the last two or three inches of black hose above the tops of his laced shoes. I'd heard the woman who worked at the grocery say that he was Mexican like her, though the Anglos said he was from Spain and that's why he spoke Spanish with a lisp.

I hadn't been born a Catholic that I knew, but it seemed like the place I should go. It was called St. Mary's, and I guess I didn't think the Mexicans like Lupe Ramos and her family would mind as much as some of the other people in town about seeing me. What I liked best about St. Mary's was that the people didn't stand outside and ask your name or try to make you sign a guest book while your hand was shaking and you couldn't think. The priest might smile, but he wouldn't stop you with conversation like a minister might. And he didn't tell you that you had to come to confession inside the box with a curtain door or communion. About half the people didn't even go.

During mass, I turned my head toward that box, wondering how I could go in there, and if the priest would believe that what I was doing to make my living was a mortal sin, though I knew it was, that mating for nothing was too close to mating for kids; that it was taking advantage of what Nature planned, and the wrong way; and that if you did that, you had to expect a family from it.

And me hoping that as long as I cared to attend church the priest would never catch on, as Doc hadn't caught on yet, me sponging off outside, bathing as best I could, cold water jerking from the rusted spigot into a pan, no matter how windy and dark it was when I got home. And me afraid of the dark ever since I was little, and knowing if a stranger came up at night, there wouldn't be a thing I could do. And that seemed strange, too, me being afraid of one more man to add to the ones I already had. Because what difference was it? The sin the priest spoke about happened the first time I'd gone down for Maury.

So I got to wear my dress to Easter mass, and I even put a dollar in the collection basket when the usher pushed it at me. That was the price of two movies, and I was giving it up for a mission they had in Colombia. But the priest had described it in his sermon, and it sounded worthwhile to me. On the way out, after mass was over, no one said anything, though maybe that was because I was leaving quick, the wind hard against the front of my dress and me holding my hair to one side so it wouldn't fly around and fill with dust. I'd thought about putting it up in a French twist. I wished I had.

One thing that troubled me was that I'd hoped that after we'd started what we had, Maury and Link and I might go places together, at least ride in the truck, but even that had to stop, since both of them thought it was too risky to be seen riding with me. I missed it, though; wasting time, going halfway to Fort Davis before Maury turned the truck around. But they were probably right. Maury and me, or me and Link, being seen together could only make people know for sure what before they'd only suspected. Link was particularly strict on that. He never talked to me except when we were at the stone house. He kept his appointment at whatever time he said, paid me, and left.

Maury was different. After he bought me the sweater and then the dress, he talked to me, sometimes even before he'd gotten what he'd come for, but more often after we'd been together, when he'd stay with me, rolling over on his back, smoking a cigarette, offering me one, and telling me his plans. He wanted a big family, he said, and a good job in a city; but his father wanted him working in the store, taking it over after a couple of years of college, so that he could retire. "I'm the only son, so it's expected," Maury said. "It'd break my mother's heart if I didn't do that, and it'd shock Jeannie, my sister, though she never comes up here to see about anything. Well, she has four kids. There isn't time." Maury was nice about Jeannie, considering. She sounded selfish to me.

He rarely asked me questions, just talked, wanting me to listen to him and be near him. Then finally saying that he had to do one thing or the other, he'd dress and leave the stone house; and after lying there awhile, thinking about what I still had to do for school, I'd leave, too.

Though often I just stayed there after the boys left me, enjoying the silence or, anyway, listening to the sounds outside. Sometimes I went to sleep in the stone house, and if I'd been there in the afternoon, it might be dark by the time I'd walked nearly a mile back to the trailer. The stars would be flashing at me; maybe there would be a rising moon. And when I got home, the door to the trailer would as often as not be open, and Doc would be lying in the bunk inside, cold, half-dressed, and with no covers. I'd straighten his bed, heat a can of something to eat, then sit next to him and feed him if that was one of those nights when he was refusing to eat.

"Where've you been?" Doc asked me once, when I came home late in the afternoon, when it was early spring and almost dark; and I'd lied that I'd been with a girlfriend, and I knew that I was going to have to find that girlfriend—though there was no big rush, since during the day Doc just sat on the sofa bench or outdoors in an aluminum chair at the foot of the steps, playing solitaire on a board he'd laid across his lap, sipping on a bottle of liquor, or else staring out at the hills, then waking up from whatever daydream he'd had (him sitting in a college lecture hall, or going to that church party because it was the only social gathering in town and meeting a pretty, soft-spoken girl named Joylyn Prescott) so he could question me.

"Did you get the things I wanted?" he asked.

"Yes, I did." That meant a box of aspirin and a pack of cigarettes. I gave them to him and went inside. The trailer had electric lights, but since we weren't in a park with hookups, we used a kerosene lantern. I opened the drawer by the stove, pulled out a match, lifted the lantern chimney, lighted it, and turned up the wick.

Over the next few weeks, Maury brought me a couple more presents, both of them boxes of Whitman's Sampler candy. Then, as the weeks drew on toward summer, he came less to the stone house. More and more often, only Link came, saying that Maury was working at his family's store; but I knew that he was with Betty, and that they were close to making their plans.

Then one cold night when the stars looked like flowers, some of them still in bud, others splashing out like the daisies that we got in Anderson after a rain, I went downtown, wearing some new shoes—store-bought this time. On my way, I was holding my jacket as close to my body as I could, looking down at the decorated toes of my pumps every step I took, watching the loops and curls of silver threads flash under the circles of the street lamps, my feet starting to hurt from them but my mind not yet caring. Because the fun had been in going into Abrams's store, sitting down in one of the chairs where they fit shoes, keeping my purse in my lap, taking my time to study each shoe that Mr. Abrams brought, turning down a bunch, then choosing these.

And now I was seeing Maury get out of a blue Ford coupe (a graduation gift from his grandparents) and help Betty Elias out; then they crossed the main street toward the movie. I noticed that he had his hair slicked back in a way I didn't like and that he was wearing a wool blazer and slacks. He had on his gold watch and his senior ring with the sapphire. I was surprised he hadn't given the ring to Betty, along with the gold football I had seen her wearing around her neck on a chain. He used to let me wear it at the stone house, but I knew to give it back before he left. I guessed he was always with Betty on weekend evenings, taking her out to Serrello's Drive-in for a Coke, then buying her a ticket to the movie, probably riding halfway to Maynard's Ranch afterward, then stopping the car by the side of the road to see how far he could get her to go, but not pressing too hard, since she was going to be his wife.

When I caught his eye, he blushed, and I saw him clasp Betty's arm more firmly than he had before; and it was then that I knew just what those times with me meant to Maury and just what they didn't.

He didn't say anything. "Hi, Stella," Betty said. "You all right?"

"Hi, Betty," I whispered.

I stopped and watched as they walked past, Maury's shoulders looking too big for his blazer, the wind blowing the brown slacks against his legs, not like the tight jeans I knew about, the front showing the man of him. I thought about clothes and what they meant. Here, last September, I'd been going to school, sitting in the rear of the classroom, not only so as not to be called on, but because I had to wear mended dresses, and slips where the straps were broken and had to be tied in little knots to hold, hair I could never get to look right because I had to wash it with bar soap instead of shampoo.

I kept trying to reason how it was that Maury had come to the decision that he and Link could make the arrangement with me that they had. Had it occurred to them at the initiation when we'd climbed the hill and I was bending over painting, and Link had seen something that set him off wanting me, the wind catching under my blouse and showing what I had in my bra; or my rump in the air like I was ready for something I wasn't even thinking about? When we started at the stone house, I didn't have my full figure yet, and I had no ways, either. That is, I didn't know anything about crying at the right time like some of the girls who had been brought up where they had mothers and aunts to watch—I mean, getting tears in their eyes when they needed them most, and knowing about smiling and then turning their heads as if they had promised something they couldn't deliver because their bodies were too precious to them.

Not that mine wasn't precious to me; it was just that I had to use it different and make it do things that weren't easy. Still, I hadn't thought about that too long, because I'd lived the other way: cleaning out toilets at the filling station, washing the writing off the tile walls, and that only until Mr. Rawl's wife got well enough after having her baby; then I was washing dishes in the railway café until my knuckles got raw and bled easy, and they had to fire me anyway because I was underage when the county inspector came through and caught me. So it just seemed that since the boys weren't married, I'd quit thinking about the reasons anymore; and I wasn't too surprised when Maury met me one afternoon when I was in the drugstore, looking at a magazine, him coming up and taking a magazine himself and browsing through it like I was; the pages before me just seeming to keep turning, color photographs of one woman's beautiful face after another, blurring until the druggist's wife asked me if I was going to buy the magazine. And then Maury reached into his pocket for seventy-five cents, scattering the coins on the glass counter, making them ring.

"I heard you quit seeing Link," he said when we were outside.

"You heard wrong." Though I planned to; I hated Link, hated him touching me; I always had. For some time I'd wanted to break with him, and seeing Maury today made me want to more.

We were passing by Abrams's and I thought he might leave me then and go inside, but he didn't. He kept walking with me, not too close but keeping abreast.

"He said so."

"It was just for a short time."

"All right. You don't need to say why."

I glanced at him sideways, sharp; I wasn't flirting. "I know I don't."

We were quiet awhile, then after the courthouse square, when we were on a street with cottages, he started telling me about college, how it was different from being down at the high school. "I miss it," he said. "Being the big fish, I mean. Where I am now, I feel like I'm nothing at all."

"Except to Betty Elias," I said soft, although not jealous. I'd be moving out of reality if I were jealous of that.

He didn't answer. When we were walking past a red-brick house, the only two-story one on the block, he took my hand, and both of us stopped. "I need to see you," he said. His jaw was set as if he was ready to say something stronger if I refused.

"You're seeing me now."

I wasn't afraid of Maury, not since the first time at the stone house, when what he did and what he didn't do told me everything about him I'd ever need to know. I just stared at him, and when that got too long, I glanced down the street at a big spotted dog that was loping through a yard, moving toward a whistling sound coming from one of the cottage doors.

"Don't you want to?" he asked.

My eyes shifted back to his, but his were so dark, you couldn't always read his intention in them. "You mean like before?" I asked.

"Yes, like what we had last year but just us."

Just us. I looked around, half-hoping and half-afraid that someone other than me might be hearing him.

I hadn't answered him then, but it worried me that Maury was always believing that people wouldn't find out about what he did. I told him I'd think about it.

At the end of the paved street, I left him and went home, waiting until that night to open the folded piece of paper he'd given me. On it was written an address: *16 Preston Avenue.* I was to turn the corner and walk a half-block down Fifth Street to the alley, then turn right. He'd be waiting. He gave the time.

I didn't go and that wasn't because I didn't want to, but because I wanted to so much. I guess I knew enough about disappointments by then, and I wasn't willing to risk another. I stayed with Doc and made dinner, boiling rice, frying a half-chicken and making cream gravy from the drippings. At first Doc couldn't eat the chicken I gave him; then I cut it up small, and he did. Afterward the trailer smelled of grease and smoke, but I didn't care. I just sat quiet and let Doc ramble on about how the ranch at Valentine was lost, him confused with nearly every detail, thinking it was because he'd been cheated out of the title by some rancher he knew, and me not bothering anymore to correct him. While I heated the water in the kettle and washed up, he tried to read an old history book he had, held it anyway, while I did my homework.

The next day, Maury was waiting for me a few blocks from the school in a spot next to some shrubs on a vacant lot. "I've been watching for you," he said. And if he was angry, you couldn't tell by his expression. He was real nice-looking then, better-looking than when we'd first met. I thought his face had filled out more, or else, since he was older, he had more confidence showing in it. He was wearing jeans but a white shirt, starched and ironed right.

"You dress up for me?" I asked.

"Sure."

I blushed. "I thought so."

He was quiet, looking at me like he was wishing for something real hard and hoping he'd get it just by staring. "It's not like you to stand me up, Stella."

"I was busy." I glanced away from him at a girl who was skating down a driveway. She waved her arms to get her balance, then steadied, squatting to her knees and turning into the street.

"Doing what?"

"Studying."

"Since when did you start studying so much?"

"I always did."

"I don't remember it."

By then he was smiling, gentle, not too full. I didn't say anything.

He asked again.

"Don't you have to work?" I said.

"I'm not working afternoons anymore."

My head tilted to the side, and I think I smiled back, so he might have thought I was teasing him. "Your daddy let you off now you're in college?" I'd known he'd had to work all summer at the store and that he despised it. He wanted to work on one of the ranches, but his father said no.

"That's right. I help him on Saturdays."

Both of us were silent. A car went by. I turned toward the vacant lot, hoping the people in the car hadn't seen my face.

"You coming?" Maury asked.

"I can't stay too long," I whispered.

"Maybe I don't need you too long." He smiled as if he loved me, and then he was stroking my hair, and when he reached for my school books, I let him take them. We walked past the girl who was skating. She looked at us, then glanced away. Neither of us knew her. I walked beside Maury, keeping his pace, soon turning with him down a shaded alley, the center overgrown with weeds so we had to walk in the twin ruts. The apartment was about twenty yards down the alley from the street. Maury took out a key, opened the door, and waited while I went in before him. "No one lives here now," he said, as if he was apologizing for that.

The light in the room was dim, the window shades drawn to the sills, but the place had been aired and smelled fresh. Maury started taking off his clothes, expecting me to do the same, and when I was behind him in that, he finished for me what I hadn't done. He held me for a moment in the cool air coming from the window, standing with me, my arms full around him now, me pressing to him tight. He kissed me, then became impatient and moved me back, my body going down while he held me; then him trying to wait and not being able, but my being the same, so it was over before I even saw the room good.

I lay with my legs spread awkward the way he'd left me, but I didn't want to move. I glanced at him. He was lying on his back, one knee bent, quiet, with his eyes shut. Across his body, through the window shades, I could see the shrubs scraping at the screens and letting in the scent of flowers. I drew up close to Maury, my body touching all the way along his. "What flower is that, Maury?" I asked.

"What flower is what?" He was smiling; he had opened his eyes, and they were following mine.

"The one that smells so good," I said.

"I don't know, honey. I don't know about flowers."

"You brought me roses." That was at the stone house, a bunch of them, the stems wrapped in wet paper to keep them fresh.

"Because I know you love roses."

My eyes moved around to see what there was in the room. On the side wall stood a sofa draped with a white sheet and pushed under two windows. In one corner, half-hidden by a print curtain, were a refrigerator and stove. Squares of gray and white linoleum covered the floor, as though the whole apartment were a kitchen. I thought of a married couple moving in, rearranging the furniture, fixing it up.

Maury drew me closer to him; I rested my head on his shoulder. After a while, he began talking about leaving Anderson. There wasn't enough for him here, he said. I tried to think of Maury being gone, how the town would seem without him.

I got up and went into the bathroom, a small space partitioned off with wallboard, so from outside Maury must have been able to hear everything I did. When I came out, he was watching me, and that made me stop and wait in the doorway to watch him back. A man like Maury can be beautiful lying sprawled in bed, dark eyes partway closed, black hair all over him, his chest rising regular with each of his breaths, his arms and legs spread, him not caring now that someone was studying him, especially me, since I'd just been with him. Because I knew some men are vain about women admiring what they have.

He held out his arms to me, telling me to come back to him, and saying how pretty I was. He was talking like he might love me.

"Well, you never said that before," I whispered.

He laughed, and I did, but quieter. "Sure I did," he said. "Maybe you didn't listen."

Then later, after he'd opened Cokes for us from the refrigerator, and he was asking me about how things were going with me since he hadn't been around, I told him that Link had tried to bring in someone else and what I'd done. It was a football player from the college. At first I said no, but when I thought more about some expenses coming up, and a debt I had at the pharmacy, I changed my mind.

Maury looked away from me, the thick brows above his eyes coming together tight while he was thinking about it; then, after a moment, he said, "You don't need to go with anybody else."

"You going to come back?" And I knew that he wasn't so much worried about the blame I might be putting on him as about me, and wishing there were something different he could do. I didn't understand about him and Betty, and I know he didn't, unless it was religion, his family not wanting him around women who were not of his faith.

By then the sun was trying to come in bright, but the leaves stopped most of it, all except some patches that were like animal prints on a wet path.

"You bring the Cokes here?"

"Yes."

"For me?"

He nodded.

"Then you knew I was coming with you when you asked?"

"I hoped you would."

"Who made up the bed?" I asked him.

"I did." He came up on his elbow and stared down in my face. "I fixed it up for us."

"And whose is this?" I asked. "The apartment, I mean."

"It's ours, my family's. My dad rents it out. It used to be a garage for the house in front, but he had it made into this. After the last tenant moved, he hasn't done anything about it. No one comes here. Don't worry, Stella."

And I didn't. Each time I met him, we'd decide when to see one another again, and I'd go there, walking over calm and breathing in the cool air deep, knowing he'd be waiting when I arrived, that he'd answer the door. He brought a radio; we played music softly, danced, and sang with it the parts of the songs we knew. Once, just after we got there, we took off our clothes, danced close, seeing just for fun how long we could hold off—Maury teased me for being the one to give up first.

Then, in a couple of weeks, he gave me a key, and sometimes I'd go early; and sometimes he'd come with his arms loaded with flowers he'd picked for me from the banks of the creek or from his mother's garden, me putting them in a glass jar I found in one of the cabinets. And for the first time something made me not want to take what he gave me, not so much the stockings and the pair of earrings that he brought from the store as the money, the regular amount that meant there wasn't anything between us. Because I know there was, and I know he thought so, too. I believe that if he had asked me to, if he had wanted me to see no one else but him forever in my life, I would have, and that that part of my past would have been over. But Maury didn't, and it still makes me sad to think of it.

So that night when I saw Betty and Maury downtown, I thought about what we'd done, Maury and me meeting twice that week. I guess I was still feeling close to him then. How could I not? Betty must have felt something else. She was still waiting for him, and by the look of her walking so proud and straight, she planned to wait until her wedding, until she'd said the words and they'd exchanged all those promises that I didn't believe I'd ever exchange with anyone.

I watched Maury and Betty go into the movie, and after a while I got chilly and moody, and went into the movie, too. Mrs. Chandler was standing behind the candy counter doing a crossword. I bought my ticket and bag of popcorn, disturbing her to wait on me and take my money. The bag was warm in my hand, and the popcorn smelled of butter. Mrs. Chandler and her husband owned the movie. She sold the tickets and refreshments, and he ran the projector and cleaned up the theater between shows. I had tried to get a job there once, and Mr. Chandler had been nice about it. "There's hardly enough profit even for my wife and me," he had said, smiling. "I guess we'll have to do the work."

I climbed the stairs and sat in the balcony, in the back where I had to listen to the whirring of the projector, but where no one else was. Starting a few rows in front of me, there were couples, the boys' arms mostly around the shoulders of the girls they'd brought, their cheeks pressed close. I noticed that Maury and Betty were in the center of the balcony on the fourth aisle back. She said something to him, and he helped her out of her jacket. His, really. His football jacket from Anderson High School, blue and gold, the one he had lent me once when we were walking together. It made me feel sick to see it. Some of the couples were kissing and not watching the show. I was sitting on the aisle, my legs crossed so that the light from the screen could hit the silver on my shoes and shine like flashes of heat lightning in a summer sky. By the middle of the movie, I was feeling too bad to stay, so I left, walked out to the street, looking both ways for something nice to come along, and when it didn't, I turned to the right and walked down the sidewalk toward a café, where I planned to order coffee.

I'd gone as far as the drugstore when my feet began to hurt, and I stopped a moment to peer into the display windows at the dark blue packages of tampons and picture puzzles of Hawaii, bath powder and lotions of all kinds. I was nearly to the turn for the café, when I heard a car drawing up. In it were some boys, probably from Marathon or Davis, not college, anyway, because they were loud and drove a car that looked like trash, decals of orange and black flames applied to the fenders and doors. Two of them were hanging out the windows; the one with long hair blowing across his face stretched out a skinny white arm in my direction. In his hand was a can of beer. "You want this, sweetheart?"

"No."

"Come on. It isn't going to hurt you."

"No." I said it as definite as I could. And that's because he was one of those boys who has a sniffy, rodent face, and who'll try to force or cheat you into getting what he wants, because he can't get it any other way. "It's free," he said. "It won't cost you nothing."

But I knew what it could cost me: his taut, sweaty body straining over mine, pinning me to the backseat of that car, his going at me fast, burning hell out of me, since he didn't know what happens to a woman and never would and didn't care—or care that I was taking all the risks. Because that's what men pay you for, much more than for the pleasure they get or a dozen other reasons I wasn't smart enough to figure out then. But I was getting there, this thing of Maury engaged to Betty Elias teaching me more about making mistakes than I'd ever dreamed possible. Because Maury needed from me, I knew, what he would never get from all the Betty Eliases in the world, and that was not my fault or hers, but just the way things were.

I took the offer of the beer, a kind of dare, my reasoning in taking it being that if I was stupid and careless about my life, still and all, I wasn't a coward. I stepped to the curb, going near the boy, keeping my body relaxed; then, in one motion, I leaned forward and snatched the can from him, so quick and clean that he couldn't have pulled me into the car no matter how fast he'd been. When I stepped back and started walking away, I heard them jeering after me. One of them said a word I hated, and it made me wonder what they knew. In my head, I had words to reply, but I didn't say anything. I just went on walking toward the café. Then, when I heard the car screech on its brakes, back up, and turn, I ducked into the alley at the side of the grocery store, crouching behind a pile of cardboard boxes. I heard the one from whom I took the beer yelling for me and beating on the side of the car. Then, after a while of riding up and down the alley, long enough for me to get my legs cramped in the squat I had to keep, they gave up.

When they were gone, when there wasn't a sound from anywhere except a shout or two from the pool hall, I opened the can and drank the beer down, a full one for the first time in my life, raising the beer can as high as it had to go for me to get the last drop. And that made me take in the sky, a bright moon, a veil of clouds sailing across its face, as you might draw your fingers as gently as you could across the body of someone you loved. That's what I was thinking about Maury, and what he did with me, and that made me know something I had guessed at but hadn't known for sure before.

I threw away the can, made certain that the street was clear, then started up to the café, me hoping for lots of people to be there talking loud and turning up the jukebox, drowning out with it whatever I knew, and whatever I didn't know, all that I could and could never have of Maury.

13

I suppose one thing I believed in Winston Valley was that if I was good, people would like me and praise Jimmy for winning me; if I took care of him and my baby, they'd respect that work; if I did my tasks steady, I'd stop getting depressed or worried about meeting people like Maureen McAuley. And I guess what was bad was that after she came so close and then didn't follow up, I quit being so careful, or thinking about what she knew, or waiting for a phone call or a letter from her with more about her sister in Prentice.

Because during the winter and spring, my life had seemed so normal—I was like everyone else, attending church, sewing clothes, making meals, carrying dinner down to Mrs. Slover when she got sick, going by the drugstore for her medicine. "You don't need to do that, Stella Jean," she said. But I did need to do it, to act with her like June did with Angie. I needed to keep up my house right, too, so anyone who dropped by after ten o'clock could wander all over and never find a thing dirty or out of place. To the people in Winston Valley, I imagined that I was just Jimmy Lester's wife, a girl he'd met in a big city, who went regular to church, served the punch for baptisms, or watched the children while the other mothers were at the service; a good girl who was always sticking up her hand to volunteer, nothing strange about her except that she seemed to have no people.

Jim and I'd been married almost four years on that summer Saturday night when June and Buck and the Pattisons asked us to go with them to a dance at Crider's. The Pattisons were June and Buck's best friends from high school, and they'd driven all the way here from Plano to stay through the weekend. The two couples were as close as they could be. They'd gone to parties together, been in one another's weddings, were godparents to one another's children. It was for old times' sake that they wanted to go to Crider's, and it was their fondness for Jimmy that made them want us with them. Crider's was sixty miles away, an outdoor dance hall set on a bluff above the Guadalupe River. We planned to convoy there, so the Pattisons and June and Buck came by our house about seven and piled out of the station wagon, Barbara Pattison kissing Jimmy and hugging him tight. "He's still the baby," she said. "Just look at that red hair."

Then she turned to me and gave me a hug. "And aren't you the pretty one?" she asked me. "Well, I guess you are." She glanced at Jimmy. "So how did you get her? Just lucky or what? Getting rich and owning half that garage?"

She hugged Jimmy again, then coaxed Darrell from my arms and kissed his face and neck until he laughed. "Well, now, you're the winner, too," she said. "Wouldn't Mommy Barbara just love to have you? I guess she sure would, that curly blond hair and those huge blue eyes." She was speaking to him in high-pitched baby talk, Darrell pulling on her necklace, his diapered buttocks bobbing up and down on the locked arms that held him.

I liked her at once, and I liked Don, her husband. Already he was talking to Jimmy about the renovations on the garage and station, praising him for doing well so quick.

That evening, I had on a print dress with a round neck and eyelet trim, my hair brushed away from my face but not curled except for the bangs. My hair was short then; and, since Darrell's birth, I'd put on a few pounds. But Jimmy liked my looks no matter what I did. He was that kind of man, cheerful just about all the time, good-hearted, believing that whatever he had was the best.

I climbed into the truck. Jim handed Darrell up to me.

I hadn't wanted to take Darrell to Crider's. I'd said that if we had to, I thought we shouldn't go. Mrs. Slover had a cold and anyway, she disapproved of dancing. June and Buck were going with us; I didn't trust anyone else with him; and I didn't like dragging him around to night spots, tiring him and risking getting him hurt or sick. June was leaving Nancy with Trix, paying him fifty cents an hour to take special care of her, but I didn't want to leave Darrell there; I was afraid of the treatment he might get since I still thought that June and Buck's kids were jealous of him.

I told Jim that we should stay home and watch the shows on TV; that if we took him, Darrell would get tired and fussy; but Jim was fond of the Pattisons and wanted to please them by going. They'd been good to him, he said, treated him equal with Buck though he was much younger; and he'd appreciated that. He was speaking serious then and not smiling, so I knew we had to go. "Jimmy, would you like to go there if you couldn't dance and just had to watch?" I asked as one final argument. "Why would Darrell want to go?"

Then Jimmy joked and pulled me down in his lap, holding me. "He can dance. Well, can't he walk? If you can walk, you can dance."

And Darrell could walk. He'd been walking since his first birthday party, when June and Buck and Mrs. Slover were watching, and I'd been squatting on the floor behind him, holding him around his waist, and Jim was crouched a couple of yards ahead, stretching out his arms, the palms of his hands up, his fingers curled to beckon. "Come on," he'd said to coax Darrell. "Right here. Daddy'll catch you if you start to fall." And then, when Darrell had taken the five or six steps he needed to get to Jim, Jim caught him, and all of us cheered, especially me.

"Oh, Jim, see what he can do! See him, honey!" I'd been screeching in everyone's ear, my voice hoarse from it and from laughing; thinking, while June was squatting down, breaking some cake in small pieces and feeding them to Darrell, how lucky he and I were to have all these people to love.

Jim and I had been to Crider's before, but never with friends. You could always find friends, see some people and sit with them, or wait until someone came you knew and then invite them to your table. And everyone, including me, always wanted to be with Jim Lester; and that was not only because he was fun, but because he worked in the center of Winston Valley and knew everything that went on there; all about the prices of lambs and calves, too, because he discussed them with Buck and men like Buck; all about politics because he read the paper every morning and remembered what it said. And since I was Jimmy's wife, they wanted me, too. Before we had Darrell, we might decide on a Saturday night to get in the truck and ride over to Crider's, the wind of a summer night blowing through the cab of the truck, keeping us cool; then our dancing until midnight or past and driving home slow, so we could enjoy the moonlight and whatever came from the stars to strike the pastures and hills; Jimmy telling me the name of each ranch we passed and some of what he knew about the people who lived there.

As we drove over that evening, the sun was going down behind the truck, burning twin circles in the side mirrors of the cab, flaring up the prairie we passed, making the high grass look like a crowd of people carrying torches. I kept looking around to see, letting the sun hurt my eyes a little, leave a scattering of spots, making the view before me brighter and less real. I enjoyed the magic of that, and I told Jim. He didn't reply much to things like this. He wasn't one to rave about sunsets or sunups or the pretty colors of warblers and jays; and, when once I pointed that out, he said, "I'll let you do that, honey. You're the one in the family good at making poems." He grinned. "Poor old Jim. He's just good at greasing cars, doing dirty jobs."

"That's not true," I said quick. "Well, you can sing hymns, Jimmy." He had a good voice for that. He kept on-key, and you could hear him for three or four rows back or front. Dr. Tellerson said that once the congregation began to sing, he always knew where Jimmy Lester was; no need to go searching with his eyes for what his ears had already told him.

I kept looking behind us for the Pattisons' station wagon, seeing its lights flare, then losing them on the wrong side of a curve. Darrell watched, too, climbing on me to do that, mussing my skirt, me straightening it and him mussing it again the next time.

"Mama . . ."

I glanced at Darrell. I could see by his open mouth and his eyes staying so fixed that he was hearing something and listening, and that he wanted me to listen. He liked live music. He'd heard it before at Buck's ranch when sometimes Buck's friends brought out their accordions and violins and played for us to dance. Even before we got to Crider's, we could hear music, first just a buzzing in the air, then the hum of fiddles coming clear, and the melody of the songs sounding like someone calling to us from down by the river. Jim didn't have to know the address of Crider's to know which way to turn. The sounds got louder with each empty vacant block that took us closer to the place to park. By the time we were trying to decide about where to leave our car, we could hardly hear ourselves think.

The lot was crowded with cars and looked full, but Jimmy found a place on the grass under a tree, and then he carried Darrell on one arm, offering me the other to help me get across the ditch in my high-heeled shoes. We bought our tickets at the gate, had the back of our left hands stamped with the *C* for Crider's, so the attendants inside the fence would know we'd paid.

By then, Darrell was riding on Jim's shoulders, Darrell laughing and digging his hands into the top of Jimmy's head, pushing Jim's hair over his eyes so Jim could hardly see. People were greeting us from everywhere: "How's it going, Jim?" "Hi, Stella!" "How you been?" People were reaching out to pat Darrell. "And how's that big boy?" I heard Darrell say he was fine while he stared at Jim's friends and smiled at them with a wide-open mouth. It was as if he were a prince riding up high on his daddy's shoulders. And I saw that all those people who had always loved the Lesters were now loving Darrell; and since I fitted in there somewhere, I figured they cared something for me, too.

We found a good table on the river side of the dance floor with places enough for all of us. When the others came, we ordered a pitcher of beer, a cup of grape soda for Darrell, then went up to the buffet tables for barbecued ribs and links and beef, all of us taking the full plate with red beans and cole slaw and thick-sliced homemade bread. I'd brought special food for Darrell.

Then, when we were eating, Darrell stood up in his chair, holding up a raw onion ring with one hand and wiping his other hand in the barbecue sauce on Jimmy's plate.

"Don't do that, honey," I said.

"No!" Darrell replied crossly.

I reached out and shook him. "Don't you say no to your mama! You hear me? I'm not going have it!"

"He's not hurting anything," Jimmy said.

"He's getting that sauce all over him," I said. "It'll stain his clothes." I talked quiet and kept my eyes moving fast between Jim and Darrell. Darrell was whimpering. Jim cleaned Darrell's hands with his paper napkin and took him in his arms. Darrell looked back at me, then put his thumb in his mouth and hid his face on his father's shoulder.

The closest that Jim and I ever came to quarreling was over things about raising Darrell, Jim wanting him brought up easy and me wanting him brought up strict. I didn't mind picking up after Darrell or cleaning up after him, either, but I didn't want him acting rude and losing friends. "You're going to spoil him rotten," I had warned Jim more than once, not pressing him too hard but warning.

And then he'd tease me to get me off it. "Like I spoil you, Stella Jean? I love you and him. If you love people enough, there's no way in the world you can spoil them into going bad."

"Well, I'm not going to have him running over everybody and getting wild."

"And who could he run over? You seen how little he is?"

"He won't be little forever."

"Maybe, but let's think about now. Forever's a long time."

Then we would quiet down, and our complaints would get in the background of something else we were talking about or preparing to do.

Jimmy asked me to dance. The band was playing a waltz, but the floor was so crowded, you had to dance close, and that ruined your steps. Following the waltz was a two-step and a polka, everyone jammed in together, trying to move. But we didn't care. That's what it was like to be at Crider's, smashed in, laughing, feeling like a million dollars because you were young and healthy, and because some man with a guitar was leaning into a microphone and belting out a beautiful love song; and because the band was playing loud and you could feel the rhythms taking you out of yourself and making you something better than you were. That man was singing now, a slow song about a woman who'd deserted him and now she was getting married to his friend. "*I loved you more than anyone/I never caused you pain. . . .*"

The tune changed. We went back and forth from the table to the dance floor, dancing until we were sweating and having to go cool down in the air coming off the river, walking between the double row of lighted paper lanterns that were swinging in the wind, then getting a beer, me of age now to buy it, having a legal I.D.; then excusing myself because beer goes right through you, and I laughed about it with the other women in the rest room, no innocent remarks like *we are like we are and can't help it,* but crude remarks, dirtier sometimes than we really meant. You can be like that before something's wrong; it's like flaunting good health when you're strong. You throw good fortune up to God when you have it and imagine that you're safe.

The band played another slow dance, just instruments this time, Jimmy and I holding on to one another as close as two people on a dance floor can get. He kissed me, too, holding me a little too long for being where we were; but I didn't say anything. Then, in a while, when we went back to our places, Buck was laughing, and he said, "You call that dancing, Jimmy?"

"What do you call it, Buck?"

"You know damned well what I call it." Buck was always teasing us about something, but I didn't mind, and I particularly liked for him to point out how close Jim and I were. I thought it made it all that better for how we stood in the family.

Buck turned to June, putting his arm over her shoulder. "Can we do that, too, honey? What do you think?"

June gave him a quick kiss, then rose from her chair. "Sure we can," she answered, "but right now I think I want to take a walk down by the water. You want to come, Barbara . . . you, Stella Jean?"

"Sure," Barbara answered, and Don and Buck stood up with her.

"We'll come down later," I said. I thought it was easier to mind Darrell here. If we went down, we'd have to hold him every second. And, anyway, I didn't want him that near the river.

We watched June and Buck and the Pattisons climb down the

steep, twisting steps to the water, slow and careful, hugging to the rail. Then we saw them standing on the terrace in the tight little group that they had always been. Likely they were talking about the proms they'd shared, Buck and June's early marriage when they were still in high school, the Pattisons marrying the following spring, just three days after school ended; talking about the fun things that had happened on the bus trips to other towns for football games, the parties in friends' backyards, where they'd roasted hot dogs and toasted marshmallows as many as they could eat, everyone in the class admiring them and treating them fair.

And I was going to have parties for Darrell, make memories like that for my son. And not just birthdays, but Fourth of July and Easter as well; and Halloween with a filled washtub in the backyard floating with apples; a witch with a tall black hat and long, crooked fingers; a horror house on the attic floor with chicken bones and spaghetti to touch, the things I'd heard kids in Anderson talk about but hadn't yet seen. Other parties, too. Maybe we could even borrow ponies so that kids could ride around the yard, or Jimmy could lead them up and down on the street before our house. Buck could take care of getting them.

By that time, I was feeling secure, perfect. I wasn't thinking about much else but where I was and what I was doing. I'd been practicing that for a long time, and it meant I didn't get anxious much anymore, nothing to tear Jim and me down when we didn't need it, when everything was going so well for him and Mr. Hendrick at the garage. And I thought I'd earned my right to belong, that God wanted me helping Mrs. Slover, getting Oona Harmon over at the house whenever I could. So nothing could have been so far from my mind than what happened. But, like I say, it's when you least expect it that the ground falls out from beneath you, like Henry Slover's playing football, planning to go to the college in San Marcos so he could be an accountant; then going to war and coming home wounded so bad that he had to live the rest of his life in a hospital, not able to think good, much less understand anything like adding up figures on a balance sheet; and Mrs. Slover, the best person I knew, having her happiness blown away like paper off a bridge.

Jimmy had taken the empty pitcher and gone to get some beer, straying back in the crowd until I lost sight of him. He was gone a long time, so I figured he'd run into someone he knew, that he was talking to him, hoping I'd bring Darrell and come see. And then at once Darrell was fussing, beginning his sleepy song that lasted about five minutes and then went into serious crying if I couldn't get him down for bed.

A couple came up to my table, Billy and Maude Raymond. Maude told me that she liked my dress, that I was looking good.

I held out my hand to her. "Thank you," I said. "I like yours, too."

She was wearing a blue dotted swiss with puffed sleeves, one that Mrs. Slover had a pattern for and was thinking about making up for me and sending one to Jessica. Maude was older than I was, but the dress made her look as young as some of the young girls dancing.

"Where's your old man?" Billy asked. He was glancing around for Jim, trying to pick him out in the crowd. "He glad to get out of a dry county?"

"I guess so," I said softly. "Jimmy doesn't drink much. He never drinks a drop at home."

Billy blushed. "Well, neither do I, really. It's only when I come out to a party."

The Raymonds were nice, I thought. Billy helped the kids at church with sports on Saturday afternoons. When Mr. Hampshire, the regular organist, was sick, Maude played the organ for Sunday service. I pushed my chair sideways to make room for them. "You want to sit with us?" I asked. "We can scoot the other chairs around and make you plenty of room."

"No, thank you," Maude answered. "We've got to find Billy's sister. She's saving us places. You seen her?"

She was talking about Thea Birdsall. I knew her from the beauty shop, the one who gave permanents and cut hair. "No, I haven't," I said. "But if I do, I'll tell her you're here."

"Thanks." Then she and Billy moved into the crowd.

I tried waiting longer; then, when Jim still didn't come and Darrell was getting tried, I decided to take him on to the truck and put him down on the seat to sleep. It was June who told me he'd be safe there because they had a watchman who went around checking cars. I lifted Darrell out of his chair, lowered him to the ground, keeping his hand in mine and leading him. "Maybe we'll see Daddy," I said.

I had to go slow with Darrell. I kept looking down to guide him, not watching the faces of people ahead of me, so not knowing what to avoid and what to go near, just making my way toward the far terrace, thinking I'd see Jim there and that he'd pick up Darrell, show him off to the person it was who was keeping his attention so long, then go with me to the trunk and help me bed Darrell down.

We were nearly to the edge of the circling dancers. I'd just turned in toward the crowd, starting to push my way through in earnest, not thinking of anything but my baby, of getting him to sleep, brushing the edge of an empty table, pushing a chair up to it so I could get by. I was all absorbed in that when it happened, when I felt a man's hand on my shoulder, biting into it, and not Jimmy's hand and not even Buck's, but one that was harsh and mean, the kind I hadn't felt for so long I scarcely knew how to respond. I turned quick—not scared but angry at someone I didn't know touching me that way.

"Sandy," I heard, blurring in with the loud drums and guitar; and my heart jumped because I knew this was bad.

At first I couldn't place the man who was holding me, and I thought I didn't know the woman pressed up behind him, either. It was my heart that knew it first, leaping up, then my breaths coming as loud and fast as if I'd been running—though I was standing in place, stiller than I'd ever been in my life; my thoughts gone like lightning to a farmhouse where Vic and I had stopped on the way from Anderson to Prentice, that place appearing out of the dust, unpainted, needing repair. "We'll spend the night here," Vic had said, explaining that this was his brother Charlie's house. And I remembered this man before me now standing on a makeshift porch that was no more than loose boards setting up on bricks; his kitchen lighted by twitching bars of neon lights; a bedroom upstairs at the head of some steep steps. And then early the next morning, there had been Vic's fat hands pulling up my gown without waking me first.

The woman was standing back, keeping her eyes on Charlie,

him saying he was glad to see me, and then talking about Vic. But I couldn't make out a thing he said after, other than he'd just learned my husband's name and that we lived in Winston Valley.

I could hardly look in Charlie's face, the blood was so much rushing to my head, filling my eyes so that I was nearly blind with it; and I heard myself panting. I must have been holding Darrell so hard he was hollering, but I couldn't have heard or stopped if I'd known.

Charlie was blocking my way. I tried to pass, but he held on to my arm and kept me still. He was stronger than his thin body and dried-out mustache would make you believe. He may have said a lot of things, too. I guess he did. But I couldn't think. The last thing that I did hear was an order, and it sounded like I'd better follow it: "Put the baby in a chair, and then you and me can dance. We need to talk."

"I can't leave him."

"All right, let him listen."

And if I'd thought long enough and careful enough, I might have come to some other conclusion about letting him go right then to Jim. On the other hand, I knew that Jim expected me pure or at least as pure as he believed I'd been. I'd heard him and Buck talk about women, just one or two of the local ones who slept around, expecting presents—though I was to think many times later that it was Jimmy who found me, Jim who was looking around for a girl in Fort Worth, thinking the place was exotic, since never in his life had he strayed much more than a few miles from Winston Valley, and then only to buy special feed for Buck's stock, or else to go to a high school ball game, he and his friends trailing the team long after they'd graduated, since, except for marrying and having children, or buying land or into a store, those were the most adventurous things they ever did. And maybe the most adventurous things that anyone ever does. I thought so then. And him loving me because everything went well there in the city: Buck's winning the blue ribbon for a calf and prize money for one of his steers.

And later, I would think that, strangely, it was Jim and Darrell who betrayed me, gave me over; Jim insisting on going to Crider's to please the Pattisons; Darrell whose need of sleep had made me believe that I should take him out to the truck; and then I'd taken the long way, choosing the lane between the dancers and the people watching, so I could show off what a perfect child I was mother to.

Jim and I were driving home. Darrell's head lay in my lap, me touching his brow and smoothing back the hair on his damp forehead, seeing that one of his shoes was untied but not wanting to reach down and tie it for fear of disturbing his rest.

There must have been tears on my face, sliding down my cheeks, because Jim said, "Anything wrong, honey? Anyone say something?"

"No, I'm fine," I answered, taking the handkerchief he offered.

"You don't act like it."

"I am, though."

He reached over and pressed my hand. "You let me know if anyone ever troubles you. I'm good at handling that kind of thing."

"I know you are, Jimmy."

"You love me?"

"Yes, I do."

He knew about these tears. When we first married, he asked about them urgently, then gradually became accustomed to some things about me that he couldn't know.

When we stopped for a light in a town, he leaned over and kissed me. Even then, we might have been just anyone, a family riding home after a dance where we'd had fun.

The truck rode fine. It was new. Jim had bought it the month before, and now he was handling it as smoothly as he always handled a car or a truck, one arm resting on the window, his fingers light on the steering wheel, the other hand reaching out to pat me, since I guess I was crying again. His hands were like that when we went into a sharp turn, Jim taking it a little too fast and the headlights of another car bearing down heavy on us, both Jim's arms jerking to take full hold of the wheel. The other car honked a steady howl; our truck veered off the road onto the shoulder, rocks clattering against the inside of the fenders like hail on a roof of tin, me bending as low and tight as I could to shield Darrell's body with mine.

And then after, when we were peaceful again, and I had quieted Darrell on my shoulder, I caught myself thinking that if we'd gotten killed, it might have been better for all the sorrow I might have to put on them and on me, to keep theirs from being worse, all of it being more than I knew Jim could bear, so he'd say to Junior and Trix if they tried to marry a stray woman: *You marry from right here, a girl you know has been to church all her life, not just taken up religion and good ways since she got a husband and child.* I was thinking that if the truck had crashed and I'd died, then I could have been down there in Judgment, because Judgment comes immediately, and then I'd know for sure the meaning of my life and theirs. "Why is God so indifferent?" I once asked Mrs. Slover. "Why is He so silent, just leaving us here alone and not even leading us?"

"He does lead us," she answered. "We just don't pay attention, and when He speaks, we don't listen."

Well, I thought I'd listened. I thought I wouldn't miss anything He wished of me, as long as I might be left with my family. I guess my wish was too insignificant, though I didn't think Mrs. Slover could be wrong. Because if she could, then nothing was certain, since I'd always believed she had to be such a faithful echo of my real mother, if not of Joylyn.

14

For all the two years that I lived in Prentice, when I'd sit in my room with the window open and feel the breeze pressing on my cheek, seeing how it ruffled the pages of my book, I would imagine that I had lived in a pretty room always and that I could dream all I wanted, that dream being broken only by Fran bringing work to me, or Ruth criticizing what I did. I got good at forgetting mistakes, though. It was as if I were two people, the one who went downstairs, the other who lived alone here, straightening up so nothing was ever out of place; reading magazines that I bought downtown or borrowed; talking to Hadley or Esther or one of the others, who sometimes knocked and asked to borrow something she'd run out of, or just to come in and sit looking out the window the same way I did.

Yet it took me a while to realize that Ruth was all business, and whatever affection she gave me came out of that and not from anything going on in her heart. "Come tell me if you have problems," she'd say to us at dinner, or sometimes when she visited our rooms; but when you did, she had a way of blaming you for what went wrong, or not listening to what you told her, so you began to realize that it wasn't you who were her ally, but the ones who came here looking for what you had, and paying her to use it.

When Vic and I walked into Ruth's office, she was sitting before a long, low table that she used as a desk, her hands touching the edges of a paper, her eyes working down the columns. Her chair had a softly curved back, but she wasn't leaning against it. Behind her were three windows covered with blinds, not raised but with the slats open. Before the desk were two armchairs, old but not worn. A lamp was on, though if she'd raised the blinds behind her, she wouldn't have needed it.

She glanced up a moment, made a gesture with her hand, then looked back at her work, sliding the pencil down the paper, her lips moving, but her saying nothing aloud. Vic took one of the chairs and let me know that I should take the other. And then she spoke to Vic, but without seeing him, I believe. She put the pencil down and folded her hands on the paper. Her eyes were blue, heavy-lidded, the pupils black and soft, like those of someone with a fever. She stared at me, taking her time.

"You had a nice trip?" she asked. "It's a pretty drive up here from Anderson." Her voice was gentle, her accent thin and whispery, not from around here. It occurred to me that you have to be a long way from where you were born to do what she did.

I looked up. Ruth's eyes had gone to Vic. "How have you been?" she asked him.

"I'm all right." He was getting out a cigarette, and I noticed that his hand wasn't all that steady.

When Ruth smiled, the skin stretched tight around her lips and neck. She looked the age of the mothers of some of the people I'd known in school, the older ones who brought refreshments for class parties and picnics or came after school to help some of the kids who still couldn't read. Her black hair was pulled high away from her face, so her ears showed. Her eyebrows were thick and black, and I could see that she didn't pluck them. On the tops of her hands were purple veins that branched out and intersected like streams.

I glanced at Vic, but his attention was on the bookshelf, as though one of the books interested him, and he'd soon rise and take it out of its place. He seemed so uncomfortable here that I wondered if he'd ever been anything to Ruth. I looked back and forth at both of them and decided he hadn't.

I'd met Vic Hansen in Anderson, one afternoon when I was walking home. He was in a flashy car, a fat man, balding, wearing a striped shirt, an opened jacket, a tie that looked like moving water, blue with streaks of white. He talked with his words clipped off like someone educated, but I knew that people dressed like him never were. He'd heard about me, he said; heard I'd been with a football player that Link Kittley had brought to the trailer one evening and that I'd said could stay. It was after Doc died and Maury had married, so when Vic drove me to the hotel in Ellison, ordered a steak dinner served in the room, paid me twenty dollars, and asked if I needed a steady income, I said yes.

"Vic says you've been working in Anderson," Ruth said to me.

I nodded.

"All by yourself there?" She was holding a pencil, sliding it slowly between her fingers.

I nodded again.

"No one to look after your interests?"

"I guess not."

She crooked her finger and beckoned. "Come here," she said.

I got up from my chair.

When I didn't move closer, she beckoned again. "Around the desk to me," she said.

She rose, took my arm, and guided me toward the window, pulled on a cord to raise one of the blinds. A bright light made a streak across the carpet and flooded the wall. I tried not to squint. Holding my chin in one of her hands, she turned my head from side to side, then spread her hands and ran them slowly through my hair all the way out to the ends. Her fingers were warm, and her breath smelled of mint. I'd seen a roll of candies on her desk, but she didn't offer any. "Vic says you won't have any of your people looking for you."

"No, ma'am."

They were both staring at me, Vic shifting his weight so his knee was bent, and that made him look awkward. Ruth said that she wanted to see how I was, using a word for that command that at first I didn't understand, and I blushed so that after I obeyed, there was a peach color to my skin that the mirror caught exactly in the brightness of the morning.

I'll always remember how the sunlight was, that I could see my naked body in a mirror, me gazing at it steady so I wouldn't have to look at Ruth's face. Still I could see beyond, her eyes on me, my skin gone white again like some sand we'd had near the creek at the ranch, my breasts falling heavy from their own weight, the nipples made stiff by the cool air that came in the windows. I heard Ruth take in her breath. I expected a compliment then, but I didn't get it. She glanced at Vic. "You been with her?"

"Yes."

Without saying anything to me, Ruth walked toward him. "She's fine, isn't she?" he said. "Didn't I tell you?" She pulled at his sleeve so he bent his head toward her. She said something. He shook his head; then at what must have been a second question, he nodded. While they talked, I was putting on my clothes, thinking back on how, no matter how bad things had been, I'd had my independence, and that I was losing it today, and all I was doing now was trying not to feel anything as I stood there on a part of the floor without carpet.

Ruth pointed her finger at the door to the left of the desk. I thought she wanted me to sit in a chair near there; but when I started to, she corrected me: "No, go wait in the next room," she said.

I picked up the canvas bag of things I'd brought with me, crossed the carpet, not looking back, opening the door, then standing on the other side of it breathing free again and steady. The room was Ruth's bedroom. I could see right away by the photograph on the night table, a much younger Ruth posing with a man, Ruth in a red peplum dress with big shoulder pads, a pearl choker; the man in an airman's blue uniform, gold wings on his lapel; Ruth's lips drawn up in a smile, while the man beside her seemed serious and tense. It might have been that he was getting photographed and didn't like it; but maybe it was Ruth's presence making him uneasy, doing what it did to Vic and me.

The bed was small and made up with a chenille spread; the dresser low and wide, with a framed mirror on hinges. All the furniture was blond wood, new; and there was a white shag carpet. On one wall were four steep windows, side by side, all of them covered with shutters. The wallpaper had beige stripes.

After a while, I sat down on a high-backed wooden chair. I

heard doors open and shut. Occasionally I heard talk. I caught some of the words, but never enough to understand. I went to one of the windows, opened the blinds halfway, and glanced out. Before me was a narrow porch, where two girls in terry-cloth robes were sitting on a metal glider. One of the girls was dark, her hair spread wide like a hood, the nails on her toes and hands painted gold. The other had auburn hair, long and straight, brushed to her shoulder blades, then curling up gently. When the black-headed girl glanced toward me, I left the window.

There was a knock at the door, I started across the carpet to open it, but the girl came in before I could. She was small and slim, her thick brown hair pulled high on her head and fastened with a blue plastic barrette, curled strands flowing along the side of her face. She had dark brown eyes, and for a moment she stared at me, looking me over nearly as thoroughly as Ruth had, and seeming not to like what she saw. "I'm Sandy," I said, the name for me that Vic had used with Ruth.

"Ruth told me your name."

She walked full into the room and picked up a bottle of perfume on the dresser, sniffing at the stopper, then putting it back and drawing down the corners of her lips. "I'll take you to your room," she said.

"Is that where I'll live?"

"Yes, it's on the top floor."

For a moment, she waited as though she expected me to object, and when I didn't, she started toward the hallway. "My name's Hadley," she said.

We climbed two flights of stairs, then went down a hallway lighted only by a window at the far end. The bedroom doors on either side were shut. She told me they stayed that way, whether you had someone in your room or not. She opened one of the doors with a key that Ruth had given her, then handed it to me.

The room was in the center of the house and had two windows that gave onto the backyard, both of them decorated with white shades and sill-length curtains of machine lace. It smelled faintly of the dry rose petals that were in a dish on the dresser. Hadley went to the windows and raised them both wide. The limb of a tallow tree swayed and pushed against the screens.

A cream rug with a wide printed border of flowers covered the wood floor nearly to the walls. In one corner was a chaise longue upholstered in blue polished cotton. Two small lace pillows lay against its arms. The bed was nearly large enough to cover the wall to the left. It had a blue headboard to match the chaise longue—no footboard, so the end corners of the quilted spread hung down on the carpet. A mirror covered the opposite wall. Hadley opened a door. Behind it was a closet with a bare rack. "I'll get you some coat hangers," she said.

I didn't want to trouble her or anyone. "I don't have but a few things. I can put my jeans and shirts in the drawers." I pointed toward the dresser.

"Nobody has many clothes when they first come here."

She came back with a half-dozen hangers and fitted them in the rack. Hadley didn't smile much. At first, I thought this was because she just didn't take to me, but later I learned that it was other things.

"You happy here?" I asked.

She shrugged her shoulders, then picked up something on the dresser. "Sure. Why wouldn't I be?"

I slid my hand along the side of the night table, then along the fringe of the lamp. "You ever work for anyone else?"

"No."

She tipped her head, her hair falling low over her shoulders, her lips parted. "You ever been with a man before?"

"Yes."

She smiled, her eyes moving away from mine. "That's too bad."

"Why?"

"You can make real money for the first time."

"Is that what you did?"

She was bending over, looking at some figurines on the dresser, picking them up. "No. Most of the ones who come here like that don't stay long. Ruth gets rid of them."

"Why would she?"

"Maybe she thinks she might get into trouble, somebody thinking they'd been brought here against their will."

"Do you think they are?"

"No, not here."

I glanced over at the dresser. It had an organdy skirt in a pattern of flowers; a card was stuck under the glass, a valentine signed with a message that made me blush. I pulled it out and dropped it into the empty wastebasket. Then I looked at the set of china figurines of serious-faced boys making love to smiling girls who were raising up their long skirts for that to happen. I touched one of them. It was slick and cold.

"You like the room?"

"It's fine."

Hadley gestured with her head toward the window. A breeze was moving the shades so that occasionally they clacked against the panes. "Ruth doesn't like dust coming in," she said. "You can keep the windows open when you're in here, but close them when you leave. It makes more work for Fran, and she complains."

"Who's Fran?"

"The maid."

"She nice?"

"She's okay." Hadley looked down at her polished nails, rubbing her finger over one of them to make it shine. "No, she's fine."

She opened the door at the end of the mirror. It gave onto a bathroom. There was another door on the other side. "Esther is across from you. You share the bathroom. If you're in here, lock the door on the other side, but don't forget to unlock it when you leave."

The fixtures were newer than the house. I'd never seen a bidet before, but Hadley told me what it was for and what Ruth expected. "You have to protect yourself," she said. "I mean, not get sick. You can't work here if you are."

In the corner was a large glass shower with a window at the top and a kind of bench. She told me what Ruth expected there, too. "We do what they want," she said. She showed me where the towels were and the hamper.

"And if you get hurt?"

"See the doctor."

"But if you do and—"

"Complain then."

"She listen?"

"No. Why should she? She can get someone else. You think she can't?"

I was standing by the dresser again, picking up the comb-and-brush set. They were tortoise-shell, and the streak of sunlight that went across the dresser melted into them like light on a stream. "Will she want me to work today?"

"You plan to live here free?" She laughed. "And don't worry about being busy. We're busy. There's no other good place near here."

For the first time, she looked at me with real interest. "You love the first one you were with?" she asked.

"No."

She stood still a moment, frowning. "That's too bad."

I didn't answer.

"How old are you anyway?"

"Sixteen."

"You don't look that old."

"I am."

"I guess it's your blond hair and the way you wear it down." She turned to go. "It's real pretty," she said softly, then she left and shut the door. I heard her cross the hall.

I sat down on the chaise, glancing out the window at the leaves of the tallow tree, gold and red, some of them beginning to fall. After a time, I got up, walked around, feeling the rug against my feet, looking again at the figurines.

When Fran came for me, it was nearly eight o'clock. The sun was gone. I had turned on the two small lamps on the dresser. I lay back on the chaise, the dusky shadow of me in the mirror, the white of the satin dress Ruth had told me to wear like an open lily in a pool, me raising my head as I heard the rustle of Fran's starched skirt, sensed her near me, listened to what she said, though not quite hearing. "She wants you in the Rose Room," she said.

"I don't know where that is," I whispered, any more than at first I'd known the whereabouts of the stone house. It was Maury and Link who had taken me there, Maury helping me out of the truck, talking with me gentle, leading me in. After that, the stone house was the part of my life I didn't look at in my mind, just where my feet led me before sunset or after dark. And when that work was finished, I usually had the dark to go through, the stars washing over my head.

"I'll take you there," Fran said. Fran's face was full black, and she was dressed in a white uniform with lace trim.

I stood before the mirror, putting the ribbon in my hair, slanting the bow to the side; and then I followed Fran down. In the hallway, the lamplight ran across her hair that she combed through with oil so it looked like a lake without wind. She smelled like that oil and like pressed cotton cloth. "You all right?" she asked.

"Yes."

We passed the living room. One of the girls was sitting on a sofa with a man. They weren't holding hands or even touching, but they watched me while I passed. I heard the man whistle softly, the girl whispered something, and they laughed. When I noticed that she was in a short dress, I blushed for this long one I wore and wondered why Ruth chose it. A couple crossed the hallway toward the stairs. I'd met the girl at supper. She'd been friendly there, asked me if I'd like to walk down to the town with her one day, but she didn't even glance at me now. She was talking to a man with a sagging face, whose arm she held. He must have been fifty. I didn't know a man that old would be looking for this. He glanced at me. I glanced down.

"It's in here," Fran said.

The Rose Room was the parlor I'd seen that morning, but now the door was shut. When Fran opened it, I saw that before each of the two sofas lighted candles stood in saucers, the shadows of their flames flickering on the dusty pink of the walls. Sitting at the far end of the room was a girl wearing a dress like mine but in a soft lilac shade instead of white. Her body showed through, but she had a scarf to cover her shoulders. On her feet were flat silk sandals, the same material as the dress. Ruth was sitting alone near the fireplace. I knew to go to her. She touched me where my dress fell tight to my hips, then led me toward a mirror, standing behind me and adjusting my hair slightly by pulling it away from my cheeks. "We may want to pin this up sometime to make you look older," she said, "but you're fine for tonight."

"Is he old?" I was thinking of the man I'd just seen.

"No."

"Fran . . ." Fran dipped her head, and the white cap flashed. Ruth asked her to bring each of us a glass of wine, then she began telling me about the man I'd meet, how he'd come here with a friend in town. After that, and when I couldn't think of anything more to ask her, we waited in silence until Fran brought the wine.

I drank a first deep swallow, then drank the rest quickly. After that, the air around me seemed to soften. The image of the candle flame beat against my dress. I put my hand over the brightest spot, as though I might stroke it away.

"A friend and I went to Florida last spring," Ruth was saying. "We stayed at Oceanside, a hotel on the beach. Then, once, when we were sunbathing, a man settled in the space beside us with a radio; and when I complained of the noise to a beach attendant, all he could do was move us to another space. . . . Why do people go to a place like that if all they want is noise? Wouldn't you think they'd want quiet?"

A man came in, small and slight in the shoulders. I thought he might be the one I was meeting, so I started to rise, but Ruth touched my arm. "He's with Gwen," she said. He glanced at us, his eyes stopping on me; then he moved toward the other sofa, sat down beside the girl there, and I saw Fran take him a drink. Later, when I glanced that way, he was staring at me. The wine I'd drunk made me stare back until he looked away.

Ruth glanced at her watch. The small hand was at nine. Gwen and the man got up to leave, him letting her go ahead through the door, indicating to her that he needed to say something to Ruth. Ruth rose to meet him. Under his breath, he asked her a question. She shook her head, though when he spoke again, she nodded. Then he went to where Gwen was, their forms passed through, and the door clicked shut.

"He wants to see you," Ruth told me. "Thursday. Mr. Campe. Will you remember that? Mr. Campe?"

I could hear music from the living room, someone playing show tunes, making mistakes and going right on. "Who's playing the piano?" I asked.

"I don't know. One of the visitors. Do you play? If you do, I can—"

"No, ma'am, I don't. Not anymore." I thought of the piano in Valentine, how Joylyn and I had missed it after it was sold.

I listened. In a moment, the music stopped. There was quiet on the other side of the door, so I thought the living room might be empty. "Maybe he isn't coming," I said.

Ruth smiled, her teeth and earrings sparkling in the candlelight. "He'll be here."

Another quarter hour passed before Fran opened the door again. A man in a dove-colored suede jacket, brown shirt, and light-colored tie came to Ruth, his gaze avoiding mine, instead holding to Ruth's, as if he'd come for her. He had dark eyes and a small mouth; his cheeks had a blue cast to them, even though he'd shaved close. Ruth got up to meet him. She introduced me to him, "Sandy, this is Mr. Lucas." I reached out my hand, and he took it, holding it and bringing me to stand beside him.

Ruth glanced around as though she was looking for someone. "Didn't Fran give you a drink?" she asked him.

"I don't want one."

Then Ruth nudged me. There was a glance between her and Mr. Lucas. I hesitated. I didn't know what I should do, if I should walk up to my room and he would follow, or if there was something more for Fran to do.

"It's a quarter past nine," Ruth said to him. "Do you want—"

"No, tell Fran not to bother us."

"You want anything sent up to the room?" Ruth asked.

"No."

Fran stood beside the door to open it for us, then motioned to me in the direction of the stairs. "We have to go up to the third," I said. "My room's up there."

"I know where it is."

I went ahead of him. One of the girls passed us as she was coming down. She kept her eyes ahead looking toward the man she was going to meet.

When we came to the third floor, I turned to the right as I knew to, Mr. Lucas still following me, the skirt of the satin dress clinging to my thighs like flowing water and making me walk in short steps. I felt awkward. I started to pass the door to the room that was mine, but he caught my arm. "This is it," he said.

I turned.

I had left on the lamp beside the bed. Fran must have pulled the shades and closed the lace curtains. It seemed forever since that morning when I'd stood in the window and felt the peacefulness of the room and the yard and the trees beyond. In the cold semidarkness, the space looked unfamiliar. I glanced toward Mr. Lucas's face, but he had turned away to take off his jacket. In the mirror, I could see both of us, the satin dress, my bare shoulders, the thin white straps, my body stretched against the thin material, the white ribbon in my light-colored hair, Mr. Lucas's dark shirt; then my arms raising like a baby's and the dress coming over my head, covering my face so that I was seeing the lamplight through the cloth, the hair ribbon catching in the satin hem, all of it falling to the floor, where I reached for it but had to stop when his arm was under me, lifting me toward him. I wanted to pick up the pile of satin, to reach down and fold it and put it in a chair because Ruth had told me not to hurt the clothes, but I knew also to let him hold me, that the less I did contrary to him, the better off I'd be, as Link had taught me that first time.

He asked me to take off his shirt, and when he didn't say not to, I went on with the rest of his clothes, until I was seeing him, the thinness of the muscular, lank body, the bony knees, the deeply tanned skin. He was staring at us both then, taking his time, his eyes moving between us, studying the differences, speaking about them.

For a time, his lips were pursed, and I thought he was going to ask me questions about how I came here and where I came from, but he said nothing more. He turned me and pressed against me from behind, covering my breasts with his hands, then watching us in the mirror wall, his silver ring shining, the stone in its center appearing quite blue. My eyes fixed on that blueness, and then I smiled.

"You're beautiful," he said. "But I'm sure you know that." My smile in the mirror became yet fuller, brighter than anything in the room, brighter than the ring; and it seemed even uglier than his peculiar expression and the way he was bending down now, and what he was doing to me with his hand.

"Anything wrong?" he asked.

"No."

I turned and caressed him like I knew to.

"Do you like me?" he asked.

I nodded.

He turned me again, then squatted a little. I felt the air from the window cold on my skin, and I guess he felt it, too, from far outside, from the lake and beyond, steady and streaming over the valleys and fields, taking the leaves with it and letting the big birds soar in its currents. While he raised me up and began, my thoughts scattered. One was of Vic, telling me about this place on the way to Ellison; one was of the Bells, the orderliness and safety of the yellow kitchen where I watched Mrs. Bell work; then I was thinking of Joylyn, fixing in my mind her face before me, so that it wouldn't move and fade out. I saw her yellow curls, her green eyes; tried to feel her holding me, keeping her hands between my body and Vic's and this one's now. Because I knew she would want to, that she had to love me at least that much.

I thought he would take me to bed then, but I felt my body being lowered onto the chaise, slowly because he was that strong, placing me facedown this time, his body going down with mine, covering me, him waiting, then lifting himself to kiss my shoulders. He pushed my hair away from my neck and kissed me there, warming me from the cold from the window, asking me if I liked what he did.

My cheek lay on the cushion of the chaise. My eyes were opened, staring into the mirror. He was looking there, too, watching what he did with me. We stayed quiet an instant; then, when he was ready, he pulled away. I started to rise, too, but he pushed me down, the flat of his hand between my shoulders, and he whispered to me to stay still.

"No," I said, when I understood; but he kept talking to me, telling me what he wanted, what he enjoyed and expected, then words I couldn't understand until his voice broke off. In an instant, the pain passed through me, and I jerked to free myself, succeeding, then having him bring me back, and afterward using the firmness of his weight to keep me. I must have been panting, and tears wet my face and the place where my cheek was. For a moment he stopped moving. He was talking again, coaxing. Over and over, he called me his pretty girl. He said he loved me, talked about the money he had and that he'd give me, taking his time. In one strong effort, I tried again to move away. For an instant, I think I did.

When he began again, I was thinking of Doc, how his buying

the ranch in Valentine was making me do this. I thought of Joylyn leaving in that truck, so that one day I'd be in this room, the bed and flowered rug, the silver brush and mirror; trading my place in Ozona for this one in Prentice, all of it as if nothing else had gone on in between.

15

One morning brought in a day in Prentice when the wind almost ceased and the air was so bright and clear that you could see beyond the cedars to the edges of the hills. The afternoon before, Ruth had stopped me in the hallway to say that we'd go shopping today, but then after breakfast, she'd sent word by Esther that we'd have to postpone our trip until later in the week. She said I didn't have to stay in the house; if I wanted, I could go out walking—I had the whole day to sleep or wander. "But if you do go out, she wants you to be sure and use the back way," Esther said.

"Is she afraid I'll soil something?" Since it made the walk shorter, I liked to use the front. I could go down the twenty or so steps to the sidewalk and not have to get my shoes scuffed, by taking the gravel drive and then the lane to the bottom of the hill. I reached inside the closet for my coat.

"She doesn't like anyone using the front but her," Esther said.

Esther hardly ever talked, and when she did, she spoke softly. At the supper table, if she said anything, you'd either miss it or have to get the others quiet and ask her to say it again. Most of the time, really except at meals, she stayed in her room, listening to her phonograph, sitting at her dresser, fixing her hair in different ways, arranging her clothes and jewelry. I didn't know much about her, only that she'd had her nineteenth birthday in October, and that before she'd come here three years ago, she'd lived in a series of foster homes in a town near the coast. I never knew how she'd come to Ruth's, and I never asked her. The girls who lived in the house stayed to themselves. There wasn't much friendship among us, and Ruth didn't encourage it. She was always watching us, interrupting us when we were together.

"Why don't you come to town with me?" I asked Esther.

"I can't. I'm working this afternoon. But I'm off tomorrow. My cousin's picking me up after supper." Her voice sounded tired. "You work all night?" she asked.

"Fran brought someone up late."

"After midnight?"

"Yes."

Esther glanced at me sharply. If we'd finished our appointments, we weren't supposed to be disturbed after twelve. "You didn't have to take him," she said. "I don't think you should have."

"He'd come a long way."

"Where from?"

I didn't want to tell her because I knew the one who'd asked Fran to wake me for him usually went to her. "Tabors'," I answered.

The Tabors owned a huge ranch near Abilene. When any of their men came in, Ruth didn't like us to turn them down. More than once, she'd asked for a favor for them, saying that though there were places closer, they preferred to come here and she wanted it to stay that way.

"Who'd you see?"

"Jake Slade."

The color ran out of Esther's face. Jake was young, eighteen, nineteen maybe, always clean and fresh-looking as if he'd just stepped out of a shower. And he was good-natured, saying nothing when he first saw you, looking almost grim; but then, after he'd gotten what he came for, he'd joke with you and treat you like a friend. He was the kind who might invite you out of here one day. I guess Esther had thought of that, and I had, too.

She turned away from me and glanced down at the things on my dresser. "He do all right?"

"Sure," I said. "Why wouldn't he?"

"I wonder why he came so late," she said.

"Maybe he didn't think of it earlier."

She sighed. "Oh, he'd thought of it."

She picked up a lipstick from the glass tray I had, opened it, and rubbed some on the back of her hand, turning her wrist in the light from the window to study its shade.

"You want me to get you some of that in town?" I asked.

She was walking out. "No, thanks, I'll get it next time I'm down there."

After she left and shut the door on her side of the bathroom, I heard some music start on her phonograph, a man singing a sad song, a harmonica whining behind him. I put on a skirt and sweater, some low-heeled shoes I'd brought from Anderson. The air outside had warmed, so I decided I could do without my coat. I went down the back stairs, passing Fran in the hall. The house still smelled of breakfast.

I used the side door, opening it easy and not letting the screen slam because I knew Ruth liked the house peaceful, whatever time of day.

I walked down toward town, past the pasture at the foot of the hill, past some houses set back from the road, their yards nearly bare of grass. A woman wearing a man's denim jacket was sitting on a porch, shelling peas. She had a paper sack and a bowl in her lap. She glanced up as I passed. I thought she might smile, but she didn't. She stared, looking right through me, then bowed her head over her work. Well, she was right not to smile. And that made me wonder why the people who lived around here didn't complain about Ruth's. I thought I would if I owned a house like that lady had—not that the house was all that nice, but just that you wouldn't want the cars coming and going at night, the doors slamming, and if you had guests, them asking what was going on up there. Maybe next time I'd do her a favor and use the trail behind her place, or at least take the other side of the street.

I passed another block of old houses, the lawns fresher and neater. One of them had yellow chrysanthemums blooming, and I saw a bright green garden hose coiled in a corner beside the steps. I crossed a park where some girls, standing in line to toss a basketball through a ring, were moaning at their failures, cheering at each success. Suddenly the one arched to shoot the basket glanced at me and then stopped all motion, as though she were playing Statues, and someone had told her to freeze. I went on.

At the next street, I crossed over to the shady side. The first storefront was nearly empty, nothing in the windows except a poster of a man and woman and some kids sitting on some matching furniture. Hadley said it used to be a furniture store that went out of business when a more modern one was built on the highway. There was rubble on the floor and a broom fallen over a dustpan. It looked as though someone had started to sweep it out, then lost heart, as I sometimes used to when I'd set out to clean the trailer.

Once more I crossed the street, this time to see the movie posters, a picture with Gary Cooper. I wondered why women like me admired Gary Cooper so much. Was it because he always acted sweet and patient, and talked in a voice that never changed tone? No surprises. Sweet, that is, until he had to be tough and defend you and his friends; and then no one could defeat him. And afterwards, when the trouble was over, he'd put his arms around you, assuring you that he loved you, and that whatever cause was yours, was his.

The movie front looked like the scooped-out middle of a shell. In the rear was the glass box to sell tickets, with a small opening in it so you could slip your dollar through, and then a ticket would slide out of a slot and you could take it. No one was there now. I saw by a sign that the movie didn't open until two o'clock. That wasn't for another hour, so I walked on past until I reached a shop where they sold sewing machines and materials for dresses. My eyes were drawn back to where a clerk was sitting on a bench before one of the machines, pulling a small piece of material under the presser foot. I'd done that, Joylyn watching me, telling me how. It occurred to me that when I could, I'd work in a place like this, teaching people to sew, making a commission when I sold a sewing machine, knowing all about how it worked; and that I'd also know all about dress materials and how to cut a dress from a pattern.

The face of a small girl appeared at the window. I smiled, and she smiled at me, then walked to the back of the shop to the clerk who was giving the lesson. She hugged the woman's neck, then turned her head so that she could stare at me.

I looked more carefully at the clerk, wondering if when I was thirty, I'd look like her, my face broad and full, the belt around my waist not making any difference, my breasts heavy with fat made from eating good food I'd cooked myself, and not having anything more than working in a shop to worry me—even having scuffs on my feet and not bothering myself about thick ankles, keeping my child near me at work, even if that meant losing my job. And after work I'd take it home to a place that was clean, feed it something good for it, and turn on the radio to something right for kids.

When the clerk glanced at me, my eyes shot straight to a pattern showing a shirtwaist dress, and displayed beside a piece of yardage upended on its bolt, so that the material cascaded down like the spring water at Balmorhea, blue-green like that water, too; filling a swimming pool as big as a lake poured out on the desert. And that made me remember that Balmorhea was where we kids in Anderson had gone for a class picnic, and that I'd ridden in the yellow bus, no one beside me, holding my towel roll tight to my lap.

They all must have known about me then. First, they'd been afraid of me because I was poor and dirty; and then, when I could dress nice and pay to use a shower at the hotel, they'd stayed away because they knew what I did: The girls were told not to have anything to do with me, and the boys didn't butt in because of Maury and Link. Link had once fought a boy for cheating at pool until that boy couldn't get up off the floor of the pool hall, and his brother had to come for him and clean him up before he could take him home.

But I remember that when we were in the dressing room at the park with its open dressing stall and showers set in pairs along the side walls, and I was pulling off my clothes to change into my swimsuit, the girls kept looking at me, though, if I caught their eyes, they shifted them to another girl or something on the wall. Then, when I'd gone out of the dressing room, and walked down the sidewalk under the cottonwood trees, where I was going down the steps into the cold water, I got different kinds of stares from two of the boys. Their names were John Douglas and Red, and they'd followed me into the water, letting me use their face mask to see the fish and plants, then teasing me, John playing with me first, and then Red trying to hold me under water until I cried.

I ran back into the dressing room, dressed, got into the bus, and stayed there until it was dark.

The next time I saw Maury, I told him what had happened, and he went looking for John Douglas, and then for Red. He told me they wouldn't bother me again, and they never did. At school, if they saw me coming, they'd move to the other side of the hall. And then Maury offered to take me back to Balmorhea so I'd have the fun I'd missed and get the memory settled out.

"You want to go there?" he asked, and I told him I did.

We met near midnight on a Friday and drove over in the truck, and he boosted me over the fence, and I jumped on the grass below and giggled, until he warned me to hush, because there was a park ranger living in the rock house not a hundred yards away. Then he came over the fence himself, while I was touching the water and drawing back my hand because of the cold. "You need to get in fast," I whispered, "but I know I can't."

Maury took off his clothes and went in quiet, and I undressed; and then Maury came for me, bringing me in the water slow, pausing each time I said I was too cold. In the moonlight, I saw the shadows of fish, Maury swimming beside me in the deep water.

I looked at the pretty dress material, and for a moment more at the sewing lesson, at the little girl standing close to her mother, taking pins out of the cushion now; then I walked on to the drugstore, bought the lipstick that Esther wanted even though she'd told me not to, then went over to the booths behind the soda fountain, all of them filled but one. I didn't know if they let someone who came in alone sit in a booth, but I thought I would try it, and, sure enough, it worked fine.

While I ate, I watched the people coming in: a woman with her two sons, each of them fussing about ordering sodas when the most she was offering was a cone; then two cowboys walked in heavy, scraping their bootheels on the marble floor, as if they weren't used to coming inside. My eyes passed over them quick. Until they sat down, I hid my face behind the menu card, figuring that they might be some of those well enough off to visit Ruth's.

And we had to be careful about that, since Ruth didn't want us talking to anyone on the outside, afraid we'd make some deal like Angela Vega had, going out to live in a cabin on a ranch near Lampasas and getting a regular salary, pooled by three of the unmarried hands who made the arrangement.

I hurried to finish my food, keeping my head bowed as I went to the register to pay. Then I walked up to the Gary Cooper movie, bought a matinee ticket at half price, and a Coke to calm my stomach after seeing those men.

After the movie, I climbed the slope to the house, breathing in all I could of the fresh air, filling my lungs time after time, wanting to feel healthy as long as I could. I wished I could be outside forever, walking like this till my legs got tired; and then I'd lie down by some pool of spring water and rest, seeing the moon, bright and clear, lighting the grass and the trees, so even at night I wouldn't be afraid, Maury above and around me, protecting me from John Douglas and Red, his face drifting strong and quiet with each of the falling colored leaves, Maury touching me gentle each time he came down.

16

Vic was driving; Sylvia and I were together in back. He had come for us about nine, wearing a suit, so I reasoned that by his wanting to make a good impression, he was worried, and if Vic was worried, I was, too. He'd told Ruth that the reason he was late was trouble with the car, and then Ruth had led him over to the door away from Sylvia and me. They'd talked alone, argued, Ruth saying no, backing down, saying no again; then Vic was pushing past her, beckoning for us and taking us down the back steps to his car.

We crossed the railroad tracks. The Jefferson Hotel was about three blocks farther, ten floors of dark red brick. Brass posts held up a maroon awning over the walk to the door. At first, because he cruised by, looking up at the lighted windows, I thought Vic might let us out in front, but he parked behind the hotel in a lot, then got out with us, taking our arms again and steering us past some garbage cans and through a heavy metal door. "We'll use the stairs," he said. "It's the fifth floor." The climb was harder for him than for us, and we were there before him. When he arrived, he was breathing heavy and his face was wet.

We waited a moment, while he'd wiped his face and neck with

a handkerchief. Sylvia was trembling, but I was quiet. I imagined that anything that happened here couldn't be much worse than what I'd had before, just having it happen in a different setting. At these times, I didn't think of what was going on. Instead, I made a game of it, played like I was someone else, older, twenty-three or twenty-four, brought up in a big city, where you learn not to be afraid of things.

Vic glanced down at a scrap of paper that he held and muttered a number I couldn't hear. At the end of the hall, he stopped before a door, glanced down at the paper, and knocked. "Be nice now," he said, while we were waiting. "They're paying good." I asked him how much, but he didn't answer.

Behind the door, I heard a radio, jazz music. A man answered. When he turned his head, a reddish light glanced off his shiny brow. He looked back and forth quick at Sylvia and me, then opened the door wider and invited us in, telling Vic that his name was Hank.

"I'm sorry we're late," Vic said, "but you know with the girls . . ."

He offered Hank his hand, but he didn't take it.

The room had twin red leather sofas facing one another; a low coffee table between them had a tall vase with dead-looking reeds instead of flowers. There were chairs with upholstered seats and curved wooden arms. A black lacquered chest of drawers stood against the back wall. On it was a tray with glasses and two half-emptied bottles of whiskey. As soon as we entered, a gray-haired man in a tan suit got up from a chair and turned off one of the lamps and then the radio. He was dressed better then the others, and though his hair had lost its color, he didn't look all that old. By the way he acted quiet, I supposed that he was the boss and paying for this. Someone called him Mike. There were four men including him and the one who'd let us in. One of them, a youngish man with close-cropped sideburns, was digging his fingers into a plastic ice bucket; the other, young, too, was sitting on one of the sofas, smoking.

"Where do you want them?" Vic asked.

"On either side," Hank answered, not looking at us now. He opened a door to the right for Sylvia; Vic followed her in, me going into the other room, Hank before me to turn on the light. It was a small room with blue walls, a maple dresser with a mirror, a large, low bed, an easy chair with matching hassock. The single window was sealed shut, a noisy air-conditioning unit wedged between the frame and sill. The carpet was flowered. When I pulled back the bedspread, I saw that the sheets were flowered, too. On the dresser was a tray of glasses wrapped in plastic. "Do I stay in here?" I asked Vic, who'd left Sylvia and come in behind us.

"No," Hank said, answering for him. "Come out and talk to us awhile. We're having drinks." He touched my cheek with the side of his hand.

I glanced at Vic. "Are you staying?" I asked him.

"No, he's not," Hank said. "I'll telephone him when we're ready to break up." He drew a card out of his jacket pocket and gestured with it toward Vic. "I have your number," he said. "This still where you can be reached?"

Vic nodded, and then vanished somewhere while Hank was telling me something about the kind of work that brought them to Prentice and how successful they were at what they did. "I'll buy you a drink," he said, laughing and patting my arm.

I followed him out of the bedroom to the tray of liquor. At first I hadn't noticed Sylvia, then I saw her on the sofa beside Mike. He was smiling at her and running his finger along one of the curls that Fran had pulled up for her in a ribbon. In a moment, he stood up, picking up both their drinks, and she followed him behind the door of the bedroom that was hers.

"We're going to have some supper sent up," Hank said to me. "You hungry?"

"No, thank you."

"You don't go in for the extras, huh?" he said. "Just business. Well, that's good." He offered me a cigarette. I shook my head, and he smiled, then sat down in one of the armchairs. The man who'd been fixing a drink when I came in moved close and asked me my name.

"Sandy."

"I'm Glenn." He asked me to dance.

I rose from my chair, feeling his arms go around me, though he didn't hold me close. I'd noticed a gold band on his finger. Most of the men who came to Ruth's didn't wear rings. Hadley said that they weren't married, since, if they were, they wouldn't need to spend good money for what we had.

I talked to him a few minutes, questions about where I was from and where he was from, both of us probably lying in our answers. I know I was. He danced with me through what was left of the song, then through another one, saying nothing more, just running his hand nervously up and down my back. "I'm sorry I'm not a better dancer," he said.

I believed that he didn't want to be here, that the only reason he was, was because the others wanted it. Some of the men who came to Ruth's were like that. They went upstairs, saying nothing, waiting behind you while you opened the door. It took a while to get them ready, and sometimes you couldn't relax them no matter what you did, so that when Fran knocked at the door, you had to ask them if they wanted to pay for more time.

Hank emptied his glass and set it down, then tapped Glenn on the shoulder. "May I cut in?"

Glenn nodded, and I believe he was relieved. In any case, he stepped aside, and Hank took me in his arms. Mike was coming out of Sylvia's room, buckling his belt. His feet were bare; the skin on them looked yellow against the carpet. Then the one on the sofa who'd been leafing through a magazine got up and went in. I heard him laugh and say something loud to Sylvia, then the door slammed shut. Hank put both hands over his ears in mock irritation at the noise, then went back to dancing, holding me close and beginning to move us toward the door that was mine, joking about dancing into the room. After we were inside, he shut the door with the side of his foot, losing his balance a little when he did, then he was whispering, "Old Glenn was going to keep you dancing all night, huh?"

He took off his jacket and began unfastening his shirt. "Either of you live with Hansen?"

"No, we don't."

He laughed. "I didn't think so. There's got to be a limit to what anybody'll do."

I went in the bathroom, hung up my dress, and folded my

underwear on the side of the tub. My stomach was hurting; a headache was starting at the base of my skull. I had to stay still for a moment before I could go out. When I did, the room was dark, and Hank was lying on the bed. He looked at me a moment, said something obscene, then rose halfway to reach for me, pulling me down beside him, breathing heavy, joking with me, then saying he liked the way I talked, slow and easy, not pretending or putting on. He was still talking when he centered me under him and came into me, taking too long, exaggerating what he got.

Then, after a few moments of lying apart from me, letting his breaths get back regular, he rose and pulled on his pants, leaving his shirt on the chair. Before he left, he bent close, his lips touching mine while he talked, saying he'd tell Glenn I was waiting for him. "Or maybe he just wants you to come back in there and dance."

I lay still, my eyes shut, listening to the music through the half-opened door. There was a knock from the hallway, the click of silverware, liquid being poured into glasses; and when nothing happened, I wondered if I should get dressed and go out to the living room again. Then one of them pushed at the door, shut it, and I could see by the light coming in from the curtain that it was the man whose name I didn't know, the one who'd been with Sylvia. He was with me a much shorter time than Hank, asking no favors, exploring a little, trying to please me with his hands. I figured by then that they would keep coming in the room like this, choosing either me or Sylvia according to what suited them and which of us was free, do that until they were tired and felt that they hadn't spent their money for nothing. When Glenn came in, he'd had more to drink, and that had taken his shyness, so he was rough. I said something, and he came at me easier.

When he left, the door closed, and I heard a train go by, moving fast through Prentice, not stopping for anything. Then the radio went up again, roaring. Someone cursed, and the sound went down to a buzz. I heard people moving around and talking, then the grating noise of a window being opened. A glass shattered; someone yelled as though he'd been cut. There was some quiet, then laughter and more talk, a knock on the door to the hall, voices I hadn't heard before. I came up on my arm, listening to those and then for Sylvia, but I didn't hear her. I got up, went into the bathroom, washed my face and sponged with a washcloth; and when I went back in the room and remembered that the bedsheets were damp, I got two bath towels and laid them side by side. I must have been asleep, when I thought I heard Vic's voice mixing with Mike's, then more silence, so I believed it was over, that they'd paid for the party and were leaving. I started to get up. I was almost on my feet, when Mike and Hank and two men I hadn't seen before came in together.

The two new ones were drunk, dirty, louder than the others, and didn't look as if they belonged to the group. At first, they sniggered like boys who've just heard a private joke, then they were undressing and talking mean, their eyes bright as lanterns turned on me.

Right away, I was up and moving fast toward the bathroom, passing through the four of them. The bathroom door had a lock, and even if I had to stay in there the rest of the night, I meant to use it. Hank caught me, asking me what was my hurry, then one of the new men tugged me away from him, hurting my arm. "We don't have to do this at Ruth's," I said firm. If a man had the money, he could ask for two of us, but it never happened this way.

"You ain't at Ruth's!" the man said, turning me around, shoving his hand between my legs, doing something with his fingers that made tears stream down my cheeks.

The other ones moved in, and I was hitting all of them with my fists, and kicking with my legs at every piece of flesh close. I felt a blow to my cheek; then a half-dozen hands moved my body backward and down, so I was lying crossways on the bed, my knees up and turned outward; then my legs free again and kicking, until Hank was holding me, telling the one who had me to take his time with me because I was worth it.

When the man turned me over and lifted me up, I screamed. Hank put his hand over my mouth and I bit him; but I paid for it after, because what he made me do with him then was a kind of final humiliation, though not as much to my body as to my mind. I don't remember a lot past that, except one of them had to hold me still and then didn't have to hold me anymore.

It was dark in the room when I felt Vic's hands pushing my flesh into my clothes, and me seeing, swimming above my eyes, his face, his lips compressed in one line, my hand pushing his away as if I were still fighting. "We got to be out of here before it gets light," he said, shaking me to bring me back to my mind. He took a sharp glance backward at the door, trying to put on my stockings, but not being able to because I couldn't straighten my legs. I was still bleeding some; my thighs were bruised solid.

He jammed the stockings down in his pocket, then put on my shoes, twisting them over my toes.

"Stand up," he whispered.

But I couldn't stand by myself, so he had to pull me up and support me while he drew my dress over my head, his fingers catching in the lace, tearing it. He ran his hands through my hair like a comb. I tried to pull away, turning my head. "You walk beside me like nothing happened," he said.

Going out, I tripped on a liquor bottle. It turned over and caused a trickle of gold on the border of the rug. I glanced toward the open door of the other bedroom. Vic's eyes followed mine. "They sent Sylvia home in a cab," he said. "Somebody went with her. Hank and the older one wanted you to stay awhile for them. I didn't know about the others coming."

He started for the stairs. I told him I couldn't walk down. We stood before the elevator door listening to the chains creak. It was one of those open cage elevators, where you can see the length of the shaft, and looking down makes you dizzy and you want to jump. When the elevator came, the floor of it wasn't quite level, so we had to step up.

When we were inside, Vic told me to get my hands off my face. He grabbed my arms and shook me then. He was nearly crying himself. "You want us arrested?" he asked.

He tugged at the door to the back parking lot, but it was locked from the inside. Then he tried to take us in a wide berth around the front desk, but the clerk standing behind it glanced up from a book he was reading and beckoned him over.

"Stupid bastard," Vic whispered. His face looked like I was seeing it from under water, his mouth pulled apart. He left me, walked over toward the clerk, and threw some rumpled bills on the counter.

About the time Vic got me past the door and into the lot where he'd parked, I started yelling. I yelled until he slapped me, my shoulders, my arms, and then my face, one side and the other, my ears ringing so that in the car I had to hold the sides of my head with both hands. "You want the police?" Vic said. "I ought to take you to them. Then you'll know what it's like." He gestured in the direction of the hotel. "What happened up there is just a sample of what they'd do to you, once they knew what you were. There aren't any rules anymore, Sandy. Once you're into this, it don't matter how much."

He paused and frowned hard, like he was trying to think of something else. "You like the money, don't you?" Then he reached over and shook my shoulder. "Well, don't you? I know Sylvia does."

He was watching the street before him, the streetlights flashing one after another in the oval lenses of his glasses. "Well, to hell with it," he said, calm now. "We won't worry. And I guarantee you that next time we'll be more careful about who's invited, and I'll set a strict limit on the time. That going to be okay with you? I know Sylvia likes it fine."

Sometimes, when he came to Ruth's, Vic went to Sylvia's room instead of mine, and I could be grateful to her for that.

"Sylvia likes making lots of money quick," he said.

"So do you, Vic," I whispered. "You son of a bitch."

I didn't cry out when he hit me this time. I don't think I even blinked.

17

It was getting cool when Darrell and I walked up to Mrs. Slover's, insects singing, birds in nearly every tree. In the Baileys' yard, a flock of grackles picked at the grass, one of them sucking water from a pool being left on the sidewalk by a sprinkler. Mrs. Bailey's car was not in its place in the shed. I started to turn off the water at the porch but thought better of it. Maybe she had some purpose in leaving it on.

Mrs. Slover answered the door, her eyes lighting up for Darrell like they always did. I was holding him in my arms then, so the dog, Alley, had to reach up with her muzzle to touch him. Darrell called her name and bent down to pat her head.

"I hoped I'd see you this afternoon," Mrs. Slover said. Darrell pushed away from me and held out his arms for her to take him. "Granma," he said. He'd heard June's kids calling Mrs. Ambler *Granma.*

"Sure he can call me that," Mrs. Slover had told me the first time he'd said it, when I'd tried to excuse his manners and his mistake. "He doesn't have any other, so why not me?"

Now she took him in her arms, kissed his cheek, and let him play with her necklace, warning him not to pull too hard. She was well from her cold, so that morning Mrs. Tellerson had driven her to see Henry. I asked how Henry was and got the usual reply that he looked too pale, she was afraid the doctors neglected him, the therapy wasn't regular enough.

We went into the living room, Darrell reciting all the words he knew, while Mrs. Slover tried to talk, him interrupting nearly everything she said. Then he was taking things out of her sewing basket, and she was distracting him with a coloring book. He pushed it aside. "No," he said, his hand diving again into the sewing bag and coming up with a yellow cloth measuring tape.

"Cookie," Darrell said, surprising himself, I think, that he had only just now thought of asking.

I went back to the kitchen and got him one, oatmeal raisin, from the cookie jar. Mrs. Slover held him in her lap while he ate it; and then in a moment he drank a cup of juice. We talked more about Henry, then about Jimmy's work and church and Dr. Tellerson.

"I need to talk to you," I said, at last. I gestured toward Darrell, and she understood at once that I had something to say to her that couldn't be said in his presence, so she lowered him to the floor.

"Take him to the porch then, and give him the basket of toys," she said.

I did that, setting him on the hook rug and getting down the basket, laying it carefully on its side so that the things spilled out gently. Darrell picked out the blocks. "House," he said, beginning to stack them.

"Yes, darling," I said. "Make a beautiful, tall house."

"For Mommy and Darrell."

"And Daddy."

I went back in the parlor, feeling stiff and tight all through my body, three sleepless nights showing on me in every move I made.

Mrs. Slover noticed and asked me if I was feeling well.

"Yes, ma'am, I'm fine."

She smiled. "You're not pregnant again?"

"No, I don't believe so." Jim and I had talked of another child, but not so soon. I wanted a girl, someone I could teach things, so that when Jimmy necessarily had to take over Darrell, I'd have the girl for myself, just as when Buck had taken over the training of Junior and Trix, June had Nancy.

I pulled up a chair and sat opposite her, my body leaning slightly forward, my hands on my knees. She was preparing to thread a needle when I told her. I spoke slowly and precisely so there could be no mistake. She was holding the end of the thread between her lips, then she let it go, so that it swirled to her lap, the needle still in her hand. As I continued, her mouth slacked, her eyes shut halfway and blinked rapidly, as if they were suffering under too strong a light. After a few minutes, when I'd finished all I meant to say, I asked her if there was any hope for it, if I might tell Jim and expect forgiveness, not at first but some time in the future, and that perhaps I could stay with her in case he didn't want to live with me for a while. "I don't think I can pay you," I said, "but I'll do whatever you want to help around here." I tried to smile. "You know I can."

She sat still, her features stiffening with each new labored breath she took. Putting the point of the needle through the lapel of her dress, she glanced down, the corners of her mouth trembling. The handkerchief that she'd been hemming when Darrell and I got there remained in her lap. She gazed at it, as though she were trying to sort things out in the regular weave of the linen. When she looked up, there were tears in her eyes. She whispered something about how cruel I had been to marry Jim, since he'd already had more sorrow than most people can bear. I remembered that she had known Jimmy's mother and admired her. "You can't stay here," she said.

I glanced toward the porch where Darrell was piling up blocks as high as he could, moaning when any one of them fell, picking it up and replacing it, working as carefully as his daddy would work on a machine or some window or door hinge he might set out to repair.

"And you mustn't tell Jimmy," she added.

"Not tell him?" I echoed. "Perhaps in a letter."

She shook her head. "No, none of it. Nothing at all."

I heard the wheeze and spin of the clock and then the strokes for six o'clock. I knew I should leave, that too much time had passed, but I hoped that Mrs. Slover might glance up at me and show by some new motion of her hand or light in her eyes that she'd changed her mind and would soon tell me.

Alley got up from her place on a folded blanket near the hearth, came to Mrs. Slover, and put her head on her lap, but Mrs. Slover waved her hand and pushed the dog away. Alley glanced back and forth between us, then turned and slowly left the room, her tail wagging gently.

After Mrs. Slover had turned to gaze out the window, not lifting the corner of the curtain but watching the declining light through the lace; when I reckoned that the interval of waiting had been too long for another and different response, I rose and went to the porch for Darrell, calming his protests at leaving so soon with a promise to get out his blocks at home. For an instant, he gazed up at me, his face wide and serious, so I knew he was calculating, weighing the rewards of this activity against the one promised. Then, with a sigh, he began helping me take down his building and replace the blocks in the basket, me talking to him soft, coaxing him on. And when he stretched his arms up to me, I bent low to embrace him, kissing his face (he kissed me back, two wet, carelessly placed kisses on my cheek); then I carried him to the front door, Mrs. Slover following behind us. She reached toward Darrell's shoulder, cupping it in her hand. "You aren't taking him with you," she said.

"What?"

"I mean, when you leave Winston Valley. You'll leave Darrell here with Jimmy."

"I'm not leaving," I said. "Why should I? This is my home. And if I were to leave, I'd certainly take my child."

"Jimmy won't allow it."

The silver rims of Mrs. Slover's glasses caught and glittered in the outside light. Her hand stretched out then, and I thought that she meant to take mine and hold it a moment, but she was only reaching for the handle of the door. She started to say something. I waited. Then her eyes went dim, and I knew that whatever thought she'd had, she'd decided not to share it.

I carried Darrell down the steps to the walk, and then set him on his feet. On the way home, we didn't talk much. Darrell was studying everything as he always did, sometimes squatting to examine some fallen leaf or to pick the head off a wildflower that he wanted to collect and take home, put in water, as I put flowers from our garden in water to make them last.

Earlier, when we'd taken our walk from our house to Mrs. Slover's, the sun had been low over the valley, bearing down, the light bursting when we passed under the limbs of trees, then coming out full again in the clear space before us. Now it was low, close to the breast of the hill, and made a long, thin shadow of my body that narrowed at the top like a steeple, breaking at sharp angles when I passed by a shed, then lengthening again when I'd passed the building. Darrell, so much smaller and with shorter, quicker steps, looked like a shadow of my shadow, my copy, dependent in the way he would have to be until his form had at least the length and breadth of mine.

"Ice cream?" Darrell asked. He said it funny; only Jimmy and I and Mrs. Slover could understand.

"Not now," I answered. "After supper. When we've finished eating, we'll walk up to the drugstore."

He came close to me and took my hand, as though the adventure had already begun. "Daddy coming?"

"Yes, Daddy will come. Doesn't he always go with us when he's off work?"

"Darrell, too?"

"Yes, darling. You, too."

Jimmy came home late. His dinner had been waiting. I'd fed Darrell, and now he was sitting on a pallet on the floor of the living room, playing with his blocks, stacking them, then knocking them down, yelling out in delight each time he did.

I'd meant to go to Jimmy, hide my face against him, and tell him quickly, but somehow I lost that instant of courage, and after that I couldn't. I was nervous through dinner, and he noticed it. "Anything wrong?" he asked.

"No."

"Where'd you go today?"

"I stayed here."

"I tried to phone you this afternoon. I thought you and the baby might walk up to the garage and let me buy you a Coke."

"We went to Mrs. Slover's."

"She over her cold?"

"Yes. She went to see Henry."

Jimmy looked up from cutting his meat. "He okay? No bad news?"

"No, he's the same."

Again I started to tell him, then lost my nerve. The thing was that he seemed so happy about his day, and I didn't want to break into that. Then, after supper, when we were going to the drugstore, walking slow because of Darrell, he put his arm around my waist. "You're my darling," he said to me, smiling down in my face. "Well, aren't you? Isn't that so?"

Darrell was running ahead of us. I yelled at him not to go too far.

"Don't be so strict on him," Jimmy said.

Another time I might have argued, but not now. Jim stopped me and kissed my mouth. Darrell glanced back, then ran to Jim and raised his arms, to be picked up. Jim swung him up to him. "There's my boy," he said. "You going to play pro football, Darrell? Or are you going to be a rancher?"

"A rancher!" Darrell shouted.

"Good. Uncle Buck and me'll get you started."

At the drugstore, we ordered chocolate cones, then sat down at a soda table with a man who was buying a used truck from Jim. I held Darrell, keeping a napkin under his chin so the ice cream wouldn't drip on his shirt. On the way home, Jimmy talked about the sale, and another one, too—not quite so final, but close. Later, we watched part of a movie on television. When Darrell fell asleep on my lap, Jimmy took him to his room.

We were in bed when I began. I'd waited until Jimmy was beside me in the darkness, so I couldn't see his expression. As soon as I spoke, my voice began to tremble, and I know my voice shook. "I don't know how to tell you this, and I guess I've put it off as long as I can, but I kept hoping that maybe—well, I thought I was free of it, but now I know I'm not. In any case, I can't keep it hidden anymore, and I guess I'm tired of being scared."

I repeated what I'd told Mrs. Slover, telling about the ones at school, and Vic coming after, and how young I still was, and not really knowing what Ruth's was going to be like. "I left there, Jimmy," I said. "I did that on my own. Well, if I'd had a family, I wouldn't have done any of it. It's when you're by yourself that something like that can happen." I quit talking then. I'd just go on excusing myself, and suddenly it didn't seem right.

At first he said nothing. I couldn't even hear him breathe. I was looking straight up at the ceiling, trying to keep my body quiet. Even in the dark, I didn't dare turn my face toward his. Then I felt him rise up in bed slow. He reached across me to switch on the light. "What are you saying?" he asked soft.

But I couldn't answer, because I'd never seen him like that, his features pulled close and pinched in a way I thought I'd never see, because nothing in our lives except maybe Darrell's getting sick or dying would ever be tragic enough to cause it.

"Where?" he asked me, hoarsely. "Anderson? I never heard of that town."

I told him where it was, naming El Paso and Stockton as the close big towns that he might know.

"Good God, Stella," he whispered. "What are you doing? Joking with me? Don't do that. You gone crazy, telling me something like this?"

He had grabbed me. I didn't pull back, not even in reflex. He held me, hurting my shoulders, his eyes all over my face looking for the lie, and then, when he couldn't find it, he pushed me backward on the pillows. "It's not true, Stella." His hands trembled violently, and he shook me to make me speak. "I mean, some of it, or what?" He shook me again. "Is it true?"

"Yes, it's true, Jimmy."

"It's not you and June, one of your—"

"No, it's not me and June."

And then he was up, pulling on his clothes and going into Darrell's room. When the light went on, Darrell howled, and I ran in there, my arms around him, me picking him up, him crying, and Jimmy wrenching him from me. Jim grabbed some clothes for Darrell, none of them right for him, then took him into the bathroom and locked the door. Darrell was yelling for me. I heard the water run briefly, then a bottle shattered on the floor. Jimmy came out, Darrell dressed wrong, Jimmy holding him so close he was whimpering from pain. Jim told him harsh to hush. Neither of them looked at me; they were watching one another. Jimmy picked up Darrell's shoes off the floor in the hallway. I kept behind them down the back porch steps to the lawn and the truck. I tried to get in. I got the door open, but Jimmy pushed me away, and I fell against the fence, pain going all through me. But that was my leg twisted underneath me, so the muscle was pulled.

I didn't phone anyone. Nor did I leave the house. The next day, the phone rang once about noon. I answered, and when it wasn't Jimmy, I hung up. I spent my day cleaning the house, watching the drive, walking outside to look up the street. I tried to read a magazine, but I couldn't. That afternoon, Oona came over. While I was making her some lemonade, she went into Darrell's room. "Where's he?" she called to me.

"Darrell's not home, honey." And when she was standing in the kitchen door, looking confused, I said, "He'll be home soon, and then you can take him out and play on the swings. You'll look out for him careful, won't you?"

I tried to be patient. I knew it was better to wait, to let Jimmy come to me with whatever conditions he had; but when the next morning he wasn't home with Darrell, and I'd heard nothing at all, I got up well before dawn and went to Mr. Copley, a neighbor that I knew drove out each work morning on the road that passed by Buck and June's. I asked him to take me there, explaining that Jimmy was helping Buck and wanted me to meet him. I suppose he thought it was strange that Jimmy wasn't coming in for me and that I'd said nothing about Darrell, but he agreed, and then let me off at the gate, since I asked him not to drive in. I'd already seen Jim's truck parked in front, so I walked up there toward the porch light, then right into Buck and June's house, June still in her housecoat, running after me, while I crossed the living room and hall and started climbing the stairs. "I'm getting my baby," I told her. Tears were flowing down my cheeks as soon as I spoke.

"Jimmy's still asleep." June said. "You can't go up there."

"Yes, I can," I said, not breaking the quick stride I'd gone into as soon as Mr. Copley had let me out. "Jimmy should have brought him home. I've been sitting there waiting for two nights straight, and I'm not waiting a minute more." Out of the corner of my eye, I'd seen Buck, but he was standing back.

I was in the bedroom then, the sun coming through the cleft in the hill, flashing its beams in the window. Jim was in bed, Darrell beside him. Darrell looked up at me with his blue eyes bright and startled. "Mama," he said, rising on his knees, while I was coming toward him. He was in rubber pants, and his diaper was wet, but I wasn't taking time to change him then. I gathered him in my arms, ran downstairs and out of the house, Jimmy full awake now and out of bed, calling my name shrill, following me barefoot, June and Buck standing in the yard, the dogs barking steady ever since I came.

"Stella—" I was on the drive, nearly to the road. Jimmy had me by the shoulder. I shook him off. Then I was running, Darrell getting heavy and squirming. Jimmy had on nothing but the shorts he'd put on quick, so he had to stop at the gate. But he was yelling at me until I could hardly hear him anymore. I'd walked about a half mile when a car came. When it stopped, I climbed in, Darrell and I sitting in back since it was a man driving and his wife in the passenger seat, me thanking God that they weren't from Winston Valley, only travelers passing through Texas to the coast. Darrell was getting my dress wet, and I guess he smelled bad to someone else, but they didn't say anything, asked no questions, either.

We weren't halfway home when I noticed Jimmy's truck coming up on us. But he stayed behind while we went through town and then again when Darrell and I were getting out at the house. I watched him come in the drive. While he parked, I took Darrell to the bathroom and started water in the tub. Then, later, when I'd dressed him, I carried him to the kitchen, where I knew Jim was. He was sitting at the table, hunched over some coffee he'd heated, his clothes rumpled, his face looking strained. Darrell's arms were around my neck tight, his cheek against mine. I noticed how Jimmy was looking at that.

"You want something to eat?" I asked him quietly.

He shook his head.

"I could fix you some eggs. You want me to scramble you some?"

"No."

I poured cereal and milk in a bowl for Darrell, cut a peach over it, then set him in the high chair. It was hot in the room, so I raised up the window, slipping the stick underneath to hold it open. I could smell the heat off the grass, though it was still early enough for the cicadas to be rattling their wings. When I went to Darrell's room to get him a favorite toy car that he'd asked for, as I was going back, I saw Jimmy in the hallway, blocking the space, his jaw set tight and his eyes harder than I'd ever seen them. "We got to talk, Stella."

"I know. . . . You tell them? June and Buck?"

"You think I'm crazy? You want me ruining Darrell's chances with them, losing him his family?"

"You shouldn't have taken him out there."

He leaned closer and spoke clear. "I sure as hell wasn't leaving him here."

I looked down at my dress. It was wrinkled, and I realized for the first time that day that I had on the same dress I'd worn ever since the afternoon I'd gone to Mrs. Slover's. There was a stain on the neck from lipstick. Jimmy was staring at the stain, like something was written there to try to understand. "What are you going to do?" I asked.

"I don't know. Not what I could have done if you'd told me before we had Darrell."

"What would you have done, Jimmy? Kicked me out?" I was crying then.

He didn't reply, but I saw the answer in his face.

I brushed past him, went to the kitchen, and gave Darrell the toy, then went into the living room, where I could wipe my eyes and try to calm myself for what was coming. Jim followed me. "We have to keep quiet," he said. "I can't have people knowing. If they do, I can't stay here. And I won't give up the business."

"No, of course not," I said.

"One thing I have to know . . . where you got that money I used for the garage. Did someone leave it to you, like you said?"

"No."

"Did it come from the work, any of it?"

"It was from the money I made, yes."

"Goddammit, Stella!"

He walked toward the front window. His back was to me. When he made up his mind, he turned. "All right," he said, "I'll give it back to you as the garage earns, make it in payments. I ought to sell the place now, but I'd have to take a loss on the improvements, and I'm not going to do that. I did talk to Buck about selling it. I asked him if he knew of any buyer, but he said no."

"What'd you tell him?" I asked soft. "You were tired of it? Or what?"

"I don't remember what I told him. I was thinking then that we had to leave."

"Maybe we could go somewhere else, Jimmy."

"And me do what? Set up a new life?" He laughed like people do when they've said the last thing in the world that would be funny. "I can't leave Winston Valley. My roots are here. My friends. Everything. And where could we go to, Stella? To some town with me knowing nobody and nobody knowing us? It'd take me ten years to get where I am now. And that with saving every penny, no one helping me or giving a damn."

He paused, staring at me. "You should have said something, Stella. Early on. Before we had a family. We might have lived together, near here or something, but not this."

"And not marry?" I felt something ugly twist inside of me. "Me having to live like I did before?"

"You didn't *have* to do nothing, Stella. Nobody does. Living is just choices, one right after the other. Haven't you figured that out?"

"I haven't figured out anything," I said. I had sat down on the plaid-covered hassock that I'd been so proud to buy a couple of months before. My legs were out straight, awkward. I rubbed my hands along them as though they were stiff. "What are you going to do?" I asked. "I mean, what do you want?"

"Just what I said. For you to keep quiet."

I looked down. "You tell Mrs. Slover?" he asked.

"Yes, I did."

"Why the hell can't you keep your mouth shut?" It was his voice shaking now, him close to crying. "Is it so much fun telling it?" His fists were clenched like he was going to hit something, but I knew it wasn't me. His enemies were his parents dying, and his marrying gone wrong, and his future in a kind of trouble he never thought it'd be in again, him thinking how lucky Buck was, getting June and inheriting a ranch, and how he had no luck at all.

"She won't tell, Jimmy," I said, standing and touching the sleeve of his shirt. "She wouldn't hurt us that way."

"You shouldn't have told her. She talks. She tells things."

"No, she doesn't."

"The hell she doesn't!" he yelled down in my face. "And since when have you become such an authority on Mrs. Slover? I grew up in her goddamned house, me and Henry. And you know more? She talks, I tell you. Who the hell else have you told? Dr. Tellerson? Maybe he'll give a sermon about it."

"No one else, Jim."

Darrell was calling to me from the kitchen. I knew he'd finished breakfast and wanted to get out of his chair. I started to go there.

Jim's hands were on me, tightening on my arms. "You think you can keep quiet?" he asked.

"Yes."

For a moment, he studied my face. "All right." Then he turned me around and pushed me forward a little. "Go see what the baby wants."

While I was in the kitchen, cleaning Darrell's face and hands and taking him down from his chair, I heard Jimmy's boots heavy on the floor, then the bang of the back screen door. The truck started up. He was late to work, I knew, and I guessed that would go down to my account, too.

"I love you, Darrell," I said.

"I love Daddy," he said.

"I do, too."

He smiled and tipped his head. "Daddy loves Mama and Darrell."

I was looking out the opened window, my back to Darrell. "We'll see."

Later that week, Vic called. The instant I recognized his voice, I hung up the phone; then the next call, after I'd told him to leave me alone, I listened. He was coming for me, he said. All I had to say was when. He reminded me that I'd determined my future long ago when I'd taken up with him and let him find me the place at Ruth's. Meanwhile if I wanted Jim Lester to know all that he, Vic, knew about me, he'd be happy to oblige.

I told him that Jim knew, and was taking it fine.

"Then he's not a man any woman would want. . . . There's no going back, Sandy. You shouldn't have left until I'd planned for it on the outside."

"Like you did in the hotel in Prentice?"

"That wasn't my fault."

"Whose was it?"

"You look here, Sandy," he said. "I've got the Winston Valley phone book in my hand. You want me calling some numbers and saying what I know?"

He was still talking when I hung up.

For the next few days, I went about my business like nothing had happened, the only changes being no calls from Mrs. Slover and my not taking Darrell up there—though I did see June that week. One afternoon after Darrell's nap, and at a time that I knew Buck was away taking some cattle to a sale, I drove out to the ranch to find out what June was thinking. When I got there, she and Nancy were watching a kid show on TV; a man dressed in a rabbit suit sitting in an easy chair, telling stories. As soon as she saw me, she sent Nancy to play outside in the sand pile with Darrell.

"You and Jimmy sure had a fight," she said.

"Yes, we did."

"What was it?"

"Something silly."

"Must have been bedtime stories, huh?"

"Something like that."

"You still love him?"

I reached out for her hand and patted it. I needed to touch someone. "Sure, I do. It's nothing like that.

"He get drunk while he was here?" I asked.

Her eyes avoided mine. "He had some beer."

She looked at me serious then and put her hand over mine. "You'd better be warmer with him, Stella. Give him what he wants. You can lose these Lester men if you don't." She told me things about her and Buck, rifts she believed she'd healed by making up that way. "I like you," she said. "I don't want to see you hurt. I really don't want to see that happen."

I nodded, but it was hard for me to look into her eyes. I'd never had her sternness directed at me before. She might have been talking to Nancy or Trix.

I guess she noticed my discomfort, because she got up then, fixed us a cup of coffee, and invited me to sit with her at the kitchen table. We talked about marriage and Jimmy's temperament, the troubles Jimmy'd had when he was young, how sweet he could be, and how that made it all the more difficult when he wasn't. When I left, she seemed satisfied that whatever fears she'd had were less serious than she'd thought. And I felt better.

The weeks went by, Jim and I passing one another in the house like people on sidewalks in big towns, our heads turned down like we were afraid that some slight wayward glance connecting might break the fragile thread that held us. I heard nothing from Vic. I figured he might have given up, and that made me regret telling Jimmy what I had.

Thanksgiving came, but there was no luncheon party this year since June and Buck and the Amblers were visiting Claude's relatives in Amarillo. Christmas came, the season changing; then Vic telephoned again, saying he was arranging things for me, he was just waiting to find out when I could leave. "Bring your son," he said. "We'll find a nurse for him. Don't worry about it."

"I can't take him from here."

"Why not? There's other towns."

Meanwhile, Jimmy and I kept living together under the same roof, him disregarding me most of the time, never talking to me except to complain: His shirts weren't ironed right; his meals weren't what he wanted. He'd push back his plate, go outside, and get in the truck, coming home at all hours, answering rude if I asked him where he'd been. I knew he was playing pool, gambling some, drinking. June told me because Kelly Joe Winkler, the pool hall owner in Boerne, told Buck. "Can't you keep him home?" June asked me. "It doesn't look good, Stella."

Darrell fussed, and I know it wasn't just because he was still recovering from a touch of flu like Dr. Moor said, but because he knew things were wrong at home. Perhaps he noticed the formal treatment his daddy gave me and that he'd moved out from me and up to the attic room; maybe Darrell even heard Jim come down once, his bare feet padding on the stairs and me holding my breath and praying. And he nearly tried it. I think he was close to reaching out for me when he gave up and moved from sitting on the edge of the bed to the dresser stool, talking to me awhile, smoking a cigarette in the darkness, telling me about the garage and some profits that were coming in, since they'd started selling used trucks and cars in the side lot that they were renting now from the Beardsleys for practically nothing.

"That's so good, Jim," I said. "I'm proud of it." I wanted to say *proud of you,* but that didn't sound right even to me. Maybe he sensed my awkwardness, because in a moment he left the room, saying he was tired, excusing himself. I heard him in the bathroom, then slowly climbing the stairs.

And the worst of it was that he was paying me back what he owed. One morning a month he'd get the deposit book out of the desk drawer, take it with him to work, then put it back that night.

Everything annoyed him: the garage, his partnership with Mr. Hendrick, the town, my presence in the house, or my not being home when he thought I should be. He complained of being tired all the time, and I knew he didn't sleep much. He didn't eat well, either. Sometimes he'd leave a plateful of food, then go into the living room and read the part of the newspaper he'd missed that morning. He never phoned me from the garage anymore. At home, he never held me or teased me. No more roughhousing or playing until both of us were laughing until we hurt, those sessions ending up in bed, finishing hard and with both of us exhausted like you need to be if you're ever going to get calm. In the meanwhile, he spoke of offenses to him and slights, people dissatisfied with his work, or their failing to pay on time, or begging for things on credit. "I'm not running a business for my own health," I heard him tell an old friend who'd recently lost part of his farm to pay debts.

June noticed, and one Sunday after church she said, "Things still okay between you and Jim?"

"Yes," I answered, "why wouldn't they be?"

She said something about my coming to our Tuesday sewing club, not missing it like I had last week. I said I would, and she left quickly, saying Buck and the kids were waiting for her in the car.

Then one afternoon, when he had lost a copy of a signed promissory note on the sale of a truck (he was certain that he'd left it at home on the desk), Jim was furious and yelled at me for losing it. "But what can you expect?" he was asking me, his voice breaking with rage. "You can't do nothing right, Stella. You ever notice it at Buck and June's? Nothing out of place. Why the hell can't you watch out for things like June does? You think she don't know where any business paper of Buck's is? You throw it out in the yard with the garbage? One of them filthy sows of Buck's is a better housekeeper!" He put his hand under my chin and made me look at him. "Don't you ever think?" He touched the top of my head, his hand on it hard. "Is there anything in there?"

"You never brought it home, Jim," I said. "I've never seen it. I always know what comes in here."

"The hell you do! You don't know nothing!"

He started for the back door. He was going to look for the note again at the garage. "You were the one used to be careful about the house," he yelled. "Is it telling me what you did that makes you neglect everything? You going back to that, Stella?"

"Maybe I will," I said. "You want to come see me there? It's more than I get here."

I was standing straight, my limbs trembling, like when I'd talked to Vic on that day just before I'd left Ruth's. I saw Jim crossing the kitchen to me, then felt the flat of his hand burning into my cheek and neck. I slumped back into a chair, my head in my hands, trying to stop the loud ringing noise that meant I was going crazy.

That afternoon he found the promissory note and telephoned, saying that Mr. Hendrick had taken it home to read it over. He spoke so softly I could hardly hear him. When he came home that night, he was quiet, and I knew he hadn't slapped me for the thing lost, but about what he knew and wished he didn't.

He said nothing during dinner, but he was nervous, and when he turned off the TV at nine before the movie was half over and came back to the bedroom where I was lying on the bed, I knew he had something to say to me. "I'm sorry, Stella. I don't mean it. I'm trying, you know. I sure as hell am."

I wanted to answer him, but I couldn't. "I'm afraid," he went on. "I'm thinking everywhere I go that someone's going to say something and I won't know how to handle it."

"About me?" I asked.

"Yes."

"About what I did?"

"Yes, about that."

I thought I might start crying then, and my voice sounded like I would. "I don't want to go, Jimmy," I said. "I don't want to leave here. I don't think I'd much want to live afterward. You understand?"

"I'm not asking you to leave, Stella. I want us to be able to keep what we have."

"Then what are you asking?"

"I don't know. Things still aren't straight in my mind. Like I say, I don't want to admit what's going on, and I feel strange. Failing, I mean."

"Failing at what?"

"At you and me. I promised to love you. In the ceremony, I mean, before God."

"And you can't?"

"I don't know."

I thought he might be asking to make love, that though he couldn't love me, he wanted me; and for me, that was better than nothing. I wasn't so dumb I couldn't see the value of getting him started back that way. He sat awhile on the bed, looking down at the rug, squinting as if there were something in the pattern he couldn't quite see. When he left, I turned off the lamp. I saw the light go off in the living room, but I knew he was sitting in the easy chair, where you could look out the window. "Jimmy," I called to him soft, but he didn't answer.

I lay still awhile, then got up, put on the gown I kept at the foot of the bed for getting up with Darrell, and went in to him. He turned his head. He could see me by the lamp in the hall, light coming through the gown. "You look pretty," he said.

"Thank you, Jimmy."

He glanced away, and I waited. I went near him, stood before him, and in a moment he pulled me down, beginning to make love rough; then he started to cry and fell away from me. I stayed beside him, listening to him quiet down gradual; then, when I knew it was right, I moved close to him, stroking him, doing what I needed to, to make him love me like he had the first time, slow, careful, like a good man does with a woman he doesn't yet quite know.

18

Flowers were starting to bloom in the valley, and the grass was nearly as green as the place in the river where we went to bathe in the summer, the light changing quick and sparkling under the yellow shade. Darrell was saying more words, scolding me, answering no to everything I asked him to do. I watched him continually, never letting him out of my sight. I was worried about stairs, cars, an unclosed gate, the slippery banks of the river.

Then one day June phoned to say that she and her mother were planning a tea to raise money for some new equipment for Dr. Moor's clinic. At first they had thought of having it in the church recreation room, but then Mrs. Ambler decided that the party would be better at her house. The living room was small, of course, but if the weather was good, they could put the tables and chairs outdoors, spread them over her yard and the yard of her next-door neighbor. June asked me in on the planning, but I said no. I preferred being home with Darrell and keeping quiet, trying to please Jimmy, dealing with Vic the best I could, believing that I'd talked him into staying away.

But June kept on. She wanted us to get into some project together, she said; and she stayed after me until I agreed. I would set up things for her, I said; help her and Angie fix the tables, arrange the flowers like I knew how, because before Darrell was born, I used to go up to the florist in the square and watch the way Mr. Curtiss did the arrangements for weddings and parties. "And we sure can't make any profit if we hire a florist," she had said.

The afternoon of the tea, the weather was as nearly perfect as June and Angie Ambler could have wished. Mild and gentle, already warm so the ladies coming in were saying we were sure to have a warm summer. I was serving the cranberry punch, standing behind the long table we'd placed between the two big oaks. I'd made myself a dress with a ruffle going down the front in a filled-in V. The skirt was full, so when I sat down, it would go long and full over my legs. I had asked June to curl and tease my hair and then spray it, so it would lie still even in the strong breeze that we were relying on to keep the party cool.

Mrs. Slover came. I thought that for appearances' sake she might speak to me, but she didn't. She gave me one quick glance, then turned to Mrs. Tellerson's sister and complimented her on her dress and hat.

Buck and his two sons had cut the grass for us and edged around the flower beds, where azaleas were blooming and begonias looked like the full skirt of a woman who'd lain out there to nap in the shade. We had placed folding lawn chairs around in both the yard.

"Angie," Mrs. Moor was saying, "I never saw your garden look so nice."

Every one of them had paid five dollars to come, so the yards had to be pretty and the food, too: cucumber sandwiches on bread we'd sliced as thin as paper, cream-cheese sandwiches the same way; and then a scoop of chicken salad in iceberg-lettuce cups and a fruit salad with fresh pineapple and strawberries, powdered sugar to sprinkle over it, a mint leaf sticking up high. We rented a big silver teapot in San Antonio and borrowed china cups from all over Winston Valley. A big blue jay was jumping flat-footed into the birdbath, diving in and shaking off. Angie laughed, and so did the lady sitting next to her. "That's a comical sight," Angie said. And it was.

And then it seemed like it was that Thanksgiving at Buck and

June's all over again—like it and not like it, but like it because I was having Maureen McAuley put in my mind, and not like it because she wasn't there to threaten me. I only heard she was coming to visit. June said so out of the clear blue sky, as if she'd never even been thinking about it. And it chilled me as if I were inside the ice block in the bowl of punch I served, and I was seeing my face surfacing, then sinking back.

Angie was speaking, and there was June, standing beside Mrs. Frazier, the woman who owned the beauty shop and operated the cash register. "I talked to Maureen on the phone last night," Angie said. "She was calling kind of urgent, Stella—from Prentice, where she's with her sister, Florence, the one who owns the dress shop. First time she's been in Prentice since we were all at my house for that Thanksgiving. You remember? She says Florence remembers you. But she says it wasn't the name Stella but pretty close. *Sandy,* Florence thinks, but Maureen told her that's wrong—pale blond hair, a real pretty girl."

She held out her empty punch cup for me to fill. I took the cup and lifted the ladle. I sensed a softness in my flesh, a slackness in my muscles. For the first time that afternoon, some of the punch spilled on the lace cloth.

"What were you doing in Prentice?" Angie was asking.

I wasn't quite looking at her, but I believe she gave a side glance to June and Mrs. Frazier. After a few minutes of shrugging and saying I didn't understand Maureen's mistake about me, I put down the punch ladle and excused myself, as if I might be going to get a washcloth to clean up the spill.

That week Vic called me, telling me that I had to meet with him. I guess I couldn't think straight because he'd made me crazy, and Angie had, and with her, since Angie was her mother, June. Yet now, especially, I couldn't anger Vic. All along, I'd worked hard not to, talking to him patient on the phone, begging whenever I had to. He said he wanted me to drive over to San Marcos. If I didn't, he'd visit me at my house here. He told me that he was at the Bowie Motel, number 116, upstairs. "I'll be looking for you," he said, and then he told me when.

I drove there slow, wanting to turn back yet going on since I had some idea that if I did as Vic asked, he'd leave me alone; that by going to where he was, I could keep him away from my family. The motel was on the old highway to San Antonio, a pink stucco building in the center of a cement yard for parking.

I left the truck at the side and climbed the stairs. Vic stepped outside the room onto the gallery. He looked thinner, lines around his eyes and mouth I didn't remember. He was wearing blue trousers, a white shirt, his shoes smudged with dust. "You think I look older?" he asked.

I shook my head.

"Sure you do. Well, time's passing for us both." He drew me into the room and shut the door.

It was nearly dark inside, the curtains drawn. The room smelled of smoke and whiskey. He handed me a jewelry box, blue and soft. My hands were shaking when I set it on the dresser. I didn't open it then or later. "I just came here to tell you that if my husband knew about you phoning, he'd be here instead of me," I said.

"Then why didn't you send him?"

I was trying to act old and steady, but it seemed to me that I was still the child that he'd taken to Ellison.

"You staying with me awhile?"

"I'm married, Vic." I could see myself talking in the mirror, nothing but shadows behind. "You asked me to come here. What do you want?"

He stared at me, smiling. "It's you and me that's married, Sandy. Remember? Don't you? We had our honeymoon. You remember where? I do. Remember that hotel in Ellison, a while before I took you to Ruth's?"

He rubbed his cheek with his fingers. "See how I shaved for you?" He took my hand and tried to slide it against his face. I jerked it away, then he handed me a glass of whiskey he'd poured for me. I brushed my hand against the glass so some of the whiskey spilled on the carpet. He didn't say anything, just set the glass on the dresser, looked down, and rubbed at the wet spot with his shoe.

He glanced up, held my eyes a moment, then poured me another drink, and I took it.

I met with him twice more, keeping him from Darrell and Jim

that way, then the next time I told him I wouldn't come back. I was standing outside the door crying. It had started to rain, big drops hopping on the gallery floor. I was yelling at Vic, calling him names that I remembered from Ruth's, him yelling back. I held my hands over my ears, then left, ran to my car, getting soaked, then having to stop at a variety store because I'd told Jimmy I'd gone to San Marcos to shop, people staring at me while I bought an armload of things I thought they'd know I didn't need.

The days that followed, I spent with Darrell, teaching him, playing with him, taking him places. I remember particularly our walks down to the river to see the "blue fish." At first, I didn't know exactly where he saw "blue fish," but he talked about them often and pointed to the rippling water, and I pretended that I could see them, too. "Yes, I see them, darling. Of course I do." Later, I realized that he was talking about the silver minnows that looked blue to him because of the sky's reflection in the water. He liked me to take off his shoes and let him wade. His eyes would tear whenever he stepped on a sharp rock, but he'd go right on, stopping to try to catch the minnows with his hands, failing, laughing nervously when they nibbled at his feet.

At that time Darrell's birthday was a week away. It occurred to me that after the tea at the Amblers', I shouldn't plan a party for him, but I did it anyway, cutting out invitations from colored paper, mailing them, then baking a cake and writing his name on it and how old he was in spun chocolate sugar, the way Mrs. Slover had taught me.

The first reply I got was from June, saying that Nancy couldn't come because she was sick. I asked her what Nancy had. A stomach virus, she answered.

"Will I see you before then?" I asked her.

She hesitated. "I'll try to get by."

"You want me to come out and help you with Nancy?"

"No," she answered quickly. "I wouldn't want Darrell infected."

"I'll leave Darrell with Jimmy."

"No, thanks."

I hesitated. "I need to borrow your ice-cream freezer, June."

"Fine. I'll have Buck drop it off at the garage."

"Why not here?"

"Oh, that might not be on his way."

But I knew it was. We'd always remarked on my house's convenience whenever I kept Nancy for June.

That night I telephoned Mrs. Slover to invite her. I did that on impulse, some vague hope popping in my head and giving me courage to dial. As soon as she heard my voice, she said, "I'm sorry I can't talk with you now."

"I wanted to invite you to Darrell's party," I tried to say, but the line went dead before I'd finished my message. For a moment, I listened to the buzzing, then returned the receiver to its cradle.

The next day, two of the mothers from church whose boys played with Darrell on Sundays called to say they couldn't come. There were six others I hadn't heard from. I made a list and started to phone, then thought better of it.

All the day of the party, my heart was in my throat, me knowing ahead what I knew but trying not to believe it. I made the peach ice cream in the freezer, then hung a piñata to a tree in back, one in the form of a white bird that twirled in the wind, the ribbons from it rippling like water. Darrell had stood under it, looking straight up, his hands reaching to catch the streamers. "The moon," he said, as if he were singing to it.

"No, darling," I said softly. "See its wings? It's a birdie."

He had turned to me and looked at me, as though to see if I was teasing, then returned his gaze to the piñata and smiled.

Jimmy came home at midafternoon, a few minutes before the party was to begin. He had to duck for the crepe-paper streamers. He came through them with his hands as though he were swimming, Darrell talking all the while, circling him, telling him what was inside the piñata. I noticed how good Jimmy looked, his red hair shining like one of the decorations, and that gave me pain to think of what we had been and what we were now, and made me remember that for nearly a month at the end of winter, he never made love to me, and then, when he did begin coming to me again, it was quick and without regard for either of us, just getting over a task he seemed to need periodically to complete.

Jim looked around, nodding his head at how pretty the house looked, smiling at Darrell, congratulating him on having a birthday, then going out with him to the yard to look at the new collie puppy.

"What have you named him?" I heard Jim ask.

"Alley," Darrell answered.

"No, that's Mrs. Slover's dog. What's your dog's name?"

"Alley, too." Then he started laughing, and Jimmy did.

When everything was ready, Jim and Darrell went outside on the front porch and waited for the guests. I sat in the living room until I heard the first one come. It was Oona, bringing a present of a battered doll that she must have wrapped herself, the paper wrinkled and no bow in the ribbon, only a tight knot that I had to cut with scissors. Not that it mattered. When she handed the present to Darrell, he hugged her around the knees. It was the first time I'd ever seen Oona in a dress. The print was faded, but it fit her nicely, and a tear in the lace collar had been mended. Her face was scrubbed clean, so Mr. Harmon must have been well enough to help her. I had meant to go down and see about dressing her myself, but with all the things to do, and Jimmy coming in when he did, it slipped my mind. I took Darrell and Oona's picture with the Polaroid camera that Buck and June had given us for Christmas. The print slid out of the slot. I held it against me until it was ready, then put it in Darrell's outstretched hand. Immediately he offered it to Oona, who folded it in half and put it in the pocket of her dress.

It was a quarter after three. I saw Jimmy glance at his watch. Then Amy Morse arrived in a blue station wagon with her little boy, Charles. They lived out of town, just this side of Blanco. Then Linda Newton and Davey. Two more kids came, their mothers with them. Jimmy didn't say anything about there being so few children, but he kept looking at me like something was wrong. Then, when we did the piñata, and since everyone except Oona was too little to hit it, Jimmy held up the kids in his arms so they could. It was Oona's second blow with the stick that burst the side and brought the candy down; then Darrell and the others scrambled for it, until the last piece was claimed. After that, Jimmy helped Darrell open his presents. He teased him. "Look at all the thank-you notes you're going to have to write." He snuggled Darrell's tummy with his face, and Darrell laughed.

"How many kids did you invite?" Jimmy asked me when those who had come left.

"About fifteen. But there's some kind of sickness going around."

I squatted down beside Darrell, who was playing with a toy spring that could walk up and down steps. "You just have your birthday at a bad time of year," I said to him. "The warm weather brings on colds." I hugged him. "Did you know that, honey?"

"How come June wasn't here?" Jimmy asked.

I looked up at him standing above us. "Nancy was sick."

"The hell she was. I saw her and June in town this morning."

"Maybe she'd come in to see the doctor."

"Nancy looked fine to me, skipping down the sidewalk, hollering at her mama to buy her something."

The phone rang. I'd hoped it might be Nancy or June calling to wish Darrell a happy birthday, but it was Mr. Harmon. He said he'd found the new wooden puzzle that Oona was supposed to bring as a present. "She wanted it for herself," he said.

"Then let her keep it," I said. "Darrell likes the doll."

"She said it was her broke the piñata. That true?"

"Yes."

"Thank you for letting her."

"I didn't let her. She—"

"Thanks just the same. . . . You're a good woman, Mrs. Lester." I'd heard a catch in his voice. "Thank you."

Darrell was fussy that evening. He kept calling for his daddy, making it clear that he didn't want me. It was as if someone had finally told him something, and he'd understood.

Early that afternoon Vic had telephoned from the drugstore in Winston Valley. He'd said that he had some photos of me that were taken at Ruth's, and that he was going to bring one set over here and leave another in the mail slot at the garage.

Then, later, when the party was going on, and we were outside cutting the cake and serving the food, I thought that I saw a car like Vic's drive by, a man in it, anyway, looking at the house.

Darrell couldn't sleep. I took him out of his bed and sat with him in the rocker, singing when I could, but he wasn't much listening. He cried some and tried to climb out of my lap, asking where his daddy was. Jim was in the living room, sitting quiet, not reading or watching television. Then in a while, when he came for Darrell, Darrell held out his arms, and I heard Jimmy taking him up to the attic room, climbing slow and heavy, whispering to him.

I figured that that meant he was staying up there again, that after the failed party for Darrell, especially the absence of June and Nancy, the time of us sharing a room, or anything else, was over. "You'll ruin us," Jimmy had said a few days before, after I'd told him about Maureen, crying while I did. "You'll do it sure. I told you. We can't live here if it gets out. At least, we sure as hell can't live together."

I had mentioned again that we might leave, go somewhere different.

"My folks lived here," he'd argued. "They're buried here. I'll never leave Winston Valley. And where would I go? Anderson? Or why don't we try Prentice? You want me to start up something there?"

"You once wanted to drive a truck and travel."

"I didn't own things then," he'd said, "and I didn't have a son. You can't go out on the road once you've got children."

"Some men do."

"Not me. I never would. If you have kids, you put them first and yourself as far behind as you can stand it. Anything else is wrong."

"You have to support them."

"I'm supporting mine."

Vic phoned again. Jimmy called down the stairs, asking who it was. "It was a wrong number," I answered.

"I thought it was one of the kids' mothers who forgot the time," he said. "Did you tell them ten o'clock?" He waited for me to answer, and when I didn't, I heard him go back to bed.

I hadn't cleaned up after the birthday. I did that then, gathering the strings of crepe paper and stuffing them in a plastic garbage bag, the paper plates, too. There were cartoon birds drawn on the plates to match the piñata, the birds wearing party hats and holding balloons. I took one of the unused plates and put it in my purse along with the two washed candles from the cake. I glanced at the coffee table. I wanted to take the Polaroid shots of the party, but I thought better of it for what they might mean to Darrell. I went to the desk drawer and took a few other pictures, ones for which there were copies. Then I went to the bedroom and packed a change of clothes. If I'd stopped for anything, I might have quit. It occurred to me that Jimmy must have heard me busying around and guessed what I was doing, but if that was true, he didn't come down.

For a time, I stood in the hallway listening for Darrell. When I heard nothing, I climbed the first three steps, waited a moment, then went the rest of the way and looked into the room. Jimmy was sleeping on his back, breathing quiet. Darrell was beside him, his hand on his father's arm, the fingers digging tight into his flesh, like he knew he'd better not let go. I stayed there a long moment, thinking about the first time I'd seen this room, when the house still belonged to Kitty and Orman Cater. It was quiet now in the backyard, fireflies winking, the piñata shining white under the night sky, the fragile bird ruined. I turned and moved toward the bed and kissed my baby. His eyes didn't open, but I could see by the faint light from the hallway that he smiled. I kissed Jimmy the same way; I don't believe he wakened, but his head turned from me as though he knew.

For a moment, I waited outside the room, perhaps for one of them to call for me, or simply to say my name in sleep, and when they didn't, I went back downstairs and slid my suitcase off the bed. I thought of Joylyn and me leaving Ozona, Doc waiting in the truck while we wandered around the empty house, taking a few minutes to fix in our memory the details of the place we were leaving.

When I walked through the kitchen, Darrell's puppy crossed the newspapers Jim had spread for it and sniffed at my clothes. I put down the suitcase and stayed a moment to pat its head.

I used the back door, passing by the new rosebushes, the honeysuckle, the sultanas and fern coming out. I shut the gate quiet, then stopped once to look back. It was dark upstairs. My eyes came down to the front windows. The puppy had climbed to the sofa back to watch me. I lifted my hand like that was someone to tell good-bye.

I was feeling the cool night down on me with its dark cover and stars. "Count them, Mama," Darrell would have said, pointing his finger straight up. I looked at their millions, counting for him a few of the brightest, then I shut my eyes so I could hear the river clear.

When I passed Mrs. Slover's, the lights were out, all but the yellow light on the porch. My ride was waiting just beyond on the road. I stood a moment gazing at the vegetable garden that, until these last few months, I'd always helped her tend. Darrell had almost seemed to have come out of that earth and from among the dense leaves of the pecans, their roots nearly to the river. I was shivering, so I pulled my sweater close around me, and then I went on.

19

It was a spring morning when I went into the doctor's office. Not my appointment time. I saw him regularly on afternoons at three, but today I had something special to tell him. He was in his easy chair, as he always was for our sessions, smiling at me, the window across from him green with the morning sun and its reflections on the slope of the hospital lawn. I told him that I wanted to leave; it was time to be on my own. Through one of the aides, I'd heard of a job in the stockroom of Justin's Department Store and I thought I could get it. He replied that it might be too soon, but he'd talk to his colleagues and let me know.

I had been away from Winston Valley for over five years then: some months wandering, finding work as a clerk in a grocery store, losing that when the woman I replaced recovered from an illness and was well enough to return; housekeeping, caring for an elderly man until his death; two years in Brenham, working in bars and restaurants, eight months here in Austin, where I'd been hospitalized instead of serving a prison term for assault and drug use. Marijuana was the drug. Actually I had rarely used it, only a few times when I was depressed or tired and someone where I worked offered it, and not even all that much on that evening when I stuck the blade of a pocket knife into the shoulder of a drunk who had pushed me into the coat closet and started taking off my clothes.

I never went to court, only sat long hours at a table with three state psychiatrists; and because they were professional and not simply friends, because the room was warm and dimly lit, and because they gave me heavy doses of tranquilizers to calm the hysteria I came in with, I made the mistake of telling them the story of my life. In any case, after two days of talks they put me in the state hospital, where I talked to yet more psychiatrists and slept out months of my life under prescribed drugs.

Then, slowly, I began to recover, to read a little, to take a class, to take long walks outside the grounds. I liked my small closet room, the iron cot that I'd made a spread for in the quilting group we had, the hook rug, the rough cotton curtains with blue rickrack trim, this room on the west side where fig ivy wandered under the sill on its footed tendrils; a room that was stifling in summer, stuffy in winter, but all mine with rarely an intruder, and where I could read or embroider flowers on hand towels and pillow cases while listening to the records I borrowed from the hospital library, loud piano pieces, whole orchestras from famous cities drowning out all the other impulses of my life that I couldn't handle.

Then, finally, after I realized that I was among the healthier patients, I began to respond to the needs of some of those around me. For the next months, I had done pretty much what the nurses had done earlier for me: taken unhurried strolls with disturbed people in the park outside the old red-brick buildings where we lived; coaxed a young woman to eat who for some days had refused her meals; talked to women who pleaded with me and anyone else who would listen to them to be returned to their families. But now, in the doctor's office, I wanted something different, and I knew that I was ready. "I can make it on my own," I told the doctor, clear and strong. "I need to leave."

A week later, a volunteer from a local women's service club drove me to my new neighborhood, took me to lunch at a cafeteria near the apartment (for which the state was paying the first month's rent), then left me at my front door with a plant of yellow chrysanthemums in a green plastic pot, encouraging words, and a wave of her hand out her car window as she drove away.

The apartment was in a neighborhood called Tarrytown. The name pleased me, since it sounded childlike, the name of a toy park. The complex was relatively new, but the builders had kept the old trees, bur oaks whose enormous acorns fell in October. Later, I learned to collect them, paint them gold and silver, and use them at Christmas. My apartment was on the second floor; a metal staircase took me down to the yard where a path led to a blue oblong swimming pool with metal chairs and tables held down by chains. In the apartment, there were two rooms, small with big windows but cool and shadowy because of the trees. The service club had supplied a bed and dresser. The first weekend I went to a garage sale and bought an odd-shaped but very cheap sofa, a lamp table, and a pine dinette. Three months later, I owned a car, a used Chevy that I paid down on one summer morning after negotiating closely with a fat man in a car lot, while triangularly shaped banners snapped above us like pistol shots and the man's wife kept calling him inside to the phone while he kept refusing, turning away from the direction of her cries to smile at me.

Each morning, I drove to Justin's, parked in one of the covered spaces reserved for personnel, then walked to work past a gift shop and an Asian boutique. I dressed for work in simple dresses and plain jewelry, a uniform I'd learned to put together by studying women whom I admired. It was easy to observe those models at Justin's: women whose husbands didn't earn enough or weren't persuasive enough to keep them home; women who thought of the job as temporary while they finished paying on a house note or sending a child through school; single women like myself, who needed to make their own way.

At first I returned to my doctor at the hospital dutifully, writing the appointment times in a date book that I kept beside my telephone. Then, gradually, I began to cancel the appointments, to miss a couple and get a friendly scolding from the doctor, then not to go at all.

By then I had a routine, and he knew it: work, movies, and evening lectures at the university, where I'd sit in the back of the hall, quiet, listening to some professor, his beautiful way of telling you what he knew, long, flowing sentences with words I often didn't know, but all of it like music. Sometimes I went to a free concert, sat in a soft seat in the air-conditioned hall of the music school, shut my eyes, and listened. Within a few months, I quit taking sleeping pills at night, and within a year I no longer needed the tranquilizers that had once been essential to start my day.

I spent four years this way. And I liked Austin well enough, the hot, dry summers, the sunny winters. In good weather, I went routinely to Barton Springs to swim in the cold waters of the pool, and then, afterward, to sun on the grassy slopes above it. Occasionally, early on a Sunday morning, I rode my bike along the park trails, the children and I and college students rushing past one another, nodding and smiling, shouting something trite but necessary about the beauty of the day. I liked to be outdoors, now and then stopping my bike to listen to the music of some bare-chested, bearded guitarist. Sometimes I walked over to the park for an event. Once, on the first of May, I went to a May Day festival at the Botanical Gardens and bought a few pots of herbs, engaging the women who sold them in conversation about these plants that I meant to raise in the small spots of sun that came to my otherwise-shady balcony.

I rarely received invitations, because I never gave any out. At that time, I preferred a book or a movie on television to any society that I could attract.

I was long out of the habit of being with men. If a man asked me out, I usually refused; though every now and again, I had a date, someone I'd meet at my apartment when I went down for a swim, or had something heavy to carry upstairs and wasn't managing very well. Once a man named Eric came into my life, a boy really, who had just started his internship at Brackenridge Hospital, and who, when he didn't have to work for resident doctors or see patients, wanted to see me. We went to movies or watched TV at my place. Often he brought steaks, and I cooked them for him on a grill that I kept outside. Sometimes at night after dinner, we'd sit on my balcony, gazing out at the black treetops, talking, mostly about the horrors of the emergency ward and those indigent patients whose troubles came solely, he believed, from vice and carelessness.

I argued that strongly; sometimes I got angry and let him know it, yet I valued Eric's company; and I guess that was because I needed people around me who were as confident and in control of their lives as he seemed to be. His attitude influenced mine, and so I was disappointed when, after the last of my several refusals to go to bed with him, he quit coming by and quit calling. After a month or two (it was three days before Christmas), I phoned him, told him I would cook him a Mexican chicken dish that I knew he liked. He'd said he'd come, and he did, and after he'd eaten, he complimented me on the meal, told me how much it relaxed him to come here, then said that his roommate had gone away for the holiday and that he'd like me to come stay with him in his apartment. I was still in the process of refusing him, trying to explain why I had to, when he picked up his jacket and a book he'd brought to lend me and left.

At first I felt the loss, the anger at discovering that you can't just be a friend to a man, then gradually I figured that I was lucky, that if I kept my encounters with any one person brief, there would hardly be anyone who knew me, and those who did would leave me to myself, believing that whatever circle I moved in was distant and closed.

It was in the winter of that year that two things happened: first, I was transferred out of the stockroom, given a raise, and told I'd be working on the floor; second, I met Mary Gayle Brinsley, a woman who was new at work, and whom they put out selling merchandise right away—no working her way up from the stockroom. She'd come in ahead of us all somehow, a pretty woman, her short hair shining, her brown eyes flecked with gold and made larger and browner yet by the big tinted glasses that she wore. When she moved, she moved fast. She thought fast, too: fine judgment about customers, good instincts.

She was shorter than I was, always fighting her weight, following fad diets she found in magazines, trying to do something about her craving for junk foods and Cokes. She had divorced her husband, Al Hagan, years before, taken back her maiden name, and was bringing up their two children alone. "I've sued Al twice for child support," she told me. "He makes payments awhile, then quits. I finally gave up begging him. And that was about the time I started meeting with a group, people having problems like mine. And then I began doing some volunteer work. On Sunday afternoons, I phone kids at foster homes to see how they are. If things don't sound right, I go over there. You should try it."

And I did. Before long I was spending a good part of my spare time sitting at a table in an agency, addressing envelopes or helping overworked counselors take children on picnics to Zilker Park or Wonder Cave, climbing in buses with the children, smelling their sweaty bodies, sometimes the unmistakable odor of filth. Once, on one of the buses, I pinned together a little girl's dress that was torn out at the shoulder. Some boy had bothered her, she said. She laid her head in my lap while I pinned it, sucking her thumb, though she was a child of nearly eleven. When the outing was finished, she hugged me and told me that she loved me, so after we parted, I asked the counselor for her address. She lived in an orphanage on the north side of town, a three-story stone building surrounded by an eight-foot chain-link fence. Several times I invited her for a swim at Barton Springs, or to eat lunch at my apartment and swim in the pool there. At first she was scared of me. When I went for her, I had to go up to her dormitory room to find her, and she wouldn't be ready. Then, slowly, as time passed and she knew she could depend on me to come, she began to wait for me on the front steps, a bundle clutched under her arm that was the swimsuit she seemed afraid she might lose, or some special game, Lotto or Chinese checkers, that she planned to teach me how to play. She'd run to the car and give me a kiss, holding my face in her hands to do it; then start to talk fast, telling me about some row she'd had with another child, bursting into tears when she told me about an injustice done to her by the housemother; and I'd try to soothe her and tell her how she might work out the problem. She listened, and then the next time I saw her and asked if my suggestion had worked, usually she said that it had, though she might mention some new problem on her mind, though gradually less serious.

I missed her when she took up permanent residence in a foster home and no longer needed me. I phoned her for a while, and she phoned me, telling me of school and neighborhood friends, the new mother who was teaching her to cook and care for the dog that she'd been given for Christmas. She was training it, she said, using a book that her *daddy* had borrowed for her from the public library. Already the dog could sit on command, she said, and shake hands. I'll never forget the sound of her voice when she told me that the family was adopting her, her telling it like a trough overflowing, breathless, delighted beyond imagination. After a few months, I quit hearing from her. But there were other children.

Sometimes Mary Gayle talked well of her ex, Al Hagan, praising him when he got a job. "Well, he's quit drinking," she said. Sometimes she even bought him presents at Justin's, nothing important, novelties mostly, but things she knew he would like. "Hell, I know his taste," she said. "I should." From time to time she met with him for lunch at a barbecue stand on Nineteenth Street, or at one of the taco shops on Town Lake. She must have had some fondness for him somehow. I asked her.

"Sure I do," she said. "Like you do for a mad dog that they say's cured. I don't trust Al. He doesn't know anything about himself."

"And how could he find out?"

"He won't. He's the type who doesn't."

"And you?" I said. "Have you found out so much about yourself?" I realized I was talking like a psychiatrist.

"Well, sure," she said.

I knew that I'd irritated her, but the next day she phoned Al, and I heard from one of the other women at Justin's that they were having dinner on Saturday at her place.

She wasn't particularly religious, she said, and she certainly would never become a Quaker, though that's where she went on Sunday mornings in a big Victorian house on a street called Washington Square. "There's no ritual," she complained. "No minister or music. It's not a real church."

That was a Monday morning when we were drinking coffee together in the snack room at Justin's. I was sitting beside her at a round table, decorated with a cut-glass bud vase filled with dusty plastic poppies. The chrome pedestal of the table felt cold to my knees. I kept trying to cross my legs, but the table's low surface didn't allow it. We were alone in the carpeted room, machines buzzing around us. "Then why do you go?" I asked.

"Because they have a good program for kids, and they're against the war in Vietnam."

"A lot of people are against the war."

"Yes, but these people are quiet and patient about it."

I laughed. "Then they won't get anything done."

Mary Gayle was stirring her coffee then, gazing into the cup. I thought she was smiling, but when she glanced up, her look was serious, stern, a surprise to me since her face nearly always carried a smile. "Oh, I think they will," she said.

Once she tried to get me to go to a meeting with her, but I refused. I wasn't going to any church then. I figured I needed my Sundays for rest, so I slept late, straightened a closet or a drawer in my apartment, went for a swim in the pool or for a bike ride in Zilker Park.

It's strange the way things come upon you when you're not looking for them, stranger yet when you have a premonition. Because I'm sure that I knew something was going to happen to me that evening at Mary Gayle's house, and perhaps that was why I nearly didn't go. In any case, it was a couple of weeks before we were to have a vacation together at her parents' ranch near Fredericksburg, and when in honor of that, she had decided to give a party. "It's just spur-of-the-moment," she told me one afternoon as she was leaving work. "I want to get some friends together. Anyhow, it'll be fun, and I promise to have some single men."

I arrived late. All that day, I'd meant to cancel, to say something about a headache, a special date; but I thought she'd know better, and I needed her friendship. I had been uneasy about the party, thinking that the guests would be old friends of hers and Al Hagan's, and that though I could fit in fairly well with the Mary Gayle who worked at Justin's, I might not with the people here.

"I'll have someone pick you up," she said, after I'd accepted.

"No," I replied quickly. "I'll come alone."

"You're sure you can find it?" I'd never been to Mary Gayle's before. After work, since she lived far from the city's center, we'd always gone to my place or somewhere in town.

"Yes."

But I had trouble. The address was on Red Bud Trail, one of those winding roads in West Lake Hills on the other side of the low-water bridge. The problem was that there are several Red Bud Trails, and Mary Gayle hadn't been all that clear as to which one was hers. In any case, I took one false turn after another, drove my car up a couple of dead-end streets, once found myself on a mini-highway called the Bee Cave Road, turned back into the neighborhood as soon as I could find a place to do so, at last finding her house at the top of a hill on one of the short streets I would have sworn I'd been on before. I felt out of place on that street, parking my old-model American car among the newer foreign ones, and out of place locking it, since people up here with their pretty shrubs and colored flowers probably never locked their cars. As I went toward the walk to the frame house, everything about my coming seemed wrong, all of it except disappointing Mary Gayle. I just hadn't fully realized this side of my friend, a suburban housewife with a house in a neighborhood where some of the houses seemed quite fine. "We were always the poor folks on the street," Mary Gayle would tell me later. "I couldn't pay the taxes on the house except for my parents helping me. After the kids get out of high school, I have to sell it and give Al his half of the equity. The thing is, staying here means a lot to Christina and Sam—they lost their daddy; I'm not going to make them lose their home."

"And you? Won't you miss it?"

"No, I've had it long enough. Once I get something, it loses its appeal." She laughed. "That's human nature."

Since it was summer, it was still light at nearly eight o'clock. I was wearing a two-piece beige knit dress and high-heeled black patent shoes. I'd tried several outfits, finally choosing this one since it was my best. Mary Gayle answered the door in a loose-fitting blue Mexican dress with white embroidery. I saw other guests milling around on the terrace in off-the-shoulder cotton dresses, one woman in slacks and a sleeveless sweater, so I knew at once that I was overdressed.

"Come in, Stella," Mary Gayle said, taking both my hands in hers. "Well, don't you look pretty? Your hair looks great. You spend the afternoon in the beauty shop?"

She brought me inside into a small, comfortable living room, double glass doors opening onto a patio, oak trees shading the grass in summer patterns of late evening, people grouped around a sofa, talking. "I guess you see that I have no garden," she said. "The deer eat my flowers." She introduced me to a couple and handed me some wine in a plastic tumbler. The doorbell rang, and she left us. I tried to talk to the couple; we exchanged a few words; then I moved out toward the terrace, looking for someone I might know. At last I saw Lucy Fritz, a woman who worked with us. She came up to me, kissed my cheek, and introduced me to her husband, a short, chubby man who offered me a smile and a kiss, too. Another couple joined us. I listened to the small talk, then the men divided off to talk about a hunting lease that the two of them would share this fall.

I was feeling happier then; the wine had helped, and so had the Fritzes' greeting. I listened to Lucy tell about a lunch she'd had with a buyer, then complain about some store remodeling that the management planned. "Customers don't like it," she said. "Habit is strong with them. They'll hate the mess and shop somewhere else; then they'll get used to the new place and forget their old friends."

Another woman had joined us, and afterward I could be at ease to focus on the wider part of the room to see the others. My eyes stopped on a man who was turned away from me. I admired him for the way his back was, the broadness of it, good shoulders, and the heavy, sooty blackness of his hair, not as neatly cropped as that of the other men here, a little too long on his neck, the wind from the opened door playing with the curls at the crown of his head. One of the men talking to him made a slight nod in my direction, and he turned. Immediately the smile left his face, and I'm sure it left mine. Keeping his eyes on me, he said something to the men with him. They nodded, then he rose and came toward me.

At first the vision of him was unclear. It was as though I might be seeing a relation of his, perhaps the figure of someone I knew fairly well approaching out of a light rain; and that's what the passage of twenty years had done. His body was heavier, his features thicker. There was some gray at his temples, his eyes darker, I thought, but his skin not so deeply tanned.

I stood stock-still, my heartbeat picking up dangerously. I tried to remember every trick in the book that I'd ever learned about self-control, while the presence of this man and all that it implied, rushed thundering like an avalanche to destroy the fragilely restored landscape of my mind. Immediately, I turned to leave, took a couple of steps, but a hand on my arm stopped me. A voice spoke to me, and it seemed from far away, asking me something I couldn't answer, since I'd been unable to concentrate on the question. I stood waiting, forced to listen then to what was being said, not replying yet hearing the familiar voice, its tone deeper and better balanced than before; gradually I accepted the fact that I knew this man and wished that I did not. At last I asked him a question in response to his lengthy and nervous greeting. "How are you, Maury?" I said.

Mary Gayle had joined us. She was holding a green jug of wine, filling my glass and giving him a fresh one. "I wanted you two to meet," she said. "I'm glad to see that's happened. How do you like him, Stella? Isn't he nice? And he's been single for six whole months."

Maury kept his eyes on me. I don't think he glanced once at Mary Gayle. "Good," she said to us both. "Well, that's arranged. . . ." She turned to take her wine to a group on the sofa, continuing her pleasant chatter.

Maury's hand shook, and wine spilled on his fingers. He wiped at his hand with the paper napkin Mary Gayle had given him.

"How are you, Stella Jean?" he asked.

I glanced up and held his eyes. "Did you know I was coming here?"

"No, I didn't. Did you know that I was?"

"No, of course not."

"And you wouldn't have come here if you had."

"That's right." I was thinking that this was going to cost me Mary Gayle. He'd tell her, or she'd sense it, and then I'd lose my friend. I knew that wasn't fair, and I was angry, though I wasn't sure if at Mary Gayle for asking me here, at Maury for intruding into my precariously arranged life, or at myself for not having learned to rely on the poise and control that had won me my job at Justin's and my place in this house. I knew that Maury was nervous, too; and not at the fact of getting caught but at something else that I liked not to think I understood.

"And what excuse would you have given?" he asked.

"How do you know her? Were you a friend of her husband's?"

"I'm still a friend of her husband's. And hers, too. We used to be neighbors." He made a motion with his hand. "Our house was at the foot of the hill. . . . She wanted me to pick you up."

"I thought you said you didn't know I was coming."

"I didn't; but she said she had a friend who'd have to drive up here alone. Apparently you said you didn't want a ride."

I glanced around the room at other women alone. "It could have been one of them."

"I don't think so."

A woman I didn't know came up to us with a plateful of sandwiches, telling us that she'd made them. She introduced herself, and I recognized her name. I took one; Maury shook his head. I saw his eyes pass quickly from my face to my left hand, looking for a ring, and when he saw the gold band I wore, he asked me if I was married.

"Not anymore," I answered.

"Then why the ring?"

"I like to wear it. I've worn it since my husband gave it to me."

"Then there's something still there."

I didn't answer, and he didn't insist. He continued speaking quietly, telling me about his life, that he worked for an insurance company, so that soon I assumed that he might be telling me about himself and asking me questions just to fill in the time while he looked at me and thought about what kind of woman I'd become that I'd be a guest here and that I could have ever entered his life on any social pretext at all.

"Have you been in Austin long?" he asked.

"Nearly five years."

"I'm sorry I didn't know that. And what did you do before?"

"Worked. Drifted."

He smiled. "I thought only men were supposed to drift."

"I don't know what men are supposed to do." There was anger in the way I said this; I regretted immediately showing him that much emotion.

He didn't seem to notice. He went on talking about his work, his other interests, as though he were presenting all this for my inspection. At one point, he covered my hand with his. "Look," he said, "I'll never say anything."

I withdrew my hand quickly. "I know damned well you won't!"

"Because I have as much to lose as you?"

"I have nothing more to lose at all," I said.

A couple interrupted us, friends of Maury's. The woman kissed him and for a moment held him tightly to her, as if there were some hurt for which she must comfort him. She reminded me of Betty, the kind of woman she was, tall, beautifully groomed. The man joked with Maury on a subject that I knew nothing about, and it was then that I excused myself and went to Mary Gayle to tell her that I was leaving. She drew me into the hallway.

"But you just got here," she whispered.

"I'm sorry."

"Do you like him?" she asked me. "Maury. I was hoping he might take you out with him after the party." She glanced back into the room as if she might try to call him near us.

"He's fine," I said quickly, "but I have to go home." And then I lied. "I told a man where I live that I'd see him later for a drink, and I don't want to disappoint him."

Mary Gayle frowned. I don't know if it was because she knew I was lying or that I'd made other plans and was leaving early.

"I'll call you tomorrow," I said, hugging her and kissing her cheek.

I hurried to my car, got in, turned it around in the cul-de-sac, the wheels digging out. As I was driving away, I saw Maury on the front porch, Mary Gayle behind him at the door, both of them watching me.

I drove down the hill fast, the right front tire sometimes hitting the rocky shoulder of the winding road. I crossed the low-water bridge going nearly fifty, and took Lake Austin Boulevard at almost the same speed. At the first light on Exposition, I began to yell, and that was because I'd remembered that this was the way Maury had driven the red truck on that first day that he and Link and I had gone to the stone house, same kind of bridge, same feeling on my part that if we went fast enough we might have an accident, and then I'd no longer have to live with a fate that was so relentless in crippling my soul.

20

It seemed to me that no matter what I did, how quiet I lay, how much I tried to relax my body like Mrs. Sneed told me, I still kept bleeding. She said I would. But I didn't know it would be this much, and I didn't know how I'd keep it from Doc, or how I could go to school the next day when I was soaking through a pad every twenty minutes, and classes lasted fifty-five.

I didn't go. I tried to, but my body wouldn't follow my mind in that, so I stayed in the bunk where I was. Sometimes my skin felt hot and dry; other times I was sweating through my sheet. I saw the sun rise behind the glass in the door, the color go from purple to dark rose, then shiny like a bowl of pearls; but still I couldn't get up. I woke thinking that maybe I'd bled so much the blood had gotten down to Doc, sleeping in the bunk below me, and that I'd have to clean it and hope he didn't wake while I did; but it didn't happen, just my blanket stained; and when finally I had to swing myself down to get to the outhouse, wincing when I lowered my body from the upper bunk to the floor, it had to be ten o'clock, because when I opened the door, the sun blasted through it, put my head on fire, and made my eyes like griddles. I leaned on the side of the trailer, digging my fingers in the window's edge to keep from falling, and hoping that Doc hadn't wakened suddenly and seen my hands, because I think there was blood on them, too, from what Mrs. Sneed did.

And then, sitting on the hole, I could hear the blood hit on the soiled paper, me leaning back a little so I could see by the light through the chinks in the wall that the yellow triangle of hair between my legs was matted and red-orange. I sat as relaxed as I could, then it got so bad again that I reached in the box for papers until I'd used most of the rest of them. Later, I'd have to go down to the Kleppers' house and collect the newspapers that Mrs. Klepper saved for me on the covered back porch, me taking home what I could carry in my arms, cutting them into squares, and slipping them in an old Kleenex box that I kept out here.

In a way, I'd been prepared for what happened. Really since my first time at the stone house, I'd had to think of where I'd go if I ever needed it, and so about a month before on a Saturday morning, when I was sitting on a chair waiting for my washing to get done, I'd listened over the pounding of one machine and the roaring spin of another to what two women were saying while one was feeding coins into a machine and the other was folding overalls and long johns on a table made rickety by people who didn't own it, bumping against it and using it hard.

"Jan Eldridge nearly died of it," the woman feeding the coins was saying. "It was her fifth. She didn't want no more, so she went to Ida Sneed. She was three months, I think."

The other woman raised her head and glanced at me. I looked down at my book. "Four's what I heard," she said softer. "When she got fever, they took her to the hospital in Midland."

The one who'd fed in the coins nodded.

"And didn't nobody turn in Ida?"

"No, because she does it right. It's Jan that didn't take care of herself afterward."

The woman shrugged. "She don't take care of nothing."

I'd known about Mrs. Sneed, that her house was a quarter-mile off the highway, one story with asbestos siding, the roof patched with tin, the back part of the fence tangled around broken posts. On either side of the front door, dusty ligustrums hid most of the porch. In the side yard, there was a cactus break, the limbs wrapped around one another like they were hugging together against the wind. The property had been kept up, until Mr. Sneed had his legs twisted and broken in a car wreck two years before, then not kept up at all.

Even before that day in the Laundromat, I'd heard people talk about what Mrs. Sneed did for a living, saying it secret, so you just heard parts of phrases shut up quick, most of them said so quiet you lacked the key word, so the truth is more something in your mind than anything you can count on. It was an afternoon in summer when I'd first gone over there. I wanted to talk to her, ask her things, especially about if what I was doing to keep safe was enough, but I didn't have the courage. Then, later, when it happened, when I had all the signs, I walked to the house, stood across the road looking at it, then decided not to go in, to wait a few more days. Every break between classes, I went to the girls' toilet, hoping for something to show up plain. So it was three weeks after I'd meant to that I went to Mrs. Sneed, every day excusing myself, thinking I was just nervous and that's why nothing had gone normal.

It was a cool fall evening when I went again. I'd felt fairly confident on the way over, walking steady, not fast but keeping my steps even and quick. I went down the driveway to the back door. It was all right until I knocked, but then when I was standing there waiting, my chin started quivering, and my eyes filled with tears. I wished I'd had another woman with me, someone with her arm around my waist, or at least holding my hand.

When no one answered, a horror came over me that I might be knocking at the wrong house: Maybe it was another cottage, one of those nearer the lane, where I'd seen lights. I started to leave; then I heard footsteps, and a face peered out the porch window through a shade held back to make a slit. In a moment, the door opened, and a woman let me in. The house smelled of cats and dried flowers. I knew Mrs. Sneed by sight. I'd seen her in town, but then she'd been in a dress and stockings, and now, at about eight on a Saturday night, she was dressed in a robe, the hem broken out of one of her sleeves so it dangled over her hand and later made her have to keep pulling on it to make the gestures that helped her to explain what she planned to do. She reminded me of Mrs. Bell in the thinness of her face and body, and how she ducked her head and looked down when she was listening to something sad.

She asked me what I wanted, and when I told her, she led me through a kitchen into a living room, asked me to sit down on a worn sofa that had cushions you sank into too deeply to cross your legs, so you had to sit in a hollow, looking clumsy. The floors were bare wood. A hook rug was crumpled in front of a fireplace, where there were still ashes from a fire the winter before. On the back of an upholstered chair, staring at me, blinking from sleep, was a yellow cat. A black cat lay curled on a mat under the table. I wanted to take up one of them and stroke it, so I'd have something to do while I talked. Mrs. Sneed asked me why I'd come.

My mouth was dry. I had to clear my throat. "I believe I have a baby," I said. My hand went low on my belly like I was trying to show her the whereabouts of that truth. "I can't take care of it. There's no one to help me, I mean." My voice had gone to a whisper. "I've got Doc, my father, but he's sick."

She reached down like she'd straighten something on the table. "And what do you expect me to do?"

"I thought you might help me."

"You the girl lives up at Whitcombs' with that man who worked awhile for the railroad?"

"Yes, ma'am."

"And you don't want to marry the one who did this?"

"No, ma'am."

"Or is it that he won't marry you?"

"No, he won't."

"He forced you? Because if he did—"

"No, I let him."

She paused, watching me for a moment from behind her glasses. She was standing close, so I had to look up. I tried to guess her next question, and I did. "Do you know now that you can't be with a man if you're not married?"

"Yes, I do."

"And you won't do it anymore. Well, I won't do this twice." I was thinking of Joylyn and what she'd think of me killing a baby, when her sorrow was that she couldn't have any of her own. "I don't like to do this unless I have that guarantee," Mrs. Sneed said.

She rose and started to leave the room, then turned back. "How old are you?" she asked.

"Fifteen."

She said nothing in reply, just stared at me a moment as if she were getting something straight in her mind. When she left, I tried to imagine that I was just visiting, that she was some friend of Joylyn's whom Joylyn had written me to look up. I glanced around at the room, the stacks of warped magazines on the floor, the cluttered table. I heard Mrs. Sneed speak to someone in the back of the house; a male voice replied deep and shaky, then she was back in the doorway waving me forward with her hand. "Better to do it right away and not worry with it anymore. Isn't that right? Isn't that what you want?"

I rose and followed her down a dark hallway that connected to the back of the cottage. "I'd rather not turn on any lights just yet," she said.

We passed a closed door, a light under it. A sound came from behind it, weight shifting on a bed. Halfway across a dark room, she put her hand down and snapped on a gooseneck lamp. The shades were pulled down, the three windows decorated with net curtains tied back with frayed ribbons. The wallpaper had a green ivy print. Near the lamp stood a long, high table. Mrs. Sneed took some books off it and set them on the floor, then she pushed up a stool at one end and set a metal tray on the seat of a wooden chair. No other furniture was in the room. "This used to be my daughter's room," she said.

It was quick what she did, slipping me down on the table, having me bend my knees and hold them apart, while she sat on the stool at my feet and cleaned me with something cold that smelled strong of alcohol. She told me to bear down, and I tried to; then she pushed up into me with something that felt like the back of a spoon. I heard her whisper a kind of warning to herself, then she made a knife flash that caused my whole body to draw up; and after, I felt a pain too strong to scream for, because there was no breath in me behind my voice, only the scalding that made me draw in air whether I wanted to or not. I lay there, trying to quiet the shuddering in my limbs, while she caught the blood in the pan she was holding, me trying not to sob, because she'd forbade it.

When the pain went down and I relaxed some, she pulled me higher on the table, placed a folded bath towel between my legs, then rolled me on my side and told me to stay still until she said otherwise. I lay there crying when I couldn't help it, lying quiet with my eyes closed when I could, wondering why I was here being punished, and asking myself why the ones I went with weren't.

I felt the presence of Mrs. Sneed, her sitting beside me, leafing through the pages of one of the books she'd picked up from the floor. When she got up, she went to the door, unhooked it, and left the room, moving away from me. A door opened in the hallway. I saw the light hit the wall and bend. Then I may have slept. I only know that when I wakened, she was feeling my forehead, then putting her fingers tight to my wrist while she looked at her watch.

"Is is over?" I asked.

"Yes."

I lay on my side, staring at the wallpaper, the ivy trailing in its sleepy curls, then the print of it starting to run together into a single color with a dancing motion to it, and I didn't know why that was. I told Mrs. Sneed, and she said for me to lie still until my sight was clear. I shut my eyes, my body rocking slow, as if I were in a boat. While I rested, she told me about her daughter. "When she married, we let her take her furniture," she said. "Her daddy built her dresser and bed, and she did the stencils on them. She always was good in art."

Later, when I could get up, she showed me a picture of her granddaughters, two frowning babies sitting in a shaded stroller. "I went to her when they were born," she said. "I spent two weeks looking after her and them."

She told me that I owed her eighty dollars. I tried to give her the twenty that I had. Her hand held back a second, then she took the money. "I'll get the rest as soon as I can," I said.

She told me that that was all right, though if I didn't bring another twenty by this time next week, she'd have to ask my father for it. "This is how I make my living," she explained.

When I was strong enough to get up, she drove me home, telling me to lie down in the backseat so I wouldn't be seen and have someone make up a story about us being together. When she left me at the foot of the path to the trailer, she reminded me again of the payment. I promised she'd have it by when she said. I cried the rest of that night, then slept for two days solid, telling Doc I had the flu. The only thing that woke me up was my crying, and that wasn't always from the physical pain. I would waken, thinking I'd heard my baby scream, but maybe it was only me screaming for the thing I'd lost.

21

The phone rang. I let it go. A few minutes passed while I watched from my pillow the red bar of sunrise push below the shade until it entered my bedroom, at last lifting into my sight the far wall tacked solid with travel posters: windmills and fields of tulips, beaches, colossal churches, castles on the Rhine. The phone rang again. This time, I stretched across the bed and picked it up.

"Stella?" a voice said. "Stella Jean?"

I rolled over on my back and stared up at the ceiling. There was a slight buzzing on the phone, and then the voice came in clear. "It's Maury Abrams."

"I know who it is."

He spoke quickly, saying how sorry he was that I'd left Mary Gayle's party; then he was asking me questions, and finally if he could take me somewhere for lunch.

I made excuses until he interrupted, and then I listened while he talked more, and not specifically about us, but about Mary Gayle and how she'd talked to him about me last night. He'd stayed late at her place, he said.

"Maybe you should ask her to lunch then," I suggested. "She's charming, and just because you know Al Hagan doesn't mean that you can't court his wife."

There was a long moment of silence, and then he was speaking softly. "Stella, will you please not talk to me like that? I really want to see if we can't—"

I lifted myself on one arm. I had wakened afraid, but that was over. When the phone had rung, I'd felt the same panic I'd felt the night before when I'd seen Maury, but now, fresh from my sleep, I could enjoy this. Suddenly, telling him what I thought seemed a bonus, as if someone might call and inform you that you were at last getting paid for something that you'd earned long ago, the payment of which you no longer expected. "How do you want me to talk to you, Maury? Like I did the last time you were with me, saying that you loved me, then telling me good-bye because you were marrying someone else?"

"That was a mistake."

"Yes, it was."

"My parents wanted it. I was young. You remember my father? I was wrong; but right then, I just couldn't deal with it."

"Couldn't deal with it! Deal with what? With your own marriage? . . . Don't play stupid, Maury! I hate that!"

I was thinking about Red and John Douglas, and what Maury had done when he'd heard from me about Balmorhea. I reminded him of that, and then I said, "Why were you not afraid to confront two boys who had insulted me and would despise you for threatening them, and not your parents who would have loved you no matter what you did?"

I didn't wait for a reply. I slammed down the receiver, my heart racing as I lay down again, staring at the ceiling and thinking yet more clearly of what that last day together in Anderson had been like, the two of us lying in bed under a blanket, the windows grown blue with the lateness of afternoon, the air smelling of the huge orange roses that Maury had brought me from his mother's garden.

For another half hour I tried to sleep. The phone rang repeatedly. I didn't answer. Later, I phoned Mary Gayle and told her that Maury had called.

"I want you to like him," she said. "Help him if you can. Be his friend. He's had a bad time. Bad choice, bad marriage. He misses his kids. His ex keeps them from him as much as she can; the younger one, he's only nine, phones him all the time, crying. Maury's suing for custody, and eventually, I think he'll win, but for now it's terrible." She paused as though to wait for me to reply, and when I didn't, she went on, "I like him. He's good to other people. We loved it when he lived around here."

I wanted her to stop talking about Maury, but I couldn't think of what to say to make that happen.

"You sure upset him last night, when you left early," she said. "I was surprised at how hurt he seemed. I didn't know you knew him. Where, Stella?"

I didn't tell her, and I knew he hadn't. In a moment, I had lured her back into talking about her party, how nice it had been, how much she enjoyed entertaining, and wanted to do it more.

That afternoon, Maury telephoned again. He asked me to go with him to dinner. I refused. Instead, I ate with Mary Gayle. She wanted to talk to me about Maury. He was a fine person, she said, industrious, a loyal friend. She told me about a charity drive he'd run the year before, the people he'd persuaded to help. I told her I just wasn't interested, so she dropped it and then we began talking about Justin's and her family.

On Monday, Maury telephoned me at work. We met downstairs briefly. He asked to see me at quitting time and take me for a drive. I told him no. He said that he had to be out of town for two days, but he'd call me when he returned. And he did. Again I refused to see him; the next day at work, I asked Mary Gayle to tell him to leave me alone.

"Why don't you go out with him?" she asked.

"I don't want to."

"Just once. Maybe then he'll give up. Won't like you as well."

"Oh, no—he'll like me."

The following Saturday night, a week after Mary Gayle's party, I went to a movie alone. I hadn't heard from Maury. It was the first time since I'd met him at Mary Gayle's that a day had passed with him in town that I'd had no word. In the theater, I saw a woman I knew, one who lived in the apartment complex where I did. She'd come on the bus, so I offered her a ride home and accepted an invitation to have coffee and cake at her place. I stayed with her about an hour, discussing the movie and her job as a typist for a brokerage firm. When I got home, there was a note on the door from Maury. On the deck was a plant, an enormous hibiscus bush with a dozen yellow blooms. The note said that he'd raised it himself from a cutting and that he wanted me to have it, since he knew I loved flowers. The next morning he telephoned.

"It looks like you're going to wake me every Sunday morning," I said.

"I was thinking about you. Did you like the plant?"

"I wish you wouldn't bring me things. It makes it more difficult."

"It's not difficult at all," he said.

"Not for you. It never was."

I told him how I felt, in answer to three awkwardly phrased questions, and when he asked me out, I said that I had plans for the rest of the day. I lay in bed a while longer, trying to sleep, at last reaching for my robe and getting up. On my way to the kitchen, I had opened the door to the deck so that the breeze from the tops of the trees could come inside pure and fresh, the blue sky caught beyond in openings between the limbs. I was making coffee, when I heard footsteps on the outside stairs and then a soft knock at the door. It was Maury, gray slacks, a blue blazer, perfect for a Sunday morning. In his hands, he held a bouquet of yellow roses wrapped in a cone of green tissue. I thought of the apartment in Anderson, our meetings there, the flowers he brought. I knew that he loved me then, that his marriage to Betty was wrong, that her chilly indifference to life would either diminish his emotions to the level of hers or else cause a rebellion within him that would erode his strength, damage his family, and break his heart. In my childish, awkward way, I had told him that then. He had not listened.

"You shouldn't have brought me these," I said about the roses. "I didn't think I'd see you."

His eyes squinted slightly, his shoulders bowed a little as though in apology. Immediately I thought of that day when we'd met in the drugstore in Anderson, his wanting me showing in every feature of his face. I glanced at the flowers. "I can't accept them," I said. I meant to taunt him, fight with him, and then throw him out.

"I don't expect anything."

"Yes, you do. You think you can just come here."

"What do you want?" he asked softly, a little afraid of me, I thought, and I didn't mind that. "Please, Stella . . . you tell me. Maybe you just need time to get used to me."

"I am used to you."

I drew the sash of my robe tight around me and pushed back the hair that was in my face. I hate melodramatics in others; for an instant, a rush of self-hate surged through my heart. I had started for my room, when he set the flowers on the table and came across the carpet to stop my retreat.

I pushed at him. "No!" I said. "Absolutely not!"

I moved away from him. Again he was asking me to lunch. "It's too early for lunch," I answered. "I haven't even had breakfast."

"Well, have some coffee, then we can drive around awhile." He looked at his watch. "It's ten-thirty. I'll take you to Michel's. It's on Lake Travis."

"I know where it is."

I'd heard of it. One of the women I worked with had gone there with her husband on their anniversary. "I can't afford it," I said.

"I'll take you."

"I won't let you."

Then I sighed and turned to him fully. "Maury Abrams and Stella Jean Landry, eating together at a restaurant on the lake. How in the hell does that sound?"

"It sounds good," he said gently, yet I refused to believe in that gentleness.

"Not to your wife," I said.

"I'm not married."

"You were. Long enough to have two children. I don't think this will look right to them, either."

He tried to smile. I knew I had hurt him by mentioning his sons. "You talk a lot now," he said.

"I always talked a lot. You didn't listen."

"All right," he said, speaking as softly as I was. "I just want to take you to lunch."

"Why, Maury?"

He hesitated and then he said, "Because I like you, because seeing you after all these years means a lot to me."

"Don't talk to me like that. It won't work."

For a moment he was quiet, staring at me as if the silence itself might tell him things that he believed I would try to keep secret. "I used to ask about you whenever I was in Anderson," he said, at last. "No one knew where you had gone, until finally a friend of Link's said he thought you'd left town with a man. He didn't know if you'd married him."

"And what would it have mattered if I had been there? You were married."

"I just wanted to see you."

"And Betty?"

"She was going on to other things."

"Other men?"

"No."

"Not sex?"

"No."

"And that was what I was to you." I waved my hand to dismiss the thought.

"I kept remembering how it was between you and me," he said quietly.

"It was hell."

I lowered my eyes then, and I was thinking how little I understood people, and how stupid this was. Maury sat down on the sofa, watching every move I made, while I arranged the roses in a tall green vase that Mary Gayle had given me, then set two mugs of coffee on a tray; Stella Jean, the lady, the well-brought-up girl, nothing in her past to upset an insurance agent successful enough to buy a woman flowers and ask her to lunch. I turned on the television. There was a news program. Neither of us watched. Yet I was beginning to sense that he had come here in friendship; that he wanted to sit down in my living room, feel at home, have the closeness of another human being who had once known him so well.

"This is like some kind of board game," he said. "Each of us making moves."

"Not for me. I'm not playing."

For a few minutes, I sulked visibly; then, at once, without being sure why, I was closing the door to my bedroom, dressing, understanding that though I'd never really accepted his invitation, I was going.

* * *

We rode in Maury's Buick sedan toward Lake Travis, the windows open, both of us wearing dark glasses against the sun. At that time, I thought there was something feminine about a man using dark glasses. I glanced at Maury; he caught that glance, and when he smiled, I knew I was wrong.

At first we tried to talk, and when that failed, Maury watched the road in silence, and I watched whatever landscape we were passing with a sharp, fake attention. I kept wondering why Maury wanted me, why he was making this switch: a man whom convention once led so strictly by the nose that he'd married a woman he didn't love; that same man courting now a woman he'd once used in the way he'd used me.

He drove to a place some few miles past the entrance to a pricey suburban resort called Lakeway. The restaurant was in an old house, the decoration studiedly simple, the cooking French—at least the dishes had French names. On a small table in the center of the room, there were desserts: custard with a gold-colored sauce, a black chocolate cake, pears standing up in a sauce, a bowl of thick country cream. Maury asked for a table beside the window, where we could see the garden and the lake beyond. The guests were talking quietly; some of them glanced up when we crossed the room. There was no menu, so the waiter, a thin, brunet man with a foreign accent and delicate hands, described what they served. I ordered the fish bisque and roast chicken.

"You and Betty come here?" I asked, when the waiter had gone.

"No."

"Others?"

"Others what?"

"Women."

"Once or twice."

"Mary Gayle says you don't go out much."

"That's so." He reached for my hand. "I'm glad you've been asking."

I turned my gaze away from his, as though something interested me at another table. "It doesn't mean anything."

"All right."

The waiter brought a bottle of wine and then the soup. I had guessed immediately that in bringing me here, Maury had planned to do two things: one, impress me; two, put me in a quiet, mellow mood. The first didn't matter; the second irritated me, and when I said so, he blushed.

Then I thought I'd tell him what I'd been thinking. "Maury, there's nothing at all left of the girl you knew in Anderson. If you're looking for her, you won't find her. . . . No, listen," I said, when he started to interrupt me, "you won't." I told him what I'd been doing since I'd been in Austin, how hard I'd worked. I was talking like my psychiatrist at the hospital, sometimes even using words he had used. While I spoke, Maury's eyes stayed on me steady. Halfway through, I saw him flinch, and I saw that slight twist come to his mouth that years before had meant that he was angry with something in his life.

Then he smiled. "We're meeting as friends or not at all?"

"We're meeting once, Maury. This is it."

"And I'm supposed to treasure it and not call back."

"You don't have to treasure it."

"And why? Because you don't like me? Because you can't forgive me?"

"I forgive you. What does that cost? Nothing, zero."

"I can get hurt, Stella. I'm not over it, honey. I think of you. I remember everything."

I set down my glass harder than I'd meant. The wine sloshed; a few drops slid to the cloth. "Remember what, Maury? That first afternoon in Anderson when you made love to me, then gave to me over to Link?" As I spoke, I paused for a moment to watch the pain come into his face, and when it had, I went on: "You're coming up from a past that I've spent twenty years trying to forget, and I can't handle it without help."

"And help means being ugly."

I stared at him an instant. "I'm sorry if I'm being ugly," I said quietly, "but I told you I wasn't interested. I don't like it that you're divorced, either; it's making a promise and not keeping it."

"Aren't you divorced?"

"No."

"But you don't live with your husband."

"I haven't seen him in years."

"Is this a war against men?" he asked.

"A retreat. I turn and fight only when forced."

"And I've forced you."

I nodded. "Now do you want to take me home before you waste your money buying me lunch in a place like this?"

"You make me wish you were the way you used to be."

"I'm sure I do," I said.

When I started to get up, he pulled me back gently, shaking his head, saying he was sorry. Then he was asking me what my life had been like after I'd left Anderson. He asked again about Vic. "You didn't want to marry him?"

"No."

"You want to tell me who that was—your husband?" He was glancing at my ring as he had when we were at Mary Gayle's party. "Does that mean you're still in love with him?"

"It means that I like the way it looks. Why I wear it is my concern."

He whistled softly. "All right. But you spent some time away from Anderson before you came here."

It was not a question, but I answered as though it were. "Yes, but I told you that last night."

"And you're not saying where?"

"No."

"Does Mary Gayle know?"

"No, she doesn't."

"That's all right with me. Anything bad about it?"

I leaned across the table. "Everything's bad about it, Maury. Now how does that fit with the vision you have of yourself in Austin society?"

"I'm not in Austin society. I have some friends. I live here. I work here. That's all."

"What if your sons knew you were having lunch with someone like me?"

"It's not their business," he whispered.

"Who you want to screw is not their business? . . . All right."

He smiled. "I haven't let on that that's what I want."

"It's what you always want."

"I'm different."

"Liar! . . . Are you going to show me around town like you showed me around in Anderson?"

His expression changed, and he looked down. "Please, Stella."

When finally he glanced up, there were tears catching on his black lashes. Immediately I called him a couple of names that would have fit better on Vic than on him, but I didn't care much about subtle distinctions right then. I understood that he didn't like my saying dirty words, not me, not the woman he'd brought here, his lady. "What a hypocrite you are, Maury," I whispered. "You take out a woman like me, pretending that she's some middle-class friend of Mary Gayle Brinsley's. I liked you better before. You and Link both. At the stone house . . . Is he here in town? You and him plan to set me up in a town house convenient to your work?"

I turned my face and glanced out the window through a lace curtain. Behind it was a garden, rosebushes with tiny flowers arranged on their stems in bouquets. In the background, the lake had taken on the silence of the sky. I could see faintly the traces that a speedboat made. I remembered from the past, thinking how remarkably passive Nature could be when some fresh disaster was ripping through my life.

Maury opened a pack of cigarettes, taking his time with the paper and seal. "Well, I understand," he said. He offered me one. I didn't take it. "And you blame me for what happened to you?"

"Certainly."

I'd begun turning my glass around in my hands, staring into the wine, a wine so nice that it had the aftertaste of flowers. I was trying not to be dramatic, but neither wanting him to see my eyes that always told everything about me.

After lunch, he ordered another bottle of wine, not to drink here, he said, though he didn't say where, and I didn't ask.

I opened my purse.

"What are you doing?" he asked.

I pushed a ten-dollar bill across the cloth to him to pay for at least part of my meal. He refused it; I insisted. He was angry, but I didn't care.

The trip home was quiet, Maury driving slowly, to extend the time, I thought. About halfway there, I turned on the radio, and when it played a cowboy love song, I changed the dial past the music stations to news. Maury shook his head. I turned it off.

"You don't like that?" I asked.

"Not right now."

I didn't know what he was feeling, but I was exhausted, and my silence let him know. When we got to my place, I told him I was sorry that I couldn't invite him in, that I had enjoyed the afternoon, but that now I had some things to do.

"Let me come in, Stella," he said. "Just for a while. Maybe I could wait while you—"

"No."

"Will you see me tomorrow?"

I had opened the car door and turned to him. "I can't," I said, "but I thank you for taking me out. I've never been to a place like that. I'll remember it."

I was out of the car, crossing the walk, and climbing the steps. I knew that he had followed me for a way, carrying the bottle of wine; and then I was inside, standing at the window, watching him stare up through the tree branches at my porch before he turned to leave. I waited until he had driven away, then in the trance that the heavy scent of yellow roses and the wine caused, I left the window, went to my bedroom, slipped off my clothes, and drew on my bathing suit, unhooking my necklace and loosening my hair from its pins.

In a moment, I was outside, going down the steps to the pool. I walked hurriedly past a couple who'd spoken to me, then dived from the side, felt the punishing shock of the cold water, and began the laps I did every day of the summer when I was home. I opened my eyes under water, the edges of blue and white shadows like arrows on the bottom of the pool, my eyes following the black stripe, fifteen meters. I swam as fast as I could, my arms dipping furiously to pull me along, my feet kicking in angry, regular beats. I'd done only three laps when I realized that I wasn't going to be able to finish my usual twenty. I climbed out, breathing rapidly, and took the steps fast. I'd forgotten my towel, but there was one I'd left to dry at the far end of the deck railing. I pulled it toward me, drawing it over my shoulders and through my hair, repeatedly drying my eyes on one of its corners. The phone was ringing. I let it ring, sometimes picking it up, sometimes not, until it stopped, and I could watch its silent black profile fade out gradually as the trees lost their final shine, and the moonlight stood patiently on my porch like a visitor waiting to be let in. I went to sleep in a chair.

I slept fitfully, trying to get comfortable yet not wanting to move. When I wakened, a coral mist was easing through the partly opened door and around the edges of the shades. The telephone was ringing again. I answered.

Maury started in at once, his voice tired but strong. It had been good to see me, he said, but maybe he should have gone slower and given me more time. He'd heard that there was a symphony concert in the park next Sunday. Would I like to go?

Outside the window, I could see my neighbor at the corner of her deck, the skirt of her dress ballooning in the morning air. She was watering her potted begonias through the narrow spout of a dented metal can.

"Maury," I said, while he was still talking, pleading his case, making plans. "Maury, I want to ask you something."

I guess my voice had an edge to it, that my words cut through the middle of his like an ocean wave in one of my travel posters cuts across another and changes its flow. I was shivering now in expectancy, so my teeth chattered a little, and I knew the story was going to come out confused, nothing real to it except the one at the other end of the telephone who would now become part of what I knew. "Maury, do you remember Mrs. Sneed?"

I paused to listen. Nothing. He might have put down the receiver, left it where it lay. "One time I went there. . . . Maury, do you remember what she did?"

22

Once I was a baby and then a child with Doc, rolling my head on his lean arm muscles, laughing way up at his face above me, my eyes nearly covered with lashes colored like sand; then anger rising in them when he teased me, then tried to make up with me and hold me too close.

And that was after he had stopped the cattle truck by the side of the road at the zoo with the hilas and snakes that I'd begged to see.

"All right, but we can't stay long," he said. "The cattle need watering."

Where he stopped the truck, we had to walk back, and I complained. "Did you want me to turn around in the middle of the highway?" he asked, close to my face, him still smelling of whiskey from the night before. "I guess you wanted to see us jackknife."

I pulled away.

The zoo cost thirty cents for him and eleven for me. I went first to the rabbits because they reminded me of the ones I had at home in the hutch, then to the coyote mother striding up and down in a chicken-wire cage, her nose dry and patches of her coat gone, so her skin showed red and crusted. "I feel sorry for it," I said soft. I could see a cub sleeping on a blanket in the corner of the pen, breathing heavy like it had run uphill.

"It's better than fending for yourself," Doc said.

"I don't think so."

I told the woman who took money that the coyote needed water. I pointed at its dry dish. She frowned at me and said nothing, but she turned on the hose and splashed water, and the coyote gulped it down, so I asked her to fill the dish again. Then Doc picked up the snake marked FOR HANDLING and touched my neck with it. The snake, a king, was feeble from being too long under glass in the sun, but it twisted just the same under Doc's hold. And Doc saw that I drew back and had a fear of it. And then the woman who watered the coyote scratched under the fullness of her flowered dress, and when Doc went to the rest room, she warned me that the way I acted shows the fear of what men got.

But I didn't believe it. "I'm not afraid of men and what they got," I said.

And the woman laughed in her eyes. "Well, you'd better be," she said, warm and misty in my ear.

And that was when Doc had the last of the cattle to sell, practically pets that I'd known since they were calves, me rubbing against them, stroking them between the lumps on their head and, then later, between the slick, shiny horns they got. I'd fed one of them with a baby bottle, the one whose mother died and that I'd named Linda. I'd lazed in the straw with Linda, cuddling her neck and head with my girl's arms that weren't worth much of anything then. And I cried to see her sold, still asking Doc not to sell her even after the bidding on her began. Because Doc and me both knew that some bastard butcher in an army camp slaughterhouse was going to hit her between her horns with a hammer, then go on to take her meat, leaving her flesh gleaming and naked, maybe hanging her up to age, her flank blood-wet as a mirror, the men eating her not knowing when they sliced into the meat one cow's goodness from another trampling its own newborn calf. It made you sick. At least it did me, though I may have mixed up that dislike of flesh with what Doc did.

Because that night after the auction, I wakened and sat up in bed in a lady's boardinghouse in a town I couldn't remember Doc's telling me the name of, only that he'd let the room for one night. "Not to be with you," he would say later, when I was crouched and hiding, and he was trying to talk to me through a door, "but because I couldn't drive home drunk." And I hadn't yelled because there was no one to yell to but strangers. Instead, I stared, not trembling, but staring, not at Doc but at the light behind the window shade where branches made a web, and wind blew sand from one end of the street to the other. And Doc forgot who I was and rose from the armchair where he'd been drinking the whiskey, and smoking, lighting the next cigarette off the one he had, until the lampshade was still drinking smoke even after he left the chair. And he came toward the bed that was mine, mumbling, "Stella, I've done so much for you. Isn't that true?"

I didn't answer, so to get my attention, he jiggled the mattress.

"Yes, it's true," I whispered.

I think he was waiting for me to say something more, but I was tired, and the middle of the night never seems like real clock time, so what happens shifts in your mind like the dream you were in a moment before you wakened. But I dodged when he came after me, because I'd never seen that, and I slipped from the bed on my knees. When I ducked behind a chair, he came after me, and the fight made losing worse. The next morning the covers were pulled out, and Doc wet a washrag and cleaned up the streaks.

I don't remember leaving the boardinghouse, but I never cried again. I fought, and whenever he was holding me still for him, I blanked my thoughts and waited till what he was doing finished. Quiet. And quiet after. That way for days or a week, Doc pleading with me for company.

"Stella, you want to go into town to the movie? We could get dinner at the café."

I said no, though I could imagine a movie.

Then Doc took to leaving me at the ranch a day, two, three. The first time I woke up from my sleep alone, it was raining a cloudburst. Then the rain quit, and the stars came out wide open and stared on the dirt before the house. I went outside, brushing past the ocotillo limbs in flowering pink since it was May. No fragrance, and just the moon to see that no truck was coming. I found Luis in his shack and asked him if he knew if Doc was ever coming back. He shook his head. "*No me habla,*" he said.

The next morning, after I curried Pete and my pony, Jay, I went inside the house and lay on my bed awhile. That night I went out again to one of the tube chairs and watched for headlights to spread over the cattle guard. I watched till the sun arrived, but nothing else. Finally Doc came home with no lights on at all, since it was full morning. My head ached from the sun's new brightness, my neck was cramped from sleeping sitting up with my head lolling. I turned and ran into the house, but at least I wasn't alone anymore.

The next time Doc left, and since he'd had to let Luis go where he could earn wages, I'd sat up straight in bed when I heard the sound of the truck jolting across the wash, the tires grinding at the dry stones, my heart pounding while the sound got louder, me hoping to see Joylyn brought back by Doc or the men who took her, but seeing Doc walking alone past the window, the chip of a new moon crisp behind him.

He waited there at the door like he thought I might invite him into this corner of the house that I called mine and that he called mine because it pleased him to think he'd made such a nice place for me. But that was no worse than waking to the sound of a belt buckle loosening at a time when there was no color yet in the sky, only the sides of the room visible just the same in that way, as in the country, you see purple after it's gone black, and then the light goes blue before it's navy blue, before the white begins. And Doc held out a bottle of beer to me, and fell, cutting his hand; then he knelt and pulled out the lining of his pockets to show me how empty they were from playing cards in town.

And I said, "I don't want any lamp on." And then I yelled, "Goddammit!" when he didn't pay attention. I reached for the bedside lamp and knocked it over so the bulb blinked and shattered on the red tile floor.

And Doc never hurried me really, but hesitated as though he was trying not to go farther, but to imagine that he was somewhere else, that maybe this was not home but a bar, where he was telling the story about the college money the Rotary gave him, the straight A's until medical school, telling it to the people he met there.

"They're cowboys mostly," he said once, while I was brushing Jay, and he was leaning awhile on the side post of the shed, then staggering to spread some hay for the few animals we had left, arranging the straw, scraping manure just once or twice with the shovel over a stall and adding that to the pile outside. And then later, he tried to play with the ends of my hair and to stroke me like I was one of the barn kittens at the Estes' ranch, and tell me where he'd gone before he met Joylyn and ask did I mind that. "Because she didn't," he said. "Not what happened before." Nice-looking girls there, stacked, smelling sweet; but after her, he couldn't do anything with them. I ran away before he'd finished talking.

Then once, Doc propped his butt resting on the edge of the walnut sideboard that had been Joylyn's grandmother's, and he cried into his hands until the water dropped through his fingers, then red-eyed and sniffling still, he sat down and leafed through a medical book, saying he was going to brush up for the exams since you could always go back. "It's never too late to finish up. Like MacArthur said," Doc said, " 'I shall return.' " He laughed, raised his fist, and gave it a jab upward. Or Doc sitting in the unpainted chair near Joylyn's copper Chambers range and trying not to let me see his face behind the cigarette smoke, and not asking when dinner would be ready, either, since how could he ask chores of me now? I could do as much or as little as I pleased. But in a while that was more than Doc did.

Sometimes he brought tequila home and swigged it like it was water from a canteen on a hot day, and he'd been laboring under the sun. And then it wasn't quite him who came to me. Not shy, yet not mean either, and still thinking. Because I was a child still, he said, his voice thick as if his tongue weren't moving. It was better without going in since there was no risk, and, anyway, I was too small. "Isn't that true, baby?" he asked. But I didn't answer because I didn't know where.

And he called me *baby*. No matter how old I grew, I remained *baby*, because that was right to go with my face: "Blue winter-lake eyes," Doc said, "always waiting for something good to happen." Doc had always said that, smiling, raising my chin with the crooked finger he broke once and didn't have set (though Luis was still there when it happened, so Doc could have given him the orders himself for setting it) kissing my mouth, and joking with me. "Well, you're not any real daughter of mine!" Though someone seeing that might know what Doc might think to do when he was drinking, and that he might run after me if I ran away, find me, then come at me slow but steady. Or not find me until I had to come home to eat or change into something clean. And every time, I said, each early morning I said, *He won't do it again.* "It was a mistake," he said. He pressed his fists into his eyes and sobbed. "I won't," he said. He said, trust him.

23

I took my vacation from Justin's with Mary Gayle, a week at her parents' ranch where her children were staying for the summer. "They're in high school now," she had told me. "Since the divorce, I don't have money for trips, so I always go home to my parents. They're nice to me, and they adore the kids. Mom and I are as close as sisters, and if my dad gets difficult, I just move out of the line of fire until he calms. He's still mad about the divorce. He took Al's side . . . sickness and health."

I had looked forward to the vacation ever since the Easter weekend when Mary Gayle had come back from there, dropped by my place, and suggested that we do this in the summer. In preparation, I bought a straw hat and two western-style shirts; Mary Gayle was lending me a pair of boots. "I'm so glad you're going," she said. "We both need the rest; a change always does good. And actually you're doing me a favor; I need someone of my own generation out there to protect me."

When she picked me up, coming to my door in tight, faded jeans and a bleached-out work shirt, her dark hair in thick plaits, gold loop earrings, I was ready. That day she was especially talkative, laughing at her own jokes and at anything I said that might be the least funny, sharing secrets, listening keenly to whatever I told her.

She drove a Ford van, and once when I asked her why she had such a big car, she explained that she and Al had needed it for all the children's things and theirs: bikes and tents and coolers. It suited their life. Al had liked to camp—not in hot summer, but in fall at the time of the colored leaves, and in spring when the bluebonnets were out. They always went equipped with all the comforts, stayed in the best parks, making reservations months ahead, inviting friends to join them, taking along field glasses, bird-study books, wildflower guides, planning recreation for every hour of the trip.

In the divorce settlement, she asked for the van and got it; and though it was fairly beat-up now, you could see what it had been: sunset and sunrise painted on the sides, the ice-blue promise of the background gleaming through. "I keep it for the kids," she said. "One of the many things I do to make up for breaking with Al."

We rode through the countryside, flowers covering the meadows and flowing at high tide over the shoulders of the road, daisies, asters, yellow and blue; fields stretched out and dotted with paint and chestnut horses that watched us from behind fences; the van coming to such hills that Mary Gayle and I could look down on valleys deep in cedars, cliffs rising above them, some with plants whose roots hung along their edges in shaggy decorations. Once when we'd slowed at a curve, a bird flew across the road before us, beautiful, two black bands around a white neck. Mary Gayle said it was a killdeer. "It's a real actor," she said, "limping, dragging a wing to distract you from a nest full of babies."

I used to love to look at birds. In Winston Valley, I'd had a book with pictures of them and written descriptions, so that I could identify them for myself and Darrell, teach us both.

"By the way," she said, in a while, "have you seen Maury?"

"No," I answered. "Just that lunch."

And when I said nothing more, she asked, "You want to talk about it?"

"Not really."

"All right." But I could see that she was frowning, and not only because of the glare. "Well, I hope something works out. I think of you together, two such good-looking people. I guess you're my favorites."

"Thank you," I said softly, realizing how completely I loved being in this car with her, and being invited to her parents' home.

We talked about the horses we might ride and a day trip she wanted to take, and then again she mentioned Maury. She spoke of his kindness to both her and Al at the time of their separation, Betty's selfishness and discontent, though she'd had every chance in Mary Gayle's opinion to be happy. "He tried to persuade her to go to college and get her degree. She took a few courses, but never finished anything. Meanwhile she was spending money like water, buying clothes, furniture, charging things to Maury that he couldn't afford. I think she was punishing him. I don't know why." She sighed and shook her head. "Maury stayed with her for years after all of his friends thought he should have left."

"Why didn't he?"

"Because of the boys. He really loves his kids and wants them with him. Betty's unfair to them, and I know Maury grieves. I want him to marry again, and if he gets them back to find his sons a real mother."

I was thinking about how good Maury looked now in his late thirties; about the success he'd made at work. "That shouldn't be too hard," I said.

"No one seems to interest him."

"Why don't you make a play for him?"

"No signals," she answered. "Not one."

She continued talking about him, praising him, taking his part against Betty. Then, in a while, when I didn't respond, and there had been a period of quiet between us, she began to talk about her kids.

I listened to her tell of how they were doing in school and what her hopes were for them. "But I don't expect much," she said. She was talking about her son, Sam. "If he gets out of school and finds a job, that's enough for me. My daughter Christina's the one who's going to keep me in my old age. It's Christina who can do anything she wants. There's not a shy bone in her body. I wish I'd had that when I was her age. I've got it now, but I had to work for it. Nobody ever gave me anything."

I smiled. I wondered what Mary Gayle knew about such gifts: a woman who'd married after high school a boy she'd known nearly all her life; a woman who thought that the greatest violence ever done to her was a divorce, she and a man denying one another the love that they had promised God and their friends to keep.

When we got to the dirt road that turned into the Brinsleys' property, white-faced cattle twisted their heads and watched the car approach, and in a moment disappeared behind us in a tawny cloud of dust that the van's thick tires had raised. Just after we passed a small fenced orchard, I saw the house, a two-story box with stone walls and tall, narrow windows without shutters, Mary Gayle's mother coming outside on the porch, then gazing down intently at the steps before the house, holding back the fullness of her skirt so that she could see her feet; coming toward us until she had opened the gate and put her arms around Mary Gayle's neck, closing her eyes, and hanging on. When Mary Gayle introduced her to me, she reached out her hand and took mine. "We're so glad to have you," she said, and I could feel in her hand that that was so.

Then the children came out of the house, the girl several paces behind the boy. Sam lifted the palm of his hand toward us. "Hi, Mom," he said. "Did you bring me the bike chain?"

Mary Gayle nodded and hurried through the gate to hug him. He was a big boy, though probably not quite at his full height. No beard yet, just a fuzz of soft hair like a chick still in the nest that a parent has made. He let her hold him only a moment, then turned away, needing immediately to get into the trunk of the car to find the chain. The girl, Christina, let Mary Gayle hold her longer; then she reached down, picked up the dark glasses that Mary Gayle had dropped on the grass beside the opened door of the car, and cleaned them on the edge of her shirt. Mary Gayle thanked her and exchanged a look with me. "I can't do anything without Christina," she said.

Christina must have been about eleven, spindly arms and legs; boyish torso lost under an oversized T-shirt that gave a logo of her Austin school, an eagle with its wings spread, and the words TRUTH AND FIDELITY. Then, suddenly, she seemed to be trying to show less affection, punishing Mary Gayle, I suppose, as some random thought reminded her that her mother had sent her away to her grandparents for the summer.

"They want to stay in town with their friends," Mary Gayle had told me earlier. "They don't like to be with my parents as much as they used to, but I can't leave them alone without an adult. Next year maybe Sam can get a job. If he does, he can stay in Austin. But Christina . . . I'll always send her out here. I'm not for leaving girls alone in apartments. I don't care how sweet they act. I mean, even if the boyfriend's nice . . . well, he won't be if no one's checking." She had laughed. "It's just the way of things."

Then in the next moment, Christina broke her tough resolve and invited her mother and me into the house to see the pie that she and her grandmother had put in the oven before we came, and that, she said, we could now see through the glass door, the cherries bubbling through the fork holes in the crust.

"Chase!" Sam called as we were climbing the front steps, and a sleek black Labrador came from behind a clump of shrubs, his coat flashing in the bright sunlight, tail wagging, mouth open in what Jimmy had always called a dog's smile: "Sure they know how to smile," he once said; and then he was stroking the flat forehead of the collie puppy he'd given Darrell. A week before Darrell's birthday, he'd brought it home from work after Fred Merriman, a man who hauled gravel, had told Jim that he could have one of the puppies in return for relining the brakes on his truck. And then Darrell had run bandy-legged after the puppy, following it, falling on the grass, crying; then, remembering the puppy, had checked his sobs, risen, and scrambled after it again. And sometimes the puppy had stopped to let Darrell play with it, rolling over on its back to be stroked, nipping at him if he'd grabbed its fur in his fist and pulled. And when I'd protested, Jim'd said, "That nipping taught him more than all the words you or I could ever say. He has to learn. Let him play with his puppy." I hadn't wanted to. I'd known a girl in Anderson whose lip had been torn by a dog, and I didn't like to think of that happening to this child that I'd brought into the world perfect.

"Hey, Chase!" Sam was yelling; and the Labrador leaped with its front paws against the boy's back, nearly knocking him forward on a part of the lawn outside the fence that was thickly embedded with stones. I wanted to cry out and tell Sam to stop playing with the dog, to tell Mary Gayle to make him stop. But then Sam started rubbing at the dog's ears, catching its front paws and making it dance, then releasing it and running with it, glancing at it over his shoulder as a quarterback might glance back for a lineman of the opposing team, yelling when it overtook him, both of them falling to the ground. I glanced at Mary Gayle; she shrugged, took my arm, and we went inside to the kitchen, crossing the wide center hallway that divided the house down the middle, shaded, peaceful rooms on either side, the air heavy with the odor of butter and sugared fruit.

After we'd seen the pie and praised Christina, Mary Gayle showed me around: the corrals, the barn, the holding pen, the dark sweet-smelling storage building where feeds were kept in barrels and burlap sacks. Then we went into the garden to the gazebo, where we talked about our childhoods, me blushing once in an exchange where I realized that what I had said wouldn't tally with something I'd told Mary Gayle earlier, and that she must surely recognize the lie.

While we were talking, we heard a woodpecker in one of the oaks, the hammering as precise and regular as a machine. I was leaning over the rail of the gazebo, trying to see where the bird was. Mary Gayle pointed to a dead limb just before a division in the tree's trunk, then guided my eyes with her finger. "There it is, just below where you were looking." The bird had a red head and mottled back; it wasn't as large as I had expected, but much prettier. "It's dazzling, isn't it?" said Mary Gayle when she saw me smile.

"Yes, it is."

Later we put on our tennis shoes and walked down the steep path to the river, wading in, kicking up water, laughing, playing like kids, at last squealing and hugging, our skirts wringing wet and clinging to our thighs. We came out of the river, our arms around one another's waists, walked up to the house in silence to take a long nap, until the air was cool again, then we went back outside and played baseball in a field behind the house with Sam and some friends of his who had come from town to visit. Afterward, we were sweating and dirty, needful of yet another bath and fresh clothes.

After dinner, Mr. Brinsley suggested dominoes, and we played a long game, drinking a fruit punch and eating the remains of Christina's pie. I won, that fact making me $2.40 richer than when I came. Mr. Brinsley praised me for my game and teased me for my luck at the draw. He turned to Sam and Christina. "You ever see anyone get so many double fives?"

The children shook their heads. "I need her luck," Sam said.

Mr. Brinsley offered me a glass of a thick, sweet port that a cousin had sent him for his birthday. "Got to share it with the grand winner," he said. We watched the ten o'clock news, discussed the fall elections, then Mary Gayle and I went up to bed in her old bedroom, a room upstairs at the back of the house, twin beds covered with green taffeta spreads, blousy white muslin curtains. "It hasn't changed since I lived here," Mary Gayle said. But I had known that.

All night long, there was a cross-breeze that stirred the covers, so cool that soon after we'd turned off the lamp, I had to draw up the cotton blanket and snuggle under it, smiling at how coddled and secure that made me feel.

I went to sleep easy, but then toward morning, I had a dream, one of those vivid, deep ones that reel out smooth as a movie. I dreamed that I was home in Winston Valley and that I was holding the bathroom door shut from the outside, my back to it, keeping Jimmy in. Jimmy was yelling for me to let him out, and Darrell was trying to open the door for him, reaching high for the knob but not being able to grasp it. I was laughing and planning to hold it forever, I said; but then Darrell started to cry, so I opened it, and Jim came out, soaking wet from the shower, since I'd taken the towels, too. I ran through the bedroom door and down the hall, Jim chasing after me, Darrell shrieking and tottling after us. I was nearly to the pickup when Jimmy pulled me down, flat on my face, since he'd grabbed me around the legs; then he was lifting me under my knees and shoulders, and I was nibbling at his neck, saying it was candy. Darrell was sucking on a pacifier. I told Jim to take it from him because I didn't want it falling in the river, the waves of which were lapping at the feet of the pecan trees. Darrell cried and reached for the pacifier, then scolded us both and watched Jim and me go inside to *the tower room.* The mistake I made in the dream was to tell Jim about Maury, that I was expecting Maury's child.

Because then Jimmy had taken his hands off me and gotten out of bed. I heard the back screen slam, then I saw him squat beside the sand pile and talk to Darrell, Darrell a young man now, wearing slacks and a white shirt, both of them frowning and gazing back at the part of the house where I was. Later, Jim was in the kitchen phoning someone, then he was in Darrell's bedroom, opening the bureau drawers, dropping clothes in paper grocery sacks, until a woman with blue hair arrived in a taxi and took Jim and Darrell away. "I'm going to work in a city!" Darrell shouted back through a cloud that swirled behind the tires.

I may have cried out in my sleep. I certainly wakened, and I thought I'd wakened Mary Gayle in the bed beside mine—if I did, she was quiet.

The next morning, we got up early to ride horseback. Christina and Sam had wanted to ride with us, but when Mary Gayle knocked at Christina's bedroom door, she told her mother that she was too sleepy and would ride later. Sam replied in groans that he was coming soon, but more than a half hour passed before he reached us. He rode with us for a time, then complained about our slow pace and broke away, yelling back that he was going to a neighbor's ranch to see if the new colt had been born. After the ride, Mary Gayle and I had breakfast on the back screened porch, talked to Mrs. Brinsley until the three of us had finished a pot of coffee; then Mary Gayle and I took the truck into Fredericksburg to get some supplies that the Brinsleys needed for the week.

We had just spoken of leaving town, when Mary Gayle saw a clothing store named the Huntsman, and asked if I'd like to go in and see what they had, how the things compared in price with those at Justin's. It was a charming place in a renovated historic building: casual clothes, tooled belts, leather shoes. I bought a denim dress and sandals; Mary Gayle, a pair of khaki slacks and matching short-sleeved shirt. We went out of the store worried about our extravagance. "If we have to buy something, we should do it at Justin's, where we have our discounts," I said.

"Oh, what the hell," Mary Gayle replied. "You have to do something crazy sometimes."

After lunch, in early afternoon, we walked out on a meadow, stopping among the flowers to rest, picking blossoms, lying back on slick, fragrant grasses and watching the clouds, napping awhile under trees, then waking to the sounds of our own voices, one speaking to the other about people we knew and things we'd shared. Later, we told Mary Gayle's mother to go out on the porch and enjoy the rest of the afternoon and the book she'd been anxious to read, while we cooked dinner for the family. And we made a big meal, one that Mary Gayle's father seemed to appreciate: roast duck, corn-bread dressing, a molded vegetable salad, followed by a delicious spice cake. While we were washing dishes, Mary Gayle asked me questions that I hadn't really answered—always the same with me, lying or failing to answer completely, then remembering how Mary Gayle had introduced me to her mother: "Mom, this is my friend Stella that I told you about." Mary Gayle's friend. And Mrs. Brinsley's warm handshake, her husband's smile and greeting, both of them telling me to make myself at home and meaning it, exactly the welcome that Buck and June would have given to any new friend of Jim's. And I understood that I needed what these people were giving me, though it occurred to me, also, that the Brinsleys might feel sorry for me, since Mary Gayle might have told them that I had no family, that I was a strange type, a little touchy, a woman in her midthirties who lived alone, still pretty perhaps, but the kind of woman who had once been fresh-faced, blue-eyed, not a pound of extra flesh on her except in her breasts where it counts for something. "And she has a son," Mary Gayle might have added. "I don't know how old he is, but probably older than Sam, or about as old."

And Mary Gayle had discovered that on our Fourth of July picnic on Town Lake, when in the afternoon she'd arrived to pick me up for the canoe ride and I wasn't ready, so she'd come back into my bedroom and seen a photograph that I had from Winston Valley. It was one of Darrell and me, the only one I had of us together. The picture had been taken in July, too, but not the holiday. Later, I think, near the end of the month when it was hotter yet, and Darrell and I were standing ankle-deep on the stone floor of Cyprus Creek, the shoulder-height dam and waterfall behind us, me in a gold lamé two-piece bathing suit that Jimmy had ordered for me from a mail-order catalog. All summer long, he'd dared me to wear it; and finally, that day, I had, my breasts spilling out of it, the bra covering not much more than my nipples. "You don't care if other people see me like this?" I'd asked Jimmy while

I was still in the car, tying one of the two strings that held up the diaperlike panties. "Who's going to see us?" he'd asked, glancing up toward the house at the top of the wooded bank. The house belonged to some people from Houston, but they rarely used it. "You see anybody here? In any case, you're mine, right? I'm not worrying about that." He had paused, smiling, teasing. "Do I have any reason to?" I'd told him no.

Darrell was wearing blue trunks, low on his hips, his belly sticking out, his small shoulders hunched defiantly at the camera, his round arms hugging a small plastic inner tube decorated with the head of a sea horse. I know he was impatient, that he'd been angry and disbelieving when Jim had delayed our swim in the pool behind us with the silly notion of taking a photograph. Yet Jim had finally gotten a smile out of Darrell by promising to buy him a Dixie cup of chocolate ice cream on the way home.

"How old were you then?" Mary Gayle had asked me.

I'd paused as if I was trying to remember, though of course I knew exactly to the day. "I think I was about twenty-four."

"And the baby? Is the little boy yours?"

I'd stood away from her, my hands rooting through a dresser drawer, my eyes intent on the search for whatever it was that had brought me into my bedroom and caused Mary Gayle to stand at the door watching me for a minute, and then coming behind me to see the picture in its silver frame, the first thing I'd bought after I'd started working at Justin's. I always kept the photograph hidden when I had anyone over, and I hadn't expected Mary Gayle to come back in my room. "Yes," I said.

"I thought you told me you didn't have any children."

"I lied to you," I said calmly.

"Any reason?"

"Yes. I haven't been able to live with him, and I don't like to talk about it."

"I'm sorry," she said. "I guess I'm just too nosy."

I shook my head. "It's all right."

"Well, he's a darling. I never saw such pretty hair."

I gave a side glance toward the picture. "Yes, it was pretty." I remember mornings, Darrell sitting in his high chair, the sun coming through the window and seeming to search for the whiteness of his hair as it might search out some bright flower for its own enhancement. More than once I'd called Jimmy to come see it, the two of us standing in the middle of the kitchen, admiring our baby, Jimmy's arm around my shoulder, Darrell laughing and slapping the flat of his hands on the tray of the high chair.

"I guess this was taken a long time ago."

I had tried to smile, but the corners of my lips just clicked on and off into it and wouldn't stay put. "Yes, it was," I said.

Then Mary Gayle had picked up the picture and looked at it more carefully, taking in every detail, as I had so many times, setting it beside me on the table when I read at night in bed, then picking it up and seeing my baby smiling at Jimmy behind the camera, remembering that Jimmy had been making faces and waving his free hand to cheer Darrell.

"His daddy have him? He lives with him?"

"Yes, he does."

I hesitated, then said something that I'd often thought must be true of a man like Jim, but which I didn't know for a fact. "He's remarried, of course."

And I had wanted to believe that—that Darrell had a woman near him whom he thought of as his mother, and to whom he brought all the joy that should have been mine but that I wanted so much still to have been his. Darrell was so young when I left. Likely I was for him hardly more than a hazy presence, a woman holding him, feeding him, coming to him to arrange things when he was hungry or hurt.

Mary Gayle had glanced at me with that look of shock and sympathy that I'd seen so many times on the faces of women who hear that a woman friend has been separated from her children. For almost any reason, the reaction is the same: that life happens to you as it should, and then luck fails and everything changes. I knew how important it had been to Mary Gayle to have custody of her children, that having the duty and delight of making their home was essential to her.

"Do you ever see your son?" Mary Gayle had asked.

"No." I had turned to her, holding a white sock in my hand. The mate to it had fallen to the carpet and lay there in a heap.

She had taken a deep breath, sighed as if in mourning with me, then set the photograph down carefully, adjusting the brace behind it. When she glanced up, she said, "If you ever need to talk to someone, I—"

I shook my head again. "No."

She tucked her mouth in tightly, nodded several times, then left me so that I could finish dressing.

"Do you have any cool water?" she asked from the other room.

"Yes, in the refrigerator."

I heard her open the refrigerator door. "You don't mind if I have some of this grapefruit juice, do you?" she called.

"No, no—help yourself to anything you want."

I finished dressing, and after we'd packed the cooler with the beer and soft drinks that I'd had in the refrigerator, we went to the lake, where Ernie Pearson, the man that another friend of Mary Gayle's named Greta Lewis was living with, had rented canoes.

It was high summer; even the shadows were sun-glazed in late afternoon. There were seven of us, three men and four women. The older we became, the more often the numbers fell that way, men wanting younger women; single women believing that they wanted any man at all. We walked in rubber thong sandals over the rocks, then climbed into the boats, holding on to beer cans and tote bags, laughing, telling jokes, a man named Ray Dowling wanting to pair up with me but me being stiff-shouldered when he put his arm around me; though soon enough he retreated and started making up to Mary Gayle, who looked lovely that day in a red bathing suit and flowery cover-up.

Tough bluish clouds stood above the lake; the sun glanced off the water, shattered by the waves the boats made, beating down on our shoulders and arms; yet the breeze eased its effects, our sweating skin repeatedly dried and cooled by dependable gusts. I put my hand in the water and watched the tiny, churning furrows in the wake that my fingers made.

Since it was the Fourth of July, First Street and the bridges were decorated for the Aqua Festival. I always went to the festival with friends, arriving a couple of hours early to find a good place on the bank, spreading out a blanket and eating a picnic, plenty of California Chablis in glass jugs, so that we were numbed and happy, when, after dark, the lighted barges filed by, cartoon floats decorated with a mixture of plastic and real flowers, fresh-faced high school sweethearts sitting on thrones, capes around their shoulders with high collars behind their necks, sparkling tiaras holding their hair at the crown of their heads, golden scepters clutched in manicured hands, imperial mantles swirled around their feet or flowing down the steps to the lower levels where the princesses stood, those girls nearly as pretty and as elaborately dressed as the queen herself. And I guessed that they were the same girls picnicking beside us now: ten, fifteen years older, but sitting on the slopes of the river beside their picnic baskets woven of polished wood, red and white ice chests from which their faintly eye-creased, muscled, suntanned husbands took dripping cans of cold beer, wiping the water off on their sleeves, pulling the tab of the can; then later holding a small child on their shoulders so it would have a better view of the passing boats, most of them laughing or telling stories, some simply smiling peacefully at the festival before them.

But I never much enjoyed these pageants. I went there because the event was something that I could talk about, plan in advance, each new time believe that the show would be, at last, as remarkable as my dream. Yet, when the time came, even the fireworks, the bursting rockets rising to the top of the sky, gave me little pleasure really; but rather seemed a wound on what otherwise would have been the night's peacefulness, like those nights when, at the ranch near Valentine, I'd gone out of the house with Joylyn, when before bed we might decide to take a walk, letting the breeze cool our faces and arms, stroke us with its softness; and the stars above us had been so still and permanent, and because of the silence had seemed reassuringly not so far away but so easily within our reach at some future date that we didn't feel it necessary to explain what we knew, or even to talk about it.

Sometimes, late in the evening near small country towns, there are no sounds but those of livestock and insects, unless, of course, you choose a road beside a stream and can hear the water rippling over the rocks or gently sucking at the banks, though even those disturbances, so slight and irregular, had seemed to make too much turmoil between Jim and me, and too much turmoil for me again now at the Brinsley ranch with Mary Gayle, when after dinner I was sitting alone with her outside on the meadow in a canvas chair, the stream below us moving down the slope to the valley of the river. Because I just wanted the quiet; then later, when the sunlight would leave entirely, the essential blackness, the planets so close and their kinship so complete that I might read in them again of some other possibility.

Yet that evening the air was coming up so fresh and soothing, memories recurring in it: the trip here, meals with the family, games, flowers and birds and animals, our indulgent trip to the Huntsman, the wide-open hot summer landscapes themselves—that it was as though Nature had become partner with me, as she never had before, the soft air touching my cheek and affirming my life. And so I did a strange thing, so strange that I knew I'd have to marvel at it later, and yet I went ahead:

"We lived on a small ranch," I began. "They were not my real parents, but people who came for me after a minister said in church that a baby had been left. My new mother's name was Joylyn. A beautiful name, don't you think? I still think so. . . ." My recitation was the same that I remembered from so many years before at Mrs. Slover's, and then with Jimmy when it had to be told again. Yet as I went on, Mary Gayle nodding for me to continue, my voice, instead of fading gradually to a murmur, steadied and strengthened. I told her about Maury, that I had known him in Anderson, and then I told her how. I talked about Prentice, all there was in a surprisingly few short sentences. "And then I left and met Jim, and I thought I could marry and live in that town. After a while I was sure of it, and then one holiday, a woman came, and she remembered . . ."

"And Vic?" Mary Gayle asked, when later I'd paused for a moment. "What happened then? You didn't ever see him again? You didn't go with him?"

"Yes."

"Why?"

"I couldn't think. I don't know."

For a time, she was silent. I could hear my own breathing.

"Stella," she said at last, "did Maury stay with you that afternoon, after the lunch, I mean?"

"No. . . . I told you."

"He's in love with you."

"I think so."

"And before?"

"Before?"

"In Anderson?"

"Yes."

"Did you tell him about Ruth?"

"Yes."

"And what did he say?"

"I don't know," I answered. "I told him in a letter."

"Would he have the letter now?"

"Yes, I took it to his place."

Two afternoons before, I'd driven to Maury's apartment. The building was a new one on Sixth Street, built along the slope of a hill, stucco walls. Each apartment had a broad balcony, some with a view of the city. I'd been nervous when I'd delivered the letter. I'd had to check to see that Maury's car was gone. A gardener, who was edging the walks, had glanced up at me as I was going to the mailboxes. I could imagine his telling Maury that a woman had been there and how frightened she seemed.

I was quiet then, and Mary Gayle said nothing more, nor did she repeat her question; then she was looking away from me, and I could imagine how she felt and what she would soon *have* to say: that her parents mustn't know, and certainly not her children; that I should have told her before and let her judge for herself the wisdom of asking me here. When I could no longer bear her silence, and the suspense of knowing her mind and her decision, I left my chair and hurried along the path that had led us here, returned to the house, and took the stairs to the bedrooms. I heard the voices of Mr. Brinsley and the children in the living room. Mrs. Brinsley had gone to bed; the light was off at the top of the stairs. I walked by her door quietly and went into the room that was Mary Gayle's. I put my suitcase on the bed, opened the bureau drawer, took the denim dress from the closet, still in its plastic wrapper. When Mary Gayle came upstairs, I had nearly finished packing. "What are you doing?" she asked quietly.

She had come near me. There were tears in her eyes enlarged under the lenses of her glasses; I'm sure there were tears in mine. "Why would you do this?" she asked. "We have more time. I don't understand. Did I hurt you with my questions?"

I shook my head.

"And, anyhow," she said, "I've heard things. It doesn't matter. I knew you had troubles." She stood before me and put her hands on my shoulders. "We make a good pair, don't we? I couldn't make my marriage work, and you—"

"We don't make a pair at all, Mary Gayle," I said, then raised my hand in the air and traced a wide arc to describe the richness of what must have been her childhood, school days, and time as a young woman. "You grew up in this house, your parents are here, your children."

I sank down to the side of the bed, Mary Gayle beside me, taking my hand, talking to me, making suggestions. At last she spoke of a way that I might see Darrell, at least make an effort to return to Winston Valley. I shook my head. I wouldn't break in now on what I'd tried so hard to mend. Even my doctor had hardly suggested that.

The phone rang; footsteps came toward us on the stairs and in the hallway. Christina knocked and opened the door. "Someone for you, Stella." She was smiling, teasing. "It's a man. Is it your husband?"

I smoothed my clothes and my hair as though she had said someone was there waiting for me. "No, honey," I said, and then I went downstairs, Christina following close behind.

The telephone was in the living room. Mr. Brinsley was still there; Sam, too. They watched me as I picked up the receiver.

Maury spoke fast, asking why I hadn't told him I was leaving. He had waited hours for me in front of my apartment. "This morning when I called at work, they told me that you were on vacation but left no word where. Stella, I had to get the telephone number from Al Hagan."

Mr. Brinsley and Sam were discussing their game; Christina was watching Sam's cards; and although I was speaking quietly, I knew they could hear every word I said. I thought I heard Mary Gayle come near, but I dared not look around.

"When are you coming home?" Maury was asking.

"Sunday week."

"Then I'll drive out there."

He waited for a reply, and when there was none, he said, "Will you see me tomorrow? We need to talk. About your letter, Stella, I—"

"I don't want to talk about it."

"Then just see me, only for a little while."

I told him that I couldn't, that for me nothing had changed, that I didn't know of any way of our making anything out of what we had to remember, and that I wasn't willing to try.

"I love you," he said, interrupting me. "I've never loved anyone else in my life. I know that. We should have married in Anderson."

"We didn't."

"But we can, Stella. Right now. I can be out there in two hours, and we'll talk."

"Why marriage? To ease your conscience?"

"Love has nothing to do with conscience." He asked again if he could see me at the Brinsley's ranch and talk with me about our future.

"I'm not interested," I answered.

"Then what would interest you? You tell me, Stella. Everything on your terms."

"A blank check?"

"Exactly."

"As it was in Anderson?"

"Please God, Stella," he whispered.

"Please God, what, Maury? Have mercy on you? I do better to consider myself."

And then I was thinking: *Here I am in this house with this family, listening on the phone to this man who caused me so much pain, who has found out more about the desecration of my life than he ever believed possible, and who now seems to be asking me to be mother to his sons.*

I felt as if I were slipping through the opening of a door that I'd closed a dozen times. "No," I said, loud and clear.

I glanced over at the others and saw that Sam was staring at me, and that Mr. Brinsley was looking way too close at his cards. Just about then, Mary Gayle's arm went around my waist, and Christina began holding my hand.

"No," I said again to Maury, and then I said good-bye.

24

It was nearly a month later when I agreed to see Maury, and this at my apartment, where I felt safe. After all, I was at home, in my territory among the trailing pink geraniums I'd raised from cuttings; the spray of trumpet vine from my neighbor's porch, and one rampant sweetheart rose.

When he arrived, I was dressed in slacks and a cotton sweater, something Mary Gayle might have chosen, simple, nothing for show. I had flowers on the table in defiance of his bringing me more.

He stood just inside the door, wearing khakis, a plaid shirt, colors that flattered every line in his body and softened the contours of his face, everything about him perfect, his speech, his stance and manner, just as it always had been. He leaned near me, gently, as if in friendship, to greet me with a kiss on the cheek. I preferred a handshake, and he accepted that; then I moved quickly past him toward the deck.

"It's cool out here," he said, a slight complaint in his voice.

"It's all right."

I leaned against the rail of the porch beside one of the geranium plants, getting my balance there, not knowing how I'd crossed to this side but aware that when Maury had reached out to guide me, I'd pushed him away. He stood close; I was looking up into his face. When he tried to take my hand, I drew it back.

"I'm going there," I said. "To Anderson, I mean; I need to see it again."

He looked as though I'd hit him, and I knew I'd been right in believing that he'd disapprove. "Because of me?"

"Partly."

The low evening sun shone behind me, bright in his eyes. He turned his head a little to avoid its glare. "There wouldn't be any point in that," he said. "It would only churn up things that you need to forget. Why do it? Shouldn't you be making new memories?"

"Where?"

"Here with me."

"That didn't help me much before. Why make the same mistake?"

"Why make this one?"

"Because I do as I please."

"You look for trouble then. Don't do that, Stella."

"I told you. I do as I please. I don't answer to anyone."

"Then let me go with you."

"No."

I moved to the edge of the porch. Maury was saying my name, trying to settle me down, telling me that he wanted what was best for me and that that wasn't a visit back home. My arms were around my waist as if I were protecting myself from the cool air. "You remember the apartment, Maury?"

I was thinking of the roses he brought to me from his mother's garden, his rebellion against his parents, who disciplined him too harshly, directed his life, and held narrow views. "Do you want me to see your mother when I'm there?" I asked to taunt him.

To his credit, he didn't flinch. "If you like."

"Does she know about us?"

"I don't know."

"Should I tell her?"

"If that would please you."

"What a coward you were," I whispered.

"Not now."

"You think you've changed?"

"I know I have."

People were using the walk below. I tried to keep my voice down. "Why do you think that? Because you're willing to take up with a woman like me? I don't understand. Why the hair shirt, Maury?"

He reached for my hand again. I let him hold it a moment, then turned away.

"All right," he said; but I knew that he hadn't given up, that he was injured but powerful still.

"Where did your mother think you took the roses?" I asked.

"Roses?"

I told him what I was remembering.

"I don't know."

"You lied to her like you lied to everyone about me."

"I didn't talk about you then. Never. I promise."

"You promise! You think it was for love of you and Link? You had money! You remember what clothes I had, the meal you bought me at the Sweet Shop? I'd never been in that place before except through the back door for food they thought was too rotten to sell up front! They didn't want to serve me, Maury, until I told them that Link would pay!"

"And you blame me? All right. But what are you asking of me now?"

"Nothing! That's just the point! I don't need anything from you now!"

I started to leave him, then I turned. "Just one question: Was Betty's knowing about me the reason for the divorce?"

"No, I wanted that."

"And Maury Abrams gets what he wants."

"It was my mistake."

"So was I."

"And Link, he—"

"Link was an idiot."

He smiled. "And I wasn't?"

"You ever tell her?" I asked. "Does she know?"

"Yes."

"She didn't mind?"

"She understood."

"That's nice," I snapped. "Understood what? That a young man needs what I had? Did you tell her family, her father maybe? Was he happy that you were experienced? Men like that, don't they— You wouldn't hurt his little girl. That you'd know know. . . . Bastard! Mating's equal, you hear me? Equal!"

Again, I moved to go inside. He grabbed for me. I avoided him; and as I did, I bumped against one of the geraniums. It teetered. I tried desperately to catch it before it fell; and when I couldn't, I screamed and raked my hand along the rail and upset the two remaining plants, knocking them off the deck. I heard them thud on the earth below, their pots bursting on the flagstones.

"Stella, Stella Jean," I heard beside me, almost a wail. "Please, honey."

"Please, honey, please!" I mocked him. "Please—for what?" And not for hurting the plants, I knew, but for hurting him! Well, I wanted to see him suffer and bleed; and if by depriving him of my body and my company and by throwing a fit, I could do that, then so be it!

Using the foulest language I remembered ever having heard, I accused him of preying on me, kicking me when I was down, and ruining my life. "And if you couldn't tell people in that stinking little town that you were in love with Doc Landry's girl, then how in the hell can you tell anyone now!"

I bolted inside, locked the door, and went into the shower, turning the water on cold, wetting my slacks and cotton sweater, crying until I made myself sick; then, with water streaming from my clothes over the bathroom floor, I staggered to the toilet and vomited up, in wild, hysterical roars, every bad memory I'd ever had.

Two days later, I went to Anderson. I took off from work early, went home for a few things, and asked a neighbor to watch out for my place.

I drove Highway 71 west to 90, stayed up all night, played whatever radio station I could find, and stopped at highway restaurants and truck stops for coffee to keep me awake. By the time

I reached Pecos, I was tired and dizzy and felt the strain of a night without rest. Several times I thought of turning back. Once, in fact, I did: I drove about fifteen miles, feeling relief at my decision, then scolded myself for cowardice, turned the car around, and continued.

I arrived at the outskirts of town, a pale, fresh morning, the wind hard and cold, the *A* on the hillside standing out clear. To my right was the college, a cluster of red-brick buildings on the west slope of the hill. The old hotel, the Brussels, was as before, its four stories rising out of the dusty street, a pile of adobe with the whiteness of sugar tinted by a lavender shade. I drove past to the café that I remembered; parked before it; glanced out the window at the town that was in some ways so different, in others, the same as when I had looked back at it from my place in the car beside Vic Hansen. The main street had been made one-way, perhaps to get trucks through quickly, though there had never been much other traffic in Anderson, and I didn't suspect that that had changed.

The café was the same, a couple of blocks down from where the movie had been; but the movie was gone, and the building it used to occupy had been made into a used-furniture-and-clothing store. Abrams's was still there, though under a different name, its display windows filled with dress mannequins in styles that echoed those of a year before at Justin's. Mr. Abrams had died three years ago; Mrs. Abrams had been with Maury and Betty for a year, but he'd told me that she'd moved back here.

When I entered the café, I felt its heat, cigarette smoke already filling the air. I looked for the waitress whom I used to know, but a young blond girl waited on me, asking me in a cheerful voice where I was from; and, when I said Austin, she said that as soon as she'd saved enough money, she meant to go to the university there.

The room smelled of fried pork, hashbrowns, and coffee. The jukebox was lighted and playing; electric blue bubbles raced through the three curly tubes that framed its shape. A heavy man with a frizzy red beard stood before it feeding it coins and searching out titles of the tunes. I didn't know him, or anyone else there, all of them men, talking quiet, the kind who sit hunched in their chairs in such a way that you know they've spent all of their lives outdoors. I sat at a booth and ordered toast and coffee. After breakfast I registered at the hotel, left my things in the room, then went downstairs. Outside, a swirl of dust came down the street, spinning; another gathered in the gutter. I hugged my coat around me and began walking, looking for landmarks to see if they might make my memory correspond to what I thought was true of me.

I walked up to the post office, turned toward the church, past houses I recognized, thinking *Yes, that's the Bells' house. The trim's been changed, but the porch is the same; and, yes, that two-story red frame house is where Sarah McCloud lived, the same green shutters; Lila Daniel's house*—those girls I had admired and wanted to be like, but where the doors of their homes were closed, the girls' mothers with apologetic words and gestures, drawing their daughters inside for projects real or invented, and that could never include a girl like me.

I moved away slowly, passing the Marsters' and then the Crites', walking down the road to where our trailer had been. There was nothing there now, only a meadow where a horse was tethered, a brown one with a black mane. It was grazing, but when I whistled, it raised its head to look at me, its liquid black eyes holding mine. It let me come close, pat its forehead and muzzle, and straighten its mane. I stroked its withers and back, both of us gazing away from the sun at the college buildings on the low-lying hills. Then, with a twist of its neck, it lowered its head to graze on a patch that had more dried earth than grass. It reminded me of a horse that we'd had at the ranch, one with a white star in the center of its forehead, so it should be called *Texas,* I had thought. I remember shouting out that name to Doc on the day we got it, then running across the feedlot to him and him swinging me up in his arms and taking me to where Joylyn was resting in a chair. "It's a good name," he'd said. "And you're my smart, good girl."

I turned and crossed the road, passing a new barn and house, constructed on a blank piece of unfenced land. It didn't make much sense being there, but then neither did the trailer's absence. I crossed roads where there were curbs but no houses, still the same after more than twenty years. But who would want to build there? No trees and not much possibility of attracting grass, since the wind gathered in the hills and then blew across the land, pushing down anything that tried to grow. I'd tried to grow here. I'd tried real hard. But I just kept putting my roots in the wrong places, or not putting them down purposefully but letting others do for me what I should have known from Joylyn to do for myself. "Nothing happens to us that we don't cause," she told me. "God gives us free will. And He doesn't put us in hell, we do that ourselves." But I knew it wasn't God who put me there. I knew who it was, and so would she.

I passed a patch of earth that had been blackened by fire, scorched metal cans slung around among singed papers and bits of curled plastic. The smell was of spoiled meat and garbage; a rat scurried by my feet and ducked into the rubble. I hurried to get away, passing into a neighborhood of cottages with cyclone fences and gravel drives. A dog stood in the yard of the house at the corner, its brown head jerking upward each time it barked. Betty Elias had lived in the house with the two bushy poplars standing on either side of the door. I tried to imagine when Maury had told her about him and me; not on purpose, but likely when he'd been drinking and was disappointed about something in his life, perhaps the oncoming truth that their marriage was his family's idea and not his, that when he'd married the daughter of a friend of his parents in a synagogue in Lubbock, he'd been in love with a derelict's child in Anderson and had never been able to push that girl out of his mind.

Ah, Link and I, he might have begun, *we had this thing going. You remember Stella Landry, the one who lived with that man who worked at the railway depot? Yes, you know, the man who used to wander into the pool hall high-hatting everybody, reciting poetry as long as his voice held, then going to sleep on one of the benches, snoring till someone prodded him with a cue and made him leave. Well, when Stella was in grade school, some of the boys thought it was fun to catch up with her on the way home and tease her, and not for her never getting all her work in school, but for something else about her they didn't quite understand. I heard that once some of them hid behind a hedge, laughing aloud and giving themselves away when she turned on them yelling. One of them laid hold of her, but she wrenched away; and then she was chucking rocks at them and landing some. There was no getting to her, and finally they had to give it up and let her go. Then in high school, the boys left her to herself, thinking she was too different. But not Link and me. Because she was as good as gold to us, sweet and quiet about taking it, meeting us on time like she was working in an office, never asking favors, except that we keep what we had there secret. Remember the stone house down by the creek bed? You ever see it, honey? You remember it? Because I do. If you don't believe me, ask Link. That was our senior year.*

I thought about how many times he may have told that. And then, at once, remembering the look on his face at the apartment and seeing his sorrow, I knew that he'd never told anyone else at all. It was the football player who told and got me Vic. "And now you don't have to think anymore," Vic had said. "I'll do the thinking for you."

Well, I was doing the thinking now; the choices were mine, and I meant to make them.

For a moment, I stood on the road staring at the Eliases' house, then I walked on the three blocks and climbed the hill to the house that was the Abramses'; smoke from a neighbor's chimney swirled over the roof; the smell of burning oak was strong in the thin, cold air. On the steps up to the front door stood flowerpots; thick-leafed daisies budded out of the moist earth. The window shades were pulled down, probably to keep the sun from fading the upholstery inside. I wanted to knock, and even if Mrs. Abrams was not there, to enter. The back door would be unlocked. People in Anderson never locked their doors. If I wanted to, I could search for traces of Maury there, perhaps a yearbook with the pictures signed by his class, a full-page picture of him for being elected one of the class favorites, then further on in the freshman group, a small picture of me, my blouse wrinkled, my eyes squinting, like one of those animals afraid of living in the light.

In the yard next door, there was a tricycle turned over across the front walkway, dirt dug out below a tree, a bent toy truck, a small pail and a spade lying there where some child had left them. A little girl, six or seven, came around the side of the house. She was wearing a sweater, jeans, chaps, and boots. In her hand, she held a lasso, the rope too thick, the coil heavy for a child her size. With a quick twist of her arm and a flourish, she threw the noose away from herself, aiming it at the upturned handle of the tricycle. It caught, she tightened it, then began dragging the tricycle toward her. She was a stout child, heavy on her legs and strong, her cheeks red with the cold.

"Hi," I said.

She turned back to the house and yelled for her mother. I wanted a daughter like that, yelling for me, me sheltering her behind me and hollering for a stranger to go away.

I took one more look at Maury's house, thinking again of my threat to betray him to his mother; then I ducked my head and walked away quickly, turning right at the corner. I went down a driveway to the street and kept on. When I came to the highway, I was breathing fast, the same as I might have been years before when I'd been going to the stone house, knowing that I was late for Link, that he'd be mad and take that out on me. A truck was coming toward me. There was just time to cross. I was walking on the other side when the driver stuck his head out the window and yelled something at me that I couldn't understand but that ended with the word *Blondie.*

Blondie. On and off, all my life, I'd been called that. One of the men who came to Ruth's asked for me that way. "Your name's not Sandy," he'd said to me the first time up in the room when we were through, and he was watching me dress. "It's Blondie. Isn't that so?" He'd kept watching me, smiling, then not smiling, coming to where I was, saying he needed me a second time.

I heard the town clock chime. I glanced down at the round blue face of my watch, at its silver hands. "Ten o'clock," I whispered.

I set off down the hill, then walked alongside the creek, my heels catching in the gaps between the stones. I tripped once, hit on my knee, and scraped the hand that kept me from falling farther. Stupid, since all I'd had to do was walk slow. And what was I hurrying to? To get money? No, I had plenty of that in the purse over my shoulder. And I had money in the bank. I'd been careful about what I'd earned over the last few years, since there wasn't anyone around to take care of me but myself. People had tried. I listened in my mind to a list of them, then I settled like I always did on Joylyn, remembering how every day after she left, I had watched the road for a dust cloud that might mean a car would slow before our house, and she'd get out of it, the wind making the corner of her cotton scarf whip at her neck, while she was thanking the driver for bringing her home; Joylyn thanking people a dozen times for the smallest favor, her voice high-pitched and quivering—what it always did when she was happy.

I tripped again on a stone, and I thought about what my falling meant. It seemed to be a voice calling to me, or something catching up to me and pulling me aside, Maury still trying to stop me from what I had decided to do. I put my hands over my ears, so as not to hear. I was thinking of the day of the high school initiation, how he'd caught me when I'd tripped, tried to carry things for me, then offered me water from a cup.

I crossed a fallen log. A pair of whistling thrushes burst up in the dry grass before me. I watched their low flight into the mesquite branches, then walked on until I was across from the stone house, looking over at its walls, the roof with more of a rent in it than I remembered. I crossed the creek and passed the window, still with its cloudy panes of glass.

The door was off one of its hinges. I had to lift it and push. When it gave way, the sunlight rushing in, I stood among the motes of dust I'd made, having to wait for the details of the room to clear. Then I thought to step into a shadow. The sofa was there, but it was as if a load had fallen on it and broken its back. In one corner of the room lay a pile of empty soda bottles and a twin set of rusted gas burners. I slanted my gaze slowly to the place where the mattresses had been. They were gone. In their place were tin cans, their labels removed. When I prodded them with the toe of my shoe, they clattered aside, one of them rolling all the way to the shattered hearth.

I closed my eyes and seemed to be hearing Link, his grunting and struggling. I could nearly feel his weight, see him draw away from me, rise from the bed, pull on his clothes, his teeth chattering with the winter cold; then I could see him walking to the door and leaving the house without thinking to stay with me awhile and talk like Maury did, only the back of his football jacket turned to me, and the heels of his boots. I shivered, lowered my face to the collar of my jacket, rubbing my cheek against it. Then I turned toward the stone chimney, drawing my hand along the mantel. Dust coated my fingers. Behind me came the flutter of wings; an orange-breasted barn swallow left by a hole in the stone wall, gone so quickly that I wouldn't have known what it was except I remembered that swallows had nested in these walls before, that I'd often heard their desperate and noisy escape when I'd first opened the door.

I sat down on a part of the broken sofa, thinking about when Vic had picked me up in Winston Valley, how I'd met him that night at the crossroads carrying nothing but one suitcase, how I'd sat in silence in Vic's car, my profile to him, Vic's face made visible by the lights on the dashboard, mine by the reflection of the headlights on the road, me never glancing at him once while he'd told his plans about the place he had for me, not Ruth's, he'd said. He'd changed his mind about that. He would ask her for my back money, of course, and he'd get it; but he'd decided on something in Dallas, a step up for me because it had a quiet, wealthy clientele. "You're older. You'll know how to handle it." The first place we had stopped to eat, I had refused the food, but he had given me something to take, a pill to stop me crying. In a while, I'd felt dizzy and then numb.

From time to time, he had glanced at me, checking, the way a farmer glances at some stock he's taking into town and wants to be sure he delivers healthy. At those moments, I particularly turned my head aside and watched the road, watched as the lights in farmhouses clicked on, watched as the sky lightened, turning from purple to pale blue. I saw a man riding fences, the flare of a match as he lighted a cigarette, someone else taking out a truck, driving it toward us on the lane that connected a ranch house with the road, the car lights bumping up and making bright platinum arches out of the morning haze. Later, I stared out the window at the fences and the cedars; then the plains and the beginning of the evergreen forest that lasted all the way into Louisiana; dogwood blossoms blowing away horizontally; corridors of pines on either side of dark narrow roads. Vic smoked nervously, flicking the ashes onto the floor of the car. It was a new car. I didn't know the make. He tried to talk about his car a little. When I didn't reply, he fell into silence except for asking me a couple of times if I wanted a cigarette and holding the package out to me. I brushed at it weakly with my hand. He dropped it, then reached to pick it up, sighing as if the bending down hurt him.

"They know about me," I said.

"What are you talking about?"

"They know in town, in Winston Valley."

"How?" He reached over to touch me. I pushed back his hand. "You tell them?" he asked. "You expect me to believe that? You're not that dumb."

"I'm not dumb at all," I whispered. "I just keep bad company."

"Well, you're not in bad company now."

Then he spoke to me as though he were a parent telling his child of a gift. "I'm going to get you an apartment, Sandy, whatever you want. When you're not working, you'll be with me."

He smiled, his lips spreading into the corners of his thick cheeks. "So how much do they know? You think they need the details? You wouldn't be with me if there weren't things that I know that you didn't want said."

"One day, I'm going to kill you," I said softly.

"Why, for taking you to a good place? Easy work. What else can you do? You don't even have high school finished. You crazy?"

"You caused that."

He put a cigarette in his mouth and pressed in the lighter. "That boy caused it," he said. "You told me yourself. The one who paid you in Anderson, and you thought was in love with you." Vic laughed. "The ones in love don't pay, sweetheart."

We drove all that morning, approached the city near noon, crossed briefly through an industrial section, then turned into a neighborhood with neatly arranged parks and houses with lawns so clean and clipped that the grass looked fake. The place where he delivered me was on the fringe of that neighborhood, not far from a university. The property had a twelve-foot wall around it; behind that, a high, thick privet hedge; then a huge yard, nearly a park itself, with hawthorn, magnolia trees, and oak.

My memory of the rest of that day is unclear, but somehow I entered the house from a back drive and was introduced to a woman named Wynette, Vic talking while I stood waiting. I agreed to everything asked of me with a nod or a whisper, my back curved over a cluttered dresser top, where there was a paper that Vic told me to sign.

She wanted me to work that night, but I said I couldn't. She asked when I could. I told her it would be two days. Then, the next morning early, before the dawn had come, without saying a word to her or anyone else, I left, using the back stairs, crossing the pebbled drive, catching a bus to the station, and buying a ticket to Temple, and not because Temple meant anything to me. It was only a name I liked, one that sounded as if it might be able to protect me.

For nearly two weeks, I stayed in a cheap motel, taking the rest of the tablets Vic gave me, sleeping and crying, going out only long enough to buy enough soda crackers and Coke to keep me alive. When I felt sane enough to make an arrangement, I rented a room, worked wherever I could, finally at a bar where I wore a skimpy satin costume, my duties being to deliver drinks and to tell the bartender when anyone was so drunk he shouldn't have more. I always wore my wedding ring, and if a man started in on me, I made sure he saw it. When people asked me where my husband was, I answered that he was in the service, that I was working until he had a good place for us, and then I'd go there.

I looked again at the clutter and litter of the stone house and where the mattresses had been. The swallows were rustling again in the walls, coming back, so I got up as quietly as I could and left, taking the long way back to town along the road, passing Ida Sneed's house, thinking of what had occurred there and the sadness I'd felt after. That child would be nearly an adult now, maybe thinking of getting married soon and having a child of its own.

Then, and nearly without willing it, I was at Preston Avenue, turning the corner and taking the alley to number 16, to the apartment that Maury and I had sometimes shared; I stopped short and stood away, since someone lived there now. I listened for a moment to a radio being played through the window, Big Band music from the war, music you want to dance to, and dance close with a man you love. I thought of Maury and me walking in that door now, dancing, having fun.

And then, without much willing this, either, but doing it like I'd made myself some kind of promise, I was climbing the hill to the cemetery where Doc was, first walking past the big granite gravestones that marked where the ranchers lay, then one for a mayor and his wife, and for a lawyer whose name I'd heard, but never knew. At last I was at the corner near the wall. I had to stoop down and pull away some bits of dry sedge grass to read Doc's name. For a few minutes, I stood beside the grave, thinking of evening suppers around the table in Ozona: white candles glowing; zinnias standing out like umbrellas in a rose-colored Chinese vase; Joylyn, Doc, Dad, and me, all of us talking polite.

When I started down the hill, I was quiet, my hands in the pockets of my jacket, brooding, until I was back at the Brussels, spending what little was left of the morning in my room, sitting on the bed, gazing out at low, marbled clouds that looked like wagons bringing in more cold. At noon, I went downstairs and ordered lunch in the nearly empty hotel restaurant, ate half a plateful of salty, steamed chicken with dumplings, then went up to my room, listened to part of a movie on TV, turned off the television, lowered the shade, and lay on top of the covers. I thought about Joylyn; I was hearing her sing to me, probably something left over from the religious music, coming in from a radio program being played in the room next to mine. And, in a while, that made me sleep, deep and heavy, dreams rushing in and out, changing subjects, none of them the kind you can remember.

It was nearly five in the afternoon when I woke to the bells ringing for church. I rose, went to the window, and raised the shade; then I looked down, watching wispy clouds hanging above the railroad station. I saw figures climbing the hill beyond, mostly women, some of them carrying babies in their arms, some leading children up the rocky path. I saw a small boy run behind a woman and take her hand, though she hadn't turned her head toward him but seemed to have her attention on a woman companion beside her.

My boy would be having another birthday soon. I always sent him a gift on his birthday, mailed it weeks early so it would have plenty of time to get there. The first year, I sent him a beautifully painted wooden sailboat, thinking carefully of how old he was and what he'd like to have, studying other children to discover that; watching them play in the park; later on watching children at Justin's for what they chose, then buying the best of those for him. Once I spent nearly a month's salary on an electric train set that I saw making the eyes of a little boy glow with delight, then look up at his mother and beg for it; his mother took his arm and led him away, the child glancing back, frowning at the train until a display of board games blocked it from his sight. That day, I bought one of the models of that train, plus tiny cars and villages and stations and the roundhouse and signal crossings with the crossarm gates. I paid for the gift, had it wrapped, picked out the paper and ribbon myself, watching sternly while the girl behind the counter tied the bow, then pulled the edge of the scissors against the ribbon ends to make them curl.

On each of Darrell's birthdays, I stayed at home from work, a ritual that I never broke. On those days, I kept on my nightgown, sat on the sofa, staring at the lighted television screen; or else I stayed in bed, thinking about Darrell with even more clarity than when I'd left: the food I'd prepared for him; games we'd created together and played; walks we'd taken in the woods and along the creek, the long, gentle branches of the moss-green cyprus shading us, the water rippling swift and clean over the creek's slippery stone floor, my removing the tiny leather *huaraches* from his feet and letting him down so that he could stand in the water, his mouth open in surprise at the feel of the current pulling at his legs; the clothes I had made for him, the sunsuit with the duck that Mrs. Slover took so much care to stitch on the bib. I remember throwing a ball to him, light as I was able, the ball falling through his hands, him screeching and running for it, then throwing it back as hard as he could, never quite in my direction. I thought of what he and Jim might do for his birthday: a party in the yard with a table covered with decorated sweets, or barbecue and pony rides at June and Buck's, perhaps even a trip into San Antonio: Breckenridge Park, a tour of the zoo, and afterward, a feast in a Mexican restaurant on a pier beside the river.

I watched the people climbing the hill. Then, in a moment, I was pulling on my skirt and sweater, taking up my purse but forgetting my jacket, not waiting for the elevator but running down the stairs, then outside to follow them, the cold wind cutting at my face and legs, taking the path now empty of people. I arrived and stood waiting inside the door, my heart pounding, my breaths so raggedly taken that I couldn't control the sound of them. A girl twisted around to look at me, staring until I knelt in back on a kneeling bench beside a tiered rack of candles, their yellow flames twitching, their red and green glass cups filled with the clear liquid of melted wax. Someone had folded a dollar bill and stuffed it into the coin slot. I pushed it down with my fingernail, then put in coins of my own. The fall to the bottom of the box jarred the silence; the only other sounds were from within the confessional, the person whispering, the priest murmuring replies, then the steady blending of the two voices in a prayer. I lit a candle for Darrell, another for Maury, and then Joylyn.

At last I heard the bench on which the girl was kneeling creak as she rose from it, her slim brown hand pulling the curtain aside. She looked young—fourteen or fifteen, I supposed—and then I was wondering what she had said to the priest that had made him keep her so long: that she was in love, that she and her lover had slept together, that she was sorry for that sin and wouldn't repeat it?

For a time, I prayed as I saw the other women do, my head bowed, my knuckles pushed hard against my forehead. I prayed for myself and Maury, for an answer that would accommodate to both the past and to my notion of God; then I rose to my feet, walked toward the confessional, and drew the curtain aside. The light from the candles behind allowed me to see a wooden kneeler, a brass cross tacked to the wall. As I went inside, the flap of the curtain fell back and left me in the dark space, in a box that smelled of musty draperies, and that had the scent and warmth of the girl who'd been there before me. I knelt, the kneeler scarcely wide enough to support me. There was a sound behind the partition of a body shifting its position. My eyes strained toward it. The window slid aside, leaving a mesh screen between the listener and me. I saw the shadow of the priest's hand as he made the sign of the cross.

"Bless me, Father, for I have . . ."

At first, I didn't know how I knew this beginning, then it came to me that I'd heard it from Luis's grandson at the ranch, when the itinerant priest had come by, and I'd asked what was confession. I spoke quickly, though I soon felt the patience of the one I faced, the lowered and steady profile, the lips moving in response. I told him about Maury, what we'd had at the stone house, and what there was now. He replied that if we loved one another and were repentant, we might amend our lives. He quoted from the Bible to show me how he knew; and then he asked if I understood what Maury was suffering; first the failure of his marriage, and second, his inability to persuade me to forgive him. I told him about Esther and Sylvia, about Ruth and me, about killing a baby, and about Doc. My voice faltered when I spoke of Jimmy, and I thought I'd have to stop; and then he was interrupting me, not blaming me but wanting to know, so he could counsel me and understand. "Then why did you marry him?" he asked me, "and why did you bear him a child?"

"Because I thought I could have something good; because I thought I had it coming due."

I told him about Jim's family: June, Buck, and their kids; about Mrs. Slover; about the house the Ormans owned and that had never seemed quite mine. I told him that I'd gone to church there and prayed for what did happen not to happen, and that I'd never understood why all of what I'd prayed against came on me just the same. Finally I asked him if he thought I could see Darrell. He said that I could; all I had to do was ask God and God would show me how.

When I returned to Austin two days later, I telephoned Maury's apartment. A boy answered. He kept saying hello. He'd be silent, then he'd try again, speaking more slowly, his voice breaking on his breath. "Mother," he said, "if that's you, you should answer." He paused a moment longer and then there was a voice in the background, words urgently spoken, a break, and I was hearing Maury on the phone. "Stella . . . May I come to see you? May I come out there?" He began to say something more; then he cursed, and not at me, I knew, but at himself and his belief that he had failed to make me love him.

I held on to the phone, listening to him speak again of permanency and marriage, to apologize in a half-dozen ways for all that had happened before; and when I couldn't listen any longer, when even the priest's advice and encouragement seemed not yet enough, I hung up, and then I began to cry.

25

Winston Valley is only fifty miles from Austin, but it has always seemed farther than that to me. That is until I recall that its nearness is why I settled in Austin at all; that I'd had some idea that on a clear, windy day those in Winston Valley and I might share some of the same air, or that when I climbed to the top of a hill and looked to the southwest, I might see a cloud overhead that was passing in the direction of my home, and that when it reached the neighborhood I knew, it might contain some small reflected image of myself.

On the morning that I drove there, the sky was a light, clear blue. I had telephoned Mary Gayle, and she'd said the weather forecast was rain, though not until afternoon. She hadn't wanted me to go, not to the funeral at least. I should wait, and together we'd think of another way, another time. But I did go, and I went early, so that before going to the church I'd have time to get my bearings, calm myself, and restore my courage.

I gazed ahead at the empty road, no one there but me, but always someone expected. At that moment, it occurred to me that I had spent my whole life searching for my family, that there would be no pause in that pursuit, that each new attempt that I made pulled me in more deeply; that I was like a person who walks ever farther into an ocean, more of me helpless at each step, knowing I should turn back, hearing cheerful voices calling to me from behind but being unable to respond, since somewhere before me I truly believe there is an island, and on it, one who holds the secrets for which I continually take this risk.

I planned to drive first straight through town, then just after Holden's pool hall or at the corner fence of the Olsens' ranch to turn around and drive back to select the things I wanted most to see. On the way, the car wound slowly around the curves. I watched for turns onto one ranch road and then another, forgetting one landmark, having a second surprise me, at last arriving at the outskirts of town, seeing places I had never known: a motel, a lumberyard, a shopping center with a chamber of commerce, arranged at the base of a hill where I used to see sheep grazing. I didn't believe that when I lived here, there had been any chamber of commerce at all. Yet people talked about Winston Valley now, making it sound smart and glamorous, though in my memory it was neither of these things—rather, it was where you had a home, a husband and son, in-laws, and all the friends for whom you could possibly ask.

So that landmark confused me, yet my car had gone on rolling in the only direction I thought it could, to what was called the square, though it was not really a square then or now, only three roads meeting together with two rather sketchy town streets.

There were new stores, the facade of a building changed, plate glass to see the quilts made by farm women, jewelry and furniture that looked like they came from Taos rather than anything I knew about being made here. The grocery store that had been owned by the Wade family was gone. Bearden's Café and the feedlot beside it had been torn down and replaced with a restaurant and a dry goods–hardware store that advertised seeds and fancy garden plants. Later, on the road to Johnson City, I would see a supermarket called Brookshire's. The parking lot before it, dotted with pickups and wide, comfortable cars, was larger than the center of Winston Valley, and so it occurred to me that it had been built in anticipation of the hill behind it being covered with new houses.

I hadn't planned to drive into the neighborhood I knew, but in a moment I found myself taking the turn to the left behind the stables, then turning again at an angle onto the shaded road that would take me to Mrs. Slover's house. At a bend in the road, a dog ran at the fender of my car, baring its teeth, barking savagely. Alley had liked to do that. I thought about Alley, how long ago she must have died, since she was an old dog even then when Jim and I were still playing with her, throwing her tennis balls so Darrell could see her run; she used to gaze up at us with her large, sad eyes that meant she was sorry she could no longer give the dazzling show that she once had. "Poor Jimmy," I said suddenly, aloud, the image and voice of my husband calling to the dog seeming to fill the car with that quick bullet shot of recall, those that so often take over in the silence.

But if there were new buildings around the center of town and on the outskirts, nothing had changed here, the old frame houses with their porches with lattice skirts and their large unfenced yards unaltered. Now along the curving lane, cars were parked, pulled to the side as far as they would go, dipping slightly toward the ditch. In Mrs. Slover's yard, there was a car parked up on jacks where we used to have the truck garden. I saw only the bed of roses beside the porch, likely all she'd been able to manage. Had I stayed, I would have cared for her garden, made her meals, helped her write to Henry. I had thought often of Henry, what had become of him. Perhaps Jim had taken over his care, he and Darrell driving up every other Sunday afternoon to visit him, as we used to do, taking him news and gossip he could never respond to, flowers he would hardly look at, presents he couldn't use. Or had his sister, Jessica, come for him? I had met her once on the only visit she ever made to Winston Valley while I lived there, a heavy, slow-moving woman with long, messy hair, her thick wrists and neck hung with tarnished copper bracelets and ivory beads, Mrs. Slover always taking her cool things to drink, cooking her meals, wishing she would talk to her more and show affection. It was through her that I had learned of Mrs. Slover's death. Apparently, at some point in time, she had moved back to Texas. Two days ago, I had seen the notice in the newspaper, Jessica's name given as one of the survivors, and Austin as her home. I wondered if, in these later years, she'd been kinder to her mother, if after Mrs. Slover's illness had begun, she'd seen to her care with the concern and interest that once Mrs. Slover had seen to mine.

I drove by the house, turning at the curve in the lane so that I might see the room that Jim and I had shared. The window shades were pulled down. I wondered if anyone else had slept in that room since, some couple as young as Jim and I had been then, having trouble getting out of bed, believing that there was nothing else in the world to do other than to be together and keep the intervals between making love as short as possible. I remember how much love Jim and I put into that room during the year we lived there. It was a long honeymoon, he and I joking and laughing, Jimmy teasing me, but nice, our playing like children, sometimes in the middle of the night getting out of bed and walking in our bedclothes down to the riverbank and making love there—though I believe that on account of the timing from after it was so hot outdoors, I got my baby in Henry's room, the fan blowing on us cool; and that made me feel close to the room even though it was empty of us now. Sometimes when Jim was at work, I had opened the window onto the yard and let the air freshen with the scent of honeysuckle or ligustrum, depending on the season, while I was in the living room visiting with Mrs. Slover or making her a pitcher of lemonade or putting out sweets on a plate, then setting it between us, so it would be as though we were old-fashioned ladies having tea. I was thinking how right that was, the family of us, and how I envied what more there might have been behind those shades in Henry's room, and grieved for my own loss; and not simply that the time had passed and plowed under the flowers of that existence, but that there was no longer love between me and the one who shared its memory.

A couple was entering the house, both of them young, a red-faced outdoor man looking uncomfortable in a shiny dark suit, the woman wearing a navy blue coat, two little girls trailing behind them dressed in corduroy jackets, their heads bent low to gauge the steps they climbed. The mother was holding a white bakery box, cookies or a cake, something to add to the table for lunch, since the guests would surely stand around in the dining room, telling what they knew of Mrs. Slover, stories about the good things she'd done. I wondered if they might not even talk about

Jim Lester, her taking him in after his parents' death, and then of Stella Landry, the one who had come here, lived with him, borne him a son, then disappeared. *It was on Darrell's birthday, wasn't it? I believe he was three years old.*

I turned the car around, ducked my head to study the house again, the drive, the shade tree under which Jim had always parked the truck. The reflection of a branch rippled along the kitchen window. I could nearly see myself behind the panes of glass watching for Jim, then running outside at the first sight of the truck beyond the bend, trying always to meet it at the turn so Jim would stop and get out, then catch me in his arms, kissing me full on my mouth, twirling me around until my head was going back and both of us were dizzy, even when I was pregnant, at least until Mrs. Slover, shouting from the porch and flapping a dishtowel, told us no.

I waited then for my mind to go through the exercise of imagining in short, flickering scenes what might have been: my walking up here from our house with Darrell, then with Jim for Sunday lunch, the weeks passing, the seasons changing: November, for the hedge of poinsettias that ran along the south side of the garage; March, when the pear trees budded and azaleas bloomed; April, for geraniums and begonias that I raised from the cuttings that I begged off our neighbors. I'd planned to watch for those changes every year of my life, until I died during one of them in my own home and among my children and these friends.

A man was walking up the road toward the house, middle-aged, gray hair, a blue suit, an umbrella rolled tight. He was looking at me with the tense, pulled face of those who are going to the house of someone who has died and have just met with another mourner. I knew that he meant to speak to me as people here do to strangers. Pretending not to see him, I turned the car around, then drove the route that I had so often walked to the garage to have lunch with Jim and then sit near him watching his able, quick hands do the work from which he made our living. When I saw the building, I felt pain in my heart: It was there, but boarded up, weeds growing between the cracks in the pavement, black curls of graffiti marking the walls, the garage's services replaced, I supposed, by the new filling station and garage that I'd seen on Highway 12. At first I was convinced that this meant Jim had left Winston Valley; then it occurred to me that he had built the new station himself. I turned and drove past it slowly. A man with tanned skin and black hair walked out of the service area where a car was drawn up high on a lift. I saw the shape of yet another man behind the glass window but knew that he lacked the height of the man who had been my husband.

Afterward, I went by the house where the Harmons had lived. The lawn was carefully tended now. The big pecan tree at its corner was gone, possibly sacrificed to give sunlight to the double row of pansies that bordered the front walk. I remembered how Oona used to walk down to our house to visit Darrell, her awkward gait. She always looked as if she might fall forward, but she never did, and I'd known better than to go out and help her, since this only drew attention from her father, who might come down, scold her for roaming, and take her home. So I found that if I left her alone, she usually made it to us, and when she did, she'd find Darrell, then rock him in the rocking chair, or sit on the floor with him and play, never apparently made uncomfortable by his shrieks about the toys being his, Oona always showing that quiet, cheerful patience that I learned to admire so much in her and in those like her whom I've met occasionally since.

After that, I had only to turn my head. I hesitated, narrowed my eyes, then found myself gazing fully at the house where Jim and I had lived, surprised a little that there were new houses on either side but surprised mostly at how our house seemed so much grander now, with its new wide porch and the long, pitched-roof addition added to the back—a family room, perhaps a new bedroom as well. I turned off the car motor so that I might hear the sounds of the morning, a mockingbird in one of the pear trees, a dog barking in the distance. The yard was clean and planted with flowering shrubs; more azaleas and ornamental trees, though less space for the cutting yard and orchard. The coralvine was still there, hanging to the porch in its heart-shaped, leafy dream. I remembered that it had been rich and green when I left Winston Valley, preparing for the pink explosion during that next summer; how I'd walked past it quickly that night, fearing that my admiration might make me stop for too long, and that even such a brief delay might ruin my family's life.

The house seemed freshly painted, the same color that Jim and I had chosen, the walkway the same, too, the stone that we'd laid one fall afternoon, a family project, Jim and Buck taking up the old cement walk with an air hammer that Buck had borrowed from a friend in Hunt; then June and Buck and I had spread the sand and laid down the stones, fitting in the angles, then planting ajuga in between, me pulling the hose out every dry summer night to water it and make it want to spread.

Near the street, there was a mailbox with the name LESTER, the letters perfectly stenciled. An expensive red motorbike was parked before the garage. Likely it was Darrell's, a gift. Perhaps an only son is spoiled, possibly to make up for what else he doesn't have, and for the mistake his father made in choosing his mother.

Just off the garage was a neatly made lean-to greenhouse, not new, perhaps added only a short time after I left, again the work precise and true, and of the best materials. The swings and sliding board were still in the yard, the ones that were there on that day when Jim and I decided to buy the house while we were in the garden, the deep grass lapping at the feet of the shade trees, the breezes cool and fresh from the river, Jim and Orman Cater drinking beer from bottles, while Kitty, her noisy kids pulling on her skirt to get her attention, brought out a glass of cold apple juice for me.

On the porch was a dog, a collie so old it hardly raised its head to see me. It lay on a rug, its head on its paws that were stretched out before it. Was that the puppy Jim had brought to Darrell? The one that Darrell insisted on calling Alley since Alley was the only other dog that he really knew?

I sat there quietly, wondering what Jim had done that morning when he'd found me gone. Had he run to Buck and June? Had he stayed indoors a day, a week? Did he go to work? And if he stayed home, was it loss or shame, or did he despise me so much that he felt no loss, and managed the shame with activities so harsh that they protected him from it? And what had Jim said to our baby? That Mama had gone on a trip? And then Darrell had searched for me and listened for the door and my step in the hallway, fussing, asking for me, watching from the porch, the fear and anger rising; then, gradually with time, forgetting. Because what had I left him? Some photographs, clothes, plants I'd set in the garden, the way the furniture was arranged.

I thought of my family going through its activities, Jim getting out of bed and pouring out cereal for him and Darrell, or walking down with him to Bearden's and ordering something hot, then leaving Darrell at school, going for him at lunch and sharing with him packaged sandwiches and chips, then picking him up at three and taking him to the garage until quitting time, until he was old enough to be given a key to a house that he'd enter alone each afternoon, as in all families where there is no woman. I could be certain that Jim had taught him to play ball and hunt, that Buck and his boys and Jim and Darrell had gone out on fall mornings and brought down birds and deer, filled the freezer with game enough to eat all year. I imagined that Darrell would have spent his summers with June and Buck, holidays, too. I wondered how Junior and Trix and Nancy had treated him, a boy without a mother, one whom they would pity but could never openly dislike, since their parents and their uncle Jim would never allow it. I wondered how they spoke of me, or if they never did, so that Darrell stopped asking questions about his mother's brief stay in Winston Valley, because they were never answered happily or with much respect: *She didn't love us. She was like some animals that don't quite attach no matter how much you pet and coax them. And she was too quiet. She never wanted to do much outside the house, unless something at church.* Or more simply: *One night she left here. We don't know why.*

A little girl came to the screened door and pushed on it until it gave way and opened. She wore black patent-leather shoes and white socks, turned down at the ankles, a pink dress and matching sweater. Her hair was in two thick brown plaits, tied at the ends with ribbons. The screen banged shut behind her. For an instant, she stared at my car, then made her way down the steps, holding out her arms as if to balance herself. The dog rose slowly to its feet, watched her attentively, but did not follow.

A young woman in a dark dress came out on the porch and called to her, but she continued moving down the stone walk. I put my hand on the car key and turned it. The motor caught and drowned out the child's reply. She was at the gate, her hand on the lever that would open it. In the rearview mirror, I saw the woman pick her up, both of them watching as my car pulled away. For an instant, I put on the brakes. I thought about going back, that I might get out and talk to them, ask directions to Comfort or Dripping Springs. But I didn't. Instead, I drove away, turning back toward the center of town. I glanced at my watch. Five till twelve. Lunchtime in Winston Valley, always the same, twelve until one, a full hour, the children taking the walk home to a warm meal set on the kitchen table: meat, vegetables, hot bread, a fruit compote stewed that morning.

A bell sounded a high, piercing cry over the valley, stopped by a brake of cyprus beside the river. That was from the school. I drove across the bridge and up the gradual slope, then turned left and passed the fairgrounds. The school was just beyond on the crest of a hill, a long one-story stone building with a parking lot before it, an enclosed football field to the left. When I left Winston Valley, the school was new. We were all proud of it, dreaming of our children being there, imagining their success. The doors were open wide. Kids poured out onto the porch, the sun catching on their young bodies and faces, most of them walking quickly toward a walkway partly sheltered from the wind by lantana and oak. Immediately, my eyes searched among the boys for a blond one, perhaps taller than the other boys, lanky, big-boned. I saw several who fit that description, but one in particular who had a wiry easiness about him that was so much like Jim. He was neatly dressed in khaki slacks and a blue jacket. His hair was short, the color of it nearly as light as mine had been at his age, his complexion fairer than most of the others around him.

I had pulled the car in a space, gotten out, and was walking toward him. His gaze passed into mine, then went on to someone else. My lips formed to say his name, when a girl came up beside him, the other boys with him dropping back. He took her arm, bent his head low to hear something she said, then smiled, and she did. As they turned the corner in the direction of town, he glanced back at me, his blue eyes reflecting the color of the patch of sky behind him, just as Jim's would have done. I made a gesture after he turned away, nearly a wave of my hand, then stood where I was until all the students had left, and the schoolyard was empty. A gust of wind blew my skirt against my legs, my hair away from my face. One sleeve of the cardigan sweater that I had pulled over my shoulders had slipped down. I reached for it.

A man in a pinstripe suit came across the lawn, paused an

instant, then turned and came toward me. "Is there anything I can do for you, ma'am?"

"No, sir," I murmured. "Thank you." I walked back toward the sound of the idling car.

For my lunch, I stopped in a drive-in grocery and bought a ham-and-cheese sandwich on a thick, crusty piece of French bread. I wasn't hungry. It was just that I had remembered I'd had no food since the day before.

"You want it heated?" asked the cashier, a man with leathery skin, sharp bones showing beneath the open collar of his faded blue shirt.

"No," I answered. In my hand were two dollar bills, which he didn't seem to want to take.

"The sandwiches are better heated, ma'am; makes the cheese melt down."

I laid the bills on the counter. "All right."

While I waited, I stood aside for another customer, and when the cashier gave me back the heated sandwich wrapped in a fresh napkin, I thanked him.

I stayed in my car in the parking lot, waiting there long after I'd finished eating. Beside the car was a metal sign advertising cigarettes. The wind caught under it, made it rock; then it clanked back to position on its base, shuttering a little, as if bracing for the next gust.

My mouth was dry, and I wanted to go back in the store and buy myself something to drink, but I didn't. I just sat there still and quiet, waiting, though for nothing specific. Or perhaps I was hoping that I might see someone pass whom I might recognize: Buck, perhaps; June. I wondered if I'd know them. They'd be older now, past fifty. I took little risk in their recognizing me. For one thing, I had short hair; for another, I was wearing black silk and a hat with a veil; and of course, I was no longer young. For the second time in my life, I wore a larger-size dress than I had when I had married Jim; and if I didn't like that extra flesh around my middle or on my thighs, I liked it on my face. It made me seem soft, not so tense and anxious.

The man who had waited on me came out of the store. He was

carrying a cowhide jacket over his shoulder. He didn't need it now but might have worn it in the cool of the morning. When he stopped beside the car, I rolled down the glass. "You need something?" he asked.

"No."

"Anything wrong?"

"No, thank you," I answered. "I'm fine."

He shrugged, then glanced down at my black dress. "You come in town for the funeral?"

"Yes."

He paused, his gaze slightly away from mine, and then he said, "Too bad about her. Everybody seemed to like her. I ain't been here long enough to meet her, just seen her once or twice before she got bedridden. You knew her well?"

"Yes, I did."

"Well, don't take her passing so hard," he said. "It's a blessing, her suffering and all. She lived too long." He tried to smile for me. "That's just something not to do."

I waited for the frown to leave his face, but it didn't. He stayed longer, as if he meant to ask me something more but couldn't quite do it; then he turned and walked slowly along the shoulder of the road, his boots mashing down the grass. It would be some time later, after I'd driven and parked down by the river, that I would put my hands over my face and feel the wetness and the heat, then realize that in my mouth there was the taste of salt, and that for some time I'd been crying.

For a while, I stared at the water of this river that I used to so much love and visit. I watched the flash of the current as it passed, the swirls and eddies starting up, going on, repeating. At last, I relaxed, the side of my head against the car window. I don't know how long I slept, but when I woke, the sun was hidden behind a bank of black clouds, my limbs felt cramped, and I felt the familiar ache in my heart that is nearly always present during the first little while after I wake.

I glanced quickly at my watch, then opened my purse and looked at my face in the mirror of my compact. Because of my rest, my features looked gentle and childish. I combed my hair back from my face, touched the puffy contours of my eyelids, reached into the rear seat for my hat, then started the car and drove through town one more time, again turning off to the right and passing by the house that Jim and I had shared. The clouds had covered the sun; there was no shade in the yard now, so everything looked one color. The gate to the drive was closed. I pulled the car away slowly, stopping once, glancing back, then driving on, down one street and another. I did this carefully, with the leisure of a person who has waited long, and who believes that this may be the only time, since the opportunity comes so rarely, and the courage to do it is so difficult to gather, that the idea of repeating it is unimaginable.

The clock struck three. It had begun to rain; big, startled splashes hit the windshield, the car wipers smoothing them out in the pattern of a fan. I drove up the hill along the rain-sweetened street that led to the church, its familiar trees and houses, then the pink brick walls of the church itself, the thick white columns, the garden at the side where June and I used to talk and make our plans, the roses leafed out but without blooms, the three pairs of twin privets still cut in the shape of baskets with handles, the terrace without a single weed.

Cars were filling the parking lot, each of them entering slowly. Two men in gleaming raincoats hurried for the entrance. I parked at the side, drew the veil of my hat down over my face, opened my umbrella, then crossed the damp grass and went inside. A woman in a flowered hat was playing the organ, no tune that I recognized, only bass chords struck and held, then resolved after long intervals. An usher came close, but I pretended not to see him and slid quickly into a pew in back. I slipped one of the heavy black prayer books from the rack and opened it to read. Only when the coffin was being brought did I lift my eyes. Six men were walking beside it, their attention on the altar and the carpet before them.

One of them was Jim, a bit taller than the others. He was heavier than he had been. His hair had thinned a little, but he still had the boyish look that I remembered. As he turned and took his seat at the front, I expected him to break out in a smile, my memory of him that he was nearly always smiling, since the things I cared most to remember took place during times when he was happy, when every remark I made pleased him, and everything I did was bright and perfect, and he told me.

I sat with my hands in my lap, my eyes down. When once I glanced up, I saw a baby in the pew before me, turning in its mother's arms to stare at me, fascinated, I believe, with the strand of pearls around my neck, the baby too far away to reach them, though it tried. The woman holding it resembled Mrs. Moor's daughter, with a fuller figure than I remembered, her hair darker now. I didn't know the minister—it wasn't Dr. Tellerson but a young man who preached long and carefully about the good that Mrs. Slover had done, her patience during the illness of her son, her willingness to help those around her to care for the poor and heal the sick, as Jesus requires. He leaned forward on the lectern, both his elbows out like wings. "There was no charity you could ask her to do to which she'd say no. And she made no transgression. If I asked now of what transgressions you may know, wouldn't you have to say none?"

There was silence except for the weeping, the rustling of people's clothes as they shifted in their seats, the preacher's eyes darting to each of us, then seeming to rush to the back of the church and fix on me. I lowered my gaze to the text of the prayers. "There'll be no sins to tell when she comes before the Judgment and raises up her voice with the angels," the preacher continued. "Lct us all bc so. . . ."

I was thinking of Maury, the times when both of us brooded in the lonely quiet over a past for which I held him to blame. If Jimmy had forgiven me, I would be living now in that house that we had shared so briefly; if Mrs. Slover had taken my part and granted me pardon, I would have been at her table this noon, sharing lunch with friends, talking to them of her kindness and good works, each of us consoling the other for his pain and loss.

I sat quictly admiring as I always had the whiteness of the church, the purity of the columns and windows. Jim had often taken my hand and held it during the sermons here, and we had sat close, never glancing at the other but knowing one another's thoughts. I could hear the rain beating gently on the ground outside. There had been other rainy days in this church, ones when, after the service, we'd taken Darrell home and spent the afternoon in our house, believing that nothing could part us, that things like a rainstorm, any accident, any sickness, only brought us closer together. And I was glad of the rain today. I depended on it to hide me when we went outside, just as night had hidden my escape from this town.

We rose to sing. I replaced the blue prayer book and took up the red hymnal. A mournful hymn began, the voices rising. I tried to think of the words, but I kept hearing Mary Gayle speaking earnestly, leading me toward this: "You have to see Darrell," she had said, when I'd returned from Anderson. "Not until that's done, Stella . . . Aren't you doing what your mama did to you? Let me drive you. I'll telephone Jim Lester. I don't mind talking to him. We'll go down there together. He'll let you see your son. And if he won't, then we'll get hold of June."

When the preaching and music and reading of Scripture was finished, the people opened their umbrellas and filed out slowly behind the coffin. I sat quietly and watched them leave, rising only when I might be among the last in the procession. I was outside then, glancing away whenever anyone looked at me, walking well behind the others along the path between the two rows of poplars, where I had walked with Mrs. Slover herself the several times that we had come to put flowers on her husband's grave. I remembered his picture, heavy, the flesh straining his jacket. We were inside the iron gate, closed in together, praying and mourning for the friend who had left us. I remembered what there'd been for Doc. No flowers or green canopy there, no crowd like this, only me and Mr. Benthall, the undertaker, him giving a reading from the Bible, then reaching down and taking up a handful of sand and scattering it on the coffin; and afterward we'd sat on a bench, drinking coffee from the quart thermos he'd brought, sharing it from a shallow red plastic cup.

The mourners gathered around the gravesite, all who had come to pay their last respects to this woman who had been so long my confidante and friend. The mound of earth beside the grave was covered with a green tarpaulin, splotched darkly with rain. We stood silent and prayerful, when the minister began reading from the Bible. Then, in a while, he handed the book to the boy I'd seen at the school. He started to read the Twenty-third Psalm, then hesitated, his voice fading. He glanced at the woman I'd seen that morning at the house, where Jim and I had lived. She touched his arm gently, and then he stood straight and began the psalm again.

After this, I didn't hear him falter; his voice was rich and true; and I knew whom I was seeing, and I felt my mouth go into a smile no matter what I meant it to do. He wore a blue suit, a thin striped tie, a nice one, and it looked new. He read slowly, taking his time, pausing at the correct intervals, going on to finish. "Darrell," I whispered, and had for a reply the sniffling of the rain, the streams of it dripping from the umbrellas to the ground. It fell on steadily, a reliable scrim between me and the others. Flowered easels swayed in the wind under the burden of their blooms.

I saw Dr. and Mrs. Moor, their profiles, their heads bent, their hands folded in prayer close to their faces. They looked old, Dr. Moor swollen and heavy, Mrs. Moor using a cane. I thought I saw June and Buck, the time changing them, too; June thin; Buck's hair nearly gray, deep vertical lines on his cheeks.

At last I glanced straight across the flowers sprayed over the coffin, my lips forming to say the name of the one I saw. Jim glanced at me, his eyes fixed, dull with grief. His lids shut an instant, tightened; and when they opened again, I thought he nodded, though I would never be certain that he did. Then he was looking at the preacher, his face flushed, the dark of the umbrella shadowing whatever other expression I might have tried to read there. The woman was beside him, the one I'd seen at the house. He said something to her. She drew the boy close to her, hesitating a long moment, then spoke again in a whisper that made him put his arm around her and smile into her face. I saw with what admiration he watched her and how his arm had circled her waist. The little girl motioned to him; he took her hand and kissed it, and she laughed. *Ah, yes,* I was thinking. *That's how it is, how it should be, what I'd hoped.*

Jimmy's mouth trembled. He spoke. The woman bowed her head and nodded. I saw Jim speak again. I was standing still, my umbrella open since I was one of those outside the protection of the canopy. I lowered my head, reciting the familiar prayer with the minister. When it was over, people around me began to speak and move away, gathering in clusters under the close roof of their several umbrellas.

"Are we going home now?" I heard a child ask, as the preacher was greeting people, shaking hands. "I don't like this."

"No, darling," a woman replied. I didn't recognize her voice. "We'll go back to the Slovers' house. Don't you want to see the cake we made again? I know you'd like to taste it."

I don't know how I did it, I had not meant to; or perhaps I believed that by now I had the right. It was chance, I think, or maybe just a change of vision to that of Maury and Mary Gayle. In any case, I took in a long breath, raised my chin just a little, and moved forward. Darrell's back was to me; the others were making their way in the rain toward the church; there was no one near. I touched him, and he turned. "You read the psalm beautifully," I said. "I've never heard it read so well."

He smiled that perfect smile of youth when there seems never to have been distress and none imagined. "Thank you," he said.

I reached out my hand. He shook it. The grasp was firm, nearly hard. Then there was the shade and shadow and blue canopied rain cover of someone else with us. I lifted my eyes to him, again to Darrell. We stared at one another, all three blinking a little, the rims of our umbrellas touching, a coolness on our faces, rain splashing at our feet, Darrell's image reflecting Jim's and mine as a pond reflects twin trees that shiver and blend together when any wind comes.

It was after six o'clock when I took the highway past Buda and Kyle. The rain had stopped, and since the sky was clear in the west, an orange sunset had taken the grayness out of the stone hills and colored the shaggy grasses where this morning cattle had stood. At the height of the hills, a bright flood stained the cedars, then climbed until it made lanterns of their peaks. I watched the blueing of the valleys, then the loss of color as if a hand had eased across the landscape and closed its eyes.

The drive was quiet, the car alone on the highway except for a few trucks. I played the radio but found that I had no heart for news or music; then, in a while, I stopped for a cup of coffee at a roadside café. I sat in a booth, watching the trucks come and go in the parking lot, watched men get out of the cabs and walk toward the lighted place. They stretched their cramped bodies, yawned fully, and lighted cigarettes. I'd known men like them all my life, hardworking, thoroughly loyal and competent, willing to discuss just about anything, ready to stand long hours with friends, talking about cattle prices, places they knew, accidents they'd seen, dangerous weather. One of them came inside and spoke to me, commenting on the nasty and inconvenient rain, then asked if he might not join me at my table; but I replied that I was just leaving, though, afterward, I regretted my unkindness in not taking a few minutes to hear what he wanted to say, and not so particularly to me, but to anyone who would listen to him after such long silences.

When I came to the highway sign for Austin, I turned left toward the bridge, its metal girders gleaming as if it were daylight. I drove into Tarrytown along the road named Exposition, then turned off on my street. There were lights on in the houses and on the porches. In a moment, a patrol car pulled out from a side street and followed me at a distance. When I drove up in the drive, it pulled in behind me, and Mr. Dovela, the neighborhood patrolman, put his head out the car window. "Everything all right, ma'am?" he asked.

"Yes, sir," I called. "It is. Thank you."

I sat in the car for a while, gazing at the apartments in the moonlight, at the low-slanted roof, lights over some of the doors, their shine as delicate and cheerful as candles. Behind the cedar garden chairs, I could just make out the roses, stiff and glistening from the rain. As I got out of the car, I heard an owl from its perch somewhere in the trees, happy with the change of the weather, the somber day making a particularly beautiful night for its exercise and profit. For a moment I let the glare of the moonlight fall on my face, and then I made the sign of the cross over my forehead, heart and shoulders, as the priest in Anderson had done for me.

The stars shook among the leaves of the oaks. As I passed it, the swimming pool rocked in the moon, racing every cloud it could. I glanced up at the deck. The light was on for me. I could see the new pots of geraniums, Maury's gifts, the blossoms on trailing stems, racing toward me like a waterfall in pink.

I climbed the stairs. Wedged in the door to my apartment was a white envelope, an address printed on the back, *1208 Sixth Street;* and on the front, *Stella Jean Landry,* made out in a masculine hand that I knew from so many other messages. As I opened it, the script, the words, ran together under my eyes, asking for forgiveness and promising me as always both friendship and love.

And then a voice seemed to whisper: *Just look at that, honey;* and it was Joylyn speaking, chanting my name; and I had the fancy of the gently strummed chords of a guitar, Joylyn singing in a high voice, *Stella; oh, my Stella Jean;* and me begging for a real song, a hymn. And then her bursting out with my favorite, leaning toward me and kissing my face, tapping her foot on the floor of the porch: *Dance, honey; dance, my baby!;* and I was dancing around the card table, my head back, my mouth open, laughing, the hem of my dress rippling around my knees.

The landscape glared off the moon plate of the pool. Bright tree patterns fell in shadows onto the deck. Up close now, the pink geraniums looked like small bows, the kind of ornament you'd like for a dance. When the phone began to ring, I was picking a wide, full blossom to put in my hair. I didn't answer it. I stood for a time, gazing out at the trees and the pool in the silence, except for a cicada and, occasionally, the full, pleasant hoot of a bird. I stared and dreamed. When the phone began to ring again, I went inside to answer.